T0323886

Praise for Abbie Williams

"Williams populates her historical fiction with people nearly broken by their experiences."
— *Foreword Reviews INDIES Finalist (Soul of a Crow)*

* Gold Medalist - 2015
— *Independent Publishers Awards (Heart of a Dove)*

"Perfect for romantic mystery lovers ... a sweet, clever quickstep with characters who feel like longtime friends." — *Foreword Reviews (Wild Flower)*

"Set just after the U.S. Civil War, this passionate opening volume of a projected series successfully melds historical narrative, women's issues, and breathless romance with horsewomanship, trailside deer-gutting, and alluring smidgeons of Celtic ESP."
— *Publishers Weekly (Heart of a Dove)*

"There is a lot I liked about this book. It didn't pull punches, it feels period, it was filled with memorable characters and at times lovely descriptions and language. Even though there is a sequel coming, this book feels complete."

— *Dear Author (Heart of a Dove)*

"With a sweet romance, good natured camaraderie, and a very real element of danger, this book is hard to put down."
— *San Francisco Book Review (Heart of a Dove)*

Also By Abbie Williams

⋙ The Shore Leave Cafe Series ⋘

Summer at the Shore Leave Cafe

Second Chances

A Notion of Love

Winter at the White Oaks Lodge

Wild Flower

The First Law of Love

Until Tomorrow

The Way Back

Return to Yesterday

Forbidden

⋙ The Dove Series ⋘

Heart of a Dove

Soul of a Crow

Grace of a Hawk

Grace

OF A

Hawk

ABBIE WILLIAMS

central
avenue
publishing

2018

Published by Central Avenue Publishing, an imprint of Central Avenue Marketing Ltd.
www.centralavenuepublishing.com

GRACE OF A HAWK

978-1-77168-043-1 (pbk)
978-1-77168-044-8 (epub)
978-1-77168-045-5 (mobi)

Published in Canada

Printed in United States of America

1. FICTION/Romance - Historical

It's love you never recover from.

Part One

I JUST CAN'T figure," the boy began, and I recognized the calculated innocence in his voice; I'd sounded the same plenty of times in the past, when I wanted more information than I knew I was rightly going to get. He stalled, peering crossways at me.

"Nope," I said, staving off his opinion. The August sun was hot as a devil on my hat, even pulled low as it was, sending slick trails down my face, burning near through my clothes. I shifted, cursing the dull ache across my low back, and reached behind, retrieving my canteen. With care, I allowed a small trickle down the front of my shirt, open two buttons and where a patch of painful red would no doubt mark me by nightfall. But I didn't give a damn. A wet, sweltering heat had settled over the land and I was already hurting far worse than a little sunburn. Never mind the healing pistol shot that had hacked a chunk from my side.

Malcolm leaned from his saddle, tugging at my elbow to force my attention. Warm water slid over my belly and I shuddered as I proceeded to sip; tepid as it was, it still provided relief from the sticky heat. While I was preoccupied downing a second swallow my brother hurried to make his point.

"What I meant to say was I just can't figure – "

"I ain't got a word…on the subject." I interrupted him, coughing on the mouthful of water, and that was that. I borrowed my daddy's tone as best I could, that which preceded a thorough strapping if my brothers and me weren't smart enough to quit pestering, or flat-out disobeying. With a fair amount of desperation, I thought, *Please, boy, shut your trap. I can't think about what you intend to say. If I do, I won't be able to keep riding away.*

But Malcolm was not so readily put off; I'd never strapped the boy, and likely would never have the heart to do so, and he knew it. He possessed a keen and earnest nature just exactly like our mama's, and pressed on with his usual sincerity. "Boyd, I can't figure why you'd leave her behind when I know it pains you so."

"You ain't old enough to understand," I muttered, which was not a fair statement, nor did I kid myself it was true. My voice grumbled, stiff and hoarse, thanks to a wedge the size of a ripe plum in my gullet, one that would not be swallowed away.

Malcolm bristled, just as I always had when Daddy said the same. His voice cracked with indignation as he sniped, "I'm old enough to see what's before my eyes. I'm old enough to see that she cares for you, even if you can't see it yourself!" And then, figuring he might have pushed too far, the boy fell silent. He eyed me from the corner of his gaze before angling Aces High, his chestnut gelding, away from my surly mood, heeling the animal's sturdy flanks and riding ahead on the dusty trail; the chestnut flowed into a smooth canter, he and the boy graceful as a dancing pair.

I let them go, for now.

Sawyer, I thought, wishing again for the comforting presence of my oldest and dearest friend. *Goddammit, you should be here with us. You an' Lorie should both be here. We wished for this together. This ain't how it's supposed to be. We ain't supposed to be riding for Minnesota without you.*

I watched Malcolm and Aces grow smaller on the horizon, dust creating a butternut-colored haze behind them. A line of muddy clouds gathered along the western edge of the prairie and I dared to hope for a soaking; though I didn't relish riding wet, rainfall would cool the air and seemed the lesser of two evils, just now. Fortune nickered and tossed her head, as though sharing my sentiments; I patted my mare's familiar neck, stroking with my knuckles.

I murmured, "There's a girl. You's restless, ain't you?" and scanned the horizon, wondering if a critter stalked us in the prairie grasses grown tall and rangy with approaching autumn, and therefore beyond my sight. The horses had been skittish all day, for no reason I could identify. I fingered the stock of my pistol, rubbing a thumb along the familiar wood grain; we hunted with the rifles and there'd been no need to use the smaller firearm as we'd ridden northward, but I was reassured by its presence on my hip, all the same. We'd left Iowa City a good fortnight past, traveling since then beneath mainly warm, dry skies; Iowa City was a town we'd meant to travel through and well beyond much earlier this summer, with no plans to linger within city limits. A string of misfortunes kept us there long past our original intent.

Things happen for a reason, son, I heard my dear mama say. *Trouble is we don't always understand until we look back.*

Aw, Mama, I thought, and a familiar lash of pain struck me at the memory of her voice. It seemed every bit of love I'd ever dared to feel was tangled up with hurt, and I did not know how, or if it was even possible, to go about untangling it.

My folks loved each other, this was a certainty I'd never questioned. Growing up in the holler in the wilds of eastern Tennessee, my kin had not been blessed with fortune – at least, not the sort you could stick in a bank. Ours was fortune of another kind, the blessing of a contented life. Daddy farmed, grew corn and flax on the ridge; many a night I lay on the feather tick alongside Beaumont, my elder brother, who always fell asleep before me, our hands callused and our napes burnt red, staring into the darkness and seeing nothing but the neat, straight rows of black earth which we'd worked all the livelong day. Even when sleep did come, at last, I dreamed of the orderly dropping of seeds into the ground.

And yet, I had not been unhappy or restless as a boy; I sure as hell never figured I'd settle farther from my family's land than I could chuck a sizeable stone. I lived for the evening hours, when Mama would ring the dinner bell and we'd gather to eat in the purple gloom of twilight. Candlelight would shimmer over Mama's hair and reflect in her bright eyes. Daddy would put his hands around the delicate notches of her waist and nuzzle her neck with his beard until she shooed him aside. There would be a spat or two between Beau and me – mild-mannered as Grafton was he could seldom be roused to fighting, and was Mama's baby long before Malcolm came along – which Daddy would settle with a cuff to the back of the worse offender's head. Mama would scold and squawk even as she clapped food upon our plates, using the serving spoon that came all the way from England with Daddy's family generations ago, and finally everyone would settle at the table for grace. After dinner, Daddy played the fiddle.

Daddy's elder brother, Malcolm, lived near in those days, and our Carter cousins were present for about every other dinner hour, along with the Davises, whose homestead ran the length of the holler on the opposite side of the ridge. Uncle Malcolm had proudly constructed the family fiddles, a trade which he inherited from his own daddy, Brandon Bartholomew Carter, who was a carpenter's apprentice in the land of his birth before he ventured across an ocean to America. Those golden evenings on the porch blend one into the other in my memory; Daddy would uncork a jug of apple pie, or buckeye bush, and he and Uncle Malcolm wielded their bows between sips, each pull longer than the next, until the stars shifted halfway over the holler. We kids stole nips when we thought they wasn't looking. Far removed from those days and that familiar place, I could still taste the whiskey on the back of my tongue, the sharp sting that prickled a boy's nose hairs, followed by the heady warmth of the booze.

I longed for a jug of my daddy's whiskey just now; I would slip free the cork with a flick of my thumb and down the top half in one good swallow. And still it would not banish the picture of Rebecca Krage's eyes from my mind, this I knew. Not all the 'shine in Tennessee could do that. I had not intended to look back as we rode away from the dooryard of her homestead, there on the outskirts of Iowa City. I meant to keep my gaze on the horizon where my future lay in wait, in the North, but in the end I disobeyed my own order.

"Please take care of yourself," she'd whispered the grim, overcast morning we rode out.

A wad of cotton batting had seemed lodged in my throat as I stood near Fortune with one hand resting atop my sorrel's hide, the other hanging uselessly. I wanted to gather Rebecca to my heart and hold her close, as I had dared to do only once before. I'd studied her face in the early-morning light, greedy for a last sight of its sweet beauty, for a final glimpse of the expression in her eyes; no one had ever looked at me exactly the way Rebecca Krage did. She held my gaze and did not cry, but her lips trembled before she bit savagely upon the lower. My eyes followed the motion and I felt kicked in the ribs at the sight of her soft, curving mouth; even in the brief time our paths had crossed, I'd imagined claiming it probably hundreds of times…imagined what I would feel to taste her kiss, to sink my hands into the thick waterfall of her dark hair…

Jesus Christ, I thought, torturing myself anew. I refused to let the vision follow through to its end. Rebecca was a lady, born and bred, and a Yankee widow, to boot. I was no gentleman, and bore little hope of ever attaining the title. I had not been the one to kill her husband, Elijah Krage, but I may as well have – a Reb bullet sent him to whatever lay beyond death back in the wretched summer of 'sixty-three. And I'd been a Reb soldier to the bitter end. Elijah Krage had left his beloved wife and home to march to War in 1862, same as me, likely for reasons just as good as I'd once believed my own, and later died on a battlefield distant from Iowa. He would never look upon his youngest son's face; neither would his elder son remember him, as Cort had been very young at the time of his daddy's death. Rebecca was the one left behind, plagued by her memories.

Before Malcolm and I left, Lorie had clutched my elbows and fixed me with her sternest brow. When she spoke, her voice held notes of both determination and desperation; she knew I was set on my course, but it didn't stop her from saying, *Becky loves you, Boyd. Do not claim you are unaware of this.*

I scrubbed a hand over my face as I rode beneath the blistering sun, swiping at sweat and painful regret, with little hope of easing either. My jaw clenched and I tasted blood from the small cut inside my cheek, which I'd bit only this morning. A teetering pile of heavy stones, blunt and cold, seemed stacked atop my heart; I could not deny the truth in Lorie's words any more than I could deny that I saw in my best friend's remaining eye that he believed I should not leave Rebecca behind.

It's what's best, I'd argued. Sawyer, Lorie, and I had been gathered in the small bedroom within Rebecca's home, debating in hushed voices that night. *She's a Yankee. Besides, she's promised to Quade.*

Growing ever frustrated with me, Lorie had contradicted, *She would refuse Quade in a heartbeat if you stayed here, you know this.*

My hands fisted around Fortune's reins at the thought of Marshal Leverett Quade, even as I continued arguing with my pitiful self.

I thought, *Rebecca wanted you to stay in Iowa, don't pretend otherwise. But… would she have chosen you over Quade, in the end? You'd be the fool if you stayed behind and she had not.*

Furthermore, I was determined to reach the place I had set out to reach upon leaving Tennessee last spring, come hell or high water as Daddy always used to say, and Minnesota was this place. The very last of my blood kin, other than Malcolm, there lived, my mama's youngest brother, Jacob Miller, who had left Cumberland County and roamed northward long before War ripped apart the country. Having forged a life in the North, Jacob now homesteaded near a lake called Flickertail, was wed to a Winnebago woman named Hannah, with four children of their own. Malcolm could not remember Jacob but I'd been near to thirteen years old before he left the holler with little more than his horse and hunting rifle, and Jacob's face and voice were both present and accounted for in my memory.

Come to us in Minnesota, boy, Jacob wrote last winter, and the draw of family was more than I could resist. I recalled sitting near the hearth in the home of my youth and reading aloud this request to my brother, and later, to Sawyer and another longtime friend, Gus Warfield. Jacob's words insisted, *Come to Hannah and me, and bring with you young Malcolm. We will welcome you. You boys can make a new start here. There is nothing left in Tennessee for you now.*

I'd written Jacob in return, painstakingly, as I was a poor student at best. I explained that I would be joined on this journey by Gus Warfield and Sawyer Davis, two men Jacob had known in the years of our old lives, those of quietude that existed before the War. I assured my uncle I would work hard, that I would earn my keep and my land, and would not be a burden to him; I'd sold that which we did not require for the journey, scraping together enough for the fee to file for a homestead in Minnesota, an amount of ten dollars. The only assumption Uncle Jacob made wrongly was the one concerning Tennessee – but what was left in my beloved home state was a deep hole of memories, raw and sore as unhealed wounds. All the Carters that had once populated the ridge were gone, dead and buried, almost as though they'd never existed. Tennessee was a place best left behind, we all four understood well and good; Gus, Sawyer, the boy, and me.

Rebecca darlin', and I dared to call her such in my mind, if not actual life. *You are better off without me. You'll see this in time, now that I ain't there. But it hurt to leave you. It hurt so goddamn much. If things was different...if I had a hope of being the man you deserve...*

You are too harsh on yourself, by far, Sawyer had said the night before Malcolm and I planned our leave-taking.

My oldest friend, who had survived the War with only minor physical damage, studied me with his remaining eye; the other had been lost to the bullet of a Federal soldier no more than a month past, and well over three years after the Surrender. The man who had done this to him, Zeb Crawford, would have liked to see us all dead. Crawford's hatred I could understand, hatred being something I grappled with myself. Dozens of times I'd fought Federal soldiers for my very life, in battles made all the more miserable for the sultry summer heat, or during winter campaigns, when the snow grew red with fallen blood far faster than the fallow brown fields of autumn. Enemy soldiers clad in the faded blue I had come to loathe, bearded and grizzled and ever thinner as the War dragged on, and on, long past all reason. Hatred I understood. It did not mean, however, that I would allow someone who hated me and mine with such ferocity to live to see the dawn. *Hell, no.* I felt no guilt, or shame, and would not, over firing my pistol into Crawford that terrible night. I only wished I had fired with truer aim, so the bastard had been dead all the quicker.

I'd said to Sawyer that evening, *I ain't harsh on myself. I'm simply speaking the truth.* But Sawyer knew me as well as any brother; he saw my faults and my weaknesses, and I knew he was right, even if I wouldn't admit it.

Lorie had stood at Sawyer's side, as befitting the two of them, and she'd sighed, leveling me with her eyes and the somber set of her chin. In a last effort to convince me, she'd whispered, *Boyd, please...*

Please what? I'd responded, too sharply, as Sawyer sent me a look of warning. Even with only one eye, he made sure I understood his look. I heaved a sigh; I loved Lorie like a sister; I'd said, *I'm sorry, Lorie-girl. But I mean what I say. There ain't no good can come of it.*

And I could reach no other conclusion, even now as I rode my sorrel through the blazing August heat. Rebecca would not leave, and I could not stay. She was a Yankee, a widow, and a truer lady I had never known, other than my own mama. Rebecca was educated, well-spoken, and unafraid to speak her mind, which I admired above all else. And I admired her nearly every moment, whether she was in my line of sight, or not. Her skin was the tint of cream skimmed from the top of the milk pail, the kind I'd licked from the spoon many a time. I dreamed by day and again by night of kissing that fine skin, of unbuttoning her dress and tasting her mouth, her breasts, her belly and thighs and what was surely the damp sweetness between her legs...

Stop, I ordered, sweat beading along the full length of my spine. I was short of breath, lightheaded at the very thought of putting my mouth and hands upon Rebecca that way; it only proved to me that I did not deserve her, entertaining such lustful thoughts about a proper lady. I was no virgin, and had not been since the age of nineteen. The first instance I'd been allowed the gift of a woman's body was with a girl who was part of a troupe the Second Corps recruits, tenderfoots and has-beens alike, referred to as camp followers.

Play yer cards right, fellas, our commanding officer had said, grinning around his cigar. *They ain't the marrying kind if you know what I mean, boys. But they's good gals, an' willing to spread their legs for the right price.*

This particular girl's name had been Sallyanne; she did indeed spread her legs and if I learned her surname I had long since forgot it. Long, hay-colored hair falling over plump bare shoulders, a wide, knowing smile with two teeth missing from the bottom row; nipples near the size and shade of ripe cherries. I'd been nervous as a hen in her cramped tent, and embarrassed myself nigh unto death when I let loose before even gaining entry into her body, at merely the sight of the treasure hidden beneath the layers of her skirts. Until that moment, I had only the stories Ethan Davis told of girls to satisfy my curiosity, and there before my eyes in the lantern light was a tangle of dark hair, arrow-shaped − to guide a man's way, as Ethan always joked − and soft folds the color of the pinkest of the cosmos in my mama's garden. Greedy, I'd wanted to touch every part of her at once. She laughed and gamely let me have another go, for no charge. Even the second time around and firmly within her body, I'd come faster than I ever had using my own hand.

I like this curly hair, she told me, fingering my scalp. *You's a good-looking fella. You'll have a longer frolic next time, honey, don't you worry none. You's just too fraught this time around.*

And since, there had been many such frolics with many such girls, the brides of no one and everyone, all at once. I was not proud of myself on that front. My daddy would thrash the devil out of me if he was alive and knew how many women had spread their legs and let me spill my seed within their bodies, unable to resist the momentary rush of flooding pleasure, the sweetness of holding close a warm, naked woman and feeling her breasts and belly pressed flush to my thrusting body. Until meeting Lorie that night in St. Louis, I was ashamed to admit I hadn't given a thought to the daily lives of those whorehouse girls. I never considered where they'd come from, or who they might have loved, or been loved by, in their pasts. They'd all seemed the same until Lorie − lusty women with coy smiles and soft thighs easily parted. That fateful night we first met Lorie was the last time I'd been with a woman.

If things was different, sweet Rebecca, if I'd never fought for a Cause your husband, and you, so strongly opposed…I need to make my way beholden to no one, do you understand? I ain't good enough for a lady with a proper way of speaking, with proper opinions…

I would be your wife, she seemed to whisper, but it was only the play of the wind over the prairie, and my damnable imagination, wishing as always for things it would never have. I supposed I should know better by now; I'd always been a fine one for wanting that which was beyond my means. I wished my daddy was alive, for more reasons than I could rightly name, but mostly – at least, just now – so that he could wallop some good sense back into me. I knew Rebecca's middle name, as I'd heard her uncle, Edward Tilson, once address her using it, and thought, fancying that she could hear, *Rebecca Lynn, I know I rode away from you but I will never forget you, I swear on my life.* I'd looked over my shoulder as Malcolm and I rode out of the yard at a steady trot and saw her, watching after us. She stood with her arms crossed at her waist, gripping her elbows; she did not lift a hand in farewell. She watched until we were out of sight, I knew, and could not force the picture from my head. I damn well realized that soon enough she would become Rebecca Lynn Quade – Marshal Quade had pursued her hand without rest – and if I knew what was good for me, I would stop thinking of her altogether.

"*I miss Lorie-Lorie*," Malcolm moaned for the fourth or fifth time, and his sobbing edged another notch higher. He was tuckered, far beyond out-of-sorts, and had lay crying for the past half hour, with no notion of stopping anytime soon. He curled into a pitiful knot with his head buried in both arms, shuddering.

I bent my elbow and resettled my cheek atop this uncomfortable make-shift pillow made of my arm. The small feather pillow that had accompanied me without harm all the way from Cumberland County had fallen from Fortune's back and was swept away in the river we'd forded just before making camp this evening. I could have galloped after the damn thing; I wished now that I had. The day's oppressive humidity lingered, unpleasant as moist palms pressing against my face; I'd shucked down to nothing but the lower half of my union suit but even being near naked didn't help. I'd erected a small canvas tarpaulin at an angle, under which we'd positioned our heads, able in this way to have a hope of staying dry; traveling light as we were, and without a wagon, I'd not hauled along our wall tent and its wooden poles. The hot, motionless air was thick as a jar of sorghum syrup.

A few paces beyond where we lay, the horses stirred with agitation, unable to sleep in the blasted heat; Fortune issued a low, uneasy whinny. I had patted Malcolm's back, as I would a small babe's, when his tears first came surging, but now I could hardly bear to listen to another wail. It wasn't that I was angry at him. It was more that I was afraid I might fold, and join him in weeping.

"I know," I whispered, aiming for a steady voice even as my throat bobbed. I felt I had to admit it, and so muttered, "I miss them, too."

"We coulda *stayed*," the boy sobbed.

"No, we could not," I said, and knew this for the painful truth. "We got weeks of travel, an' weeks more of work to prepare for winter." I ground my teeth to keep from ordering him to hush the hell up. It would do no good to be harsh when he was hurting but I clamped down on my tongue, all the same.

Wheezing between every other word, Malcolm moaned, "I miss…Stormy. What if…the boys…don't watch out for him? I want to sit…at the table… with *ever'body*."

I bit my cheek for the second time this day with my infernal tooth-grinding, cursing under my breath. I squeezed tight my eyes and gripped my forehead until it hurt; against my better judgment I let my thoughts stray to the dinner surely taking place back at Rebecca's hearth, in the house where we'd lived for the better part of this past summer and where Sawyer and Lorie would continue to live until next spring, when they intended to continue onward to Minnesota. I pictured Rebecca placing dishes on the table, loading it with her delectable cooking until it all but creaked. She was always the last to take her place, untying her apron strings before sitting, with the ease of an oft-repeated gesture. I'd noticed every last time, watching as she reached behind her waist to release the ties before hanging the apron upon its hook near the woodstove, the exact same way she would reach back to unbutton her dress at day's end. The mere thought of being privy to such an intimate moment threatened my resolve. I pictured the way her dress would slip from her shoulders and sink slowly to the floor, becoming a puddle of material at her bare feet.

I growled at my brother, "Hush the hell up."

Malcolm hushed his words but not his crying. My arm prickled with stitching needles, numb beneath the weight of my thick skull, and I flopped to the opposite side, my nose but a few inches from the slope of the dirty-white canvas. I was determined to tune out Malcolm's sobs; I knew he would tucker and give way to sleep after a spell. I closed my eyes, thinking I might lose my mind before this night was through, what with the heat and Malcolm's lamenting, and my own damnable thoughts – the one thing I couldn't outride. I was accustomed to sharing a sleeping space with my brother. Back along the trail, before we'd reached Iowa City, nothing had troubled me this way as I lay awake, not Malcolm's sawing snores or the rasping crickets, not the horses' shuffling or the ever-present rush of the river near which we always set up our evening camp; even the hushed rustlings of Sawyer and Lorie making love half the damn night hadn't kept me from eventual sleep.

I ground the heels of my palms against my eye sockets and thought, *I wish I'd not left the fiddle behind.*

Making music filled me with great and unbridled joy. I'd learned at Daddy's knee, first by listening and later with an instrument of my own, made for me by Uncle Malcolm. If asked to, I couldn't rightly explain just *how* I made the fiddle sing; I only knew that when I took up my bow and skimmed it over the strings, music flowed forth. It seemed that the notes were in my head already and that my hands and fingers knew what to do with them, moving of their own accord. *You's a natural talent*, Daddy proclaimed when I was just a sprout, and hadn't I been as proud as a peacock, there beneath his beaming praise. Music resounded from one side of the holler to the other in those good old times, and plenty of nights there'd be dancing and singing, too. Whiskey, and bright stars against a blue-black canvas of night, Mama's sweet smile and the love of a family of my own. Knowing I was safe, a blessed time when I was not the eldest member of the Carter family; when there was someone else I could depend upon to make decisions. Christ, it had been so damn long since I'd had that security. I hated to admit to needing comfort but I was lonely as hell, even with Malcolm at my side.

He'd finally quieted and I drew a slow breath through my nose. Just as fast I went cold, eyes opening.

What in the hell?

In response, a gust of wind heaved against the tarpaulin and I sat with a jolt, startling Malcolm. The air over the prairie had altered from oppressive and humid to late-autumn frigid in the span of time it took me to sit upright.

"*No*," I whispered, staring dumbly at the canvas, which obscured my view of the western horizon. I lurched to my knees, grabbing for my rifle and boots.

Over the rising scream of the wind I heard Aces and Fortune in a sudden frenzy of snorting and stomping; any creature with a lick of good sense would already be running hell-and-gone in the opposite direction. Fortune reared, issuing a high-pitched whinny, and I finally stumbled to the conclusion that the horses had reached much earlier this day; I'd been too preoccupied with my own misery to heed their warning. From the distance came a sound like a steam whistle, growing ever louder. My heart burst into my throat.

"Christ Almighty," I croaked. "Malcolm –"

"What's –"

"Grab your boots an' *c'mon!*" I cried, lurching from beneath the canvas, never minding my lack of clothes; we had to get to safety. Distracted I may have been, but it was no excuse – as I would learn all too soon. The wind's chill stole my breath as I tugged on my boots without releasing my rifle. Lightning sizzled and its brief illumination showed me the towering funnel cloud. For the space of a second flash, a trio of rapid heartbeats, I stared, slack-jawed and mesmerized. The sight was one of certain doom, a rank of Federals charging with muskets at the ready, a mounted cavalryman closing fast, saber angled to strike…

"Sweet *bleedin' Jesus*," I muttered, but barely heard my own words over the raging, teakettle-shrieking of the wind. My fingers clenched around the stock of my rifle, as though I had any chance of preventing the advance of such a creature with bullets. It seemed to me that I moved through a swamp, my heels sunk in tar, when in truth my feet hit the ground like those of a cantering horse. I clenched hold of Malcolm, who was carrying his boots, too stunned to jam them into place, and hauled him along behind. Wind scraped our hair and blasted our faces with what felt like small pebbles. There was a sharp cracking of thunder and hail exploded from the sky, near the size of marbles. These bounced from the ground and gathered in piles, striking our heads and shoulders as we freed Aces and Fortune. They could not be left tethered beneath the trees.

"Follow me!" I shouted in Malcolm's ear, making certain he followed. Then I ran, carrying my rifle, leading my horse. Once away from the cluster of cottonwoods beneath which we'd set up camp, I stopped running and grabbed for my brother's shoulder. I understood that we could not huddle here and hold fast to our horses; they were spooked and could kick us to death, even if that was not their intent. An agony of indecision ripped at my gut – I could not set them free to bolt and leave us stranded, but mounting and attempting to ride frantic horses through the dark was foolish, at best. I spied a stand of brush close to the creek and yelped, "Yonder!"

Malcolm did not hesitate to obey and we tied the horses to the wind-whipped brush, fingers fumbling with the familiar task in our haste; I prayed it would be enough to hold them. Both Aces and Fortune reared and danced, fighting their tethers, but we could do no more for them just now. I would not risk harm to Malcolm.

"Stay put!" I yelled to my horse, resting a palm briefly to her neck, praying she would heed these words.

My heart beat too swiftly to fall; instead I clenched Malcolm's elbow and dragged him a goodly distance, shoving him to the wet ground and laying atop him, bracing my forearms about his head, protecting him just as I had the night Zeb Crawford fired his rifle into our wagon. Hail clattered around us, loud as artillery rounds. The grass crushed by our bodies scratched my face and bare torso while the rest of the prairie flapped in a frenzy of motion. I could not resist looking up into the storm and lightning seared my eyeballs. When I blinked, crooked blue-white lines jangled my vision.

Holy Jesus, I thought, ears ringing with the storm's fury. *The sky is screaming. It's screaming at us. Holy Jesus.*

We can't die here, I thought next. How many times had I thought the same goddamn thing, as a soldier? Sawyer at my side on the battlefield, both of us covered in filth and gore, begging for grace. I'd been as good as dead a hundred times as a soldier, and yet here I lay, less than a day's ride from the Minnesota border, at the mercy of a goddamn storm.

The thick black column roared our direction from the western horizon, perhaps a hundred feet from my nose. I stared, overcome with the horror and wonder of it – both at once, a strange mix of feelings – unable to tear free my eyes. I caught a better glimpse each time lightning flared. Driven forward by its swirling momentum, the twister appeared to pulse and grow, snapping trees as though the heavy trunks were nothing but spindly matchsticks, creating noise as violent as that of twelve-pound howitzers. Our canvas tarpaulin flew and disappeared like a moth into a flame; the twister appeared to have eaten it. I gaped, my skin stark and wet. A chunk of hail gashed my forehead. Our clothes and blankets, and then – *holy God* – the small creek was sucked into the storm's mouth. I struggled to believe my eyes, watching water flow upward into the air, a spell cast by an illusionist, something not real, certainly not possible. The water rose, danced, twirled like a dust devil, and became part of the whirling madness.

It'll pass, I thought, finding a measure of calm even as the howling of the wind seemed to rip the thought right out of my head. Surely it was the Carter vanity, or perhaps my own foolish pride, but I'd always figured I'd know my time of dying, and this moment was not it. Death had aimed for me plenty in the past and I well understood that there would come a time when I could no longer dodge its reach, God help me.

But not this night, I thought, and bent my face to Malcolm's hair, damp beneath my cheek, beset by love for him. *Not this night. Hold tight, boy. It'll pass.*

If there was one lesson that had penetrated my stubborn head in this life, it was that. Whether it be a storm or a battle, the anguish of combat or love, and eventually life itself – everything passed.

F ALLON'S RUN AWAY," was the first news Charley Rawley bestowed
upon arriving in the dooryard.

We had not been blessed with Charley's company for over a month and
he appeared unexpectedly this evening. Leaning on the corral fence, daw-
dling for a spell in the intoxicating sunset light, I had watched him approach
since his horse blinked into view as a small black dot on the horizon, glad
to see him but cautious nonetheless; only news of significance retained the
power to draw Charley from his family and their homestead many dozens
of miles south. The single word creeping through my thoughts as I watched
him cantering in had been *Yancy*, but the Yancy of whom I sought news, and
deeply feared, was Fallon's father, Thomas. Sawyer, in the barn brushing down
Whistler, came out into the evening at the sound of Charley's greeting. As
ever, at the sight of my husband a powerful surge of love, and simple gladness,
quickened my pulse. I thought of what I'd told Sawyer just last night and felt
a renewed flooding of tenderness.

"Run away?" I parroted, standing clear of the corral gate as Charley dismounted and led his gorgeous blue roan within. I closed the gate and summarily climbed the bottom rung, as was my habit, so that I could latch my
elbows over the top-most beam. Wearing the trousers Malcolm had left behind for my use and Sawyer's broad-brimmed hat – my own inadvertently
stomped upon by Hattie the milking cow, and now unwearable – I regarded
the intelligent, well-spoken man we had come to trust as a friend.

"Rawley," Sawyer said, shaking Charley's hand.

Charley resettled his hat and tipped the brim at me, murmuring, "Good
evening, dear Lorie," reminding me of the first moment of meeting him last

summer, when he mistook me for a boy. It did strike me as somewhat humorous that to Charley it must seem as though I was clad far more often in garments intended for men; even now, with my braid tucked under Sawyer's hat and a length of ribbon securing the waistband of my boyish trousers, I was far from properly attired. But Charley grinned, acknowledging my lack of concern over the matter, before his mustache fell back into the somber, half-frowning expression he'd worn as he rode into the dooryard.

He explained, "We have not seen hide or hair of the boy in, well, close to a month now, I would suppose, unless he has returned in my absence, though I haven't the sense that he shall have. Fannie is quite beside herself with worry. Fallon disappeared in the night hours, taking his horse with him. Stole a saddle from the tack room. Or perhaps I shall use the word 'borrowed,' until I am able to prove otherwise." Charley, a kind soul with five of his own rowdy boys, remained magnanimous as ever. He continued, "The boys and I rode at once to their homestead, but it remains unchanged. I do not believe Fallon ventured there, or if so, he did not linger long, as not a thing was disturbed. We'd since taken in their livestock."

"And of his father?" I ventured, hesitant to speak aloud Thomas Yancy's name, as though to do so would be to summon him. When I caught myself wringing my hands, I summarily ceased the motion. Sawyer came to stand near me, on the opposite side of the corral fence. The last of the sun shone over his golden hair and the angles of the face I loved more than all else in the world. He cupped my shoulder, stroking with his thumb, knowing I needed the reassurance of his touch.

"Not a word," Charley confirmed. He rested four fingertips briefly upon my forearm, braced along the corral, his touch conveying compassion; he knew how I feared Yancy, the vindictive marshal whose whereabouts remained unknown. Beneath his hat brim, Charley's dark eyes scrutinized my face. He spoke quietly. "His absence troubles me greatly, as well."

Edward Tilson, local physician and Sawyer's and my savior in more ways than one, appeared in the open door and called, "Rawley! Good evening to you, sir. I s'pose you smelled supper on the air."

"And a fine one, from the scent!" Charley returned; he was familiar with Tilson's bantering.

"Lorie-love," Sawyer murmured, offering me his arm, and the three of us walked through the dusky air, tinted a warm rose as the sun sank. Lightning bugs, which I'd been silently admiring before Charley's horse appeared on the horizon, flitted in the tall grass and late-blooming wildflowers nodding their blossomed heads in the roadside ditches. We were dining late this evening, as Tilson had only recently returned from setting a broken arm.

Tilson stood wiping his gnarled hands on a length of huck toweling, watching us come near. His gray hair hung past his jaws on either side, in need of combing as usual; Tilson was not one for fussy grooming. In his rasping voice, courtesy of a Yankee rope about his neck during the War, he demanded of Charley, "What news have you?"

"Yancy's eldest has disappeared," Charley said.

"Who has disappeared?" Rebecca asked, joining her uncle at the door, peering around his left shoulder. Spying Charley, she invited, "Do come in, Mr. Rawley."

"And not a word on the location of Yancy himself, either," Tilson said, in a grim undertone. "At least, not in town. He ain't yet reappeared on his homestead, is that right? It's already September the first and shortly it'll be two months gone since he rode away from this very yard."

Charley nodded affirmation. "There has been no sign of the man, despite the efforts of several searching parties. I shall wash quickly and join you. I've other news, as well," he said, and detoured around the north side of the house, to the hand pump. Beneath its dripping spout, a cluster of rangy white daisies had grown to the height of my thighs.

Unable to resist the urge, I leaned against Sawyer's warm, strong side, thankful for the security of him; he tucked me closer at once, kissing the top of my head. I heard the thought he sent my way, *Don't fear, love.*

I don't mean to…

Two dozen steps beyond the house in which resided Tilson, Rebecca Krage, her sons, Cort and Nathaniel, and her brother, Clint Clemens, there squatted the emerging structure of a small shanty cabin intended for mine and Sawyer's use this coming winter; all that was required was a last row of shingles over the tar paper. Although I knew Sawyer longed for us to be on the trail with Boyd and Malcolm, and chafed at the circumstances which forced us to remain behind for a time, I cared only for his recovery. Physically he was repairing well – the burns and bruises ravaging his flesh had slowly faded as they healed; his shoulder bore no more than a rounded red scar on the front, roughly the size of my thumbnail, and a thin reddish line along the back, where Tilson had neatly stitched the incision he'd sliced to free a bullet from Sawyer's body.

Sawyer's distress, and subsequent frustration, was born of the limitations forced upon him by his missing left eye. His head ached, fiercely at times, and he grew dizzy riding Whistler; numerous times I reminded him that only a short span had passed since the grievous injury, and that it would ease with time. I worried so for him that some nights, even after the intensity of our joining, I lay sleepless and fretful, listening to him breathe and praying he would be fully able to come to terms with the injury. For my sake, I knew he minimized his pain and strove not to complain, but as well as we sensed each other's thoughts I understood what he kept from me. And Sawyer knew this, too. His internal agony was as potent to me as my own.

Stormy, Malcolm's gray cat, paced near the woodstove; the animal had been left behind to traverse northward with Sawyer and me, come spring. It had been weeks since Boyd and Malcolm departed for Minnesota, armed with rifles, pistols, and rounds, food, bundles of winter clothing, and little else, prepared to ride hard, intending to reach Jacob Miller's homestead by September's end. The ache of their absence stung as nettles dragged over my skin. Each night I whispered a prayer for them, calling to my sweet Malcolm in my mind, wishing him safe. I knew Boyd would care for and protect the boy, but I longed for Malcolm in the way of a mother, imagining him hurt – an arm twisted, a knee scraped – his freckled face wet with tears before he fell asleep, for I knew he missed me every bit as devotedly. Who would sing with him? Who would pet his hair and hold him? Boyd loved him, this I knew without question, but Malcolm needed a woman's touch; since very nearly the first night we had met I'd imagined myself a surrogate mother to him, his own mama having succumbed to illness years ago, during the terrible last year of the War.

Sawyer drew out my chair and I took my customary place, to Rebecca's right. She placed the last dish upon the well-laden table and hooked her apron near the woodstove before curving a hand over my shoulder, an affectionate gesture so common to her. I smiled up at her, this woman I had grown to love as well as a sister, who had opened her home to us without question, offering friendship and kindness and acceptance. Her hair, dark and lustrous as polished walnut, was twisted back from her face, her green eyes taking on a fetching golden cast in the lantern light, a lovely shade much like Sawyer's.

Her lips softened at the sight of my smile and then became wistful, whether she knew I recognized it or not; she glanced at the chair which Boyd had always claimed, and swallowed with difficulty, before turning abruptly away. Rebecca loved Boyd, this I knew as certainly as the full moon would shine, a seamlessly-sculpted ivory circle, in this night's sky. And if his absence hurt me, it was miniscule compared to her pain; I would see Boyd again, come next year, whereas Rebecca had resigned herself to a life without him. I struggled to accept this truth; I wanted so badly to beg her to accompany us in spring, to forego her unspoken promise to Marshal Quade and instead reunite with Boyd, but I understood the irrationality of such longings. Rebecca was a mother and a lady, rooted in the security of the comfortable home she had made here in Iowa, and Marshal Quade had courted her in earnest now that Boyd was absent. Whether Quade harbored ill will towards Boyd, I knew not; Quade had never behaved as less than a gentleman in Boyd's presence, though I suspected he had at the very least sensed the imminence of Boyd's threat to his position in Rebecca's life, as he'd never been *exactly* friendly with Boyd. Now that Boyd had departed for the Northland, Quade's bearing grew daily less imposing and more relaxed; only a few nights past, I'd witnessed him laugh.

I knew Rebecca cared for Quade; I had grown to recognize him as a kind and honorable man, though I continued to struggle to refer to him as Lev, as did Rebecca, or even Leverett, as my first interactions with the man, which had been so formal, continued to color my perception of him. But I acknowledged Quade's overall decency, and his devotion to both Rebecca and her boys was as evident as the nose upon his face. These truths were, however, coupled with my knowledge that Rebecca's feelings for Quade paled in comparison to those she harbored, and would continue to harbor, for Boyd. During our frequent conversations, which I cherished, Rebecca and I shared hushed confidences in the way of sisters but even had she never spoken aloud her longing for Boyd, I would have known.

Peering at Rebecca from the corner of my gaze, I thought, *Dearest, I would do almost anything to bring him back for you. I know he loves you. He was just too damn stubborn to admit to it.*

I stretched my mind out across the endless miles even as I comprehended the futility of such an undertaking, picturing the prairie racing beneath my gaze, faster than any speed possible by man or horse. It was a wishful attempt, at best, as I knew Boyd and Malcolm could not sense my thoughts as could Sawyer. Still, I entreated Boyd, willing him to hear. *Come back for her. Please, come back for her.*

Of course there was no response; though I had not truly expected one, a small, cold chill centered itself at the base of my neck. I was unduly troubled that I failed to perceive a sense of either Boyd or Malcolm, not the faintest inkling. I refused to pose the question of their potential whereabouts just now, for fear of upsetting Rebecca; though she already worried for the same reason, even if she had not voiced it in so many words. We had received no letter from Boyd, no note hastily scrawled – he was not given to lengthy letter-writing, I knew, but there had been exactly nothing thus far, not so much as a scrap posted from a town in either Iowa or Minnesota to inform us of their progress. By now they must certainly have ridden near enough a settlement to post a letter; based upon our collective calculations and subsequent detailed examination of the mapped route, we assumed they had by now reached the Minnesota border, but we'd received no evidence to offer reassurance.

I would ask Sawyer later, when we were alone in the shanty cabin.

Charley entered from outside and Rebecca made certain her boys, Cort and little Nathaniel, were settled before taking her own place, the last to be seated. Tilson led grace; I slipped my hand into Sawyer's, to my right, and he curled tight my fingers as Tilson said, "Amen."

"Fannie sends her regards," Charley said, as everyone fell to passing dishes.

"I imagine her hands are full," Rebecca said, and then, to Nathaniel, "Do not feed the cat at the table, young man."

"That they are," Charley acknowledged. "And now with the distraction of Fallon's disappearance she is in an inconsolable state of nerves. I do confess I am angered at the boy's seeming lack of concern for what his actions have caused. To leave, with no explanation, not even to his brother. And to what end? I intend to place an ad in the town circular, seeking any word of the boy's whereabouts. Otherwise I should not have ventured so far from home in the midst of such an occurrence."

Sawyer knew, and shared, my dislike of Fallon Yancy, only compounded tenfold now that we knew of what his father, Thomas Yancy, was capable. I tried, chiefly in vain, to remind myself Fallon was only a boy, no more than fourteen years of age. As a young runaway he was bound for potential danger, no matter what his motives for the decision.

With his usual gruff and impertinent humor, Tilson observed, "Rawley, if one plans to run away it hardly seems wise to inform another party of the intent."

Charley snorted a laugh, shaking his head. "Tilson, you've a point, I shall not argue, but it concerns me greatly that a youth in my charge, however tentative, has gone missing."

"Do you believe the boy has attempted to reunite with his father? Or perhaps his father has made contact with him?" I inquired; it was the first explanation that occurred to me upon Charley's announcement.

"I was about to ask the same," Sawyer said. Beneath the table, he rested his hand upon my right thigh, patting me twice.

"I should like to believe Thomas would present himself to me, and to Fannie, in the manner of a grown man, not to mention that of a United States Marshal. Yet, given recent circumstances, I've come to realize I know very little about the man's intentions. It stands to reason that he could have made contact with his elder son between now and last July. But Dredd spoke nothing of such, and I would presume that Yancy would attempt to reach the both of them." Charley sighed and seemed to dislike the pall cast over the table at his words; he turned to me and politely changed the subject. "Fannie is especially interested to hear how well you have enjoyed learning to midwife."

Tilson's kind, blue-gray eyes alighted upon me and he beamed with all the pride of a father. "I've said it before and I'll say it many times after your absence, Lorie. You are indispensable. An admirably fast learner."

"And you have been a most gracious teacher." I smiled his way with genuine affection, my cheeks flushing with both pride and the joy of my own recent discovery, ever so new and precious. Edward Tilson, Rebecca's uncle, had doctored his entire adult life, first in Tennessee, the land of his birth, and through the duration of the War, and now attended to those in Iowa City and its neighboring farms; he had relocated after the Surrender, to live with his sister's children in Iowa. Rebecca and her younger brother shared with Tilson the homestead where Rebecca's father brought the family many years ago, and in which she had lived as a new bride, and later a widow, after her husband, Elijah Krage, was killed in 1863.

Their home was already cramped, even before the unexpected arrival of four complete strangers, as Boyd, Malcolm, Sawyer and I had been to them earlier this summer, and so the shanty cabin constructed for Sawyer's and my use would be more than welcome upon our vacating it come spring. I knew Rebecca intended to remain on this homestead after she married Marshal Quade; following the wedding, Tilson would occupy the shanty cabin, and Clemens spoke of renting his own room, nearer to town, where he was employed as deputy sheriff. Clemens had not joined us for dinner this evening, as he was on duty, and also possessed of a rather shy, solitary soul.

"Even sound teaching is only as effective as the pupil's abilities," Tilson said modestly. "You've a fine natural talent."

Sawyer caught my gaze and asked, *Would you like to wait?*

No, I said in return, a smile seeming to split my face. I'd spoken with Rebecca this morning, but no one else knew.

Tilson set down his fork at the sight of my expression and observed, "Lorie, you've the look of the cat that stole the cream. What are you about this evening?"

Rebecca, delighted, clasped my forearm and squeezed.

"We…that is, Sawyer and I…we are…" Tears surged to my eyes at the notion of something so wondrous.

Sawyer took my right hand into his left and folded together our fingers. Everyone had stopped eating, even Cort and Nathaniel, watching with expectant excitement. His deep voice rife with elation and pride, Sawyer said, "Lorie told me just last night that we are to be parents in the spring."

The table erupted with congratulatory chaos. My tears overspilled and I leaned against Sawyer, who kissed my forehead. I remained a bit ashamed of my own failure to notice my monthly bleeding had ceased nearly six weeks ago. Occupied as I'd been with the traumatic events of the summer, it took Sawyer's half-teasing observation to trigger the realization that there was a very good reason for this absence.

"I swear I am not imagining it, darlin'," he'd whispered only last night, as we lay snuggled beneath our quilts.

"Imagining what?" I'd murmured in lazy response, savoring the feeling of my backside tucked against the solid warmth of his thighs, so tired my upper eyelids seemed tethered to the lower.

He pressed his lips to my nape, sweeping aside my hair to do so, and settled my breasts within his broad palms. Gently circling both nipples with his thumbs, he murmured, "That your breasts seem to grow fuller with each passing day."

My eyelids parted at this, my hands moving to cup his much larger ones; his knuckles made unyielding ridges beneath my palms and I fitted my fingertips in the valleys between each. It was not until that very moment I counted rapidly backward, racing to recall when last I'd dug my bleeding-cloth bindings from our trunk. As awareness dawned I'd eased to a sitting position, the quilt falling to my hips. Sawyer, mildly alarmed, rose to one elbow. "It's been...it's been...I haven't..." I stumbled, unable to gather enough wits to coherently explain.

"Haven't what, love?" he asked, resting his hands on my bare thighs. He watched as I counted on my fingers, forward through the months this time, my heart fluttering with an exquisite, fledgling happiness.

"May," he understood, even before I spoke, and I nodded, tears brimming in my eyes. He whispered reverently, "Our child, next May."

"Fannie shall be overcome with joy," Charley pronounced, grinning at us here at the crowded dinner table. "What wonderful news. I am delighted to be present for this happy announcement."

"I could not be gladder for you," Rebecca said, tears glistening; she touched the edge of her sleeve to her eyes, each in turn. "And that I shall be able to help you through the process brings me much relief."

Tilson's gaze was ever shrewd, the physician in him emerging forthwith. "No more toting water or riding horseback for you, young lady. I'll warn you right now, I'll be as tetchy as your daddy," and I nodded acquiescence.

Sawyer admitted, "It brings me great comfort knowing there is an abundance of birthing knowledge in this household. I know plenty about the birthing of horses..."

I elbowed his ribs. "I expect it may be a slightly different experience when it is our child. Though, to be quite honest, there are many similarities between birthing a foal and an infant. I thought as such from the first."

However ill-prepared I was at the time, I'd assisted Tilson with the difficult delivery of firstborn twins in July; it brought me great pleasure to occasionally visit them and their soft-spoken mother, Letty Dawes, a girl younger than myself. She and her husband homesteaded west of town. Their twins, named Ulysses and Mabel Lorissa, had grown sweetly round, plump, and kissable; Mabel was my unspoken favorite, as she bore my first name as her second, a gift from Letty to me for the assistance at bringing them into the world. Since that day I'd helped birth seven babies, nowhere near Tilson's overall total, of

which he claimed to have lost track long before the War, but enough to recognize a pattern to the process, a progression consisting of methodical ways in
which to watch for and subsequently read signs; each of these births, though
messy, proved blessedly uncomplicated but Tilson carefully schooled me, most
often as we shared the wagon seat riding home, in the understanding that
babes, and often mothers, were lost in the birthing process. He confessed that
such deaths affected him as badly as any he'd ever witnessed.

"There *is* a certain amount of similarity, however unwilling I should be
to make the observation with the mother in hearing," Rebecca agreed. Her
posture appeared speculative and I could very nearly hear her silent plea;
that of her desire for Sawyer and me to remain in Iowa City rather than
venturing away from her forever. I recognized once Sawyer and I departed it
was unlikely we would ever again see Rebecca or Tilson, and no matter how
frequent and earnest our future correspondence, it could never compare to
the daily relationship we now enjoyed. A small, sharp point needled my heart
at the notion. I dearly loved them both and was overwhelmed with bouts of
guilt, as this was not enough to negate the desire to continue onward, to our
original destination in the wooded lake country of northern Minnesota.

If only they could accompany us...

Charley was saying, "That reminds me. I bear a bit of good news, as well. We've
new neighbors. They purchased Zeb Crawford's claim only a fortnight past and
to my surprise they are a family with whom you've been acquainted, Sawyer. And
you as well, dear Lorie. Their name is Spicer. Henry and Una Spicer."

This surname, Spicer, had the effect of easing, if only minutely, the thrust
of agony the word *Crawford* stabbed into my heart; Zeb Crawford, a beast of
a man, had been the one to rob Sawyer of his left eye.

I nodded in response to Charley's words. "Yes, we had the pleasure of
meeting the Spicer family in Missouri, months back."

Sawyer said, "We did indeed, but I understood them to be traveling farther west than Iowa."

Charley set down his fork and wiped his lips before replying. His tone was
somber as he related, "They intended to reach the Western Territory, that is
true, but were forced to change plans when their two youngest fell ill. They
wished not to remain in Missouri and upon hearing of the availability of so
many farmable acres, instead ventured on into Iowa. For now, they shall set
aside their plan to reach the Rockies."

"And the children?" I asked, ceasing to eat in my sudden concern, clearly picturing the energetic bunch of youngsters we'd met upon the prairie that June evening, under a splendid magenta sunset; together, we'd witnessed thousands of fireflies winking over the wild grass as evening became night. Malcolm had rapidly befriended their eldest son, Cole, while I'd taken great joy in holding their youngest, Susanna, a tiny, golden-haired girl who might have been mine and Sawyer's daughter. Even without being aware of doing so, I'd acknowledged the fact that very night; I cupped one hand over my belly, in a sudden onslaught of protective zeal.

"They seem to be on the mend. Bad water along the trail, Henry believed. The youngsters are severely weakened but my boys are helping Henry to clear out the shanty cabin that remained on the property, so at least they shall not have to build a new structure before the snow flies. I shall also offer a hand upon my return home."

I restrained a shudder at the thought of Zeb Crawford's homestead, where Thomas Yancy once intended to hide me so I could not testify against Jack Barrow in defense of Sawyer; however stone-dead Zeb, and indeed Jack, now were, my monstrous loathing of both had not been as successfully destroyed. I found room to be gladdened that the Spicers, a kind and loving family, could make use of his former homestead. Surely all essence of Zeb and his fanatical hatred would be summarily eradicated.

Tilson said, "There's a blessed amount of work to be contended with before winter, that is certain. I'm right glad for the addition of such a strong back and knowledge of horses as yours, Sawyer, my boy."

The endearment was heartfelt and I sensed Sawyer's quiet pleasure at being so affectionately addressed. I knew, as Tilson had confided to me, that Sawyer reminded him a great deal of his own sons, all but one lost in the War. I further recognized that Sawyer was similarly struck by a sense of his father, James Davis, when he spoke to Tilson. In truth, my husband and Tilson resembled one another well enough to claim genuine blood kinship – both were tall and imposing in their physical build and each maintained a strong sense of calm capability; they each possessed beautifully-shaped jawlines and observant gazes. I imagined Tilson's hair, currently pewter-gray, had once been as fair as Sawyer's. And I knew both mourned the loss of the easy, familial camaraderie that exists between a father and his beloved son.

"Well, I aim to be of as much assistance as I am able," Sawyer said, with a gentle note of humbleness in his deep voice.

"Your job is to rest, and continue healing," Rebecca admonished, in the solicitous, mildly hectoring manner of an elder sister. "Your wife, as you well know, cannot do without you."

Sawyer said quietly, "I am not much good without Lorie, either." He continued, "And I am ever grateful for your concern, dear Becky, but there comes a time in the process of resting when a man starts to feel a mite useless."

Charley said, "That is something to which I am able to attest, wholeheartedly. I was laid up many a long week when my hip was injured. I grew quite as fractious as a newborn and am indeed fortunate that my Fannie did not turn me out on a nearby hillside, to fend for my unfortunate self."

His words inspired a laugh around the table.

With good-natured exasperation, Tilson griped, "Sawyer, you are anything but useless. You pull your weight and then some and I must admit I've grown downright dependent upon our conversations. I quite enjoy them."

Sawyer sent Tilson a grudging smile. "As do I."

"What word of the Carters? My boys hardly go a day without asking after Malcolm's whereabouts. They were only that much more overjoyed to learn that young Cole Spicer had likewise made Malcolm's acquaintance. I believe I shall hardly turn around before they'll be riding out to find him. Grantley and Miles speak of little else."

No one besides me, and perhaps Sawyer, who knew of her feelings for Boyd, noticed Rebecca's need to draw a slow breath at this inquiry; she subsequently busied herself with serving her boys second helpings. I fancied I could hear her heart in its sudden powerful beating and felt ill with the desire to make possible that for which she wished – Boyd to come riding down the lane at an agitated clip and fling open the door. I could picture it as clearly as a waking dream; Boyd's dark eyes seeking Rebecca, his perpetual and unabashed intensity filling the little house as he strode inside and dropped to his knees at her side. He would gather one of her hands between both of his and bring it to his lips.

I should not have left, he would say, and for an instant the words seemed so real I fancied I could hear him speaking them, from a distance.

I shivered.

Tilson was answering Charley, Cort and Nathaniel contributing to the lively conversation, and no one but Sawyer noticed my sudden quiet; his hand moved to my waist, where he squeezed with gentle pressure, the gesture asking what was wrong.

I'll tell you later, I returned, without speaking.

"Not yet a letter?" Charley persisted.

Sawyer said, "None that we've received but they are traveling hard. We expect them to arrive at Jacob's homestead by the end of September and Boyd will know we're waiting for word, though he isn't the fondest of composition. I trust he'll send a note as soon as he is able."

I knew, at least in part, that Sawyer was attempting to offer Rebecca relief from her worry with these assurances, and tried to glean a sense of comfort, as well. I could hardly wait for the chance to inform Boyd and Malcolm of the news of our growing family; Malcolm would have waltzed about the table, begging me to join him, if they were here. Boyd would play the fiddle for us and we'd have an impromptu dance lasting well into the wee hours. The ache of missing them swelled anew and I squared my shoulders to repress a second shudder in as many minutes.

"Mama, I miss Malcolm," said Cort, heaving a sigh and seeming to read my mind. "And Mr. Carter. He played music right nice."

At my left, Rebecca seemed as tightly wound as a pocket watch; she replied in a calm non-sequitur, "Finish your food, dear one."

Conversation continued and I was the only one to observe the slight tremble in her fingers as she tucked a wayward strand of hair behind one ear before resuming eating.

In the dimness of our little cabin, hours later, Sawyer undressed me with motions both adept and tender. As ever, my blood quickened, pulsing with anticipation; he knelt, pressing his face to my naked belly, and I threaded my hands into his silken hair. It had grown just enough for me to twine within my fingers, as I would a horse's thick mane; it was a sensual pleasure I had long enjoyed, that of hair in my grasping hands. He kissed my navel, whispering, "Our child is here, within you. I could not be happier, my sweet love."

"Nor could I," I whispered, clasping his head to my body. His tongue created a small, hot circle and I giggled and gasped at the same moment, which then made me laugh. "That tickles," I murmured, stepping deliberately free of my trousers. Bare, I stood before Sawyer in the lantern's glow, watching as he smiled up at me, both hands curved around my backside.

"My Lorie-love," he whispered and I lowered my fingertips to his cheeks, tracing over the strong, angular bone structure, removing with great care the patch he wore over his absent eye. He flinched only a fraction – I might have missed it, was I not so attuned to him. I caressed the puckered ridge of scar tissue there left; he watched me without speaking.

"I am thinking of the first night I looked into your eyes. At the fire, while Malcolm went with Gus to fetch the presents they'd bought for me."

He said softly, "I remember well."

I stroked his face. His hands tightened their grip on my hips.

"When I dream, I am still able to see with both." His words were hoarse. "I almost wish I did not, that it would stop."

"It is only that much worse, when you wake and cannot," I understood, and he nodded and bent his forehead once more to my stomach, resting his temple. His wide shoulders gleamed in the golden light; he still wore his trousers, and I requested, "Come with me, love."

He stood, lifting me into his arms, depositing me upon the surface of the bed, constructed of tightly-woven ropes stretched taut over a wide frame, then topped with a down-filled tick; our very own bed, for which I had been shamelessly grateful every moment since its placement here in the space intended for us. I rested on my elbows, crooking both knees and savoring the sweet and intimate delight of witnessing the desire on my husband's handsome face as he removed the last of his remaining clothing. The same desire melted over my limbs and erupted in my heart, setting it to thrashing. My nipples formed rounded peaks and a wordless invitation rose from my throat.

Sawyer rested one knee upon the bed, between my bent legs, and a certain large swelling brushed my thigh, his cock firm and so familiar, beckoning to me. And then his expression changed markedly; I sensed the nature of his concern as it crossed his features.

"I only just..." he began.

"It was nearly the first thing I asked Rebecca," I reassured, amused and touched at the amount of disquiet present upon his face. "There is no reason we cannot make love."

"Are you certain? I feel like a selfish lout. Wanting you this way, needing you so much, that you must think it is all I think of..."

"Sawyer James," I scolded, smiling now at his uncharacteristic fluster.

He drew a fortifying breath and summarily ceased his anxious rambling. Instead, he cupped a knowing hand between my legs, stroking within, where I was slippery heat; his strong fingers grew quickly wet with my need.

"Lorissa Davis," he murmured in response, kissing my neck, plying his tongue upon my breasts, one after the other, until I gasped and cried out.

Eyes closed as pleasure coursed along my skin, I faintly recalled my original intent, which was to take him into my mouth. This was a gift we alone shared, one I felt was sacred to our marriage, to our joining. With Sawyer, lovemaking became far more than a satiation of physical need; it became a consecration – holding him deeply inside, witnessing his powerful release, experiencing my own – there could be no more holy act. I had never known lovemaking could be a thing of beauty and grace, not until I had fallen in love with Sawyer and learned to trust him.

"Let me," I whispered, and he recognized my intent.

"*Darlin'*," he groaned, as I rolled to my knees and grasped him, caressing with my thumbs the hollows created between his hipbones and groin. There was a small pearl of white at the tip of him and I opened my lips over this, swirling my tongue; it was a taste I knew well, that of his aroused body. His fingers dug into my hair. I felt him swell even more fully within my mouth and he shifted at once, lifting me into his arms and taking me instantly to my back. My legs tightened instinctively around his hips as his length, the splendid hardness of him, filled me.

He held momentarily still as I quivered beneath him, taking my lower lip into his mouth and lightly suckling. He murmured, half-teasing, "I must pause, or I'll be finished…" and bit my earlobe, sending a spasm of pleasure along my jawline on the same side.

I loved that we were able to jest and laugh in the midst of loving. I arched my neck so that he would kiss it, which he did, grasping my hips in his strong hands and taking up a slow, steady rhythm. Smiling at him, clinging to his shoulders, I said innocently, "You are so thoughtful, love."

His grin deepened. "Your sweet mouth on my…well, I can hardly contain myself."

I snorted a laugh this time and he laughed as well, almost uncoupling our bodies. I squirreled closer, wrapping my arms and legs all the more fiercely about him, meeting him thrust for powerful thrust as our laughter died away, our motion taking us all across the surface of the bed. Sawyer lifted my right ankle and hooked it over his shoulder. I gripped the bedclothes with both fists. Sweat trickled along his temples and to his jaws, gleaming upon his chest. I bared my teeth as I shuddered with the force of what his body called forth from mine – the pulsing surges that spread outward from my center and swept through me, leaving me weak, sated in their wake. He kissed the inside curve of my lower leg, opening his lips and lightly clamping his teeth there as the intensity of focus rendered us wordless, so completely entwined that I could not tell where I stopped and he began.

"You," I murmured, utterly replete, holding close his exhausted form some time later, the candle guttering in its holder.

Sawyer rose to his forearms and smoothed tangled hair from my forehead. I studied his mangled eye socket and tears leaked over my temples as I lay flat on my back, loving the satisfied weight of him draped atop me; my joy that he was alive, that he had not been taken from me, would never cease. I caught hold of his ears and tugged closer his face so that I could press my lips to the disfigurement of his scar, which he allowed. At first, when he was no longer required to wear the poultice beneath the eye patch, he'd been hesitant to let me touch or kiss the spot. But I insisted. I wanted to show him it did not upset or repulse me in any way. Simply telling him was not sufficient; I knew my actions must speak for me.

"Yes, you." His voice rasped with emotion.

I was fearful to reply in absolutes, to say that we would never be without one another again; life had taught me that to speak of such things was to perhaps negate them. I clung to him and whispered instead, "Let us take no days for granted, not ever."

He kissed away my tears and shifted us, so that I was sheltered against his chest rather than directly beneath him. I ran my palms along his ribs, coming to rest around his torso. After a spell, he murmured, "I always worry that I crush you, after."

"You do not crush me." I adopted the tone I thought of as *wifely*, and then, with the inevitability of longtime habit, synonyms riffled through my mind: *wifelike, uxorial, filial.* Sawyer and I had entered into this particular discussion before, and so with no small amount of asperity I reminded him, "You have said yourself my hips are ample."

Sawyer snorted this time, which tickled my sweating skin; I squirmed, giggling in my half-hearted attempts to escape. He allowed no evasion, instead pressing little kisses along the side of my neck as he agreed contentedly, "That I have, my sweet wife. You have lovely ample hips."

Atop our churned-up blankets I attempted to jab his ribs, where I knew it deviled him to be tickled. I would be dishonest if I did not admit that I loved provoking him to tussle with me, delighting in the strength of his warm, nude body curling around mine; he pretended to let me have the upper hand, allowing me to pin his shoulder blades to the feather tick. "That sounds like a compliment intended for a breeding mare!"

Sawyer's laughter rendered him momentarily incapable of defense and I dug my fingertips into his ribs for good measure. My hair fell all around the two of us. "Does that make me, by default, the studhorse? I am so very flattered…"

"You are in need of a strapping!" Laughter hampered my efforts to smack his backside. At last I fell across his chest and closed my teeth about the powerful ridge of muscle that sloped between his neck and shoulder. He was so magnificently made, firm planes and strong, muscular angles, his long bone structure sturdy beneath his skin. I knew every last part of his body, every ridge of scarred skin, every mole and freckle; the length of his limbs, the taste of his mouth, the scent of the hair that grew low on his belly, the changeability of his cock. I was fascinated by all of it, possessive of him to perhaps an obsessive degree; but I knew it was the same for him. Many hours had he spent, tracing his fingertips over my bare body, nothing held back, exploring and marveling, tasting of me as I did of him; how many times each of us had whispered, *I never knew it could be like this.*

"I am in need of just such," he acknowledged, gliding his touch downward to capture my waist in both wide palms, tucking me neatly beneath him. "My daddy would take a strap to me for taking such pleasure in being pummeled by a beautiful naked woman. Holy God, woman, you are beautiful. You near do me in."

"Don't you sweet talk me," I griped, even as my thighs parted in undeniable invitation. Sawyer caught my wrists lightly in his grasp and pinned them to either side of my head, biting my chin, placing heated kisses upon my collarbones. I trembled, gooseflesh rippling along my limbs at his answering grin.

"But you are so very sweet," he murmured, and claimed my mouth for his own.

Much later, the candle having blinked out of existence, the room flooded with milky moonbeams in its absence, Sawyer admitted, "I am worried about them."

I lay with my temple pressed to his heartbeat, nearly asleep to its steady rhythm, but at these words I shifted to one elbow to regard him in the meager light. Sawyer continued stroking my back, digging his thumbs along the hollows of my shoulder blades, and I shivered at both his welcome touch and his concerning words.

"I am, as well. I figured that Boyd would have sent word by now. He knows our worry."

"Can you get a feel for where they may be, Lorie-love? I've been attempting every day, to no avail." Sawyer and I had been able to sense one another from the first night we'd met, but the strength of the bond seemed exclusive to us. Try as I might, I could not establish even a fleeting awareness of their current location. *But wait.* I thought of how I'd imagined Boyd returning only earlier this evening; for a second I'd thought I heard his voice...

"I nearly forgot to tell you. At dinner, I had the strangest sense."

"When you shivered?"

"Yes, just then. I imagined Boyd coming into the house and telling Rebecca that he should not have left. It seemed so real in that moment I swore I could hear his voice."

"I'm sure those are his feelings. Not that he would admit it. Regret is a sort of weakness, in his opinion."

I closed tighter my eyes, straining with everything in me to fix a lock on Boyd and Malcolm; I envisioned the deep reaches of the sprawling prairies to the north of us, cloaked now in darkness, picturing the two of them curled close beneath the paltry shelter of their canvas tarpaulin. But the picture remained a product of my imagination, not an actual sensing. I whispered miserably, "I cannot say where they might be, not with any certainty."

Sawyer held me as I would always need holding, tucked close to him, protected in his embrace. His lips near the side of my forehead, he said, "Don't fret, darlin'. Boyd is a cautious traveler. He'll look out for them." He released a soft sigh, the familiar scent of his breath against my eyelids as he whispered, "I miss them both, a very great deal. I haven't been much apart from Boyd since we left home together in 'sixty-two."

I knew this, and that he depended upon Boyd perhaps more than he would admit. I understood there were experiences they shared as soldiers to which only Boyd was privy. Boyd was the last living soul present in the heart of the War with Sawyer, and I compared their friendship to that which I'd shared with Deirdre; she had known what it meant to work as a whore, without words or explanations, just as Boyd knew what it meant to be a soldier. Sawyer did not have to explain himself to Boyd as he often did to me, but I did not begrudge this; it only deepened my desire for us to reunite with them.

"Malcolm will be lonely, even if it is an adventure," I whispered, and longed for the boy; my arms twitched with the craving to cuddle him close. I tucked my chin at the juncture of Sawyer's neck and shoulder, which I'd bitten earlier, in play. I kissed the spot now, lamenting, "I wish they were here to know our news. They would be so happy. They'll be uncles!"

"They will know the moment we see them again, sooner if we can get a letter to them." Sawyer wound a strand of my hair about his index finger in a slow, rhythmic motion. "And Malcolm will find many things to occupy his time, of this I've no doubt. He'll be all right. But I miss the sound of his voice, I'll not deny. I do love that kid."

"I love him so. I love both of them. It's the same as being apart from family. But despite everything I am gladdened to think of them reuniting with Jacob. I wish I could see their faces upon finding him. Malcolm said once he hoped that Jacob resembles Clairee."

"I don't recollect that Jacob looks much like her, though I wasn't more than a boy when Jacob left home. I was much better acquainted with Clairee. She was fair as a spring flower, but with a temper to light a fire." Sawyer chuckled and I felt it rumble against my cheek. "She and Bainbridge were well-matched in that regard, I suppose, both possessed of strong spirits. Boyd's daddy was…well, my mama called him a handful, I recall, and once a devil, though she never knew I overheard this. It would not have been seemly. But she said so to Daddy, and he laughed and agreed."

"Your daddy was sweet, wasn't he?" I pictured the Davises so well from Sawyer's detailed stories that I fancied I had truly met them outside of my imagination. A loving family, with brothers full of mischief and a shared love of horses. I envisioned James Davis patiently teaching his boys the ways of smithing, of properly caring for hoofed animals, and comforted myself with the knowledge that our own sons would likewise be instructed by Sawyer, someday. A small, warm flame flickered anew in my belly; I was so grateful that we would be allowed this future that, at times, my exquisite happiness bordered on pain.

"He was," Sawyer agreed, resting his chin atop my head. "Daddy loved my mama so, and now that I have you, *mo mhuirnín milis*, I understand in new ways every day how very much he loved her. And how he loved us. I will never forget the sight of my daddy's eyes when we three boys told him we wished to be soldiers. Lorie, if our boys ever come to us and say they are leaving to fight, I will promptly hogtie all of them and barricade the door, and they will not be let out of our home." He wrapped me closer, placing a shielding hand over my lower belly. "I understand now that at the time I did not let myself see how much it hurt Daddy and Mama to let us go. How much courage it took for them to watch us ride out, realizing we may never return. Oh God, I beg for the same never to happen to us, Lorie-love, and yet *I* did that to them. I rode away and knew their devastation."

I held fast, not speaking, only listening. I knew nothing I could say would offer as much comfort as holding him, our bare skin warm upon each other's. Sawyer pressed his mouth to my shoulder and I stroked his hair. At last he vowed, "I have ridden away from those I love and have allowed them to ride away from me for the last time. I aim to get us to Minnesota next summer and build our home, and then let us never travel away from it again. Let us sit upon our front porch, in rocking chairs, as did those of advanced age in Suttonville." I sensed him smile and knew a measure of relief.

"You'll be obliged to take up catfishing and whittling, as did all of the elderly gentlemen back home."

"That sounds about right," Sawyer murmured. He resumed caressing my back and I rested my nose against his bristly, unshaven jaw, nodding acknowledgment.

After a time I whispered, "I worry so for Rebecca."

"She loves Boyd." Sawyer understood exactly what I meant. "It's plain as daybreak. I know it hurts you to think of leaving her behind. She's a good woman and I don't much like seeing her sad, either. Boyd should have…" He trailed to silence, surely feeling that to speak against Boyd's decision was in poor taste.

I knew what he intended to say, of course, and finished for him. "He should have listened to his heart. He's stubborn as a cloud of horseflies."

I sensed Sawyer's smile. "He always said I was the stubborn one." He was silent for a time before murmuring, "At least some things can always be counted upon."

※

I SWEAR – " I started to say, but then thought better and bit back the words.

Malcolm, uncommonly quiet since the night the storm destroyed nearly all of our supplies, sent a curious look my way, clearly awaiting the rest of the sentence. While I took a moment's time to be thankful the bulk of our belongings remained behind with Sawyer and Lorie, to be carried along in the wagon come next spring, there was no denying we'd been left in dire circumstances. I kept my fears from Malcolm, best as I could, but he was sharp, too long burdened by the cares of a grown man. I was fooling myself if I thought he failed to understand, even without my directly saying so, that our journey had been made all the more difficult. The twister had destroyed our provisions – extra clothing, my pistol and a box of rounds, and much of the food store. Our money was lost, not even a coin scavenged from the remains of our belongings, of which a few not torn to shreds were scattered for the pickings on the prairie. But far worse, fathoms worse, was the ten-dollar note I'd carried all the miles from Tennessee, which I intended to use towards the filing fee for our land purchase.

Now gone.

I'd debated turning back more than once since the storm but kept this possibility from Malcolm, as he'd no doubt bend my ear in favor of it, without letup. A part of me felt that returning to Iowa City would be akin to a kicked dog slinking home with its tail tucked between its hind legs, and I'd had enough of that feeling to last a lifetime, and then some, after the Surrender. Neither could I ask Jacob for the money; not only did my pride prevent this, but he hadn't such an amount to spare. Further, I understood I could not return to Iowa to be a burden to Tilson or Rebecca. The thought of being near Rebecca for the length of a winter sent me into a near-seizure of hunger for her, but I was wise enough to acknowledge that she would be married to Quade by then, if she wasn't already, and witnessing her as the wife of another would serve to torture me. Better that there remained distance between us. And I understood well and good it was up to me, and no other, to determine a solution to my lack of funds. God knew I was no stranger to getting things done on my own.

Malcolm continued to study me from beneath the brim of his hat, wordless, and I figured I might get lucky, that he'd let my words drop just as he would a prickly weed accidentally plucked, but my shoulders sank as he pressed, "You swear *what?*"

"I swear if you ask another question, I'm gonna tie a cloth over your mouth," I said, my tone not quite as severe as the words would suggest; Malcolm rolled his eyes heavenward but I ignored his rudeness. We were, as of this moment, flat penniless – unless I counted our mounts, but I refused to consider selling either Fortune or Aces High, animals I loved, and that without we would exist in even worse condition. We'd been goddamn lucky the stand of blackberry bushes to which we'd tied the animals kept them stationary that night; what food we did possess had been stowed in our saddle bags.

"I *know* that ain't it," Malcolm groused. And then, truly pushing his luck, he grumbled, "*Jesus*, Boyd, I ain't stupid."

I closed my eyes, thinking on what Daddy would do if I'd dared to sass, let alone curse, in his presence at age thirteen; just as swiftly a memory struck, of myself somewhere near that tender age, hiding around the side of the stock barn with Beau as we shared Granny Rose's clay pipe. The pipe was a lovely thing long cherished in Granny's family, the bowl once carved with a delicate tracery of interlocking flowers, worn smooth as silkwood from six decades of use, though my eldest brother and me didn't spend much time admiring as we passed it to and fro between drags, coughing with every puff. The memory sparked the acrid taste of raw tobacco leaf along the back of my tongue.

Why'n the hell do folks smoke this stuff? Beau had wondered aloud, then choked on a wheezing laugh. *It's right foul. Think I'd rather chaw tobaccy any ol' day.*

In our boyhoods there was scarce a fellow in the South who didn't dip; later there were many, myself included, that claimed tobacco leaf kept them sane during the War. A fella unable to accurately aim his plug was fair game for disdain, and likely near as much chaw created muck along the roadways as mud in those days, churned to a slogging mess under many thousands of booted feet. Most smoked a pipe in addition, including many a woman. Our granny was no exception, though she smoked on the porch out of respect for Mama's window curtains, edged in fine white lace. Beau and me dipped when we could steal a pinch from Daddy's quid, but Beau was fonder than me of the taste of the juice; to this day, I preferred to roll my own smokes rather than pack my lower lip.

Goddammit to hell, I ain't having no luck, I'd responded to Beau on that long-ago afternoon, irritated upon realizing the bowl no longer burned. It was my misfortune that Daddy found us just as I spoke these words, the left corner of my mouth clamped around the pipe stem while I tried in vain to relight the tobacco with the end of a small, dried reed we'd first jabbed into the woodstove.

Boys, you's fixin' to get yer hides walloped, Daddy said conversationally, holding out one wide, gnarled hand for the pipe. My daddy was a big man, *fifteen stone* as Mama liked to tease, with a full beard and a thick black mustache that hid his upper lip unless he smiled, dark eyes that could snap like the devil's own coalbed.

I didn't dare refuse and handed over the pipe, which Daddy tamped with the ease of a knife through warm butter. I dropped the reed and hastily ground it beneath my boot; Beau looked as though he meant to run, but then considered the outcome and thought better.

Daddy's gaze moved between us, his two elder sons, and there was a gleam of humor in his eyes as he used Granny's pipe to gesture; he rumbled, *Now, I seen you boys bare as eggs since you was born, an' when you got hair on your chests an' ballocks to match the hair on your heads, then you can smoke yourselves pipes, we clear as a May mornin'?*

We's clear, Daddy, Beau and I said, in near-perfect unison, and I scrubbed a knuckle over my chest in the here and now, thinking, *Well, I got plenty to match these days.*

What I'd been about to say to Malcolm, but had not, was that I swore someone was following us. The thought was a little niggling beetle chewing at the back of my mind. Had Sawyer been riding Whistler at my side I would not have hesitated to speak my suspicion, but despite everything he'd contended with in his young life, Malcolm was a boy, not a man, and under my protection to boot. I would not rouse his already fractious nerves even more with mentioning what was likely a result of my tired, over-addled mind. But then, I wasn't one to second-guess myself. I'd not survived the War by pure good grace; at least a part of it came from learning to trust my instinct, and when I felt that certain coldness on the back of my neck, it wasn't a thing to ignore. I shifted position, casual-like as I could, and peered over my right shoulder. I half expected to catch a glimpse of a telltale flash of blue.

There was nothing but waving prairie grasses, across which we'd traveled since first coming upon the Mississippi River, way back in Missouri, and I felt a mite foolish at my tetchiness. The prairie was a sight rather pretty in its own way, I'd not deny, endless fields of blooming wild grass, land that sloped gradually from one rise to the next; now, as August dwindled, there was a fair amount of gold amongst the green. Yellow daisies, those I recognized, and coneflowers of deep pink and creamy white. The clusters of pale purple blossoms, spiked like spears, Rebecca had called hyssop; these grew beyond her dooryard back in Iowa City, and I'd imagined picking great walloping armloads and presenting them, as I would if properly courting her.

I gritted my teeth, refusing to finish that thought.

Malcolm and I had crossed many a small waterway here and there on the trail, where the road petered out and took up again on the far side. Copses of trees, mostly willows and cottonwoods, whose leaves shivered and rustled in a companionable fashion, grew near the creek banks; though I felt a certain comfort in the occasional thick stands of trees, I was suddenly glad they had thinned some on the main route, as I reckoned fewer trees meant fewer places for anyone trailing us to seek cover.

Yancy? I wondered, and my upper lip curled at just the thought of the man's name. But it seemed unlikely that he would venture northward, when his kin – his two boys – were still in Iowa, dozens of miles south from Iowa City. There'd been no word of Yancy's whereabouts as of the day Malcolm and I departed. I would not know, one way or the other, if the man had since surfaced until I could send word to Sawyer, or receive word from him. As we were on the move, I could reliably post a letter, but would be long gone from any posting office before one could make its way back from Sawyer and Lorie. I had promised them I would write when I could, to assure them that we were safe…and so that Rebecca would know the same. I tightened my knees around Fortune's flanks, as though the mare could possibly carry me beyond my memories. My horse responded accordingly, increasing her pace. Malcolm cried, "Hey!" and heeled Aces, riding to catch up.

The prairie provided good grazing for our animals and I patted Fortune's solid neck, in pure affection. I'd purchased her upon returning from War, one of Piney Chapman's stock and kin to Whistler, and a better horse I'd never had, saving Arthur, the blood-bay gelding I'd ridden to War. Malcolm and I had entered into the state of Minnesota a day past, as we'd learned from a rider we met, a man whose homestead was just north of the Iowa border. Friendly folks thus far, even after hearing our Tennessee drawl; I felt the Northerners were the ones that spoke with a strange rhythm, their words that clipped along like spooked mules, near foreign to my ears, though they seemed ready enough to poke a bit of fun at our speech, if not outright misunderstand what we attempted to say.

You are saying 'guard,' as I recently came to realize, I recalled a Yankee prisoner telling me, sometime in the autumn of 'sixty-four. *I thought you were attempting to say 'god' until just this very moment's time.*

"You ain't no fun without Sawyer an' Lorie-Lorie," Malcolm griped, wiping his right hand on his thigh. He'd polished off the last of the penny candy Rebecca packed for him, tucked into a kerchief and stowed in his haversack. The boy was armed with Gus's Winchester, secure in its saddle scabbard, which he'd used to fire after Yancy that terrible night, and with which he was a good shot; before we'd left, I considered allowing him a pistol, but was still hesitant – pistols were a gamble, at best, a chance for a misfire or injury, and spoke of close-range shooting. And if it came to close quarters, I intended to be the one doing the shooting, not the boy. Besides, we were goddamn lucky to have the rifles still in our possession; the twister had stolen my pistol.

I tried not to let his words needle me; I was eldest, after all, not a young'un who could be provoked to bickering. Diverting his attention like I would a crayfish I intended to snag, I said, "Maybe there'll be a chance for a hot bath, once we reach St. Paul." Never mind that I couldn't afford it unless our fortune changed markedly before then.

Malcolm sighed, perhaps seeing through my trick. "I'm just tired, is all. But I like being on the trail, I truly do, Boyd. I like seein' what's beyond the next rise."

"I do, as well," I allowed, feeling a small lifting of spirits; the boy was a good one for that, whether he knew it or not. I said truthfully enough, "I like riding over the prairie, looking to the next horizon. I aim to settle, I do, but I know just what you mean."

"What if I can't remember Tennessee?" he asked then, on a winsome note. "Sometimes I feel like it's been years since I lived there. Do you s'pose we'll ever get back that-a-way?"

I took great care with my response. "I'd like to believe someday, boy. I do. But it ain't gonna be for a long time."

After a spell, "Boyd?"

"Hmm?"

"Do you wish you weren't never a soldier?"

My brother knew how to throw out a question to catch me smack in the gut. This one was even tougher to answer than the last. I tried for evasion. "There ain't nothing can be done about it, either way. Whether I wish it, or not."

"But do you?" he pressed, shifting on Aces. His chestnut gave an impatient whicker; Aces High was a good horse, greatly in tune with his master.

"I wish a great deal of things was the way they used to be." Damn, I was acting like a sidewinder with these sorts of answers. "I wish I ain't seen half of what I did as a soldier. But I believed in defending our home state, our home-land. I thought I was brave, boy, an' leavin' the holler to be a hero. Back then I thought – *shit*, we all thought – we'd be home by New Year, don't you recall? Beau aimed to marry Sara Lynn LeMoyne by that next spring, in 'sixty-three. He said at dinner, only the night before we done left, that he planned to make her a happy woman." And I could not help but smile a little, at the memory of my brother's boldness.

Malcolm murmured, "I recall."

I held in my mind a picture of my eldest brother, Beaumont Anson Carter, whose brimming confidence aggravated me to no end when we were chil-dren, but in which I'd later found comfort, as a soldier alongside him. He died in a charge only arm's length from my left flank, taking a musket ball to the forehead. The force of the impact unseated him from Charley Bean, his horse; from the corner of my vision, through the gathering smoke of cannon fire, I'd watched him fly back as though dragged by an unseen fist, head arched at an unnatural angle, arms pinwheeling. He'd been dead before hitting the ground.

Aw Jesus, Beau, my brother...

You should be married to Sara Lynn, with five or so young'uns by now, an' we should be playing fiddles side-by-side of an evening in the holler, sippin' hooch, just like Daddy an' Uncle Malcolm.

I figured such thoughts would never stop plaguing me – that which should have been, but never would. Grafton, some eighteen months my junior, born the year after Sawyer's twin brothers, had died clasping my hand, not long after Beau in the sweltering summer of 1863; weather to make a pig sweat as Granny would have said, Grafton stretched on a threadbare blanket in a battlefield doc's tent as he slipped from this life. Quiet, gentle Graf, who suffered through an amputated arm, a sawing of his bones, before passing; whose remaining hand stayed clenched around my own even after the light in his eyes faded to nothing. He died without wearing his boots, stocking-footed; I remembered a hole in the left sock, which two of his toes stuck through. I also recalled thinking that Mama would be sadder to hear about Graf than any of us, as she worried most about him – his softhearted ways earned him the dearest spot in her heart. And Mama loved all of us to pieces, a near violence of love.

Sawyer and I were the only ones left to each other; already close, the deaths of our kin bonded us that much more. I loved Sawyer as I would a brother of my own blood – we survived the duration of the War together, rode into Georgia and witnessed hell. The hell that existed there, following Sherman's path, overrode even the horror of seeing our brothers slaughtered before our eyes. Sawyer knew what I knew – because we had witnessed it, together. Parts of our Corps earned a bad reputation in Georgia, thanks to the actions of a negligent few, but I had long learned that folks, and history itself, tend to judge a group on the worst of its lot. Perhaps we were all to blame. God knew I partook in my share of whoring. And killing – but in battle, killing could be justified. There was no joy in it, even when I hated the men coming at me with a passion borne of dread, and pride, and raw terror.

Malcolm said, "People here been kindly to us, so far. I was worried some. I ain't heard anyone call us 'Rebs' yet."

"Not so far," I agreed. "But then, we ain't come across that many folks yet, neither."

IT WAS nearing dusk when Malcolm announced in a whisper, "I hear voices."

He had uncommon good hearing. There was little wind as evening advanced and I leaned forward, cocking an ear in the direction the boy indicated. To be sure, I heard the rise and fall of a man speaking, and a younger person, perhaps a child, responding. Within a minute's time I also smelled smoke and roasting meat and the latter was enough to spur us ahead. We'd bagged a couple of rabbits, always plentiful on the prairie, now tied by their ears to Fortune's saddle. Perhaps these folks would be willing to share their fire.

I stood in the stirrups and called a greeting as we approached, not wanting to startle them; Malcolm and I watched a man stand tall and gaze our way, shading his eyes against the setting sun – two unknown riders coming his way through the gloaming. His right hand hovered near a piece strapped to his hip but he did not palm the pistol. The evening was a fine one, weather-wise, calm as a mill pond and with the sunset burning yellow-gold in a great sweep over the prairie; its beauty made my chest ache, thinking of watching the fireflies in Rebecca's yard beneath a similar evening sky. Behind the man and child were tethered two sturdy mules, whose heads lifted before they fell again to grazing. A fire crackled and the man called, "Hallo there!"

"Boyd Carter," I said, drawing Fortune to a halt a goodly distance, perhaps ten strides, and dismounting. I tugged my hat brim, a gesture so deeply ingrained I reached for the brim even when I wasn't wearing my hat, and said, "We's been on the road since Iowa City. Saw your fire an' hoped for a bit of company."

The man said, "Kristian Hagebak," pronouncing his first name with a strong emphasis on the front half of it. In a deliberate way that suggested English was not the language he'd been raised speaking, he told us, "You may join our fire, if you wish. We are making our way home, just now. We have been visiting with my sister and her husband, some fifty miles from our homestead."

"Thank you kindly." I led Fortune closer. Malcolm dismounted and followed a few paces behind, drawing Aces after him. "This here is my brother, Malcolm. We's bound for the northern part of the state. Never been this far up the country, to be sure."

"Then let me welcome you to the state of Minnesota," Kristian acknowledged, and offered a grin, exposing a prominent front tooth, brownish with rot. I felt no sense of threat from him, a stout man perhaps ten years my elder, with hair of such a pale yellow it was nearly white, and a full beard to match. He indicated the child. "The young fellow is my son, Theodore."

"Good evening." The youngster bobbed his head in a nod. He was not Malcolm's age, perhaps only five or six.

Kristian said, "Please, do take a seat. I see you have two fine hares for your dinner."

In short order Malcolm and I staked Fortune and Aces by their lead lines, removed their saddles, and joined Kristian and his son. I gutted and skinned the rabbits, Kristian spitted them over the fire alongside their roasting prairie hens, and I tried, without much success, to quell a powerful surge of longing for Rebecca. It struck so forcefully that I clenched my jaw. In my mind's eye I saw her settling at the table to my right, where she'd customarily sat, in her warm house with its sense of cheer, hundreds of miles back along the trail; she always sent a smile my way as she sat, her cheeks blooming with roses, and I'd felt so damn lucky to receive this flushed smile I could hardly sit still at her table. I pictured her unlaced apron hanging near the woodstove. I thought of Cort and little Nathaniel, who'd pestered me with endless questions and who I also found myself missing just now, fiercely. Unshed tears burned my eyelids and stung the inside of my nose, but I would as soon receive a severe beating as let them fall in front of strangers.

You know you ain't supposed to be thinking of her.

Malcolm caught my gaze and his brow wrinkled. I could tell he was asking, *What's wrong?*

I'm right as rain. I narrowed my eyes and Malcolm heaved a small sigh, not believing me for an ever-loving second.

Addressing Kristian, I said, "We was in the path of a twister, big as I ever seen, a few days back. It ruined a goodly amount of our things."

Kristian nodded, listening despite his busy work of dividing the small, tasty prairie hens. I was more than a little stunned at the level of what seemed like homesickness in my gut – it was akin to what I'd felt the first few weeks away from the holler, as a recruit in the Army of Tennessee. At least then I'd had my brothers, and the Davis boys, to joke and share memories of home with. This evening, even with Malcolm nearby, who I dearly loved and would defend to my last breath, the gaping loneliness threated yet again. The sense of it settled deep into the cellar pit of my belly.

Kristian filled the boy's tin plate first, before his own; I thought this a kind gesture. The rabbits were almost ready – Malcolm could scarce take his eyes from them. Our diet had been slim these past days and guilt swiped a paw over my heart. I straightened my shoulders, sucking a painful breath; I was the closest thing to a daddy that the boy had, and I did not mean to shirk my duties. I would get us safely to our kin and I would make a life for Malcolm. I would see him grow to adulthood – he was already a fine boy, with the makings of a good man. I would make Mama and Daddy proud, wherever it was that their souls lingered, whether they was privy to our doings here on an earthly realm, or no.

"You said you were bound farther into Minnesota?" asked Kristian, settling with his plate, nodding to encourage a conversation.

I turned the rabbits on the spit. "We's got at least a month of travel yet, best I can figure. We plan to stop in St. Paul to petition for a homestead. My uncle is settled north of there. We plan to join him as soon as we's able."

Kristian nodded again. "Family ties are the strongest, and the best. When did you begin this journey, if I might ask?"

"Last April," I said. I slipped my small boning knife from its pouch about my neck and Malcolm gladly accepted the meat I sliced for him. He tucked into his meal, watching me speak with Kristian, but not speaking himself. The boy Theodore was likewise quiet, eating and observing.

"You are traveling light." Kristian sounded concerned at this observation. "For a journey so far, and with winter but months away, certainly you need more supply than you have? Was it the storm?"

I briefly explained about Sawyer and Lorie, and their plan to join us next summer. Just now, 1869 seemed a good two hundred years away, an unimaginable length of time before we would see them again. I concluded, "We brought along a winter coat each, an' extra clothing, but much of it was lost in the twister. We's running low on money." This was an outright lie, as we weren't just low; we had exactly none. I did not say how frightened I was at being unable to provide for my brother. Jacob was our blood, our uncle, but I could not arrive at his home with no means, dependent as a nursing calf.

"There is work in St. Paul," Kristian said, with an earnest tone that helped stave off the aching tension in my midsection. "When we first arrived to the state last year, we worked until we had saved enough to apply for land. It is a fee of ten dollars, for the filing. The Minnesota Valley Railroad Company runs the land department. My brothers and I have acquired land, what a tremendous thing! Our family never dreamed of so much land, back home in Norway. We come from Norway. We arrived in America to the town of New York. We come to Minnesota when we were able. We do not like New York so much."

I had heard tales of this port city on the coast. "I would imagine not."

Kristian spread wide his arms; the gesture seemed to encompass the entire sprawling prairie. "Here, there is space. It is uncrowded, and clean. It is a balm to my heart. It is no small task, minding a farm, let me tell you, but you have the look of a fellow who knows hard work."

I allowed a small smile, aware that Malcolm watched my every move. I knew the boy's mood was hitched directly to my own, that when I was upset, or troubled, he was as well. I agreed, "Me an' hard work are longtime friends."

"You will find work in St. Paul, a few days' steady ride from here. There is much work for able-bodied men. You will shortly save enough for the filing fee."

And I tried my damnedest to believe him.

I WAS thankful we'd been blessed with clear nights since the twister. It was cold, though, and the mosquitoes were thick, but wrapped in a blanket and aligned with the banked fire, it was tolerable. I lay awake long past everyone else nodding off, as usual; Malcolm's snores were so familiar to me I scarce heard them anymore. I rolled to my back and studied the heavens, seeking the pattern of stars I fancied was the souls of our families, the Carters and the Davises, all together in the beyond; I found a small measure of solace in the thought. Sawyer insisted this notion was the truth. I still did not know whether to believe his experience was one of an actual near-death, though he'd been mightily ill after losing his eye last summer, or a vivid dream come to comfort him; I wanted to believe that our families were safe, having found one another and henceforth continued on, together, without the pain and turmoil, or physical wounds, inflicted upon them in life. That they were happy in this place beyond, watching over us. Sawyer relayed to us the messages from each of them – Mama's kisses and Daddy's words of pride, even that of Ethan wanting me to know he could still whup me.

You's gone daft as an old man, I thought, as tears again threatened. I pressed my knuckles to my eye sockets, unrelenting, until I saw swirls of bright color, thinking of Sawyer's missing eye, thinking of my family together in the holler somewhere in the afterlife. And thinking of Rebecca; realizing I should not think of her did no good. I whispered her name to the night, *Rebecca Lynn,* and my breath grew shallow, my palms slick, as though I was a youth who'd never touched a girl. I thought of all the pretty, proper words she had spoken in my presence; she saw straight through my teasing every time and returned it, with relish, dished it right on back to me. I could never get away with a blessed damn thing in her kitchen. I pictured her face, alight with merriment as she slapped at my wrist for stealing a swipe of cake frosting; I remembered the fiddle-curve of her waist between the fullness of her breasts and hips, which always invited my grasp (though of course I'd never dared to be so bold). I kept my eyes closed to better glut myself on the memories.

You's vain as hell, I thought, of my sorry self. *You love the way she looks at you, like she's seeing an angel, or a hero. Like you's somethin' special.*

And there was no denying, Rebecca had a way of looking at me that seemed to suggest she believed all of these things. Her eyes, a rich green flecked with brown and gold, and with a gratifying lacking of guile, had rested upon me so adoringly. I savored her gaze, I could not pretend otherwise. Outspoken as she was, Rebecca was no good at hiding her feelings; what she felt showed upon her face. The evening the circuit judge declared he would overturn the order to hang Sawyer, I'd damned it all and taken Rebecca in my arms the moment we'd returned from town, unable to resist the temptation. She had spoken aloud my name and that she was glad I was back; she'd been so worried. Her soft voice came in urgent bursts, as though she was being struck. Her lips had been at my ear. She'd dug her hands into my hair. I'd crushed her close and had not wanted to let her go. If truth be known, I'd wanted to do a hell of a lot more than that – I wanted to carry her to the closest available bedding, feel her thighs glide around my hips and hear her cry out my name, repeatedly.

You are a goddamn, lowdown fool, I raged, rolling restlessly to my right side, away from the fire. My face was hot enough as it was; my body swelled with insistent need, almost against my will. *You don't deserve her. She is a lady and even imagining such wanton, lustful things about her is wrong.*

I aim to reach my family, my uncle, the last of my kin.

I get where I set out to get. Carters do not give up.

And then a new thought struck, and I flopped to the opposite side, studying the embers.

Perhaps you ain't the marrying kind, like Captain Coll.

The thought, once expressed by a former commanding officer, set my jaw in a firm line; Captain Coll was a seasoned leader but admittedly altar-shy. Even nearing two score in age, he had never settled down with any one woman. When asked why, he laughed and said, *I ain't the marrying kind, boys. I want my women when I want 'em, God love 'em, an' I don't want no fussing, when not. Henpecked, that's what married men are. You boys ready to be henpecked all your livin' lives?*

At the time, I admitted I was most assuredly not ready for any such thing. Over six years ago that was, and I'd since been with more women than I could rightly remember. Seemed there were always willing girls for the right price, as I'd been told as a green young recruit. Never once had I felt something stronger than lust for any of them – lust being a formidable temptation I had trouble resisting, I'd not deny – and all of these things contributed now to my understanding that Rebecca was far too good a woman, decent and pure and ladylike, to truly consider the likes of me.

Not everyone can have what Sawyer an' Lorie have. There ain't many that do, you know this is true. Lorie accepted Sawyer even though he's been with women too, though not near as many as you. Not for the ladies' lack of trying with him, of course.

I paused in my thoughts, realizing I considered Lorie nothing less than a proper lady. It was more that I could not think of her as a whore; the word I'd never flickered an eyelash over using now seemed base and offensive. It made me wriggle like a hooked worm to think on it, but certainly Lorie had lain with far more men than Sawyer had with women. Girls had always fought over Sawyer, even in our boyhoods; the night we'd first met Lorie in St. Louis, two of the whores in the fancy, lantern-lit saloon came close to blows over him, I saw with my own eyes. I'd always teased Sawyer about being a ladies' man, even though Ethan was the true ladies' man; no one got under more skirts in our growing years than Ethan Davis. It seemed all Eth had to do was offer a few compliments in the Irish that he, Sawyer, and Jere had learned as boys and girls went all breathless and doe-eyed. I'd been jealous as hell.

Sawyer, unlike his younger brother, had never been much for sweet-talking and had contented himself with only a few dalliances during our soldiering years, when he could bear the pain and solitude no longer and sought momentary comfort, whereas I was a downright fool for the company of whores. Until now, I'd not felt more than a nudge of guilt over it. But Lorie, who was the closest I'd ever come to a blood-kin sister, had worked as a whore for near on three years. It pained me something fierce to picture Lorie doing any of the lusty things I'd done with those whorehouse girls.

Aw, Jesus. You'd kill someone for trying to take advantage of Lorie that way, now. For even lookin' at her like they meant to think of her that way.

What would Rebecca have to say, if you told her these things? Would she cringe away from you? If she was your wife, would you have the courage to tell her the truth about all them women in your past? All them whores...

She ain't never gonna be your wife, so's there no point thinking on it. Shit, you gotta figure out how you's gonna get ten dollars to buy a land voucher.

This last thought left me sicker still. I was a Carter, near the last of my daddy's line, and I meant to do him proud.

You taught me everything you could, my father. How to be a man, a good an' decent man. I mighta failed in some regards, but I aim to make you proud. I want you to be proud of me. I swear if I ever marry, my first son'll be named in your honor.

I drifted, near to dreaming though not fully asleep, thinking on my father; for a spell I thought he was really sitting alongside the fire and there seemed to be two of him, the one in my mind and the one lit by embers. He sat whittling a chunk of blackgum wood, shaping it with his smallest paring knife. His features were highlighted by the red blaze, lit from beneath; his nose created a long shadow and his pupils were tinted orange. *Goddamn*, he muttered, and used the knife to skillfully nick a little mistake from the wood in his hands. Humming under his breath, as he always did.

Daddy, I whispered, and my boots twitched as though to get up, scraping the ground with a quick jerk. I wanted to go to him and feel him put his hand over my shoulder. When he put his hand over my shoulder I felt safer than a fox snug in its den for the winter. I felt loved, and cherished. I felt as though my life meant something beyond what it probably rightly did. And it had been so damn long since I'd felt that way. I craved it, the way a body craves a soft bed and a solid night's rest. A different craving than for that of a woman, but equally as potent, in its own way.

My boy, Daddy whispered, and seemed to be crouching near my head now, the glittering ruby mass of embers visible between his boots. And I was his boy in that instant, no longer a former soldier and full-grown, but a boy who wished to burrow and be enclosed in the protection of his father's embrace. I fancied, half-asleep, that I had been poured into a warm cup, neatly contained and unable to be harmed, from that moment forth. I wanted my daddy to take that cup and hold it between his palms, forever.

A man ain't nothing without a family, you hear me, boy?

He spoke in his low voice, close to my ear. I caught the familiar, comforting scents of him, tobacco leaf from his clothes and whiskey on his breath; I was exhausted and slipped a few inches further along the low grade that descended into the cavern of sleep. I tried to ask him another question, but my jaws wouldn't flap. Eyes closed, I promised, *I hear you, Daddy.*

Wake up, son. Wake up, he insisted, and I heard the sudden marked change in his tone, now urgent. He put his hand on my shoulder and shook, his gaze directed away from me now, out into the prairie.

The boy Theodore made a small groaning sound and kicked in his sleep, jerking me to sudden full consciousness. I sat upright, staring wildly about for my father, but of course he was gone – a dream, nothing more. Conjured up to comfort myself as I lay in a doze. The prairie was dark as a length of cloth cut for a burying suit, the nearly-full moon having tumbled beyond the western edge of the world. Turning away from the fire sent a chill over my exposed skin and I made certain that Malcolm was rolled tightly in his blanket. He was, and snoring as usual, the last of the red glow highlighting his freckles and serving to clench up my heart – he looked his age, younger even, in sleep, and it scared me.

Beyond me, a few dozen steps away, Fortune whickered as if she knew I was awake. Crickets scraped their tuneless song and all around the tall grass sighed and rustled; I reminded myself, twice, that I was no longer a soldier. No more would Federals, real or imagined, creep close as I slept, wishing to pierce my ribs with a musket blade. I sighed and rolled back into my blanket, but hardly a minute ticked past before I relented, admitting that I could not shake the distinct sense of watchful eyes somewhere out in the darkness. I leaned and drew my rifle closer to my body, keeping a hand curled loosely about the receiver, and felt a measure safer.

Then, uncertain exactly why other than to quiet a small but persistent voice in my head, I rose without making a sound and stepped deliberately away from the fire's faint glow, allowing nothing more than a gut feeling to guide my feet. Keeping my rifle in the crook of my arm, aimed low, and the fire where my brother slept at the corner of my sight, I crept southeast, staring intently as my eyes adjusted, peering at the wavering line where the grass met the sky. Mundane objects, trees and the like, took on monstrous forms – just as they had when I was soldiering and the half-sick fear I'd felt at any given moment distorted the natural shape of things. Treading with care over the uneven ground, slightly hunched, grass scratching knee-high at my trousers, I thought, *Where the hell are you? I know you's out there.*

My silent, wary steps carried me well away from the fire; I felt as though I was hunting, stalking game that might at any given second spring to motion before my eyes. Not wanting to seem a fool and yet unable to cease the motion, I went to one knee and swiped a handful of loose, dusty dirt, spreading this carefully along the barrel of my piece, to smudge out any telltale metallic glinting. I brought the stock to my shoulder, sweeping to the right, peering down the barrel. I wanted to taunt, to call into the night that I knew he was there, but that would give away my exact position. Whoever in the goddamn hell he was, I longed to flush him as I would quarry – quarry I would then corner and claim. Despite the chill in the night's air, a belligerent stubborn heat kept my bones adequately warm.

You's acting right ridiculous. Letting your wits get addled, like you always done as a boy. Acting no older than Malcolm, an' even he'd know better than to let his imagination take hold this way.

I swept the barrel slowly to the left.

Nothing.

The night was still. I strained to listen, ripples of awareness creeping along my scalp. He was close. I hunkered lower and it was then that I heard the low, muted hoot of an owl – my hair near stood on end – and immediately after, the faint but distinct sound of shifting grass stalks. Someone was out there, trying to muffle the rustlings as he crept along the prairie. Not far south of my position – I'd been right in this assumption; someone tailed us. Sweat slid down my temples and dampened my neck.

I'll find you, bastard, I thought, edging closer. For once in my sorry life, I took no satisfaction in being proven right. If I caught him in my sights, I would take him out – no time for questions. Shoot first, ask questions later, in my opinion. My heart galloped, striking my ribs as solidly as a horse's rearing hooves. I crept forward, watching for any hint of movement ahead.

Where are you?

Who are you?

And then, sudden as a deer bolting from cover, he flew to his feet, a smudge only a little darker than the night sky, roughly ten yards from my position. The crack of a discharging rifle shattered the quiet and I roared in anger, the sound lost in the bullet's report. I returned fire, the stock slapping my shoulder with gratifying power. I chambered a second round and fired after his retreating figure, to no avail – *some hell of a shot you are* – and then I was in pursuit. I heard nothing but the swollen bursts of my angry breath, my ears muffled from both shots, the world narrowing to a furious, red-gray corridor.

The ground slammed the soles of my boots, my throat dry and tight, the rifle slick in my grasp. He fled afoot, a blur of motion only paces ahead, the both of us trampling prairie grass as we ran. My free hand bunched into a hard fist, ready to beat him to death the moment I clenched hold. He was a fleet sumbitch, I'd give him that, and this thought had scarce cleared my mind before he leaped to the side, seeming to disappear. My brain stumbled to the conclusion faster than my feet; I skidded to a halt and then to a instant crouch – not a moment too soon, as his rifle discharged again. The bullet made a high-pitched zinging whine in its deadly flight. I prayed, *Please let Malcolm stay put.*

The round struck the dirt only arm's length from my right side.

Goddammit, the bastard is a good shot.

I cursed, ducking lower still, my blood hopping. A few seconds passed, in which I heard only my labored breath. Then another few, until an unmistakable sound met my ears.

A horse.

I surged to my feet to spy him running again. His mount was tethered out there, waiting. He appeared scarcely bigger than the top joint of my thumb by now, a blur in the distance; he'd bought time by firing at me. I knew I had no hope of running many yards back to Fortune and then overtaking him on horseback, especially in the dark. I aimed the rifle as squarely as I was able on a moving target and fired. My shot missed its mark; he kept running. I wasted another round, cursing the darkness, but he was out of sight.

The excited stir occasioned by my shooting match allowed for no chance at stealing a few hours' sleep. Malcolm ran to meet me as I stalked back to the fire; he was hollering fit to wake those already dead and buried, clutching Gus's rifle. His eyes were wide and agitated; he insisted upon knowing everything that had happened before I could even open my yap. Kristian stood over Theodore with his pistol at the ready – the boy cowered low to the ground, surely at Kristian's instructions – both father and son watching me with stun as I neared, Malcolm dogging my elbow.

I ran a hand through my sweating hair and admitted, "I don't know what in the hell just happened."

"Someone was shooting at you, that is what happened," Kristian said, his voice shaking with concern, but I detected anger as well. "Who was shooting at you?"

Irrational though it might be, my temper flared. I yelled, "Whoever the hell it was intended to kill us while we slept, for all I know! Likely I saved us!"

"It is my belief that ill luck stalks you." Kristian holstered his piece and motioned to the boy. "Come, Teddy, let us go. We will stay no longer with these people."

I could hardly believe my ears. "What do you mean, *ill luck?*"

Collecting their gear, clearly preparing to depart despite the early hour, Kristian kept his eyes averted. "Storms destroy your belongings and steal your money, and now men shoot at you in the night hours. I have not heard of such ill luck striking one man in a week's time and this is why we will take our leave from you now. Son, fetch your mule," he said, more kindly, and in short order the two of them were ready to ride.

Rigid with angry energy, I watched in speechless disbelief; even Malcolm had no words. Kristian made sure the boy was settled before claiming his own saddle and then regarded us with a long face. Theodore watched silently. Consternated, I offered no farewell.

"May better fortunes find you," Kristian said somberly, and heeled his mount.

A cold thread seemed to tighten around the bones in my spine, but I refused to let his words otherwise upset me. Malcolm and I stood side-by-side and watched them depart. Theodore, his mule trailing a step or two behind, looked back once before they disappeared from our sight.

❀

C AROLINE HEMMING STRAINED with knees bent and spine curled forward, loose hair hanging lank across her forehead, obscuring her vision as she labored with chin bent to chest. Teeth bared, eyes closed, she issued a low, continuous grunt that I had come to anticipate as indicative that delivery was eminent. Sweat darkened her birthing gown in wide rings. The room smelled of boiled onions and bacon fat from their earlier dinner, prepared by the eldest daughter, a girl of eight years. Outside, beneath a crisp, late-October sunshine, the children now waited for my word to return indoors; I'd told the girl to mind her younger siblings and keep them from wandering from the dooryard.

"Good work," I murmured to Caroline, then repeated myself in a louder tone when I understood she had not heard, watching as a steady trickle of pink liquid emerged from between her thighs, followed almost immediately by the crown of the newborn's head, bald and wrinkled, the slit from which he would shortly be born bulging to a preposterous girth, stretching the mother's tender skin. Even having viewed the event nearly a dozen times, I felt a distinct twinge in my nether regions, a sharp recognition of a woman's extraordinary ability to bring a child forth from her body.

Next spring this will be you was a thought never far from my consciousness.

Often, riding home on the wagon with Tilson, I reflected and indeed marveled upon the notion, however obvious, that all people, through all time, had entered the world in just such a manner. I found it difficult to believe that I had never actually witnessed a birth before that of Letty Dawes' twins. It seemed to me that babies must never cease to be born, that at any one moment hundreds, if not thousands, of them were being brought forth into

existence. I'd witnessed many a foal enter the world, forelegs emerging first
if the birth was routine, followed by the hindquarters, usually still encased
in the birthing sack before the new colt or filly broke free and attempted to
rise to its delicate hooves for the first time; that I viewed such earthy events
had unendingly offended my mother's refined sensibilities. I reflected that I
would teach my daughters the ways of nature in a more straightforward fashion than Mama, and briefly rested a palm upon my swelling belly, fancying
that I knew with certainty the child within was a girl.

*I promise, little one, I will teach you the ways of the world, without compunc-
tions. And I will protect you to my last breath.*

It's a real sight, ain't it? Tilson had asked after the second birth in which I'd
assisted him. Both of us exhausted, he let Kingfisher, his pinto gelding, take
his own pace along the road home. Tilson had mused, *Kinda unpleasant at
times, but beautiful, too. Downright miraculous, wouldn't you say, honey?*

"He's crowning!" I announced, applying another fingertip of chamomile
oil from a nearby wooden bowl, earlier prepared, to the ring of widening
flesh, as Tilson had demonstrated; it aided in preventing a woman's tearing
and eased the child's way. I was proud of how I'd shed all qualms regarding
that which was required of me, though I continued to depend very heavily
upon Tilson himself, so far graced with routine births and all in his reassuring
company. In the event of a complication, I would not know the proper course
of action and would be forced to rely completely upon the entities of common sense and pure instinct; fortunately for all concerned, Caroline's fifth
child was not proving difficult.

Tilson, called out before dawn to treat what sounded like a possible rup-
tured stomach, was therefore unavailable when Caroline's middle son came
calling for the doc; in this way, it was the first birth I'd attended without him.
The boy waited with little patience, hopping foot to foot while Sawyer helped
me to hitch Whistler to the smaller buggy, rather than the heavy buckboard;
though I knew his head was aching he smiled as I took the reins, one hand
resting on Whistler's rust-and-cream neck. He understood well the nervous
energy gathering within me at the prospect of delivering a child with no
assistance from Tilson, though Rebecca agreed at once to accompany me.
Because the Hemmings' claim shanty sat within town limits rather than one
of the outlying homesteads, and it was early in the day, I'd elected to drive the
buggy into Iowa City.

I'll be careful. I'll return as soon as I am able, I promised Sawyer without words, reading his face. I knew how difficult it was for him to allow me to ride from his sight, and therefore from his protection – neither could I easily bear the prospect of him riding away from me, no matter the circumstances. I'd been much plagued of late with exhausting bouts of vomiting, further increasing his concern.

I know, he'd said, in return. *I know.*

Positioned near Caroline's right shoulder and helping to brace her against the pains, Rebecca encouraged, "Once more!"

"And again!" I ordered.

The infant's head slid forth, red face bunched like a fist. I cupped my hands to receive the child as a shoulder nudged free of Caroline's body. She groaned and heaved, and stool stained the bed beneath her; without further delay, the tiny form slipped into my palms.

"A boy!" I announced, hurrying to insert the tip of my smallest finger into his mouth, making a gentle circular motion within the tiny sleek confines, cleaning out birth fluids.

Caroline's face split with the grin I knew to anticipate, one which never failed to stun me in the totality of its delight, an expression that denied the pain so recently suffered, the indignities enacted upon the mother's body to deliver the child all at once negated as a mother reached for her child. Satisfied the boy was breathing on his own and having wiped fluids from his eyes and nose, I placed him into Caroline's waiting arms to attend to the afterbirth. Rebecca helped me, the two of us making loose fists to knead Caroline's belly; I watched, hawk-like, assessing the amount of blood as Caroline's last link with her child slid free of her body. Assured that she was not bleeding an excessive amount, I dried my hands and fetched a length of string, measuring two fingers above the child's taut belly to tie off and then snip the birthing cord.

"He's beautiful," I congratulated Caroline, whose joy lit her entire countenance.

"Thank you, Mrs. Davis," she murmured, eyes on her new son. She rocked him in her arms while Rebecca and I worked to tidy both mother and child, and the space about them.

What should have been, only minutes later, a placid, happy scene was summarily interrupted; an intrusion as ugly as it was uninvited. The door opened with enough force to startle all of us; I nearly dropped the bundle of linen I was carrying and looked up to behold the figure of a rotund woman framed in the afternoon light, small heads peeking around her skirts in attempt to catch a glimpse of Caroline. This intrusive woman made no attempt at introduction and instead swept officiously into the room, slamming closed the door in her wake, the gesture communicating obvious anger.

"How could you allow this?" she demanded of the room at large, a voice harsh in its accusatory overtone, though clearly this woman was acquainted with at least the idea of me, for her question was meant to be rhetorical; she answered her own query by gasping, "This is deplorable! This..." Gesturing in my direction, she stuttered over perhaps a series of cruel and offensive descriptors before settling upon, "This...*woman of ill repute* attending to your delivery, Caroline! You are my brother's own wife, not some common strumpet!"

All air in the room – or perhaps only my own lungs – seemed to thin and dissipate. In the process of tidying the delivery space, my hands encrusted with drying blood and the bedclothes still soiled, I stared without blinking at this belligerent stranger who stood with arms akimbo; I clutched a linen towel, damp with water from the basin, and its wetness created patches on my sleeves in its journey down my wrists. A small burst of white dots flared in my vision ahead of a small knot of pain, centered behind my right eye.

"Mama!" crowed the little boy who'd no doubt occupied the role of youngest before this afternoon, scurrying around the hostile figure filling the doorway and darting for the bedside. This movement, inserting a certain amount of realism back into the space, allowed me to exhale; objects seemed to snap back into their proper places. I was aware that Rebecca had drawn herself up from the bedside and stood with fists bunched.

"Alice Doherty, you call yourself a Christian?" Rebecca challenged.

Alice Doherty's chin lifted a good two inches; she was so angry and affronted the skin beneath her chin quavered as she cried, "My soul is not the one endangered, Mrs. Krage! You may choose to open your home to a...to *this woman* and her *Rebel soldier husband*," Alice Doherty may as well have been describing vermin, "and thereby expose your own sons to such filth –"

"Alice!" gasped poor Caroline, so recently delivered of her newest child; her face gleamed pale as a pearl as she slumped against the pillows stacked behind her.

Rebecca moved so swiftly that her skirts flowed in a blur; she clamped a hand around Alice's upper arm and turned her about to face the dooryard, an impressive feat, as Alice was a good several-dozen pounds heavier than Rebecca. In no uncertain terms, her tone calling Tilson to my mind, Rebecca ordered, "You shall shut your despicable mouth and leave this house."

Alice wrenched free her arm and despite my condition I acted without thinking; I felt certain in that moment the self-righteous woman intended to strike Rebecca. I darted between them, displacing Rebecca; as I did so, I was granted a regrettably intimate look at Alice Doherty, noticing minute and unpleasant details – the grain of her sweating skin, nostrils that resembled those of a creature in the porcine lineage, fair hair swept beneath an unadorned white bonnet. Her eyes, a watery blue, widened and she reared away, as though proximity to me might sully her flesh.

"Keep away from me, whore!" Alice hissed. "And you, Rebecca Krage! How dare you call me despicable! I speak the truth." Her cruel words landed like blows upon my face but I refused to give her the satisfaction of flinching; little did she know I had faced far worse than her.

"The truth? You should not recognize the truth were it to fall from the heavens and land upon your personage!" Rebecca cried before I could respond, and stepped in front of me, both protective and furious. "Apologize to Mrs. Davis this instant!"

Alice faced us with no hesitation, no sense of remorse. Her brow beetled as she regarded Rebecca anew, with an expression of taunting calculation. "Rebel soldiers and shameless whores. Are these heathen what you allow at your hearth?"

Rebecca's face appeared carved of pale stone as she stared bullets at Alice; I was gratified to observe the slightest suggestion of apprehension pass across Alice's brow. Maintaining her composure with great effort, Rebecca said, "You know *nothing* of what you speak."

"Your sister-in-law has just been delivered of a child, Mrs. Doherty," I interjected, my tone flat and unprovocative; Rebecca was trembling with anger and I edged around her, suddenly conscious of the stunned, gaping manner in which Caroline and her children were observing this unfortunate exchange. The infant was Alice's newest nephew but she did not appear to wish for congratulations. Forcing myself to hold her spiteful gaze, which reminded me of Ginny Hossiter's, I mustered the calm to say, "We are upsetting the both of them."

"Then you shall take your leave, at once," Alice ordered, bristling, her lips white with sanctimonious anger. "*I* should have been called for this afternoon. I've spoken out against the doctor allowing you to attend births in our area. This is a community of upstanding people."

Rebecca's composure shattered like a brick through plate glass. "How *dare* you circulate rumors concerning Mrs. Davis or my uncle, or any person in my home? What right have you to judge those you are unacquainted with?"

Alice ignored these shouted questions, brushing past us and sailing to the bedside, where Caroline watched with speechless astonishment the drama unfolding in her house.

"Mrs. Hemming, I do apologize," I said. And then to Rebecca, "Come, let us take our leave," unwilling to allow Alice a chance to discern the tremble in my hands; my heart beat with an erratic refrain but I refused to allow Alice to witness the way her words affected me, turning my attention to gathering our supplies. Assured that Caroline and her newest son were managing well, I left the house clutching Tilson's satchel, Rebecca at my side.

Evening, and its subsequent chill, had advanced while Caroline labored. Rebecca and I sat alongside one another on the buggy seat, a heavy shawl tucked over our laps, Rebecca holding the reins while I leaned against her side, allowed the chance to crumble as I could not in the presence of others, dry-eyed but drained of all energy. Words retained their own singular capacity to injure, and devastate, this I knew well. I fixed my gaze on Whistler's familiar rump as she drew the little buggy along the road that led to the bridge over the Iowa River, along the southern road and back to our homestead. I cupped both hands over my belly, offering wordless apologies to my unborn child.

Yes, I was a whore. But I am no longer ashamed, and I pray you need never be ashamed of your mama.

"I am so very angry, Lorie," Rebecca said for the second time, and clutched my left hand in her right, winding our fingers together. "I am sorry she spoke to you in such a manner, dear one. I wanted to strike her malicious face. Please, do not believe for a moment what she says."

I held fast to Rebecca's hand, unable to respond. Insults directed my way were painful enough but this was not simply an affront to me, which I could have tolerated, but also one to my husband. My Sawyer, who had come so

close to death, whose scarred body and missing eye could be attributed pre-
cisely to what Alice Doherty suggested – the hatred directed at former Con-
federate soldiers, undying amongst those who'd fought on the opposite side
of the conflict. Had not Zeb Crawford wanted each of us dead for that very
reason, our Southern roots? He'd wanted us to pay for the grievous wrongs
enacted upon him through the deaths of his soldier sons, all lost to the Cause;
the brutality, the ravaging of soul after soul, the long-unhealed wounds, those
both physical and emotional, likely incapable of mending in the span of my
lifetime. Here was additional proof.

More quietly, Rebecca continued, "Though it is no excuse for her miserable behavior, Alice Doherty lost her husband in the War and has never
remarried. Her father was the minister to these parts for many years before
he passed away and you shall never meet a more solid hypocrite than Alice.
She is small-minded, and vicious in her opinions."

"But she speaks for the town, I am certain," I whispered at last, feeling
I must acknowledge this truth. Horace Parmley, an unctuous local journal-
ist, took a morbid interest in our story back in July, producing, to date, two
pieces in his broadside circular concerning my past as a prostitute, however
reformed, and the continuing search for Thomas Yancy, federal marshal, who
had not resurfaced since the night Zeb Crawford was killed in Rebecca's
dooryard. Yancy had ridden away like a demon that night, and Malcolm believed the shot he'd fired after the man struck true. But as much as I wished
for Yancy's subsequent death, instinct warned he was still alive somewhere
out there. The physical state in which he currently existed, and his exact location, remained a mystery to this day.

"Please do not believe that," Rebecca said, squeezing my hand. "There
are some equally dogmatic as Alice, this is true, but she represents a small
minority, at best."

"But she said…"

"She hurt you, and spoke against you and Sawyer, and for that I wish to
hurt her," Rebecca declared, with tender loyalty. "Oh, Lorie, you believed
Alice was about to lift her hand to strike me, did you not, and rushed to
defend me. I am ever so moved, dear one, though I was not in jeopardy. My
intent was to drag Alice from the house and set her upon her large backside
in the street."

Though the bitterness of Alice's punishing words stung badly, I smiled at

Rebecca's frank pronouncement.

"She did rather resemble a pig," I agreed, and Rebecca laughed too. I squeezed my dearest friend's hand and whispered, "Thank you for standing up for me."

"Horace's absurd articles have stirred up the mutterings in the first place. I am certain the furor would have died away by now, as it has been months," Rebecca groused. "He is ever less man than weasel."

"Yancy's prolonged disappearance keeps the story alive." I despised the man's name on my tongue and restrained a shudder at the notion of him hiding somewhere, plotting his revenge. And neither had his son, Fallon, reappeared. Quade, himself also a marshal, kept us well informed of any unfolding developments; indeed, Quade had inquired after Yancy at the federal level, seeing to it that Yancy's role the night of Zeb Crawford's death was well documented. Sawyer, Rebecca, Tilson and I had each given testimony before yet another marshal, a lean, mild-mannered fellow sent from Des Moines last August to take our official statements.

We had tied off all ends as best we could, here in Iowa City.

It is finished, I thought, wishing the words did not inspire the hollow ache of ambiguity in my gut.

Rebecca said, "You are possessed of an extraordinary soul, Lorie. Please, do not let a bitter woman such as Alice Doherty cast a pall over today. You were astonishing in your calm while Caroline labored."

"I'm thankful that it was an easy birth." I drew the shawl farther over my knees. The hours of sunlight shortened with each passing day and there was a bite in the air not present even a week ago.

"Do not be modest," Rebecca chided.

"And I remain most especially grateful that you will be in attendance when my turn comes."

"I am thankful for that, as well," she said, and kissed my cheek. The homestead appeared on the horizon; two cabins of solid, rough-cut logs, the sprawling barn and adjacent corral, a curl of smoke from each chimney, gingham curtains adorning the single window, stately pines guarding the northern edge of the dooryard. The cheerful place beckoned with an undeniable sense of home. Rebecca indicated a particular horse in the pen and said, "Leverett has arrived. I had forgotten he was to dine with us this evening. I do hope he has been good company for Sawyer, and that the boys have not deviled them too terribly."

"Sawyer loves those boys," I said, knowing this for truth. Cort and Nathaniel tagged along at his heels, just as they had at Boyd's last summer, asking questions and getting in the way, but I knew Sawyer enjoyed their company.

"He is most tolerant with them," Rebecca agreed. "Even Lev is not always so, though I know he cares for my boys as well as could be expected."

Rebecca and Marshal Quade planned a March wedding. She wished for me to witness the marriage before Sawyer and I left for Minnesota and I found myself grateful for the buffer of the winter months before our inevitable separation. I ached at the thought of the rest of my life without Rebecca or Tilson present in it; even Deirdre, whose friendship and strength I would never forget, had not been as dear to me as Rebecca. And though she had not spoken the words aloud, I understood Rebecca's fervent wish to delay her marriage to Quade until the last possible moment. I tucked my arm through hers, with love, and deep regret.

She inferred the direction of my thoughts, to a certain degree. "I shall miss you so, Lorie. I try my best not to think of it."

"And I, you. I wish..." But I broke off the sentence, as one snapping a dry twig.

"Lorie..."

I looked her way at the imploring whisper, finding her cheeks mottled as she studied Quade's horse in the corral, as though the gelding represented the inescapable reality in which she found herself. I could discern the pulse in her neck and knew who truly occupied her thoughts just now.

"Not a day...hardly an hour...passes when I do not think of him." The words were thick with choking pain.

I wrapped my arms about her waist and held fast; she knew I understood she meant Boyd. There was nothing I could say to offer comfort and so I simply held her. The continued strain of having received no word from them bit into each of us, with increasing concern. A dozen times a day I manufactured excuses as to why Boyd had not posted a letter; or, I tried to rationalize, perhaps a note *had* been posted and then, for whatever reason, failed to make it all the way back to us here in Iowa City. But with each sunset drawing us closer to winter snows our fear for them grew, quiet and insidious. Sawyer paced a nightly trench along the earthen floor of our cabin.

Rebecca declared with quiet passion, "I know I have no right to continue to feel for Boyd – Lorie, only you are able to understand this, as I could never admit such to another living soul – but I do feel for him." She issued a gasp, as though stabbed by an unseen knife. "I love him, oh dear God, *I love him so*. I believed, indeed I have prayed so desperately, that with time the feeling would atrophy within me but it seems to have only grown stronger for the passing of time."

Her words ran like blood from a deep gash and I gathered the reins from her grasp in the dusky evening light. Rebecca covered her face with both hands. The air around us shone with a tranquil copper glow, pristine with autumn beauty, chill and crisp as darkness advanced, the prairie's greens having long since given way to gold; dry gold grasses lit by clear golden beams, only dust motes appearing to be in motion. I knew saying anything about Boyd and his intractable stubbornness would only serve to hurt her; I acknowledged softly, "He should not have left."

"But he must, I understand this," Rebecca insisted, swiping at her tears. Her lovely face disclosed such deep longing I felt wounded. "He means to reach his kin and I only admire him for that. He needs them. I should never stand in the way of such need. But, how I miss him. The house and yard seem so terribly empty without him. And I miss dear young Malcolm, to be sure, but it is Boyd I think of all through the night."

"Oh, Becky," I mourned, resting my cheek upon her shoulder. If Boyd were to appear before us just now I would dress him down in the manner of the dourest schoolteacher, administer a thorough scolding for the distress he had caused Rebecca. I knew anger was unjustified, and certainly selfish, but it coursed anew in my veins; I did not want to lose Rebecca. If Boyd had stayed to marry her, she would be my sister forever after.

Whistler whickered as we approached the familiar yard, hastening from a walk to a trot. I murmured, "There's a good girl," to my horse, and looked up to see the door fly open, emitting Cort and Nathaniel, who approached us at a run, waving and hollering; Sawyer appeared in the doorway behind the boys. He lifted one hand to shade his vision and I felt his relief at our appearance as palpably as a touch. I had brewed willowbark tea for him this morning, in hopes it would ease his headache.

I'm home, sweetheart. I sent this thought to him straight as an arrow in flight, my heart thumping with gladness.

Rebecca squared her slender shoulders and regained her composure, discreetly drying her nose with the back of her hand. Her dark, eloquent brows and her soft mouth quirked with concern as she turned to me to ask, "Would you rather I recount the afternoon's unpleasantness, or allow you?"

"I will. I wish I did not have to speak of it at all, but likely they'll hear anyway, before too long."

"Evenin', darlin'," Sawyer said, coming to my side of the buggy. "And good evenin' to you, Becky."

I drew Whistler to a halt and smiled at him, despite the stress of the afternoon. Golden as the evening around him he appeared, his fair hair becoming spun gold in the glinting light, his eye a wealth of the rich color. His eyepatch was in place but I saw the way he observed the traces of my earlier distress; of course he could sense it. He reached to help me down as Quade stepped from the house to greet Rebecca; Cort and Nathaniel darted about her skirts, anxious to claim her undivided attention, and in the ensuing hubbub I wrapped my arms about Sawyer's waist and unapologetically absorbed the solid reassurance of him.

"What happened?" he murmured, gathering me closer.

"I'll tell you in a bit," I whispered, eyes closed as I rested my cheek to his heartbeat. "How is your head, love?"

"Much better, especially now that you're home." He cupped my elbow in one hand, bracketing my lower back with the other, and I understood anew I could never be thankful enough for my husband.

"THAT REPULSIVE, higher-than-thou old biddy." Tilson spoke without compunction. "I'll tell Alice Doherty a thing or two, next we meet. She's a problem with my decisions, does she?" His thunderous expression softened into its usual tender benevolence as he looked my way. "Lorie, my dear girl, I am ever so sorry. I wish I would have been with. I'd be curious to know how opinionated she would prove in my presence."

"Rebecca was most forthright in my defense," I said. The five of us surrounded the dinner table; it was late into the evening and Tilson had only just arrived home. He sat smoking his pipe while Rebecca warmed coffee for him. Quade lingered over dinner and then dessert, during which Rebecca and I related the events at Caroline Hemming's, keeping in mind the two little boys, both listening with ears perked. Now, hours later, Cort and Nathaniel were safely retired to their loft bed and speech flowed more forthrightly. Stormy lay on my lap and his purring rumbled pleasantly along my thighs as I stroked his cloudy fur.

Placing a steaming cup before her uncle and reclaiming her seat, Rebecca explained, "And Lorie believed, after all of this, that Alice was about to strike me and darted between the two of us, to protect me. I tell you, Sawyer, your wife is the bravest woman I have ever been privileged to know. Of course, I have known this for some time."

Though I recognized Sawyer's distress that I'd put myself in potential harm's way, he only said, "That is God's truth. Even still, Lorie-love, I'd like to find this woman and demand she apologize to you, and then I may very well knock the teeth from her head."

"Sawyer James," I murmured; I'd harbored a similar urge but as his wife felt compelled to admonish.

He replied, "This Alice woman sounds on a level with Parmley, speaking of teeth I would not mind forcibly displacing."

Quade, opposite us, snorted a laugh. The marshal sat to Rebecca's left, hatless, though he never removed his marshal's badge; it winked in the firelight, the symbol of his station. He was a somewhat stern, long-faced man; I'd been surprised to learn he was, at thirty years, not nearly as old as I would have guessed, and in fact only three years older than Rebecca. I'd mistakenly placed Quade closer to two score. His hair was thinning, the lines of his face sharp, but he smiled readily enough, especially at Rebecca. Sawyer and I had come to enjoy his company, despite his initial introduction into our lives, when he'd arrested Sawyer. I comforted, if not contented, myself with the knowledge that Quade cared deeply for Rebecca and would provide for and treat her as befitting a proper lady, all their married life.

Quade rested a proprietary arm along the back of Rebecca's chair and commented, "Parmley envisions for himself an illustrious political career, beginning with mayor of Iowa City. He was speaking of as much, just yesterday."

"Politicking seems a fitting occupation for such a weasel," Tilson said around his pipe stem. He mused, "Or dentistry."

Quade asked, "What have you against the dental arts, Edward?"

Tilson grinned. "You mean to tell me you ain't ever had a tooth pulled?"

Only just seated, Rebecca rose, almost skittishly, and crossed to the woodstove, pouring herself a cup even though she rarely drank coffee after dinner.

Quade was saying, "I've never had a tooth pulled, only knocked from my head by a well-aimed fist or two." His eyes followed Rebecca's movements as he spoke and I noticed the faintest of frowns crease his brow as he attempted to make sense of her restlessness. Not for the first time, I wondered if he'd ever suspected Rebecca's feelings for Boyd. Quade was perceptive, but for him Boyd's absence was surely in line with the old adage – *out of sight, out of mind.*

Tilson invited, "Becky, honey, have a seat, won't you?"

Quade stood to draw out her chair, as would any gentleman, and Rebecca reclaimed her seat only to spill coffee on her skirts. Much to the collective stun of the men, she exclaimed, "*Goddammit!*"

Quade uttered, "Rebecca!"

With a completely different capability for understanding the rising tide of her flustered frustration, I thought, *Oh, Becky...*

Before she could reply hoofbeats sounded on the lane, further cause for alarm, as all expected persons were currently in the house. Sawyer and Tilson rose at once, while Quade strode to the window and observed, "It's only Clint, no need to worry."

Clint Clemens tapped on the door before entering; though reared from boyhood in this house and indeed still occasionally residing within it Clemens was unfailingly courteous in his actions. He ducked inside, wearing a heavy cloak against the night's chill, his narrow, fine-featured face appearing as he removed his hat. Tilson was there to take his nephew's cloak and cup a hand over his shoulder; though Clemens was a grown man and a deputy, Tilson always behaved protectively towards him.

Rebecca was already on her feet, moving to her brother's side. She placed a hand on his back and asked, "What brings you? Is anything wrong?"

Clemens shook his head. "All is well. I am on duty this evening but I wished to deliver this letter to you, Mr. Davis." He referred to us with consistent decorum; I surmised that he always would. Referring to the proprietor of the general store, which also housed the post office, Clemens explained, "Mr. Sedum bestowed this letter upon me. It arrived this afternoon, though I've not found a moment's time until this late hour, I apologize."

"Thank you for delivering it," Sawyer said, relief abundant in his tone. "It must be word from Boyd."

"No, I believe it is a letter from Jacob Miller," Clemens contradicted, extracting an envelope from his vest pocket, and Rebecca's entire being seemed to coalesce into a knot of tension.

From Jacob? I wondered. Sawyer met my gaze, the selfsame question in his mind.

The once-ivory envelope, addressed to *Mr. Sawyer J. Davis*, was much tattered. Sawyer and I hardly knew which of us should read it first and settled for my reading aloud, everyone crowded around. Rebecca was containing her distress with true effort, her knuckles white and strained as she gripped together her hands. I observed that the post date, the twenty-fifth of September, was a solid month past. The grim question hovering over our heads descended, swift and frightening – why had not Boyd written this letter himself? It was almost November and he and Malcolm should have long reached their destination in northern Minnesota. Fingers trembling, I nearly ripped the letter extracting it from the envelope; steadying my composure, I began to read.

Less than a minute later we sat staring at each other, wordless for the space of a horrified, disbelieving heartbeat. Rebecca brought one hand to her lips but a gasping cry rose before she could muffle it – before there was a hope of attempting to offer an explanation. None of us knew what to think. I grasped the letter, sweat collecting along my ribs and temples, and studied the slanting lines of one particular sentence of Jacob's precise handwriting, willing it to be untrue:

I am greatly troubled that my nephews have not yet arrived, nor have I received a word as to their current whereabouts.

"I WILL not bring you and our child into unknown territory with winter advancing. And I will never ride away from you again. Not ever." Sawyer's voice was taut with angry tension. I knew from past experience that such a tone indicated he would not be moved from his present mindset, despite anything I said.

"But where could they be?" I sobbed, sprawled atop our bed; Sawyer paced in worry, incapable of remaining still, while my knees gave out. Another bout of weeping seized me, as did nausea. I was quite unable to staunch the surge of terrible images, those of the two of them hurt beyond repair; I could conceive of no other reason Boyd would fail to send word to us or to Jacob. He was a reluctant letter-writer, this I knew well, but he loved us; he was not thoughtless. He would know how we worried, how we waited for word. Such silence could only suggest he and Malcolm's circumstances had grown unquestionably dire; all evidence in our possession suggested that the two of them had inexplicably vanished between here and Minnesota. I refused to harbor the idea that they had been killed. I insisted, "Oh Sawyer, we *must* go after them. Why wouldn't Boyd write unless something dreadful has occurred…"

"I am every bit as worried!" Rarely did he raise his voice to me. "I am sick with worry. I would ride from this place as quickly as I could saddle Whistler but I will not ride away from you, not even for them. Do you hear me?"

"We must do something!" I cried, unwilling to heed his words, however sincere and reasonable.

Sawyer continued to pace the floorboards, clutching his temples, the picture of agony. He'd removed his eyepatch but not one other piece of clothing, even his boots, too overcome since Clemens delivered the letter only an hour ago. I lay in my shift, miserable with helplessness; I could only imagine Rebecca's present state. She had left the house almost immediately after I'd concluded reading the letter, wrapping into her shawl; when Quade moved to follow her, more bewildered than concerned, I caught his arm and implored, "Please, let me."

I found her in the barn, leaning her forehead against her bent arms, braced along the top edge of the stall Boyd had used for Fortune last summer. She cried with quiet fervor, slender frame heaving, and flinched when I put my hands upon her back.

"I should not have let him go," she wept. Her face was hidden from me, her voice muffled, but I discerned each painful and self-punishing word. "How could I have let him go away from me?"

Still gripped in the coldness of shock, I found I could not offer comfort by any other means than wrapping my arms about her, as I had earlier in the buggy; I pressed my cheek to the soft, loose weave of her knitted shawl. Her words seemed to fall to our hems and spread across the barn floor.

"I shall never forgive myself, oh Lorie, never." Rebecca gulped and moaned at the same instant. "Boyd rode from this place and I was too cowardly to tell him I love him, or to stop him. *I should have stopped him.*"

"Becky," I whispered. It did no good to remind her little could stop Boyd when he set his mind; this she already knew. I did not wish to cause her more pain, praying I did not as I said, "He knew. He is in love with you but he was too stubborn to say so."

She lifted her head. The delicate skin beneath her eyes was swollen and purple as a new bruise but hope burned in her irises; hope which she buried at all other times now flaring to the surface, bright as a line of fire along a nighttime horizon, before she could submerge its passionate presence. She whispered, "I must find him. I shall not rest until I find him."

"We'll find them together," I had vowed.

"Sawyer," I implored now in our sleeping quarters, the space made tense with our worry, coiled like wire springs between us. I rose to my knees upon the bed and reached for him. "Come here, please let me comfort you."

He came at once, bringing me to his chest, cupping his right palm over my belly; in the past few weeks the child's presence had created a firm bulge, a round smoothness like that of a summer melon tucked beneath my skirts. I slipped the suspenders from his shoulders with deft movements, drawing the shirttails from his trousers, removing every stitch and then pressing my lips to the juncture of his collarbones. He took us to the bed's surface, drawing the quilt over our hips. In the meager light we lay on our sides, studying one another. Sawyer's mouth was solemn, his face cast in flickering shadows. I latched my right leg over his thighs in a gesture of possession, hooking him closer to me as he traced his thumb along the top of my shoulder, pressing into the hollows near my neck.

"I do not believe they are dead," he said after a time, his throaty voice so familiar in its intensity. "Though I admit I am unable to sense Boyd as I sense you, *mo mhuirnín milis*, I believe he is alive. I truly believe I would feel it if he no longer walked the Earth." His sincere words struck at my heart. Sawyer was, as always, so powerfully dedicated to those he loved.

"I do not believe them dead, either, I promise you," I said, scrubbing at the last of my tears. We'd been at odds with one another ever since the letter's arrival, arguing over the possibility of heading for Minnesota without delay. I'd observed the disquiet on Tilson's face as Sawyer and I took our leave, retiring to bed; I knew Tilson feared we would depart with morning's light. Rebecca had not reemerged from the barn; Quade went to her there and I could only speculate what words were exchanged between the two of them. Surely her distress indicated to Quade that she harbored stronger feelings for Boyd than he'd suspected; I recalled that Quade had not been wildly fond of Boyd during their brief acquaintance, though he had not allowed this to color his obligations as marshal. Perhaps Quade had ascertained an undertone, sensed that which existed between Rebecca and Boyd, even if neither of them ever gave words to their sentiments; Rebecca's reaction to tonight's news was further evidence, had Quade been seeking any.

"They've been delayed and I have been considering why, without letup." Sawyer cupped a hand over my calf, applying soft pressure along its length. "There is one conclusion I fear more than others…"

Yancy, I heard him think, though he was reluctant to speak the name aloud, as though to do so would be to give Thomas Yancy additional power over us, more than the despicable man had already claimed.

I whispered, "Could it be that he followed them? Would he have been tracking them? Searching for them?"

Sawyer shook his head even before I finished speaking. "I don't believe Yancy is searching for them, at least, not the Yancy we're thinking of. Ever since the night Charley related to us that Yancy's eldest ran away, I've been unduly troubled. You know," and I did, as Sawyer had mentioned these qualms, which I shared. He continued, "The boy, Fallon, is fourteen. At that age I recall being easily provoked. Most boys are so, and on the lookout for even the slightest insult. I have tried, many a time, to imagine my feelings upon knowing someone shot at my father, perhaps grievously injured him. Would not I attempt to find this man…this boy…and force from him my retribution?"

A bitter dread clamped hold as I considered his words. Malcolm had fired the rifle after Yancy's fleeing form that dreadful night last summer, but we'd been granted no knowledge of the damage rendered. My mind leaped again through possibilities – those of Yancy wounded beyond repair that July night, furtively calling upon his eldest to seek revenge. Heaven knew revenge had long motivated Yancy's desire to destroy Sawyer, and anyone close to him, as Sawyer had killed Yancy's brother, long ago in the terrible days following the Surrender.

"Fallon's eyes were so very empty," I whispered, recalling the evening of our first meeting, July the Fourth, at the Rawleys' homestead. Fallon fought with Malcolm the next morning, over matters no doubt petty; unfortunate animosity bristled between the two boys, as I had plainly witnessed. And if Fallon knew, somehow, that Malcolm was the one to fire the repeater after his father's retreating figure...

Sawyer read my thoughts as effortlessly as I read his. "And this is a matter far from trifling. I should have considered the seriousness. I should have figured the boy would possess the gumption to go after them. Why else would he run away?"

"But we are only speculating," I said, unwilling to believe what I suddenly knew was true. I sat straight, a band of fear cinching my ribs as would a leather strap.

Sawyer studied me as understanding grew between us; we both realized the time for speculation was past. He saw the gathering determination in my eyes and reiterated, "No, Lorie. I will not allow it."

Flames licked at my cheeks. I demanded, "What of my opinion on the matter? What if I believe we should go after them without delay?"

Recognizing potential danger as would any sensible man when confronted with his angry wife, Sawyer softened his tone. "The fact remains that winter is fast approaching. You are carrying our child, love. I will not risk harm to you or our babe, as you well know."

My heart scraped over a small, sharp rock and I cupped his jaws, overcome. I whispered, "I know. I know, Sawyer."

He decided, "We will ride in the morning, to Iowa City. We'll write to Jacob. And next, the land office in St. Paul. Perhaps we can even wire the land office, rather than wait for a letter to arrive. We'll begin there."

S EPTEMBER THE FIRST," Malcolm recited with great deliberation, holding aloft a daily circular printed with fancy script reading *Saint Paul Dispatch*. His other hand remained wrapped about Aces' halter rope.

"That's yesterday's date, if I don't mistake." I slid my boot free of the stirrup and braced it against the hitching rail; I remained astride Fortune, stretching my sore back, taking a moment to marvel at the sprawl around us. St. Paul appeared a bustling river town, much like St. Louis far to the south, situated near limestone cliffs that soared in a majestic fashion, catching my eye. The wide Mississippi churned grandly through the center of town, the wide levee of its banks a crowded network of bridges and dock works, steamboats and paddlewheels, and many people. I'd not seen so many folks gathered in one place in a damn long time, not since my soldiering days; I prayed that amongst them I would find a man to pay me for work. Ten dollars' worth and God only knew how long it might take to save that amount. My head ached just considering.

Exhausted and drooping after my relentless push to reach this place, Malcolm stood quietly and examined the circular, his solemn eyes roving with care over the printed words as he shuffled his boots on the dusty ground. He murmured, "It's all talk of the election."

"I s'pose it is," I said, twisting at the waist and then hunching my shoulders. I felt raw and knew I'd pushed the boy and our mounts too hard with this ride, reaching St. Paul in only two days. Fortune and Aces High were in need of care, Malcolm and me in severe want of a bath and rest, in that order; we all four needed food. I had not a penny to my name. I felt cold and desolate despite the hot evening sun spilling over the river's murky surface, blinding my eyes. And then I felt a slash of guilt at the word *blind*. Never again could I use that word without being reminded of my oldest and dearest friend; reminded, and greatly humbled.

What I wouldn't give to talk with you, Sawyer, I thought, grim and sad. *Goddamn, I miss you. You always put things in perspective for me. You coulda sat up with me nights, waitin' for the bastard following us, an' I woulda felt all the better for you at my side, as always.*

I would post a letter to him and Lorie, as soon as I was able. Today, if possible. Malcolm and I had drawn to a halt before a wood-framed storefront in the downtown district; passersby spoke in a variety of languages. I beheld ladies with parasols, men in stiff, fitted collars and brown hats with narrower brims than mine or Malcolm's, folks who appeared proper. Amongst these genteel persons were men dressed much rougher, in stained trousers and dusty boots, some with buckskin leggings; there walked a man with tightly-rolled silver cones dangling from his ear and a line of tattooing across his forehead. I spied a stout man rolling a barrel, trailed by two youngsters. There were indeed many children, and dogs, horses, and mules; buggies, buckboards and canvas-topped wagons and rising dust, an array of color and clickety-clacking sound. I felt a jolt of dizzy confusion. My vision tilted and swam.

Malcolm dropped the circular and put his hand on my leg. He questioned, "Boyd?" and I heard the way he begged me to be all right, with just that one word.

I bit hard on the insides of my cheeks and sat straight, with effort. I hadn't eaten proper in days, and my bowels were all the worse for this fact. Keeping my voice steady, I muttered, "I just had me a twinge, is all."

"Can we get us a meal?" he begged.

"Wait here," I said, dismounting and tying Fortune to the hitching rail. I narrowed my eyes at him. "Right here an' not a step away. I'll be back directly."

Malcolm nodded, absently patting Aces' nose, leaning against his horse for the familiar comfort of it as I climbed the front steps leading to the general store. The interior of the structure proved muggy and crowded; the air a jumble of strong scents. I smelled over-ripe fruit, molasses and wheaten flour, starch, tobacco leaf, lye and lavender oil, hair pomade, and unwashed bodies. That, in particular, threw my soldiering days to the forefront of my mind but I girded my nerves and moved through the crush of people and items, to the front counter, where stood a man with waxed mustaches.

"Sir?" I inquired.

He looked my way as fast as he'd flick a gnat and said dismissively, "Saloons are a block west, nearer the river."

"I need a job," I attempted to explain, but he moved farther down the counter, unreachable from my current position. I bit down on the anger ready to well to the surface; when I considered it, a saloon might be a better bet for employment, anyway. The penny candy, as bright as promises, snared my gaze on the way out of the store and I wanted suddenly to smash the line of round-bellied jars to unsalvageable shards. The goddamn things represented nothing so much as my failure. My failure to provide for my own brother, whose face had appeared so fearful just now. He depended upon me and I must be stronger than this. It was my duty to see us through; there was no one else, no matter how I longed for my daddy to ride in and save our skins.

Malcolm followed me one block west, the two of us leading our horses. We passed many buildings, including a grain depository, a seed store, feed lots and boardinghouses, the jail and the sheriff's office, establishments of both wood-frame and stone construction. The saloon district was only steps from the steep, narrow paths leading to and fro from the levee. A flow of foot traffic moved steadily, men enjoying both the fair weather and the promise of a drink and a woman. I knew these pleasures well and had once craved them but there was nothing on my mind this night save finding work. Piano music and the sawing of a fiddle met our ears, and the sounds of laughter.

"Wait here," I told the boy for the second time, feeling the sting of guilt as he sighed and slumped against Aces High, resting his temple on the chestnut's long neck. I entered the nearest saloon, The Steam House, a squat stone structure; it was immediately cooler as I stepped inside. The space was dim and packed, as noisy as the general store, but a different kind of noise. The sounds in this place suggested the absence of restraint. I shouldered my way to the bar, where a man, bald as an egg and wrapped in a bibbed white cloth such as a butcher might wear, gave me no more than a moment's attention before being diverted by the raucous group before him. I wanted to slam my fist to the bar, or perhaps his shiny head, and prayed for the grace not to do so.

Before I could command the barkeep's attention a warm hand snaked about my waist, anchoring along my ribs. I turned to see a woman upon whose mouth was pasted a smile I knew all too well. She was skinny, the lines of her face sharp and angular. A gold-painted feather danced in her pinned-up hair, as if caught in a breeze. She did not appear much older than Lorie and my insides got all the worse twisted up, for noticing. I wondered things I never would have considered when I was a younger man – where this poor skinny girl had come from, what miserable circumstances led to her working in this dingy saloon in a river town.

"You new in town, mister? I swear I know all the regulars, and you ain't one," she said, pressing a pointy hip against my side. I caught the scent of whiskey on her lips.

I drew a deep breath, expanding my torso so that she was forced slightly away. I didn't want to be ill-mannered, but I hadn't the time for this. "I just arrived, yes, ma'am." Figuring it couldn't hurt, I elaborated, "I'm lookin' for work. You know of anyone –"

But she interrupted, "Ain't that funny? I'm looking for work, myself. I got a room right out back of here…"

"Work, you say?" A man loomed beyond the girl's shoulder.

"Shoo, Bill," she scolded. "This feller ain't looking to skin buffalo for you."

I set the girl gently to the side, where she pouted at my distraction, moving on down the bar. The man who'd asked regarded me from beneath a battered hat with one narrowed eye, as if appraising horseflesh. He wore dusty leathers that spoke of hard riding and I did not appreciate such a speculative gaze, squaring both my jaw and my shoulders; he lost the expression but continued to study me.

"I am in need of it," I explained, taking note of the scarring on his left cheek, a small entry point with a larger, triangular exit a finger-length away, the surrounding skin patched with small black powder grains no water would ever serve to remove; I recognized the wound left by a musket ball. He'd been damn lucky to survive such a shot to the face.

"A Southerner," he observed, without answering my question. He drew out the word, his tone bordering on confrontational, and I thought, *Goddammit to hell. Not now.*

"That's right," I said evenly. I felt a muscle in my cheek twitch. I was in no mood.

"Why's a Southern boy looking for work this far up-country?" he wondered next, shifting so that his right hand was nearer his holster; he'd emphasized the word *boy*, hoping to provoke something. I couldn't see his pistol but knew it was there; was this bastard itching that much for a fight? I glanced beyond him, at the exit with an oblong patch of outside light showing above its swinging doors. I was not any too keen to brawl, not when I had so many other concerns weighting my mind.

The skinny girl with the feather in her hair reappeared and tugged at my shirtsleeve. Tense as banded wire, I sprang to my feet and half the heads on the saloon floor snapped our direction. I barked at her, "I ain't got the time!"

She looked wounded and retreated several steps, and I felt like a right lout, speaking so rudely to the poor thing. Before I could apologize she lifted her chin and spoke with quiet dignity. "I only meant to tell you that Luc Beaupré might need a hand in his saloon, The Dolly Belle, two doors down yonder," and she indicated by pointing west. "My friend Emilia used to work there, see."

"Thank you kindly," I said, after a beat of silence. I felt doubly guilty for being so impolite and offered her a smile, ignoring the man with the musket scar as I took my leave, refusing to relent to the urge to drive my shoulder into him as I walked past.

"So long, Johnny!" he called to my back, his tone that of jeering gaiety; there was a low ripple of laughter. My footsteps faltered. I would be a liar if I didn't admit that I wanted to turn on my heel and slam the bastard's ugly face repeatedly against the edge of the bar counter, feel his teeth splinter with the impact –

"I'd rather have a Reb cock than yours, Bill," the girl proclaimed loudly, inspiring riotous laughter.

I did turn then, and tipped my hat with all the courtesy I could muster, keeping my gaze fixed on her as I said, "Thank you, ma'am," before exiting the place, glad twofold; one, that I'd kept hold of my temper, and two, that Malcolm had not borne witness to such a foul exchange. I found him waiting outside, scuffing the toes of his boots in the dust, one after the other. Forcing a bit of cheer, I said, "C'mon, there's a fella in the saloon over there that might need help."

The front entrance of the saloon two doors down, bearing the grand name of The Dolly Belle, was strung with red paper lanterns that seemed to sway to the rollicking thump of a piano. The sun resembled a sliced melon as Malcolm and I made our way there, its scarlet light casting the town in a fiery glow, bathing our faces. We tied Fortune and Aces out front and I debated only seconds before deciding, "C'mon inside," not wishing to leave the boy alone in the gathering darkness or the bustling, rowdy streets.

Malcolm could not help but whistle faintly through his teeth as we entered, his wondering eyes roving without letup over the wall opposite the batwing doors – a wall whitewashed rafters to floorboards and adorned with a large and ornately-framed painting of a woman sprawled naked upon her back in a field of flowers. Both plump arms were raised above her head, ample breasts with nipples red as raspberries, legs spread just enough to allow the briefest glimpse of that heaven which lay between; she reclined as though drifting in dream, eyes half-closed and lips parted. For a split second even I hesitated to gape before shaking my head, cursing myself for allowing the boy inside. But neither could I leave him out of my sight as night descended.

The mood in this place was even more raucous than the last. A woman with red garters beneath her skirts twirled upon a small platform in the corner. Other girls circulated the floor. Men pressed close, cat-calling and drinking, laughing and jostling one another to gawk. I imagined Lorie present in just such a space, alone and afraid as she must surely have been in that saloon back in St. Louis, and my gut felt kicked. I thought of Rebecca seeing what I was seeing at this very moment, and wanted to cover my face in shame. It was bad enough Malcolm witness it; ten times worse was the way I once would have reveled in just such a night's activity. Though, I'd not ever seen the likes of the nude painting on the opposite wall.

"*Messieurs, quel est votre plaisir?*" inquired a voice to the left, and a bearded man with a blue headscarf and hammered-copper hoops in either ear swooped near and bowed elaborately, giving Malcolm a wink. The silver adornments pinned to his scarf clinked like tiny bells. In heavily-accented English he observed, "A bit young, *non? Vous avez de la chance! Ici, il n'y a pas de règles!*"

"I am looking for Luc Beaupré," I said, not about to be distracted from my course, aware that my own accent distorted the French surname. I waited for this gaudy man to comment upon my Southern origins, but he did not.

"You like my Dolly Belle, do you not?" he asked Malcolm, gesturing at the painting with a grand sweep of his arm. "She is a lady of no secrets, *non?*"

Malcolm's earnest eyes remained wide, fixed on the naked woman. "A lady oughta have a few secrets, I'm of a mind to believe." And then, worried his words may have caused offense, he said, "But she is beautiful as a starry sky, that's for certain!"

I pressed, "Sir, do you know this fellow?"

The man was too busy laughing at Malcolm's words to respond and I had the sense that everything he did was calculated to earn the most attention possible; even now, he made a show of his merriment. He clapped Malcolm's shoulder. "Wise words from a boy so young."

I reached to commandeer my brother from this bizarre man's grasp when he observed my growing anger. He beamed anew and extended his hand to shake mine, gushing, "*Monsieur*, forgive me. *I* am Jean Luc, and this is my établissement. You and I were once young and so innocent as the boy, *non?*"

I shook with him and his grip was firm, despite his simpering mannerisms. He held my gaze and his handshake suggested he was not a man easily crossed, but I would have said the same thing of myself, with no false pride.

"Boyd Carter. The boy is my brother, Malcolm." I withdrew my hand. "I need work an' was told to talk to you by a gal across the way."

Jean Luc clamped his lower lip with his top row of teeth, restraining a smile. He explained this immediately, saying, "*Monsieur* Carter, I hate to disappoint, but you have been misinformed about the nature of the work. You see, I am short a girl since the lovely Emilia sought employment elsewhere, and you, sir, are most certainly not a female."

I snorted a surprised laugh and then laughed even harder, the man's outrageous humor and my own exhaustion combining to bend me forward with mirth. Malcolm was shocked, I could tell, but I could not regain control. Jean Luc joined me in laughter, clapping my back. "May I offer you a drink, at the very least?"

I gathered my wits. "No, thank you. We ain't got time."

"*C'est gratuit, pour ce soir.* For your trouble. On the house for tonight, I insist!"

In short order, Malcolm and I found ourselves at a small round table near the dancing woman, her red garters flashing. Malcolm was all eyes. Jean Luc glided behind his bar and procured two shot glasses and a brown bottle, setting all three upon the tabletop with elaborate ceremony; I reached and curled my hand over the one he'd placed before Malcolm. Mesmerized by swirling skirts and flashing legs, the boy did not notice, let alone protest.

I said in an undertone, "Thank you kindly, but none for the boy."

"I understand," he said graciously, glancing with amusement at my brother; Malcolm had turned his chair sideways to better observe the dancing woman. Jean Luc noted, "You have the look of hard travels and the sound of the Southern lands, most uncommon here. Where are you bound? Why do you seek work in this town? I am most curious, forgive my questions."

He filled a glass for me, with a flourish but still neatly, not wasting a single drop. I brought the alcohol to my nose and inhaled with a twinge of pleasure. I was not one to accept charity but found myself unable to resist the offer of such fine Kentucky bourbon; I would have known its origins even without seeing the bottle's black label. I drained the glass, pressed my lips together to fully savor the silken liquid, and then sighed, allowing a measure, however small, of indulgence. The bourbon was smooth as melted butter. My shoulders relaxed a mite and Jean Luc poured a second round.

"We was caught in a twister, a piece back," I said as the Frenchman settled upon the chair opposite. "We lost our supplies, our tent, and our money, including the ten-dollar note I'd brought to file for land. We's in a fix." Two shots of bourbon on an empty stomach had loosened my tongue. "I intend to get us farther north, to our uncle, but I can't with no means. I need to earn enough for the filing fee an' a few supplies. The boy ain't got a soul but me to look after him."

Jean Luc appeared to be listening intently. He leaned forward over the table. "When did you last eat? May I offer you and your brother a meal?" Perceiving my immediate resistance, he hurried to say, "It is no trouble. I insist," and at last I nodded, so far beyond weary I felt I may collapse over the shot glass and bust a tooth. But I could not relent to exhaustion, no matter how the booze smelted my bones. Malcolm needed food.

Jean Luc turned to beckon to a woman two tables away, ordering in rapid French, "Isobel, *chercher quelque repas pour ces hommes, tout de suite!*"

The woman nodded, expertly disengaging herself from the man who'd hooked an arm about her hips. Her curious gaze roamed over both Malcolm and me, but she disappeared without asking questions through a wide arch, trailed by complaints from the men at the table. The red-garter woman finished her dance, ending by throwing several kisses to the room. There was raucous applause and foot-stamping, and many pleas for her to stay even as she took her exit, but the man at the piano kept right on pounding the keys and the lively mood did not diminish. I realized suddenly that the lighting in the room was distorted because the lanterns' inset glass panels were tinted with a strange mix of colors, from the deep green of pine boughs to a rich maple-gold. Nearer our table, there were two lanterns set with rippled vermilion glass, casting us in fire. If I let my imagination have free reign – and how many times had I scoffed and poked fun at Sawyer's vivid imagination – I could almost believe Malcolm and I had stumbled into hell.

This odd thought caught hold of me and I felt a distinct stab of misgiving. Kristian Hagebak's pronouncement about ill luck had troubled me greatly as the boy and I continued our journey, and sitting in this saloon, far removed from everyone I loved save Malcolm, I was uneasy to the point of discomfort. My gut ached with anxiety and the scarlet-tinted glow only exaggerated this bad feeling. My eyes felt grainy. Jean Luc, whose bearded face flickered in odd patterns of light and shadow, seemed at once an image from the Carter family bible that Mama had kept tucked in a drawer and which noted all the family births, marriages, and deaths – the one lost in a fire during my absence in the War. It had contained elaborate illustration plates, one of which portrayed the devil. The Frenchman sitting across from me bore no small resemblance.

Jesus Christ, I thought, with a cold shiver. *You's got better sense than that. He's offered a meal, which Malcolm needs. Stop actin' like a superstitious old woman. You's as bad as Granny Rose, God rest her dear soul.*

Malcolm leaned nearer to me and muttered desperately, "Boyd, I gotta make water."

This matter-of-fact statement blessedly restored my senses. I nodded, jerking a thumb over my shoulder. "C'mon, I seen a necessary on the way." To Jean Luc, I added, "We'll be back directly."

When the boy and I returned, two plates had been set for us, each containing a slab of sliced beef, calico beans, and a thick square of cornbread, dripping with golden butter. My stomach lurched with a keen, all-consuming urge to tear into that food like a wolverine in snowmelt; Malcolm's stomach too, from the look of him. Jean Luc leaned on one elbow, still seated at the table and with the woman named Isobel perched on his knee, the two deep in conversation. I was heartened that the strangeness I'd felt only minutes ago, the sense of entering into hell, had faded like a bad dream upon waking.

At our appearance Isobel stood. "Gentlemen, please make yourselves comfortable." She also spoke with a French note to her words, not as pronounced as Jean Luc's. Her eyes were a brown so dark as to appear black; quick and attentive was her expression. Her teeth were small and crooked, her chin pointy as a rake tine. She reminded me of a small critter one would find in a barn, a peculiar little thing that would watch from a distance, missing nothing. Heavy black hair was twisted atop her head; it seemed the weight of it would bow the stalk of her neck.

"We are indebted. Thank you kindly," I said again, and my hand trembled as I reached for the fork placed near my plate, I could not quell it; my hunger was potent.

Malcolm let his hat dangle down his back and proceeded to shovel food directly into his mouth with his fingers until I kicked his ankle beneath the table.

"It is not often we are visited by a boy so young," Isobel said, positioning between mine and Malcolm's chairs, curling her palms around the top curve of each. Her quick-moving eyes came to rest on me as she noted, "You are looking for work, *monsieur*, Jean Luc has told me."

Mouth full, I nodded. She smelled of an oil I could not identify, not unpleasant, but strong. I felt I might sneeze, and pinched the bridge of my nose.

Jean Luc, who seemed incapable of not smiling, a trait I found repugnant even as I sat shamelessly eating his food, said, "These gentlemen are our guests for the evening, Isobel. I adore, do I not, the unexpected, *quelque chose d'interessant?*"

Isobel let her thumb trail lightly along the back of my neck, up and down. "*Oui*, this is true." Her caress provoked an unwelcome shudder along my spine but I stilled it, refusing to allow a woman's touch to upset me; I wasn't that far gone, for Christ's sake.

"Isobel, may I introduce Boyd Carter and his *petit frère*, Malcolm. And gentlemen, this *femme charmante* is Isobel Faucon. She will entertain you in my absence. Please eat well, enjoy our many comforts," and he winked again at Malcolm before rising and addressing those at a nearby table. The Dolly Belle was packed tight as a jam jar with customers, and Jean Luc ingratiated himself amongst them.

Isobel claimed his abandoned seat, straight into my line of view. Her watchful eyes flickered between us as we ate and I wanted to ask her to stop the nervous drumming of her fingers atop the table, but would not be so impolite. She surprised me by asking, "How did you learn there was work to be had, here at The Belle?"

I indicated in the general direction of The Steam House. Once I'd swallowed, I explained, "Yonder gal let me know. Said her friend used to work here but had since left." I did not mention the bastard with the musket-ball scar, the one the skinny girl had called Bill. God and good graces willing, Bill would continue his drinking next door and not set foot in this saloon tonight.

Isobel studied me without blinking; her pale face was fixed in its lines, as though carved from smooth white wood. I withstood her gaze even as I wondered at it; surely Malcolm and I weren't so strange. She seemed to be attempting to read my thoughts, or perhaps make sense of her own. Finally she spoke. "I believe I have an answer for you, *Monsieur* Carter, concerning the matter of work."

I looked hard at her, searching for deceit, but sensed she was being straight with me. "How's that?"

"Grady Ballard was here only this morning, offering cash money for able-bodied men to accompany him into the Territories," she said, and her tone grew unmistakably suggestive. "You look to be more than able-bodied, *Monsieur* Carter."

"West?" I repeated, ignoring her saucy gaze. *The Territories*, she'd said.

Isobel nodded and dropped the lewd expression, adopting an aloof air. "You would have to speak to Grady yourself, but as he and Virgil frequent The Belle when in town, they may reappear this evening." I did not believe I was mistaking the sudden note of expectation in her voice; I watched her sharp-eyed gaze pin the swinging doors as she said, "I do not believe they have yet departed but I will ask Mary for you." She nodded towards a lanky woman a few tables away, and a titch of envy colored her voice as she added, "Grady *dotes* upon Mary. She will know his whereabouts."

Isobel rose and edged through the crowd, while Malcolm asked with outright concern knitting his brows, "West?"

"Let's just talk to the man," I said, the words *cash money* thundering in my skull.

Isobel returned with the tall, leggy woman she'd named as Mary trailing a few steps behind her. A third woman, plump and pretty, with an enticing line of cleavage that caused Malcolm's lips to drop open, earning him a second kick, proceeded to surround our table.

"Gentlemen, may I present Miss Mary and Miss Cecilia," Isobel said, with ironic formality.

"Ladies," I acknowledged, tugging my hat brim.

Isobel announced, "This is Boyd Carter and his brother, Malcolm."

"He is *un petit chéri!*" cried Cecilia, closing in and ruffling Malcolm's curls, twirling one about her index finger. I refrained from rolling my eyes, even as my brother could not help but grin and shiver at this unexpected female attention. Cecilia's knowing gaze next came to rest on me, her eyelids lowering; she angled her breasts in my direction.

I looked pointedly at Mary. "What do you know of this fella Grady?"

Mary leaned one thigh against the table and jutted her hips my way, but answered forthrightly. "I'm expecting him this evening. You wish to speak with him?" Her voice was low and curt, no trace of a flowing French accent like the other women. She sounded like a Yankee, but I appreciated the lack of simpering.

"I do, indeed. I'm looking for work. Would you be so kind as to point him my way, when he arrives?"

Mary nodded, smoothing both wrists along her corseted waist. "Late as it is in the season, he's driving cattle west into the Territories. He's half-crazy." But she spoke with plain affection. "They need another hand, unless he or Virgil was lucky this day. What experience do you have with cattle, mister?"

"None," I admitted. "But I've a fine hand with horses."

"Well, you're a sturdy-looking feller, Mr. Carter," Mary said, and a half-smile unbalanced her wide mouth. "If you can ride a horse, Grady would consider you, I'm certain."

Cecilia sidled around the table, her breasts leading the way as would the cutwater of a ship. From behind my chair, she glided her fingernails along my upper arms and murmured, "A fine hand, indeed, *non?*"

All three women laughed at this playing. Malcolm, well fed after days without, appeared restored, hiding a giggle behind his cupped hand. His eyes were merry and hardly a crumb remained on his plate. Cecilia, obviously encouraged, continued smoothing her palms over my shoulders, resting her generous bosom against the nape of my neck. I reflected that once I would have felt nothing but the thrill of what was to come – but not tonight.

"Cook baked a crumble with the last of the gooseberries, just this past afternoon," Mary said, eyeing Malcolm's clean plate; the boy lit like a firecracker and she winked at him. "Perhaps there's a piece left. Izzy, won't you go and see?"

Isobel heaved a small sigh, put-upon, but obeyed nonetheless, and Mary produced a deck of playing cards from a silk pocket attached to the waist of her dress, the deck tied neatly with a bit of white ribbon; I'd spent many an hour as a solider losing my pittance pay to fellow recruits with just such a deck of cards, emblazoned with selfsame blue eagle and printed with the manufacturer's name, *L.I. Cohen*. Mary dropped to a chair catty-corner to Malcolm, unselfconsciously hiking her skirts to situate herself, crossing her long legs and asking him, "How's your hand at five-card stud, young feller?"

Malcolm sat straighter, setting aside his plate. He said, with enthusiasm, "Fair enough!" and Mary grinned, shuffling her deck.

Cecilia bent and wrapped her arms around my upper body; she smelled of the same oil as had Isobel, strong enough to make my nostrils prickle. She put her mouth to my ear and whispered, "You are lonely, *bel homme*, are you not?"

Likely she said the same to all men passing through this place, and likely nine of ten was lonely; it wasn't exactly a tough bet.

"I ain't," I muttered, but it was an outright lie. I tilted the shot glass in the glow cast by the lanterns, watching the ruby light gleam along the single drop left in the bottom. I studied the sight as though mesmerized.

Cecilia continued her persistent ministrations, moving her hands down my front side. When she reached my belly, I took her wrists gently into my grip and eased her away with as little fuss as I could manage. She was undeterred, wedging her hips between the tabletop and my lap, claiming a spot there before I could stop her. She latched her wrists about my neck and forced my regard, blocking out all other sights with her generous curves.

"Let me help you forget your loneliness, *monsieur*," she implored, pressing close.

Desperate to cast aside my longing for Rebecca, I settled my hands about Cecilia's ample waist. She smiled coyly and murmured, "*Oui*, this is more like it."

"Boyd's in love with a woman named Mrs. Rebecca," Malcolm chirped with his usual earnestness, somewhere beyond Cecilia; I could not see past the woman. I gritted my teeth at his willingness to announce his opinion before strangers.

"*Mrs.* Rebecca?" repeated Mary, guffawing, and I hated hearing her speak Rebecca's name in such a mocking tone. She carried on, "Ain't that a bit of a concern to her husband?"

Cecilia was angled so that her palm was not visible to the others; she firmly stroked my lap, lowering her lashes. She murmured, "*Viens avec moi*," and though I did not understand the words, the meaning was clear enough; my body responded to this touching and her smile grew ever lewd. My refusal would embarrass her, but that could not be helped; I had no intention of accompanying her upstairs and exhaled with relief when a sudden raucous voice lifted above the crowd, a man demanding, "Where's my sweet Virgin Mary?"

Cecilia disengaged her immediate attention from me. Mary, cards arrayed in her hands as she leaned on her elbows, directed a welcoming smile at the man approaching through the crowd, a man of height but lean as a strip of jerky, clad in buckskin leggings, much worn. He doffed his low-crowned hat, revealing dirty yellow hair and ragged side-whiskers, a sunbaked face perhaps of an age with myself. That face split with a grin as Mary lazily placed her cards facedown and stood to hook her arms about his neck. Malcolm watched this exchange with wide-eyed fascination.

The piano music was so loud I could not hear the murmured words between Mary and this yellow-haired man, but Mary turned shortly in my direction and spoke to Cecilia, ordering, "Give Mr. Carter a bit of air. I'd like him to meet Grady."

"You're in need of work?" he asked eagerly, stepping around the table. His brows were furry as autumn caterpillars, yellow and tufted as his hair, above eyes pale enough to resemble water in a glass. He said to Cecilia, "You can soak his willy later, girl, I need to talk business."

"I do thank you for the offer, ma'am," I told Cecilia, who rose with an impatient jerk of her skirts; her cheeks bore an angry red flush as she swept away.

"Grady Ballard, born in Texas, raised in Kansas," he said amiably, sliding into a chair. "My Mary tells me you're handy with horses."

"That I am," I said, feeling as though I'd plunged into the river that flowed only a short descent from The Dolly Belle – plunged and then swept against my will. I cleared the husk from my voice. "Boyd Carter, late of Tennessee."

Grady said, "I coulda guessed. I knew I heard that liquid in your voice."

Before he could speak another word I wanted to make one thing clear. "I ain't ashamed of where I was born and brought up, I'll have you know."

Grady's forehead wrinkled. "Somebody give you guff?"

"Near had me a run-in with a scarred-up fella in The Steam House," I admitted. "The girl there called him 'Bill.'"

"Bill Little," Grady confirmed, tipping his chair on its back legs as he nodded. "I know him. He served under Grant. Nowadays he's paid to skin buffalo."

"He a friend of yours?" I kept my tone neutral.

"He ain't." Grady sounded sincere. "I know him for a jackdaw. Him and his brothers roam the Territory to hunt and trap, see, but they're opportunists. They're clannish, too. I don't like accusing a man when I've only heard tales and such, but the Littles take money where they can get it, you take my meaning?"

I nodded that yes, I sure as hell did. I shifted enough to gain a better view of the entrance so that my back was not the first thing a man intending harm would see upon entering The Dolly Belle.

Grady settled his chair to all four legs and said in a different tone, "Well, listen, Tennessee, I'm short a wrangler. I'm headed out at sunrise whether I have a man or not, but I'd rather have him. We got some two hundred head of young heifer and steer in addition to a couple bull calves to drive, which ain't a big herd, but if I don't get them to Royal Lawson's ranch by mid-October, I don't get paid. We've been delayed since the death of Dyer Lawson, my employer's brother, and it's a late run to make, but I ain't worried. I run late before. What do you say? You willing to manage the remuda?"

"Hold up," I said. My ears were near to ringing and I was unfamiliar with the last word he'd used. Before he went carrying on again, I told him, "I ain't bringing the boy through any territory that ain't safe. I got me my brother to care for."

"You want territory that ain't safe, I'll march you straight down Texas way. *Shee-it.* Them Comancheros in the hills are the most vicious bunch you'll ever meet, I goddamn *guar-an-tee.*" He drew the word into three distinct parts, reclining comfortably in his chair and accepting a glass of bourbon from Mary, with a grin at her. He patted her backside and continued, "Since the treaty-signing at Fort Laramie this past spring there ain't been as much trouble in these here parts. The Sioux got their sacred land in the western Dakotas and more land since opened up to white settlers, including my current employer, Royal Lawson. Them trade and stock routes are safe enough, I figure. I've never had trouble along them, and I've traveled a-plenty."

"How long until we's back this way?" I asked. "What's the pay?"

Grady tossed back his shot and swiped his mouth with a thumb. "I can offer you fifteen dollars now, and fifteen upon delivery, plus your grub. We'll return this way once the cattle are safely delivered to Lawson, putting us back in St. Paul roughly the end of October, unless the snow comes early. In that case, we'll winter at Lawson's, but I don't relish the idea of being in such cramped quarters for them months. The old-timers are saying we got a cold winter ahead, even after the swelter of July in these parts – hottest July on record in Minnesota they say – but my hope is to avoid the snow. Lawson's spread is a few dozen miles past the Missouri River in southern Dakota Territory, some four hundred and fifty miles from where we sit tonight. Alone, I could ride me the same just shy of ten days. With the herd and the wagon, we make anywhere between fifteen to twenty miles a day, so a solid month, give or take."

I considered myself a fair judge of folks. Grady talked fast but even with the scarlet lanterns oddly highlighting his pale eyes, I sensed he was a trustworthy fellow. I calculated rapidly, the bourbon haze receding. That was thirty dollars, but meant another delay in our arrival at Jacob's; I clamped down upon the words *ill luck* as they resounded in my head, with some effort. If we accompanied Grady, by November the first I could have the filing fee, plus some twenty dollars for supplies. And by next spring, the latest I was willing to concede arriving, I would get us to Jacob's, and without empty hands. It would be a far better start than I'd figured. I tried to convince myself that a few more months was not much in the span of things, that Malcolm and I could manage this unexpected westward detour in our journey; a dizzy rush, same as earlier, flowed across my vision. I closed my eyes to clear it away.

"You said you need a wrangler?"

"I do. You'd drive our spare horses, a dozen head. I ride point and Virgil is the night watch. I got Quill to cook and I need another man to manage the remuda – that'd be you, if you take the job." For the first time he looked toward Malcolm, who sat eating the gooseberry crumble Isobel had placed before him, lips decorated by crumbs and shiny with fruit juice. Grady said, "And I don't mind the company of this here boy. Got me an unexpected sprout on this run, Dyer Lawson's little girl. She ain't got anyone now that her pa was kilt, and he was my employer's brother, like I said. Dyer planned to bring her along with us so I figure I oughtn't to leave her behind. I don't relish having to deliver the news of Dyer's death to Royal. He and Royal was close."

"You's familiar with the route?" I asked, trying to keep up with his swift explanations.

"I am. Rode it many a time now since the War. I served under Royal Lawson until I was mustered out. I trust him, and he trusts me to get his livestock to his ranch. He aims to grow his herd with the heifers and bulls in this bunch, and sell the steers to the mining towns. Royal and his brother planned to go into business together, but now that Dyer is gone, his plans'll change. Damn shame he got kilt. Horse-kicked, of all things, and him so good with horses. I still can't hardly believe it." Grady sighed, lifting his hat to plunge a hand through his hair. "I tell you, beef is in demand in the Territories and the demand is only increasing now that the country is finally moving on from the blasted War. I include myself in that sentiment, if you take my meaning, Tennessee. And with the way grain prices have soared these past two years, folks'll spread westward like ticks on a hound, see if they won't."

"Thirty and grub?" I repeated; I didn't want him to think I was a dolt, but I needed this confirmed. I quieted the word *Federal* that snarled, beast-like, in my mind.

"And we'll even feed the boy," Grady said, with another grin. "I don't recollect if I got your name, little feller…"

"Malcolm," he said, nodding politely, tugging a lock of hair over his forehead in place of his hat.

"Pleased to make your acquaintance, young Malcolm. Maybe little Cora will talk to you. Poor thing ain't hardly said a word since her pa died," Grady said. And then he slapped the tabletop in a friendly, conclusive way and inquired, "Might I buy you a drink to seal this here deal, Mr. Carter?"

I stood at the edge of a cliff, peering down. The dizziness, the sense of hell, the fear of someone trailing us even now all collided in my mind, causing me to question every choice I'd ever made. Each and every one seemed wrong. I felt crippled by the sum total of my poor decisions. Surely there was a decent goddamn explanation for why I sat here this night in the company of strangers, long gone from the holler I once thought I'd never leave.

I found my gaze returning to the nude painting on the opposite wall; I battled the urge to drape my jacket over the frame, to hide and therefore protect her naked, sprawling limbs, the appalling sense of her vulnerability. There was a familiarity to the feeling, a raw helplessness I'd first encountered during the War but that plagued me ever since in those defenseless gray moments between waking and sleeping; so many unprotected innocents, the earth seemed covered with them, above and beneath. It was more than a solitary man could grapple with.

What do you want? What choice do you have?

What the hell is there?

I felt hollow as a dead tree.

Malcolm said faintly, "Boyd…"

I cleared the ache from my throat and addressed Grady. "I'll take that drink, thank you."

G RADY AND HIS men were bivouacked west of town on a small rise overlooking the Mississippi. Malcolm and I followed him to this camp, leaving behind the pulse of activity along the river, the arrayed steamboats' many deck lanterns and the flickering streetlamps becoming as tiny as the dots of fireflies as we rode out of St. Paul, following a rocky outcropping. Two men sat near a small, crackling blaze, over which hung a kettle. One of them was sopping a biscuit through gravy and both their heads lifted at our approach; the biscuit didn't make it to the man's mouth as he watched us draw near. Behind them was a large covered wagon much like the one we'd brought along from Tennessee.

"What's that groaning sound?" Malcolm asked as our horses climbed the rise.

"It's the cattle," Grady explained. "'Lowing' is what you'd call it. They make the sound much of the time but you hear it more at night, when everything is still."

"They don't run off?" Malcolm wondered, and I was glad he'd asked. I wondered the same, but felt foolish voicing the question.

"We chase a few strays now and again," Grady said. "But they don't get far, most usually, and they're tired after a day spent walking. Though, we do keep the horses on a picket line." He called a greeting to the two men seated about the fire. "Got us a wrangler!"

"And another young'un?" asked the one with the biscuit, setting aside his plate.

The older of the two chuckled. "We'll need us a schoolmarm next thing, Ballard."

Grady laughed, tugging his palomino mare to a halt and dismounting with nimble grace. I followed more slowly, Malcolm sticking near me as we approached; Grady was a companionable fellow from what I could tell so far but all of these men were strangers to me, and I was wary. Tired and wary, but at least the boy and I had been fed, thanks to the generosity at Jean Luc's établissement; I tried to count our blessings, even as amusement colored the garble of hoity-toity French words swirling through my mind.

"Quill, Virg, I hope you two ain't too drunk to greet Boyd Carter and his little brother, Malcolm," Grady said, in the cheerful manner which seemed well-suited to him. "Fellas, this is Quill Dobbins and Virgil Turnbull."

They stood. The one called Quill was elderly, wrapped in a fringed woolen blanket and with a thick white beard, sturdy but short, barely reaching my shoulder, while Virgil was closer in age to me and Grady, wiry of build and with a drooping mustache that ate up the lower half of his face. There was a jug situated on the ground between them, on which they'd been pulling, but they regarded us soberly enough.

I offered a hand to shake with them; Virgil's mustache twitched as he extended his left hand instead of his right, muttering, "Lost it in the War."

Grady said, "But you kept your life so you oughtn't to complain, I figure."

"It's clean gone?" Malcolm inquired in his usual curious fashion, bending closer to examine the arm with its missing appendage, even though Virgil kept it tucked close to his ribcage.

"One fell-swoop of a cutlass," Grady answered for his friend. "But as luck would have it, Virg has always favored his left side."

"Did you save the hand? Got you a hook to tie over the stump?" my brother asked, peering at the man's forearm, not seeming to realize these questions pestered Virgil.

"Boy," I muttered in warning.

"I did not," Virgil said shortly.

"You shoulda kept it. You might've made a finger-bone necklace like them Ojibwe fellas wear," Grady said, with plain amusement. "You'd clatter when you walked along, so we'd know you were coming."

"You boys hungry?" asked Quill, gesturing at a kettle hanging over their fire, and his tone reminded me of the way Daddy would stave off bickering between my brothers and me. "We got beans and biscuits and there's a wee bit of bacon left. Coffee and a whiskey jug, too."

"We ate at yonder saloon, but I thank you kindly," I said, wishing to be polite, even though I could have downed a second plate with no trouble. I tried not to stare at the whiskey, reminding myself the last thing I should do just now was proceed to get lit.

"What did you think of The Belle, little feller?" Grady asked Malcolm, removing the kettle's lid. The iron spoon within it clacked against the tin as Grady loaded his plate, sending a merry grin in Malcolm's direction. "I reckon it's an eyeful for a sprout."

"My daddy would thrash me for lookin', but I sure looked," the boy said, and even I had to smile, imagining Daddy's response to the cavorting in the saloon. The others had a laugh and Grady elbowed Malcolm's ribs as we all sat around the fire, the men reclaiming the hewn logs they were using as seats. Virgil hooked a finger in the jug's round handle and took a long pull.

"Aw, it's only natural to look," Grady said. "The nude on the wall is something else, ain't she? And the gals at The Belle are pretty and clean, which ain't always the case. 'Course, some men don't mind if they ain't clean."

Quill observed Malcolm eyeing the food; he fetched a plate and passed it to my brother without a word, nodding at the kettle.

"Might'nt I?" Malcolm asked and I nodded permission; the boy made short work of a second helping.

"How about you, son?" Quill offered me.

"Thank you kindly, but I'm full up," I lied. I longed for a smoke. My fingers twitched with wanting one, but the goddamn twister had eaten all my tobacco.

"These fellers are headed into the Northland," Grady explained. "You said your uncle lived up there somewheres?"

"He does." I nodded with a slow movement, gaze stuck in the fire, picturing Jacob as I'd last seen him; I'd spent plenty of time wondering on how he might have changed since. Moreover, how *I'd* changed since. I wouldn't be surprised if Jacob failed to recognize me upon first sight. The boy Uncle Jacob remembered was green as grass shoots; that green boy had never been to War, had never imagined such horror existed. "He homesteads west of the headwaters of the Mississippi near a lake called Flickertail. He left Tennessee when I was just a young'un. We ain't yet met his wife or our cousins."

"Mostly In'jun country up that way," Virgil commented, resting his forearms on his thighs, the jug dangling from the crook of his remaining index finger.

"That's right." I heard a cantankerous note in my voice; I found I didn't like Virgil's presumptuous tone but bit back my irritation as I explained, "My uncle was raised in Tennessee, same as the boy an' me. He left home some ten years back. Favors the North now. He's wed to a Winnebago woman, name of Hannah." I kept a side-eye on Virgil as I spoke, wondering just what it was about him that served to stir my ornery side. He appeared harmless enough, skinny as a string bean. I could take him in any sort of fight. *His gaze*, I decided. I figured he was half-drunk and that this was contributing to the unpleasant set of his features. *Peevish*, Mama would have called him.

"One of my brothers married a Paiute gal back in the 'forties when he was panning for gold out California way," Quill said. "The two of them have a passel of young'uns I ain't ever met. I do believe they're right content, but our ma, God rest her, would've had conniptions to know Robert took up with a woman who weren't Christian."

I allowed, "My mama had much the same to say about Uncle Jacob."

Mouth full, Grady said, "They all but cleared the Winnebago people out of Minnesota, to my understanding. After the Dakota War there was a big push to get the red folk relocated." He paused to swallow. "I ain't no philosopher, but it don't seem quite right to me, running folks off their land like that. That's all the army does nowadays, it seems, since the War ended."

"Rightly so." Virgil's expression became outright hostile. "The red folk are a brutal lot. They're best cleared out, in my opinion."

Grady's brows lifted in an earnest fashion, reminding me of a schoolteacher I recalled from childhood. "That ain't the point, Virg. They've been driven from their homes, their hunting grounds. What man wouldn't fight back in such a situation?"

"Sending raiding parties to scalp innocents is what you mean," Virgil bickered, his narrow cheeks taking on belligerent heat. His shoulders had squared. "Attacking in the dead of night, slicing folks up like they're cattle for butchering. Goddamn wretches."

I was about to object to such talk in Malcolm's presence, stranger as I was to these men or no, when Quill cleared his throat and sent a pointed look at Virgil; Malcolm, though busy eating, was soaking up every last word.

Grady released a small sigh and sat back with the air of someone pushing a chair away from a table. "I ain't trying to upset you, Virg. And I ain't speaking lightly. We've fled arrows in our travels, as you well remember. I'm speaking of the *injustice* of it. I feel the army has better ways to spend its time than running men off their own land."

"In'juns shot arrows at you?" my brother asked, and his tone was riddled with awe as he seized on this statement; Malcolm had already been in danger too many times in his young life but here was proof that he still considered peril and adventure one and the same.

I thought, *They ain't the same an' I wish it was a lesson you need never learn, boy. I swear to keep you from harm, from this night forth, God help me.*

I'd kept as watchful as I'd been while soldiering the past nights pushing north to Minnesota. I'd sat up near the fire, remaining vigilant, stealing a broken hour's rest at most, peering into the gloom, alert for any hint of someone approaching under cover of darkness, but the shooter had not returned for us. I did not, despite hours of speculation, know what to make of this fact. Malcolm had talked of nothing but the incident as we rode, until I made him stop, weary of questions when all I wanted was to close my grainy eyes. Several times I found myself riding in a daze, losing focus; I knew it frightened Malcolm if I admitted to weakness and so I shoved aside all thoughts of rest. Now, at a fire with three other grown men, I found myself able to settle a little; perhaps this night I could sleep for a few hours in a row.

Grady said to Malcolm, "To be fair, little feller, I was in their territory both times, so who's to say I didn't deserve to have my hide skewered? That's not to say I wouldn't have fought for my life, to the last. I know all the rumors about the red folk, but from what I've seen and heard from those who know better, scouts and trappers and such, even my own limited experience, they ain't the savages that folks in the big cities believe them to be. But hell, even the army calls them savages. That's what our fellow soldiers have turned to in the years since the War, cleaning out the Territories, shooting at unarmed women and children. It's a terrible, shameful business."

My brother nodded seriously while I considered Grady's words, ignoring Virgil's glowering; I'd heard rumors of the same sort and found his compassion heartening. At the same moment there was a small stirring from inside the wagon.

"Little Cora will be glad of a playmate," Quill said, nodding towards the sound. "Come morning you can meet her, son."

Malcolm's gaze jumped to the wagon, his eyes curious and wide, lit by two tiny orange flames. Juice from the beans stained his mouth in addition to the gooseberry juice from the crumble. His hair stood on end; I thought of Lorie so lovingly trimming it for him and my heart bumped with homesickness, potent as a toothache.

You'll see Sawyer and Lorie again, before you know it. Think on that.

"I thank you for the job," I told Grady. My voice sounded harsh and I cleared the grit to insist, "Sincerely."

Grady nodded a wordless smile, busy with another bite of food. There was something about him that reminded me a little of Ethan Davis, a sort of ease to his personality, no doubt spurred on by the way he'd joked and flirted so effortlessly with the girls at The Dolly Belle. I further realized, with a small twinge, that I sat at a fire in the company of at least two former Federals.

They ain't all bad. You's surely smart enough to understand that. Look at Charley Rawley, a fine fellow who's helped you plenty.

"I need to post a couple letters before we ride out," I said, at once reminded of this necessity.

"I'd best ride back to town tonight then," Grady replied, backhanding his mouth.

GRADY LENT me a few sheets of paper from a leather-bound journal he fished from the wagon. I heard him murmur to the single occupant, low and comforting, but there was no reply. He also provided a short lead pencil and the journal itself, over which I could brace each letter in turn. I sat near the fire's glow, Malcolm at my elbow, to compose the letters to Sawyer and Lorie, and to Jacob and Hannah, the boy adding details as he read every word over my shoulder, most aloud. The men continued their conversation as I labored over my pencil-scratching, speaking with the familiarity of longtime friends; I was either desperate or daft, or both, but I found the rise and fall of their voices reassuring.

"I'd like to leave with the dawn," Grady said after I completed my writing. I'd done my damnedest to explain my decision to delay our arrival, wishing I possessed even half the eloquence required to do so. I knew both Sawyer and Jacob would understand my reasoning; it was logical to earn what money I could before settling to homestead, come spring. At the end of the letter intended for Sawyer and Lorie, missing them so terribly that my hand shook,

I'd written, *Malcolm and me are counting the days 'til we see you all again and will await with great eagerness your arrival in St. Paul, next spring.* I imagined Lorie reading theirs aloud near the woodstove. I imagined Rebecca listening. There wasn't more than an inch left at the bottom of the torn-off paper. I wrote, *All my love to you* and then scrawled my signature, *Boyd Brandon Carter.*

Grady was saying, "I'll leave your words with Mary, she'll see to it they get to the post office by morning's light."

"You trust her?" I asked, looking over the fire at him.

"I do," Grady confirmed and his grin reappeared as he winked. "This here gives me a good excuse to see her once more before we leave town. It's a long, hard winter otherwise, if you take my meaning. You joining me, Virg? Isobel has a hankering to see you again, Mary told me, and you ain't been to town since Emilia run off."

Virgil took a long pull from the jug, eyes in the flames. "I ain't spending my last dollar on a whore. Besides, I got watch."

Grady cajoled, "Last chance to see a lady in months."

Virgil snorted. "I'd hardly call any of them ladies. They're *whores.*"

Before I could think to stopper my mouth or tamp down the fire therein, I challenged, "Meanin' what? That they ain't got no feelings?"

There was a prickly lull. All eyes had swung my way but I wouldn't wriggle; Malcolm's forehead crinkled, forming horizontal furrows along his brow. I thought of sweet Lorie being spoken of so coldly, like she weren't even fully human. I knew what Sawyer would say, were he here with us. Many a night along the trail, sitting alone at the fire while the boy slept, I'd thought hard on the terrible power of name-calling. *Reb* or *whore*, it didn't matter; the derision in the voices of those who'd call us such things made the two words nigh indistinguishable. This very afternoon I'd been derided for my roots and damned if I'd be ashamed for speaking up just now.

"Carter has a point," Grady finally acknowledged, and I released a tense breath; more slowly, hoping they wouldn't notice, I let my hands relax from bunched fists.

Virgil muttered, "Whores are whores. I don't know what's wrong with me speaking the truth."

"You and the boy can sleep beneath the wagon," Quill said after Grady and Virgil rode out, in different directions. "My old bones prefer to stay near the fire."

Malcolm tucked close to my side once we were situated, as was customary. I'd never let on that this habit comforted me as well; in our tent, he couldn't sleep unless he stuck out a foot to touch my leg. Quill stretched beside the banked fire and was soon snoring. In the near-distance, the cattle made their low, moaning sounds and horses stomped and shuffled at their picket line, settling in for the night.

Malcolm was quiet for a full five seconds before whispering, "What do you think Sawyer an' Lorie will say?"

"They'll be a mite surprised," I acknowledged quietly. I lay on my back, rifle within reach, hands stacked under my head instead of a pillow. Quill had proved kind enough to give us an additional blanket. Our boots stuck out from beneath the wagon; I hadn't slept without wearing my boots since we'd left Iowa City. No more than a dozen inches above my gaze was the hard wooden crosshatching which made up the underside of the wagon – if either of us sat up too fast, we'd have a goose egg for days. Malcolm faced me, his knees bent against the ground.

"When will we meet up with them?" he wondered.

"That's a good question. Depends on whether we spend the winter in the Territories or journey back to Minnesota. My hope is that they'll meet us in St. Paul early next spring, an' we all four ride on north together, like we been." This thought cheered me, if only slightly; just now, I wasn't sure I could make it until then without them. I draped the base of both palms over my closed eyes and pressed hard, seeing swirling patterns of dark red and muddy yellow.

"I'd like that," Malcolm murmured. He seemed to be thinking hard; I could almost hear his mind churning. At last he whispered, "It's kinda funny there's a girl right above us."

I uttered a low laugh, opening my eyes; the child Grady had mentioned was the last thing on my mind, too mired as it was with my own troubles. I agreed, "It is, at that."

"Grady said her name is Cora," Malcolm went on, almost too faintly for me to hear; my eyes drifted closed again. Exhaustion made dense my arms and legs. After a spell he whispered, "You think we's doing the right thing?"

"I do." I mustered all the confidence I could. "We'll have a good thirty dollars to our name when we return this way. We won't have to be dependent on Uncle Jacob. That always rubbed me wrong, as you know."

"I do. I truly do, Boyd. I think you's brave. Brave as Daddy."

I felt the weight of responsibility crushing my chest at his innocent words. "Thank you, Malcolm." I rarely used his given name.

He shifted, nudging my leg with his toes, leaving them pressed against me; he had removed his boots, as was his habit. He whispered, "Boyd?"

"Huh?" Sleep served to smother my senses.

"That woman who done sat on your lap at The Dolly Belle..."

Dammit, I thought, coming awake as though to a rasher of cold water upturned on my head. I ordered, "Time for sleepin'," even as I realized there wasn't a chance in hell the boy would let it drop so easy.

And then, out of the clear blue, he inquired, "Do ladies *like* it when a man puts his tongue in their mouth? I mean, right *in* it?"

"Jesus *Christ*," I uttered. Had he somehow seen that very thing at the saloon? I'd explained the rudiments of lovemaking to him earlier in the summer, considering it my duty, but purposely avoided details for such awkward reasons. But, I reflected, even though we'd stayed on the ground floor we had just come from a whorehouse. I felt like a crook.

"Well, do they?" he persisted.

"What makes you ask?" I demanded, hedging.

Malcolm caved as would a collapsing root cellar, and began fast-talking. "I seen Lorie an' Sawyer, that's why." Hearing my indrawn breath, ready to scold, he raced on, "I weren't spying, I swear on a stack of bibles, Boyd. I heard me strange sounds, is all, an' I come upon them twos out behind Mrs. Rebecca's corral, of an afternoon before we left Iowa City. I seen Sawyer runnin' his hands all along her back, an' Lorie had her hands all up in his hair, an' they was kissing. That's why I wondered..."

"About tongues," I finished for him, releasing a sigh that was part exasperation, part amusement. I could hardly scold; I'd stumbled upon the two of them making love in the barn, of all places, late one evening not long before we left. I glimpsed my best friend's bare backside, moving with energetic rhythm, Lorie's slim legs wrapped about his hips as they lay together on a quilt spread over the hay in an empty stall, and could not decide whether to laugh and cause a scene, or slip quietly away; being such a gentleman, I let them alone. I even refrained from teasing Sawyer the next day. I finally said, "Well, I s'pose that depends altogether on the woman's opinion of the man."

"It appeared Lorie-Lorie's opinion of Sawyer is right good," Malcolm said, muffling a giggle, and his tone was an equal mixture of sincerity and downright waywardness. He issued a snort trying to restrain laughter, bunching his knees, holding the tops of them as he wheezed, "What if...what if you'd been eatin' something disagreeable, just before kissing, an' then you let out a burp while you was –"

"*Sleep*," I growled, heading off this trail of thought right at the pass.

All was quiet for roughly the time it took a secondhand to tick once around a clock face. But then, in a tone very unlike the one he'd just been using, Malcolm whispered, "That woman on your lap...she was a whore?" He spoke the word with curiosity and hesitance, surely thinking of the earlier exchange between me and Virgil.

I sighed again, ashamed to recall the many times I'd used the word without a wisp of guilt. "That she was."

"Was that..." He trailed to silence and I looked his way in the dimness, the familiar slender outline of the boy I would do anything for. He gathered courage and asked, "Was that what Lorie-Lorie..."

My heart sank like a ripe plum dropped in a creek. I kept silent, not sure how to answer what he intended to ask. When it was clear Malcolm could not finish the sentence, I spoke low and solemn. "Lorie was forced to do the things she did. She didn't want to work as a whore. It was the last thing she wanted, or ever figured would happen to her. She was just a young girl when the War come along." Coldness settled along my spine and I drew my forearms closer to the warmth of my chest. "She lost her entire family. I don't rightly know the whole story of how she came to be in the saloon in St. Louis where we found her that night. Thank the Lord we *did* find her."

"*We's* her family now," Malcolm whispered. "Us an' Sawyer. Damnation, I miss them."

"Myself, as well," I whispered, praying, *Let the year pass quickly, oh Lord.* If I thought too long about the coming winter months apart from them the despair weighting my chest only gained in mass. I closed my eyes and was belted by a sudden picture, as starkly defined as if unfolding a few yards south rather than many hundreds of miles. I lay as still as a felled tree, witnessing Rebecca's dooryard back in Iowa, the selfsame lopsided moon low in the night sky, rising to adorn the eastern horizon. Rebecca stood framed in the wide double doors of the barn, wrapped in her shawl, watching the pale moon. Her abundant hair was loose, falling over her shoulders and down to her elbows, which she kept clutched close to her waist. Tears streaked her upturned face like summer rain.

My heart lurched, becoming a hot coal behind my ribs. My lips pursed up as though to speak her name.

Beside me, Malcolm shifted with a restless sigh. "But *why* did someone make Lorie do them bad things? Why would someone try to hurt her? Why would someone *want* to hurt her?"

Angry righteousness threaded his questions and I was forced to reconcile this moment with the one in my head. Rebecca seemed so very near I couldn't bear to open my eyes and lose the sight of her. Before I answered my brother I offered up a second silent prayer. *Lord, protect Rebecca Krage. Oh Jesus, protect her for me. I can't be there to protect her no more.*

I fought off an onrushing sense of panic.

"Why would someone hurt any girl, Boyd?"

I drew a breath and opened my eyes. I put my hand over his shoulder, just like I figured Daddy would have done. "Listen here. You's a good-hearted boy an' I know it pains you. It pains *me*." My heartbeat hadn't yet calmed. "There's all manner of terrible things in this world. I seen many of 'em when I soldiered. Things I pray you won't ever have to see. Things I wish you never had to *know*. But you's on the way to being a man an' I can't shelter you for always. Shit, you's seen more by this age than I ever dreamed of. The truth is, sometimes women ain't got a choice but to work as whores, to survive. But Lorie is a strong woman, stronger an' braver than I ever knew a woman could be. She loves Sawyer. An' he loves her like I ain't ever seen. Them two can move on from what was, do you understand?"

I sensed him nod.

I squeezed his shoulder and concluded, "There ain't nothin' more important than protecting those you love, boy, especially your womenfolk. That's a man's job in this here world, you see? Protecting his kin from the terrible things out there."

Malcolm was silent for so long I figured him asleep; I was almost so myself. But then he murmured, "You shouldn't have left her behind." Hardly had the words cleared his mouth before he gave over to snoring.

I gritted my teeth.

Rebecca is better off without me, boy, that's God' truth. That's what being an adult is, and what you ain't learned yet. Doing what's best for someone else.

But it was goddamn cold comfort.

MORNING PAINTED the air a muted gray. I woke from a hazy muddle of bad dreams and to observe that I lay alone beneath the wagon; Malcolm was not in sight. I sat without thinking and the crack of my forehead meeting the undercarriage shuddered through the entire frame of the thing. I groaned as I rolled from beneath, staggering to my feet and stumbling forward, shouting hoarsely for the boy. My eyes bumped and strained over the sights before them – the smudge of yellowing sky to the east, the ever-waving tips of the prairie grasses. It appeared I was alone but for the livestock; though coffee boiled in a kettle hanging over the fire, no others were in view.

"Malcolm!" I bellowed, bending forward in pain, clutching my forehead. *"Answer me!"*

"I'm here!" I heard the faint reply, upwind of my position, and my shoulders sank in immediate relief.

Seconds later he appeared as a stark-black figure against the rim of the eastern horizon, none of his features perceptible as light washed him from behind. He waved one arm and I clenched my jaw against the rush of angry words I wanted to direct his way; it was not his fault I was tetchy as a mother hen these days. He ran near, hatless and breathless, and explained, "Me an' Quill was out gathering eggs for breakfast." He showed me the small burden of quail eggs held carefully in the hammock he'd made of his shirt, then looked closer at me and observed, "Why, you's bleeding."

"I bumped my damn head," I mumbled, withdrawing my hand to see a dark smear of blood. Another streaked along the side of my nose, unpleasantly warm.

Malcolm's eyes jerked to something beyond my right shoulder and his face went blank. He said, "Well, hello," and his voice, which had deepened a little with every passing month, rang high with surprise.

I turned to see a small figure standing silent as a wraith near the tailgate, which she'd used to climb to the ground; not having heard a sound, not even a jingle of the linked chain dangling from the tailgate, a twitch nudged my spine at the sight of a little girl where there hadn't been one only a second ago. She was a tiny thing, ragged in appearance, with long, tangled hair no one had bothered to comb or braid for her. There was something strange about her face but I couldn't tell just what in the early morning light.

"You must be Cora," he went on, with his usual cheeriness. "I'm Malcolm Carter. This here is my brother, Boyd."

There was no reply from the child. She simply studied us, hands hanging at her sides, unmoving as a threatened deer. Maybe she was half-witted.

"Me an' Quill been gathering breakfast," Malcolm explained, untroubled by her continued silence. "He was telling me a bit about you. I hope you don't mind none. He said you was a mite shy but that you like eggs cooked up in a pie." He rambled on, "My mama used to make egg pie for me when I was a sprout."

He might have been speaking to a carving. When Cora suddenly pointed my way a jolt of pure trepidation shot through my gut. But then my heart went soft – the little thing was crying. Quiet as a field mouse, but most assuredly crying. Malcolm dropped the eggs, which landed with a dull splat, and went straight to her. He was head and shoulders taller than she, but he bent his face to hers and took her elbows in his hands. He murmured, "Hey there, it's all right."

"*My pa,*" Cora moaned.

I felt like a lout for thinking she was half-witted. The blood on my forehead frightened her. Of course it did; her daddy had been horse-kicked. Likely he bled over his face before he died and she must have witnessed it. I hurried to use my sleeve to staunch the flow. I thought of Cort and Nathaniel as I said, "It's all right, little one. I ain't hurt bad."

Malcolm hugged her, just as he so often hugged Lorie, the unconscious tenderness as natural to him as breathing. He rocked her side to side; her tears were muffled by his dirty shirt. I hurried to dip my hands in the basin near the fire, seeing Quill headed our way with a basket, using a walking stick to aid his progress. I scooped water to clean my face, scrubbing over what felt like a hell of a welt.

"Little Miss Cora," Quill said, sounding downright stunned as he slowly approached the camp. "Whatever is wrong?"

"She was scared of the blood," I explained, gesturing at my forehead.

"She spoke?" Quill set aside his walking stick. "Well, I'll be."

Cora clung to Malcolm, who looked at me with his eyebrows raised, plainly asking what to do next.

Quill said in the calm manner of a father, "If you'll give me a moment, I'll have a fine breakfast for all of us. Miss Cora, would you like to crack these eggs into the pan?" He scrutinized my wounded forehead and indicated his haversack. "I've a leather needle you could use to stitch up that gash. Someone try to scalp you while we was gathering eggs?"

I had to chuckle at this, after our talk of Indian folk last night. Embarrassed at my own clumsiness, I said, "No, I done sat up too fast and smucked my head."

The four of us were momentarily joined by Virgil, in from his night watch, and Grady, just returning from town. Both men had the look of a long night, though for different reasons. Grady called good morning, making a point to address Cora; Virgil ignored everything but the coffee. Grady joined us first at the fire, eyeing the heavens and deciding, "Looks like a fine day headed our way."

"And I'll be enjoying it with my eyes closed," Virgil muttered, scraping a knuckle under his nose.

"Cora's been speaking to young Mr. Carter," Quill said, serving each man a plate of the egg pie, which he'd cooked up with salt and dried green onions. After weeks of what amounted to hardtack for breakfast, I restrained myself from scraping the leavings from the pan.

Virgil and Grady each registered surprise at this statement, looking at Cora with near-comical unison; I figured they were so accustomed to her silence they hardly noticed her presence at all. Grady's caterpillar eyebrows lofted high and a look of approval crossed his features as he regarded Malcolm. He murmured, "Good for you, little feller. I was hoping she might."

At this compliment my brother grinned around a bite of breakfast. Cora sat near him and did not offer a smile, nor had she spoken other than to quietly answer Malcolm's persistent questions; thus, before breakfast we had learned she was eleven years old, liked eggs but disliked onions, and agreed with Malcolm that Aces High was a fine horse. She did, however, decline the invitation to ride the animal, appearing frightful at the mere notion of approaching a horse. She was small for her age, pale as skimmed milk, near ghost-like, with a sweetly pretty face; what made it appear strange was her eyes, each of a different color, one a mossy green and the other dark as ground coffee. I tried my best not to stare at this irregularity; my grandmother would have insisted that a little girl with such eyes was marked for trouble.

Superstitious claptrap, just like Granny Rose's hoop snake tales, I reminded myself. I'd loved and respected my dear granny but she'd frightened the bejesus out of my brothers and me many a time with her tales of the Old World, delivered in the hushed voice of a born storyteller, tales inhabited by strange

and clever creatures that tormented humans. I recalled Mama once admon-
ishing Granny, who was in fact her mother-in-law, not to scare us so, and that
afterward she and Granny were put out with one another for a solid week,
until Daddy threatened to sleep in the barn instead of a house with fractious
women. I smiled a little at the thought of Daddy's blustering. I understood
now, as well as Mama understood then, that Daddy wouldn't last a night
away from her; it was an empty threat at best. And to the end, this proved
true; Malcolm told me Daddy died only hours after our mother.

"I knew you'd be good company," Grady said to Malcolm, with a continued air of satisfaction. And then, indicating my forehead with his fork,
"What'n the hell happened to you?"

"Wagon an' me had a bit of a fallout," I said, earning a round of laughter.

"I gave your letters to my Mary," Grady said. "She or one of the other gals
will get 'em posted."

"Thank you," I said, but immediately wondered, *Oughtn't I to have done it
myself? What if Mary just plain forgets?*

"You'll have no word until we return, but I do hope to get back this way
before spring," Grady said. "I posted a letter to my ma, in Kansas. She'd worry
sore all autumn, if I hadn't." He looked at Virgil. "Isobel said to bid you
farewell," but Virgil only shrugged one shoulder, not glancing up from his
breakfast.

"My daddy had him a mare with one blue and one brown eye," Malcolm
was saying to Cora. He ate the egg pie with enthusiasm even as he spoke and
the little girl did not seem embarrassed at his words. He studied her with
keen interest, peering into her slim, fair face. He carried on, "My sister, Lorie,
got eyes of green an' blue mixed together, but yours are rightly two different
colors. Was you born that way?"

"Malcolm," I warned, and his guileless gaze flashed to me; I beetled my
brows, conveying as best I could that he was being rude, even if it was not
his intent.

Cora nodded in response to his question, stirring at her eggs with her fork.
The utensil made a metallic scraping over the tin. She didn't seem upset at
Malcolm's endless blathering; maybe because he was closer to her in years. I
reflected that loneliness knew no age limits.

"I was once acquainted with a feller with one blue and one brown, just like
the horse you mentioned," Grady said, scarfing his food. "And your pa, Cora-

bell, once said his mama's eyes was just like yours."

Cora shyly ducked her chin. Her hair, dark as winter oak, fell in long, heavy tangles around her cheeks. I wasn't sure what drew my gaze Virgil's way just then – maybe because he'd fallen so still – and spied him eyeing Cora even as he kept his head bent over his plate. His sideways look was guarded and reminded me of Isobel's, the selfsame girl who'd asked Grady to bid Virgil farewell. Just as swiftly, Virgil looked back at his food.

"My ma had a gold patch in one of her eyes, like a little sunbeam," Quill remembered. He held his coffee cup loosely between both gnarled hands. The sun skimmed the earth now, streaking over us. He spoke of his mother with a note of sadness.

"I don't remember the color of my mother's eyes," Virgil said, shaking his head. "She passed when I weren't but a young'un."

"Our mama too," Malcolm said, and Cora stopped stirring her eggs, peering up at him.

"And mine," Quill said, with a small sigh.

"You boys are making me sad," Grady said, clunking his empty plate in the washbasin. "C'mon now, we got miles to go before dinner. We got cattle to drive."

The remuda consisted of an even dozen horses, sturdy head tethered to their picket line. Grady outfitted me with a faded blue bandana to tie about my neck and a fine lassoing rope, and together the two of us sat horseback, surveying the cattle herd. By morning's bright, unclouded light, the prairie to the west of camp teemed with bovine stock, tones of brown to rival a hillside in early autumn. The animals bellowed and moaned, shifting their forelegs and stirring up dust, long tails twitching.

"I never seen so many at a time," I said. "Horses, sure, but not cattle."

"Shucks, this is nothing," Grady said knowingly. "You should see the herds coming up from Texas way. Thousands of them, stock stretching out for miles. Of course, them drives have more than a dozen men, give or take." He sat his saddle with ease, forearms crossed at the wrist and braced on the saddle horn; I didn't get the sense that he was bragging over these facts, just speaking from experience. "You was cavalry, you said?"

I nodded once, avoiding his gaze, not wishing to talk further on the subject.

Grady seemed to understand without words and changed the subject; he spoke with a teasing air. "Cecilia was a mite put out that you didn't return with me last night." I felt my teeth come together at their edges and Grady nudged my arm. "Aw, I'm just funning you a little. Don't mind me. The gals there like a new feller. Isobel was right disappointed too, but more that Virg didn't come. She's sweet on him, though he won't admit it. Virg was sweet on Emilia, but he won't admit that, neither, not since she run off from The Belle with no word to him." Grady glanced my way when I did not respond and asked with a different tone, "You got a gal, Tennessee? My Mary said something of the sort."

I lifted my hat and swiped at my forehead; the gash there hurt as my knuckles scraped over it. I hardly knew Grady and yet I felt I could trust him to an extent; still, I didn't rightly know what to say about what Mary had told him about Rebecca.

Grady shifted in his saddle. Quartermain, his fine palomino mare, whickered and sidestepped. He tugged her gently back into line, murmuring, "Hold on, lady," and then asked in a quieter tone, "Your gal's wed, is she?"

My voice was hoarse. "Not yet, she ain't."

"Promised, then?"

The bite of this went deep. I nodded, keeping my eyes fixed on the distant horizon.

Grady shifted again. After a spell he said, "You shoulda joined me last night, Tennessee. Nothing takes a man's mind from his troubles better than a willing woman. Or two!" So saying, he lightly cuffed my shoulder with a closed fist.

"I used to think so," I muttered.

DRIVING A large herd was solitary work, I soon discovered. Grady rode point, roughly a mile ahead, keeping the lead bull moving; the rest of the animals fell into line as mannerly as children at a schoolhouse door, pairing up in twos and threes. It was an amusing sight at first and eventually just a tedious one, unchanging as the sun hammered down from a whitewashed sky. The cattle picked over the uneven ground with sure-footed diligence, heads bobbing with the rhythm of their steady progress, round hooves lifting a fine cloud of dust and cutting a wide swathe through the yellowing prairie grass; even the most novice of trackers could follow the trail we were leaving, and I wondered, for the first time, if I should have mentioned to Grady what had happened before we reached St. Paul. Malcolm remained quiet on the subject without my having to tell him, but he too must wonder why I hadn't offered a word on the matter.

Absently patting Fortune's neck, I reasoned, *You seen neither hide nor hair of the fellow, whoever the hell he was, since that night. And now you's headed in a completely different direction. Ain't no reason to believe he's still following.*

My main duty was to keep the horses in a bunch and not let them give over to grazing. I rode at a small distance from the cattle, keeping the herds separate, as the horses were faster-moving altogether and it did not do well to mix them with the ponderous cattle. The sun rose along our backs; we would not stop until it began setting. Breakfast and dinner were both large meals; Quill explained they were not in the habit of breaking for a noon meal on any given day. We had to make time, as Grady insisted, and he was already chafing at the delay caused by Dyer Lawson's death. Far behind me, Malcolm rode on the wagon seat with Cora and Quill; the old cook handled the team of mules, bumping tediously along, bringing up the distant rear. Virgil slept until late afternoon, on a narrow cot in the wagon, the one upon which Cora slept at night.

The afternoon sun shone in my eyes for hours, creeping beneath my hat brim; I was coated in dust and my spine ached. I reflected that while the day's work kept me occupied physically, riding alone was a terrible thing for more than one reason. I missed the company of my brother and Sawyer. I missed speaking with someone besides horses. I was never one for quietude; talking kept me sane after the War, back when all I could see when I closed my eyes was broken, torn bodies stacked up like hewn wood left in a hard rain. Gut-shot horses and muddy bogs gone sickly, murky red with spilled blood. Field tents and severed limbs and my brothers ripped from life, the smell of death thick in my nostrils.

Goddammit, I thought, and ground my teeth, willing those ugly memories back to their hidey-hole. I wanted to smoke, and grew ever more grim in temper. I hadn't gone so long without tobacco since the War. I longed for my oldest friend riding Whistler beside me. I longed for my fiddle and its bow, and the sharp, pleasant scent of rosin. My restless thoughts turned over on themselves.

May I compliment you? Rebecca had asked.

We'd stood together in the dimly-lit intimacy of her home; Lorie, Malcolm, and Tilson remained out at the fire, from which Rebecca and I had just carried her sleeping sons. The boys had been tucked in their beds and I'd stood politely to the side while Rebecca descended the loft ladder behind me, clutching her skirts with one hand. As she'd come to the lowest rung I'd reached one hand and bracketed the air at her back, as I would were she climbing from a wagon seat. I did not dare touch her in that moment, too afraid such a bold gesture would startle her – or, worse yet, that I'd relent to the urge to grasp her elbow and tug her into my embrace; she would have been shocked, likely would have slapped my face.

She stepped to the floor and shook out her skirts; the banked fire in the woodstove lent her front side a red-gold glow. Small flames flickered in her eyes as we stood in silence and I swore on my very soul I was not imagining the invitation present there. I opened my mouth to speak when she did first, asking if she could offer me a compliment.

You may indeed, I'd replied, and felt my chest grow tight at her soft words, my vanity swelling.

Her lips parted and the tip of her tongue stole out to wet them. Her long lashes threw patterns of warm light across her cheekbones as she studied my face, which was cast in shadow while the fire danced over hers. Her breasts lifted with an indrawn breath. It took the strength of a goddamn saint to keep from crossing the mere two feet of floorboards separating us. I felt like a criminal for my lustful imaginings, damning myself even as I gave over to the thought of taking her waist in my hands and closing the distance between us, of claiming that sweet, lush mouth and tasting all her secrets.

She'd whispered, *You play with such sincere passion. It is a joy simply to observe.*

Thank you kindly, I'd whispered. The tension in the air was so very taut I believed it would resonate if I drew my bow over it; I wanted to show her other ways in which I was sincerely passionate – oh Jesus, I had wanted that with a keen, finely-honed ache.

Rebecca, oh holy Lord, woman.

What would she say if she knew how exquisitely she tortured my thoughts?

You made your decision, I reminded myself, and passed a hand over my face. *She'll never know. There's no point thinking on it any longer.*

Riders approached my right flank when the sun was roughly an hour from setting and I turned to see Grady and Virgil cantering near. Grady lifted one arm in a wave. He rode Quartermain; Virgil's mount was a fine, blue-roan gelding with raindrop patterning on its rump.

"Hot, ain't it?" I asked as they rode abreast of Fortune and me, glad for the company.

Grady nodded. "And there's still trees in these parts, where there's some hope of cover from the sun. The farther west we venture, the fewer the trees."

"The country here is different than what I know, I'll say that." I scanned the horizon as though I hadn't been staring at it all damn day, picturing instead the cool, shady forests and rambling creeks of my youth.

"But not unpleasant," Grady said. "I spent my growing years in Lofton, Kansas, along with Virg here. We knew each other long before the War. There ain't much for trees on the Kansas plains, neither, not for miles at a time."

"It is quite a sight when you can see all the way to the edge of the prairie, unabated," I allowed. "Back home, in the holler, the sun set early an' you could see about as far as you could chuck a heavy stone."

Grady chuckled. He mused, "I was in Tennessee during the War but I reckon I wasn't appreciating the countryside then. I feel I should return there, in peacetime, and see what I missed."

His words served to startle me, but I said only, "I'd like to return there someday myself, but I can't rightly imagine when that might be."

Grady nodded slowly and there was a beat of silence between the three of us; I understood – perhaps for the first time, a slow dawning of awareness – it was strange for the two of them as well, conversing so civilly with a Johnny Reb. Had we met at such close range only a few years' back, we would have been grappling to drive musket blades into each other's flesh.

Grady finally said, "Your kid brother could talk the hind leg straight off a mule, if you don't mind my saying so."

"He is a jabberer." A smile pulled at my mouth. "You can feel free to tell him to shut his yap."

"Naw, I don't mind none. Quill gets a real kick out of him. And it is a fine thing to hear Cora-bell talking again. Not that she was ever much of a talker, but she's been a church mouse since Dyer passed."

"Was she there when he was kicked?" I asked, thinking of her distress this morning.

Neither immediately answered and I figured they were troubled at my rude, overly-familiar question, rightly so; after all, Dyer Lawson was a stranger to me and had been their friend. My mama and Granny Rose would deliver a sound scolding for this impolite mentioning of the deceased, especially a deceased man I'd never known.

"Not as such," Virgil said just as I opened my mouth to apologize for my rudeness; he drew a breath that lifted his narrow shoulders.

Grady elaborated, "Dyer passed in the morning hours, in the boarding-house. I didn't want Cora to see him like that, near to death and battered as he was, and ordered her kept away. But she must have crept into his room after waking that morning because we found her there at dawn, her little head on his chest. He was already gone. Poor thing, Dyer was all she had left in this world."

"We had no business bringing her along on the trail," Virgil said, gruff with impatience. "It's no place for a girl-child, as I have stated many –"

In the tone of someone taking up an old fight, Grady interrupted, "Dyer would never have wanted Cora in an orphanage. She ain't of a strong constitution. There was no option but to bring her along to her kin."

"She seems to have taken to Malcolm," I said, hoping to stave off their bickering.

A smile ghosted over Grady's face as he nodded agreement. "That she has. He's a likeable little feller and I'd hoped as such. Even my Mary had a thing or two to say about young Malcolm the other night." At the mention of Mary, Grady's smile broadened. He continued, "And Quill's grown fond of him, encourages his chattering. All of Quill's sons was killed at Gettysburg. He's got two married daughters back in Pennsylvania, but no more boys. He said Malcolm brings them to mind."

"Malcolm and me lost our whole family during the War, the entire lot. I know he's starved for the company of family, even family not his own," I said. "Our uncle is the only kin we've left in the world."

"But Malcolm has spoken of a sister," Virgil said, producing an apple from his pouch and crunching a bite of the yellow-red fruit.

"Lorie," I confirmed, wondering why even this simple statement from Virgil served to irk me. "She is my friend Sawyer's wife, an' very much like a sister to the boy an' me. Closest I'll ever come to a sister, I figure, until maybe Malcolm takes a wife."

Virgil said, "I've three sisters, all married, and all a fair piece older than me. I reckon they still have plenty to say about me roaming the country like I've done since the War. They filled my ears when I first came home, wouldn't let up for nothing. I had to escape outside to get away from them."

"They believe you should be settled?" I guessed. I'd not heard him string so many words together since meeting him, and resolved to set aside my dislike.

"They do indeed. Settled near to them, if they had their way," Virgil said.

Grady shifted, crossing his forearms on the saddle horn. "The thing is, they *couldn't* understand, nor could my family, even if we went blue in the face explaining, why we feel the need to travel. Why we can't stay in one place for any stretch of time. I tell you, Tennessee, when I was first home from soldiering I could hardly stay the whole night in my own bed. Here I was in the bed I'd longed for while sleeping in mud and guts, and yet I couldn't rest for all the gold in them hills yonder. I ain't too proud to admit I feared I was crazy, finding myself outside looking up at the moon in my underdrawers, figuring I was tetched for good."

Grady's words landed with enough impact to leave behind bruises. How odd it seemed that he felt the same way I recalled feeling, back in 'sixty-five. Like a ghost in my own home, crawling with an ill, oily discomfort. Back then Sawyer spent the nights in the Suttonville churchyard, lying alongside the newly-turned earth over the graves of his family, whiskey bottle in hand, believing he belonged there with them rather than amongst the living. And Gus, who rode Admiral along the quiet streets all through the lonely nights of that awful summer, unable to sleep in the house he had once shared with his beloved wife; a house now empty and echoing, full of naught but memories that ripped at his heart.

"I know just what you mean," I said, and meant those words more than Grady knew. He couldn't know the strangeness of realization rising like a sun inside me, piercing through an ancient-seeming darkness.

Virgil no longer appeared to be paying attention to our words, instead watching the horizon with an expression I couldn't quite read, dismal somehow, the kind Mama would have called a 'mug lump.' He murmured, "Spent my last penny on drink and gambling once I got home from the War. Lingered in Baxter Springs for a spell before…"

Again Grady interrupted. "Before I found you, with the offer of a cash job."

Virgil's expression lost its distant look, gaze sharpening as it returned to his old friend. I wasn't sure if I was imagining the resentment in his tone or if he was just poking fun at Grady as he said, "Grace has *always* shined its light on you, Ballard, since we was kids."

Grady's easy smile again brought Ethan Davis to my mind. Ignoring Virgil's irritable tone, he explained, "We signed on to drive some eight hundred head to Topeka that very day and we've been on the move, ever since. I figure someday I'll feel able to settle in somewheres, but no time soon."

I said, "There's plenty of time for that, I reckon," and sensed Virgil's sideways gaze flicker briefly to me.

Then he looked back Grady's way and muttered, "Yes. Plenty of time."

THE LANDSCAPE GREW rugged, the hills gradually steeper as we angled northwest. We drove the herd around the solitary fort on the border, where western Minnesota gave over to unclaimed wilderness, and then pressed on into Dakota Territory.

"Statehood may be a long time in coming to these parts," Quill said as we left Minnesota behind.

September waned and the nights passed clear and cold. Malcolm and I continued to sleep beneath the wagon, tucked close for warmth beneath our two blankets, while Grady and Quill lay near the fire, wrapped in theirs; Virgil remained the night watch. When I woke before dawn on the third morning of our journey, each breath a foggy cloud about my mouth and nose, I was more than a little startled to observe that Cora had crawled from her cot in the wagon bed to lie near Malcolm.

She was curled in a small knot on the far side of my brother, under both his blanket and her own woolen shawl, arms crossed over her narrow middle and legs drawn inward. Her nose and Malcolm's was a mere two inches apart as they slept, his arm tucked around her waist. I felt a stitch in my gut at this evidence of his protectiveness of her, battling the sense that I should prevent this whole situation from continuing, but as I studied the little girl's face in the gray dimness I found I hadn't the heart to demand she return to her own sleeping place.

Instead, I rolled to the other side, catching another half-hour of sleep. When I'd woken for the second time Cora was gone, leading me to wonder if she'd been an apparition I'd only imagined. But then, the very next night, Malcolm whispered in the darkness, "Boyd, Cora come to lay by us last night.

She done said she was scairt."

"I saw," I admitted.

"I don't mind," Malcolm confessed, his tone questioning whether *I* did. When I didn't reply, he whispered, "It's all right, ain't it?"

Uncertainty tugged at me, but Cora was only a child, no threat to anyone; it hurt to think of her being scared or lonely, or even cold. I further considered how much Malcolm, who craved being snuggled and petted, hugged and loved on, missed Lorie's tender affection. How he had never stopped missing our mama; Malcolm had been Mama's baby, after all.

All of these things were in my head as I finally relented, promising, "I won't say nothing."

And ever since, Cora slept with us through the night hours, creeping back to her cot before anyone else woke; the only difference was that after my approval, she claimed the spot right between the boy and me. I didn't know exactly what it was I felt with a child not my own curled to my side. Protective, to be sure, and yet somehow having her so near forced my consideration in other directions, to dark places. It was her vulnerability that troubled me most – the recognition of how powerless she would be in other circumstances. What if Grady hadn't taken her under his care? When I'd been a solider I'd seen children left without means, without kin; thin, peaked children ailing and ill, dying in the starved-out towns in the land of my birth. There was nothing as helpless as a child, and children did not ask for birth; God knew they didn't ask to be orphaned. A child could beg for grace, could pray for mercy, but no amount of praying could alter a regrettable circumstance or restore a parent to life.

I felt I'd never truly understood the impact of such things until lying under the wagon with a little orphan girl's elbow pressing against my ribs. Half-asleep, my mind stirred with disjointed images and shadowy nightmares; I drifted again through the terrible time I'd sat at Sawyer's bedside with Lorie, before we knew if he would survive his wounds, admitting to Lorie my fear of being unable to protect a family of my own, and her quiet response, that love worth having was one part pain. And my own reply – that it was worth the pain, or we would never love. I remembered how Rebecca said her memories, the ache of missing her husband, Elijah, hurt as badly as holding both hands in a fire. I was ashamed of the damnable burning sting of jealousy I'd felt ever since I realized how much Rebecca had loved Cort and Nathaniel's daddy.

Exhausted, I wondered, *Why is love so goddamn punishing? Who can bear it? Who is strong enough?*

No one. But we love, even still. Maybe we's just...plain crazy.

WE FORDED the wide James River over the course of an afternoon, with blessedly little trouble, and then followed an offshoot as it slanted westward; according to Grady, this tributary would lead the way to the larger Missouri, and eventually Royal Lawson's homestead. By early October he said we were more than halfway to our destination, having left Minnesota far behind. Grady kept track of each day in his leather-bound notebook, spending a few minutes' time at the fire each evening, recording the day's events. A journal, the likes of which I'd never in my life considered keeping, a small thing which seemed to bring him a sense of peace at day's end.

The weather remained remarkably fair and fine as we plodded along day after day; we were fortunate to continue avoiding nightly frost and Grady was optimistic about the prospect of returning to St. Paul before winter. The earth and sky appeared grander than I'd ever beheld them, with nothing to block the view in any direction. The offshoot of the James River, a swift, deep blue, kept us company; while a pretty sight, the water was also bitter-cold, and so did not encourage frequent bathing.

I was somewhat surprised to find I felt at ease, if not exactly content. The plains were beautiful in their own way, rolling with tall, yellow-brown grass that caught the wind, swaying as far as a man could see; clouds sailed along like sheep chased by a barking dog as I kept the remuda in line, day after day. Who could have guessed a boy from the Bledsoe holler, who'd never dreamed of living more than a few leagues from his childhood home, would someday ride the Territory plains over a thousand miles to the north and west, beholding sights unimagined in his youth. Thinking of Grady's journal, I often narrated what I observed as I rode; I did not put these thoughts on paper but instead spoke them in my mind, as though Sawyer rode at my side or – damn my vivid imagination – as though Rebecca rode before me on the saddle.

I ain't thinking so much on our days with the Second Corps, I'd tell Sawyer. *There's something about this open land that stretches out my thoughts, makes them thinner somehow. I don't rightly know exactly how to explain it, old friend, but I think you'd understand. Remember the time we talked about how we wished we*

could turn from men to hawks? Late that December night in 'sixty-four? Neither
of us cared a fig no more about pretending to be brave. We joked that we could fly
home then, to our mama's hearth fires, and there alight. No more War, no more
death. Just grace. The grace of hawks.

More often than I should have, I imagined brushing aside strands of Rebecca's hair, tucking them behind her ear as I murmured, *I wish you could see*
the way the clouds look just now, darlin', with the sun coming through them an'
turning the whole prairie gold. I wish you was here with me so I could hear your
voice an' feel you sitting there in front of me. Oh God, how I wish it. Likely you
don't think much on me since I been gone but that's for the best, I reckon.

To my continued surprise I enjoyed the company and conversation of my
Yankee companions, Grady and Quill especially, and even reticent Virgil, a
great deal beyond what I figured myself capable. Grady reminded me more of
Ethan the longer our acquaintance, with his easy nature and plentiful love of
womenfolk – and constant, enthusiastic talk of his own exploits. Grady was
kind to Malcolm and spoke with affection to Cora. Though on night watch
and not near as loose-jawed, Virgil was companionable enough as the weeks
wore by; he carried a tobacco pouch and was willing to share. I'd promised at
least a dozen times that I would purchase a new pouch for him the moment
we returned to St. Paul. Or any place with a decent dry-goods store or a hope
of trade; Grady spoke of a fort staked out on the west side of the Missouri
River, though it was not a place we intended to venture on our route to Royal
Lawson's homestead.

"It's nothing," Virgil would say, of the tobacco.

Malcolm was distracted from missing Lorie and Sawyer, finding in Cora
a kindred soul. The little girl grew less wary each passing day but seemed to
prefer letting Malcolm jabber rather than contributing to their conversations.
I was pleased to notice her cheeks fill out and take on a little color; she appeared less like a spirit and more like a human child. I'd grown accustomed
to her peculiar nature; her mismatched eyes still gave me an occasional start,
especially as she tended to stare fixedly at things, including myself and Malcolm, but I found that I attempted to encourage a smile from her, and felt
rewarded at earning one in return.

We all looked out for the girl, but no one more than Malcolm. He and
Cora rode by day on the wagon with Quill, and the old cook liked to tell me
as we all sat about the evening's fire what they'd discussed as the miles rolled

past beneath the wheels. Quill was older than my daddy would have been, had he lived, closer to the age of a granddaddy, and though I would not have admitted it to anyone, I liked the way Quill sometimes referred to Grady, Virgil, and me as *son*. How it spurred feelings of belonging, of being part of a family rather than an orphan. Even as a grown man I found I still longed to be someone's son, someone's grandson; to know an older generation watched out for me, and shared my joys and struggles. It seemed to me a longing that would never fully cease; a deep internal pit in which rain or mud washed away any hope of solid earth.

"Ballard said you left behind a woman you care for," Quill commented at the fire one late night, keeping his gaze fixed on the flames. Near us, Grady lay snoring; as was my habit, I tended to linger awake long past everyone else in the vicinity. But I'd found in Quill a fellow troubled sleeper; many a night had we sat up, talking with the hushed voices common to the darkness.

"Y'all gossip as much as old ladies," I complained, though I wasn't really angry that Quill knew this. Maybe it was a relief, not having to explain. I shifted, leaning back on one elbow, the fire warming my legs. I crossed my ankles with the fleeting thought that soon enough I would need new boots and turned up the collar of my jacket. Quill chuckled at my observation.

"Well, there ain't much else to do along the trail, if you're lucky."

"Meanin' we should be grateful for the lack of excitement," I understood.

Quill nodded, stirring at the embers with the end of a fire-hardened stick, one he kept and stowed in the wagon as we traveled. I'd watched menfolk prod at fires for the whole of my life; it seemed an urge common to men, to rearrange the blazing coals or the position of the kindling, trying so damn hard to feign control over anything in life. "I seen enough excitement to last me two lifetimes," he acknowledged. "And then some. Enough to know I'd rather live without it. As I'd reckon you'd say of yourself."

"I reckon that's true," I agreed. Because it had never yet worked its way into our conversations, and because I wanted him to know, I felt now was as good a time as any to say, "Quill, I weren't anywhere near the Gettysburg Campaign. I was in Tennessee during the summer of 'sixty-three."

I heard him draw a slow breath and didn't dare look his way. When at last he spoke, his voice was quiet and held no trace of anger or blame. "That never occurred to me, son. I got no hard feelings against you, even if you fought as a Reb. It ain't your fault my boys was killed. They done their duty for our country and I will be proud of them to the day I die." He sighed a second time, before murmuring, "Much as I'd like to blame someone, no good can come of hanging on to such hatred."

My shoulders lowered from an anxious hunch. I glanced his way to see his eyes on me, studying my face the way my own kin might have done, with compassion. As if Quill, in that moment, truly gave a damn about what I was feeling. Wrinkles misshaped his eyelids and lined the sides of his mouth as he remained somber. I sensed he was about to speak and heard myself blurt, "Were you ever in love?"

My words took him by surprise – I watched his shaggy white eyebrows lift and his head cock to the side, an altogether new regard in his expression. He rubbed a thumb over his beard and looked to the heavens. He was so long silent I did not expect an answer, and was a mite startled when he said with quiet ardor, "I loved my second-cousin Eleanor when we were both fifteen. We were very much in love."

"Where is she now?" I asked, already gathering that the end of this tale wasn't a happy one.

"In Harrisburg, where we was brought up," he said, and there was a grate in his voice not present earlier. And then he uttered the sort of low, half-laugh that has far more to do with pain than humor. Abandoning his fire stick and cupping his knees with both hands, he whispered, "I ain't been back that way in many dozens of years."

"What happened?" I asked, and then immediately upbraided myself. "It ain't my concern, you ain't got to tell me…"

"It's been over forty years since the day her pa took her from me," Quill said as if I hadn't spoken, staring much further than at our low-burning fire; there in the flames, he witnessed his past. "But to me it might as well be yesterday, no more than the blink of an eyelid. Funny you should ask such a question this night, young Carter, as I was thinking of her only this evening, for the first time in weeks. How odd. But then, life is often odd, ain't it?" He paused to run a hand over his face. "Her pa made sure to keep us separated until long after Ellie was promised to another."

"Her daddy wouldn't consider the two of you marrying?"

"No. And not a word I spoke would convince him otherwise. Ellie and me talked of running away together but we were so young, with no notion of what that truly meant." He snapped a kindling stick with an abrupt motion and then sat holding both halves, in utter stillness. He muttered, "Damnation."

My chest felt banded with iron as I figured, "She married this here other fella."

"She wrote to me of it. Letter came for me that next winter, envelope reading 'Mrs. Benjamin Donnelly,' but she signed it 'Ellie.' *Your Ellie* she wrote, even as the rest of the letter bid me a polite farewell. For the longest time I meant to burn up them words, but I never found the strength."

I found I couldn't speak; Quill, too preoccupied with his own thoughts, remained quiet for a long time. My spine twitched when he finally said, "But everything worked out fine in the end, I'll have you know. I married a good woman of my own two years later, my Minerva, and she and I were blessed with half a dozen young'uns. Minerva was a good wife to me, God rest her. We had a good life before the War, and I loved her dearly, I did. It weren't her fault that somewhere in the back of my mind, I couldn't altogether forget Ellie. I'd never have dishonored Min by confessing to it and she never suspected, dear soul that she was. I figure it's a fool notion to cling to the idea of another when there's a flesh-and-blood woman right before you."

I felt a freshly-honed razor pass over my soul at his words.

Silence surrounded us for another spell before he murmured, "But a heart's a fool thing, that's God's truth. What would I have done if Ellie appeared at my doorstep during them years, looking for me? Would I have had the strength to turn her away?"

Would you? I longed for an answer.

In a low whisper, Quill concluded, "I'm glad I was never asked to make the choice. And I've never been brave enough to venture back where I might run across Ellie, not in all these years."

The stars resembled glittering stones scattered along the top side of a threadbare blanket; beneath their meager light I walked far away from both our camp and the herd, unable to sleep long after Quill settled in for the night. A recklessness overtook my sensibilities – few though those might be – and I let it, allowing my mind to flood with pictures of Rebecca, memories a better man than myself would have left well enough alone. Many paces distant from all signs of life, I knelt in the darkness and pressed both palms to my face, my thoughts flung back to Iowa, last July, when I'd only known Rebecca for a few days.

"Green," I had said, with satisfaction, leaning over the corral fence, unable to keep from grinning at the woman walking my way in the dawning light, no matter how much a fool I must have seemed, out in the dooryard waiting for her to emerge into the day. Fortune nudged my arm with her long, warm nose, reminding me that I'd been currying her hide before being so thoroughly distracted.

"You might offer a simple good morning, Mr. Carter." Rebecca appeared unruffled while my blood grew hotter the closer she walked. She shifted a milk pail to the opposite hand, tucking back a stray lock of hair the wind teased across her nose, while I tried not to stare at her in the manner of an undisciplined youth. She elaborated, "Rather than such an enigmatic statement as 'green.'"

"Good mornin'," I whispered obediently. The rising sun revealed copper in her dark hair and struck the gold in her hazel eyes.

"Shall you tell me what you meant?" she pressed.

I knew even then that no good could come of our preoccupation with one another but still prayed that she asked this question in order to remain longer in my company, only arms' length away. I admired anew the prim and proper way she always spoke. I studied her face, leaning on my forearms over the topmost beam, her lips with a soft bow along the upper, a strand of hair caught in the corner of her mouth before she slipped it free with the smallest finger on her right hand. I could hardly swallow, weak-kneed as a boy who'd never touched a girl. Her gaze was equally steady in its regard.

"Your eyes," I explained at last, thrilled to watch a rose bloom in each of her cheeks. "I can't rightly decide if they're green or brown or gold, exactly. But so very green, this morning."

The wind blew chill on my neck here tonight, far away from her on the lonely Territory prairie; from the inside out, I stung with cold. I pressed harder against my face, punishing myself.

Why would you say such things when you was planning to leave? Offering compliments when there wasn't a hope of anything but hurting her. A selfish bastard is what you are.

Selfish I surely was, there was no denying, but when it came to it, I'd kept quiet about what I'd truly longed to confess to Rebecca – that her face struck at me as powerfully as the sweetest music I'd ever coaxed from my fiddle, how my fingertips ached in the same fashion, to touch her and draw forth passion and joy and contentment, each with its own series of notes. That there was a tone in her half-teasing voice which reminded me of home, of the way my mama spoke to my daddy, that of a woman who knows without a doubt that her man loves her more than all else.

But I had not spoken these things aloud. I'd ridden from her dooryard a coward, exiting her life without confessing.

Another memory sliced across my mind, this one far from sweet, as though reminding me why I so little deserved such a lady as Rebecca. A rowdy, crowded saloon in the river district of St. Louis, the night we found Lorie, a building with ornate gold letters painted on the front window, spelling *Hossiter's*. Flat on my back atop a frilly white spread stretched over a rickety bed on the second floor of this place. Naked as the day I was born, grasping the ample hips of a woman whose name was Lisette, a woman with a chipped front tooth and breasts the size of ripe musk melons, nipples gleaming from my earlier thorough tasting of them. Piano music rising up from the ground floor, headboard thumping the thin-set wall. Lisette laughing and bucking faster, curling her fingers into the hair on my chest while I gave her backside a slap and enjoyed the energetic frolic, half-drunk and with no notion of what was to follow in less than an hour's time.

You's nothing but lowdown, treating women that way, as if they ain't worth a thing but a place for you to spill your seed.

But even as this reproach thundered in my head I replaced Lisette, instead picturing Rebecca, blissfully nude and straddling me, dark hair loose over her soft shoulders, beautiful eyes alight with pleasure and love. I bent forward as if decked in the gut with a closed fist, groaning with longing, ashamed of myself even as I gave over to the vision, holding nothing back, overcome by the rush of images. I fumbled open my trousers, at last coming hard in my own hand, gasping as heat flooded between my knuckles, so goddamn guilty that I would resort to such measures when Rebecca was a lady, when I felt half-animal in my lustful actions. I was certain Elijah Krage had never lain with whores, had surely never dreamed of it. He'd taken only Rebecca to his bed; he'd loved her as his lawful wife and never wanted for more, I was certain of this as well.

Did he bring her pleasure with their lovemaking?
What about Marshal Quade? Likely he never lay with whores, either.
Rebecca deserves no less.

Stop this. You's a pitiful wretch, wondering things that ain't your concern.

I wiped my hand on the scratching ground. Stalks of prairie grass swayed about my prone body as I sprawled with arms widespread; the stars wheeled and spun and my head reeled with a dizzy ache. I fancied, for a strange moment, that I lay at the bottom of a fresh-dug grave, the grasses bending their topmost tips like the curious heads of mourners who'd come to see Boyd Carter buried. I ground the base of my palms into my eye sockets until checkered patterns flared in reds and blacks, blacker even than the darkness behind my eyelids.

I believed if I uncovered my vision and looked downward I would behold the dust-gray uniform I'd worn so proudly in 1862, that of a recruit in the Army of Tennessee. All buttons fastened proper-like, rips mended, stained material freshly pressed to swathe my dead body. Surely my old Enfield rifle would be at my side if I reached to the right, closing my fingers about the familiar hardness of the barrel. Properly laid out for burial, armaments tucked close, rifle oiled and musket blade polished to a blood-free shine. I was so cold I may as well have been dead.

"*Rebecca*," I whispered.

C ORA DON'T MUCH like horses, as you know, but I been telling her about how Lorie-Lorie rides Whistler, an' how much she loves it. I told Cora I do believe she might like a ride on Aces."

I eyed my brother across the breakfast fire; he chewed industriously, as if unaware that I intended to disagree with whatever else he was about to propose. He appeared innocent as a preacher's wife, freckles and all, but then he couldn't resist and peeked at me; one corner of his mouth lifted in a knowing grin that reminded me so much of Beaumont I shook my head. I could not help but smile, in return.

"You want to scare the bejesus outta the poor little thing? Her daddy was horse-kicked." I kept my voice low, leaning closer to Malcolm and pointing my fork at his nose for additional emphasis.

Malcolm shifted and his brows arched as he began his wheedling. "I know. But I figure I'll ride along with her so she'll see that it ain't near as frightful as she thinks. I figure if I was scairt of a horse then I'd wish somebody would get me on one so's I wouldn't be scairt no more. Boyd, I swear —"

"You swear what, little feller?" Grady asked, coming up from the creek bed carrying his shaving kit. Despite the decided lack of womenfolk for him to impress, Grady suffered our teasing and shaved if he woke early enough. My own jaws itched with a beard near eight weeks gone; it was mid-October by now and had I access to a hand mirror I'd surely behold Daddy's face looking back at me. But then again, a beard kept me a mite warmer.

Malcolm pleaded, "Mightn't I let Cora ride with me on Aces High? We spoke of it only just yesterday."

Quill joined us in time to hear the last statement. "If anyone could talk

her into it, you could, son. I believe you could talk a bird from a tree to light
upon your hand."

Malcolm beamed at this compliment, sending me a pointed look with
brows quirked, one that clearly asked, *See there?*

I set aside my plate and was about to respond when, over Malcolm's right
shoulder, I saw Cora climbing awkwardly from the back of the wagon, hampered by her shawl. My heart issued a *twang* similar to the sound indicating
a fiddle string needed tuning; her hair fell in snarls, as not one of us possessed
a brush or comb, including Cora, and the weather was far too chill to allow
washing its length in the river. She owned one dress and it had long ago
grown ragged with wear, torn at the waist along its seam. But a genuine smile
spread over her thin little face as she looked Malcolm's way; he dropped his
fork with a clatter and rose to meet her, kindly taking her hand into his and
chirping, "I was wonderin' when you'd wake. You recall what we talked about
yesterday, about you ridin' Aces with me?"

Cora nodded, looking up at him with near-heartbreaking devotion, lacing
their fingers and cupping Malcolm's hand between both of hers, patting him
almost as though unaware of doing so; I felt a powerful lashing of guilt. She
was so attached to him and we planned to leave her behind in the Territory,
forever; with her family, to be sure, but even so…

"I ain't got no extra trousers for you, but you don't mind ridin' in a skirt, do
you, Cora-bell?" Malcom had adopted Grady's nickname for the girl. "What
do you say?"

"I don't know," Cora answered slowly, tilting her chin in the direction of
the picket lines, hardly able to contain a flinch at the sight of the horses.

"C'mon," Malcolm encouraged, bouncing her hand in his, determined to
boost her confidence. "You ain't gonna get hurt, I swear. I'll keep you safe."

I thought of how tenderly Rebecca and Lorie would mother her, were we
all together in Iowa. I thought of Rebecca's no-nonsense tone and the feeling
of calm always surrounding her, that of things getting done because she said
so; with her abundant capability she would mend Cora's dress and see to it
that the little girl wanted for nothing, ever again. I knew this, and pictured it
all so clear it stung as would nettles dragged over my bare hide.

I imagined Rebecca settling Cora on the stool near the woodstove to
comb through those snarls, murmuring softly, her touches gentle and reassuring; the selfsame stool where she had once worked so diligently over me,

assisting Tilson as he cleaned the wounds on my back, gashes left behind by splintered fragments of the wagon. Rebecca had rested her hand on my neck that morning, in an unmistakable caress – a soft touch that flew straight as an arrow to my tailbone.

My heart began clubbing as one question screamed through my head with enough force to rip my hair by its roots.

What in God's name are you doing out here, so far from the woman you love?

Overtaken by the need to rise, to move, I stood, fork falling with a clatter. The conversation at the fire was focused on convincing Cora to give riding a try and no one paid me mind as I skirted the wagon and stalked a few dozen paces away, angling southward. Hatless in the early day, I stacked my wrists and rested them against my forehead, studying the horizon, a wavering mass of golden-brown grasses far as I could see, rimmed in orange-tinted light.

Too late, too late, you're too late.

The words beat an ugly refrain against the inside of my forehead; forcing them aside was like trying to drive a shovel blade through parched earth, but I did it, contradicting, *No. It ain't too late.* And maybe it was nothing more than the strength of my desperation to believe it was true, but a flicker of awareness alighted upon me. The feeling was so strong that the hairs on my nape stood straight, all at once. Hope spiked my heart.

If you's lucky as you ever been in your life, she ain't given up on your sorry hide yet.

Are you crazy? Are you vain as a peacock? She's more than given up on you. You left her behind! Quade is there, and he cares for her. What makes you think she would consider you, anyhow?

But these excuses ceased to matter as I stood there staring at the prairie to the south.

Go back! The notion was as powerful as the twister. *Go back to her, before it's too late. Before Quade makes her his wife and you ain't got a chance in hell.*

You are hundreds of miles from her. Weeks of hard travel.

It don't matter how long, how far. How can you not know this?

I imagined turning Fortune in the direction of Iowa and riding hell-for-leather, all the way back to Rebecca's dooryard. I clenched my teeth, panic mounting in my gut and swelling under my skin – what if she and Quade were already married? Somewhere in my mind was the memory of Lorie saying they planned a spring wedding, but plans often changed. It was mid-autumn already. Behind me, Malcolm's high, delighted laugh rose like smoke on a fair day; Cora had agreed to ride with him this morning. I turned in a helpless circle, seeing nothing but a grayish haze, riddled with indecision – what further risk would I bring to my brother if I acted on this sudden intent to return, all the many miles back to Iowa City?

Without getting the cattle to Lawson's you ain't got a penny to your name.

But without Rebecca you ain't got a life worth living. You'd be poor as the most pitiful wretch you could imagine.

I could ride twice as fast alone. I could get back to her within the month.

My entire frame, inside and out, ached with want of this, even as I knew it was not an option I could consider.

You can't leave behind Malcolm, or the girl.

You'll be lucky to return to St. Paul before winter strikes.

But –

Oh Jesus –

"Tennessee! Shake a leg!" Grady called.

We'll get to Lawson's, I decided, gritting my teeth. *We ain't more than a week away now, Grady only just mentioned, an' you owe it to him to finish the job. You can get your pay an' then you an' Malcolm can lit south as fast as the horses can gallop.*

But what about Cora...

I turned back for camp, shutting out all other thoughts with every scrap of determination I could muster. I would explain my choice to Grady this morning, as we rode. I would talk to Malcolm. He would understand – hell, he'd be outright glad. Right then I convinced myself I could do this thing; right then, I truly believed it could happen. As though conjured by my thoughts, my brother ran and caught at my elbow, tugging.

"I'm gonna fetch Aces. You help Cora up," Malcolm ordered, excited at the prospect of riding; he'd set so dutifully atop the wagon seat these past weeks, just to be near her. He grinned at the girl and ran in the direction of the horses. Grady had saddled Quartermain and Quill was busy tucking away the last of the cooking tools, ready to move out; Virgil appeared as a small dot in the distance, riding in to claim a few hours of sleep. Cora stood near the remains of the cookfire, silent, looking up at me with her peculiar eyes. She was so small I felt like a giant in her presence, a creature from one of Granny Rose's old stories.

I longed to ask her, *How'd you like a new mama, little one?*

But of course I could not make such promises. Royal Lawson was Cora's uncle, never mind that he was a stranger to her; Lawson would not want his brother's child riding away, and in the company of non-kinfolk, so shortly after arrival at his homestead. Though, for all I knew, Lawson would welcome someone willing to take on the burden of a niece unknown to him. I was determined to try. If Lawson was willing, Cora would return to Iowa with the boy and me. I owed that much to Malcolm and to her.

I crouched way down so our eyes were on a level. "You certain about this?"

Cora worried her lower lip with her teeth, at last nodding.

"Best set aside that shawl, honey, an' I'll help you up."

Malcolm approached, his steps jaunty, leading Aces. He called, "This here is my boy! Like I told you, he's about the best horse there is. He's been wanting to meet you."

Cora stowed her shawl in the wagon bed and I lifted her into my arms; she was slight as a sparrow. I swore I'd hefted a sack of potatoes heavier than her. A hard knot of protectiveness formed in my chest as her small hands rested on the sides of my neck, with such trust, the same trust that allowed her to sleep so soundly tucked between Malcolm and me.

Quill hitched the mules as I carried Cora to Aces; he called, "You're a brave lass, Miss Cora!"

"Mr. Boyd," she whispered.

"Yes, ma'am?" I smiled at her formality; she never failed to add the title before my name.

"I can't…" she muttered desperately, and hid her face on my shoulder.

"I got you," I assured, settling her over my right forearm so I could reach out with my left hand. With no words, just a look, I told Malcolm to keep quiet a moment; he was bouncing with energy but nodded his understanding. I took Aces by the bridle, the chestnut horse so familiar to me; I'd known him from a foal, same as Fortune, and bore the animal no small affection. He was a tall horse, high-strung with youth, but as good a boy as Malcolm claimed. Aces lifted his upper lip, exposing the top row of his big yellow teeth in a horsey grin.

I murmured, "Hold up now, fella. See there." Aces whickered and snuffled his nose against my waist, expecting a treat. "You's a bit spoiled, ain't you? Now listen," and I sensed Cora peeking at the animal. "I'd like you to meet this here young lady."

Malcolm coughed and adopted an unnaturally low tone. "Well now, good morning. My name is Aces High. Might I ask your name?"

He could hardly finish speaking for laughter, and Cora lifted her head. Seeing a ghost of a smile on her face, I played along. "Good morning to you, Aces High. How are you this fine day?"

"Right as the rain," Malcolm said in the deep voice. "You ain't told me your name, m'lady."

Cora giggled, the first I'd ever heard of such a sound from her. Heartened, I said, "This here is Miss Cora Lawson. She'd like to take a ride with you this morning, if you's of a mind to let her."

Virgil rode into camp. It was only because I held Cora in my arms that I noticed a strange expression eradicate her smile as her eyes flickered to Virgil. He didn't take especial notice of what we were doing as he dismounted and headed for the coffeepot, as he always did upon returning from night watch, but I did not believe I imagined the way Cora's slight frame went suddenly rigid, far beyond that of her concern over our proximity to Aces; surely I was mistaking what appeared to be trepidation in her eyes? What could she have to fear from Virgil?

"I would like that," Malcolm said, drawing my attention back to him and the matter at hand.

Cora shifted position, reaching to pet Aces' neck with a tentative hand, but shied away as he nickered and poked his curious nose in her direction. Her abrupt withdrawal startled the chestnut and he danced to the side, neighing; she hissed a frightened sound in response. I stepped back and decided, "Maybe later this morning."

Malcolm's shoulders drooped with disappointment.

Quill invited, "Cora, you join me and we'll watch young Malcolm take the saddle. Mayhap he'll stay near and keep us entertained."

"Sure thing," Malcolm said, mounting with his usual grace, gathering the reins.

Virgil had disappeared within the wagon.

I set Cora atop the wagon seat and told my brother, "Ride with me for a spell, first."

"These are some fine horses," Malcolm said, admiring the remuda as the sun climbed our spines; for as chill as the night hours proved, the days remained warm and pleasant.

"I'd like to propose somethin'," I said.

Malcolm squinted one eye and looked my way. He snickered. "You meanin' to ask for my hand?"

"Don't make me kick you," I groused, freeing my right boot from the stirrup and jabbing at his lower leg.

"What you proposing, then? You ain't gotta be sore at me," he said, making like he meant to knock my hat askew.

"I aim to go back," I said, and Malcolm swung in the saddle to face me, lips dropping open as he heard the quiet sincerity in my tone.

"Back to Iowa, you mean? Oh, Boyd, truly? When? This day?"

His brimming enthusiasm heartened me; gladness swelled anew in my chest. "I figure as soon as we deliver this here livestock to Cora's uncle. We signed on with Grady to do that an' it shouldn't be more'n a week now. We'll collect the pay an' then ride south. I mean to ride hard, get there fast. What do you say?"

Malcolm bounced on his saddle, causing Aces to snort and toss his head. Further agitating the gelding, he yelped, "I say, *yessir!* You can finally tell Mrs. Rebecca you mean to marry her…" He threw a concerned glance my way and hurried to ask, "Ain't that right? You mean to marry her, don't you?"

I grinned at these words, proclaiming, "I surely do," momentarily giddy. Relief slid over Malcolm's face like warm water. He nodded joyful agreement. But then, fast as spring snowmelt, his mood took a turn. I reckoned I read my brother's expressions better than anyone else in the wide world; I knew his thoughts had turned to Cora, and sure enough, he angled to peer over his right shoulder at the wagon lagging far behind.

He squared his shoulders. "I ain't leaving her behind."

I looked heavenward, hoping for inspiration – oughtn't I to tell the boy what I planned? Or would it only cause him more hurt if Royal Lawson denied my request, as he would surely do? *Wait*, my sensibility cautioned. *Wait until you's talked to Lawson before you go making promises.*

And then, for no other reason than a small stab of instinct, I asked, "Does Cora ever talk of Grady and Virgil?"

Malcolm pursed his lips in consideration, forehead beetling, wondering where I was leading our conversation. "Some. More of Grady, I reckon. I do most of the talkin' when we's together, but Cora don't mind that, she told me. She likes my stories."

Not without caution, feeling a mite foolish, I pressed, "She don't seem scairt of anyone, does she? That you's seen?"

Malcolm's brows knitted and I knew my question caught him unaware, offering me a sense of relief. Surely, as close as they were, Malcolm would suspect if Cora feared any of our traveling companions. Instead of asking why the hell I wondered such a thing, he blurted, "I ain't spoken of what happened the night we camped at the Hagebaks' fire, when someone shot at you, I swear I ain't, Boyd."

It addled me that he was worried I might be angered over this, or figured I was goading him into a confession. "That ain't what I meant, boy. I know you wouldn't say a word about that."

"Me an' you ain't spoke much of it," Malcolm acknowledged, and hesitation slowed his words. "About what went on that night or who you think mighta done it."

I nodded, unease stirring in my gut; yet another poor decision I'd made, keeping something of such significance from Grady or the others. I finally said, "It's because I don't rightly know what to make of it. I thought at first perhaps Yancy had it in him to follow us from Iowa. We don't know his fate an' that's troubled me since the night he rode from Tilson's yard." I wished again for the capability of conversing with Sawyer, of knowing what had transpired in Iowa in our absence; we had no hope of a word from them, which tormented my imagination. What if Yancy had returned there, in our absence? What if they were still in danger?

They ain't unprotected. Sawyer is there, and Tilson, and even Quade, I thought, though I despised the notion of Leverett Quade being the one to offer Rebecca his protection; I wanted her protected, no matter what, but I hated the self-assured poise Marshal Quade had always exhibited, like a skunk trailing its scent. Despair tore at my senses, washing away the foolish giddiness. *Goddamn fool that you are. If you get there too late, if they's already wed, it's no less than you deserve.*

"I don't believe Yancy was kilt." Malcolm spoke quietly but a fire burned in his voice as he continued speaking, standing in the stirrups to stretch his legs. "But I wish otherwise. I wish my shot woulda pierced his rotten heart."

Instead of reprimanding, which I had done in Iowa when Malcolm made a similar proclamation, I muttered, "I wish so too, boy, I ain't gonna lie. I wish I woulda shot that bastard Crawford to death before he took out Sawyer's eye. I ain't likely to forgive myself for that. I pray Sawyer can forgive me."

"It ain't your fault. Sawyer knows that," Malcolm admonished. "It *ain't*, Boyd."

"Maybe not, but it's the reason he an' Lorie had to stay behind. He's half-blind now. He ain't ever gonna be the same." The thought left me ill with guilt. It was unjust on a level I could not accept and the fact remained if I *had* fired my pistol with truer aim that night, Zeb would have been dead all the faster.

"It don't matter to Lorie," Malcolm insisted. "She don't blame you, nor does Sawyer."

"It matters to me," I whispered, then challenged, "Close your left eye an' give sittin' the saddle a crack."

Malcolm did so at once, cocking his head to the side, birdlike. He rode for perhaps a quarter-mile before reopening his eye. He muttered, "It makes me dizzy as a fish."

"A fish?" I repeated, amused.

"When I open both eyes under the water I get right dizzy. I expect it's how a fish feels." He blinked, then studied me. "You think it was Yancy, bird-dogging us in Minnesota?"

"I do not." I was certain of this; I'd spent many a sleepless night thinking on the matter. "I don't believe a marshal, and him a former soldier, would tail us so ineffective-like. Besides, he woulda taken me out from a distance, would not have risked creeping near a fire where at least two armed men slept. I'd sensed someone following us for a good few days before that night with the Hagebaks. A marshal wouldn't draw it out that way, not if he was so close to his quarry. Makes me think whoever he was, he was questioning the best course of action. Not rightly sure of himself."

"But if not Yancy, then who?" persisted Malcolm. "Who would tail us for days on end? Ain't no one in them parts knew us from Adam. We hadn't a lick to steal, neither!"

"I wish I knew," I muttered.

"Granny used to say, 'If wishes was horses,'" Malcolm remembered, drawing from me a small smile.

"'Beggars would ride,'" I finished.

The mention of his horse sent Malcolm's thoughts in other directions and he picked up the thread of our earlier conversation. With no room for argument, he stated, "I ain't leaving Cora behind when we ride for Iowa."

"I know you worry for her, and so do I. I care for her, a great deal. But she ain't our kin, Malcolm Alastair. We can't rightly claim responsibility for her, especially when she's got family to care for her."

His jaw bulged with a stubborn set I knew all too well; it was a purely Carter trait. He understood how serious I was simply from my use of his given names and therefore went right for the kill. "Lorie an' Mrs. Rebecca would care for her, you *know* they would, Boyd. When you an' Sawyer went after Lorie and I stayed with Mrs. Rebecca, she told me how she always wanted a daughter."

I gripped the reins all the harder. *God willing, I will give her daughters. And sons. More young'uns than we could count.* And then I begged, *Dear God, allow this to happen. Please, don't let this be too much to ask.*

I chose my words with care. "Cora belongs with her family, with her kin. You know this better'n anybody."

Malcolm rode in silence; I watched from the corner of my gaze, wary of an outburst of emotion. His lips made a tight line; he chewed on the lower. Just when I thought I might get lucky and he'd let the matter drop for now, he threw me a whopper. With all manner of calm he announced, "Well then, I expect I'll marry her. Cora'll be kin to us once we's wed, ain't nobody can say otherwise."

I refrained from sighing, gritting my teeth instead, unable to think of a reasonable reply.

Malcolm continued, gaining momentum. "We's a mite young, I know, but Mama an' Daddy wed when Mama was but fifteen, she done told me many a time. Daddy said he knew Mama was the girl for him the first he clapped eyes on her."

"I know the story," I said on a sigh, quiet and tired. "They loved each other something fierce, ain't no one could deny." I paused before asking gently, "You believe Cora is the girl for you?"

Malcolm nodded vigorous agreement.

He was so damn young, and would not admit to any sort of fickleness; even so, I felt compelled to point out, "What about Lorie? Wasn't you fixin' to marry her, last we spoke? Ain't *she* your girl?"

"She's my *sister*," Malcolm said, the emphasis suggesting my stupidity. "Besides, I do believe Sawyer might have a thing or two to say on the matter."

"You's right about that," I muttered.

"Boyd, c'mon! I ain't gonna leave Cora behind." There was a plaintive earnestness in his tone I could not doubt.

I tried for a different approach. "Can you rightly imagine explaining to Uncle Jacob that you brought along a wife? A boy of thirteen years, with no money or means, an' his bride even younger? You gonna build your own cabin, homestead your own acres?"

"We can be promised then," Malcolm insisted, and there just weren't any point arguing with him in this state of mind.

"Go on now, go on back an' ride by the wagon," I griped, unwilling to further discuss the matter. "We can chaw on this later." Malcolm couldn't quench the angry glint in his eyes but he wisely said nothing, angling Aces around and heeling him into a swift and graceful canter.

"Much later," I muttered, then heeled Fortune to catch up with Grady and Quartermain, the two of them riding a few hundred paces ahead, at point. Might as well let Grady know my plan before Malcolm blathered word to everyone.

"You know the route well enough?" was the first thing Grady asked, somewhat taken aback at my announcement. He studied me from beneath his hat's wide brim, furry yellow brows lofted high. "The weather's been fair and I don't reckon we'll be forced to spend the winter at Royal's. Why not ride back to St. Paul with Quill and Virg and me? We'll make fine time without the herd. Why lit out on a path you ain't familiar with, Tennessee?"

"It's what I must do." I was unwavering now that I'd set my course. If I was too late, everything else be damned; I knew, down to my bones, I must try. Grady's opinion was of value to me but I would not be swayed. There was, however, another matter I wanted his estimation upon. "What of Cora? Will she be welcomed into her uncle's home?"

Grady heaved a sigh, swiping at his forehead. He admitted, "I been wondering that, myself. I do hope so. Dyer loved her dearly, I know, and Cora doted on her pa. Virg insisted we oughta leave her behind, as you know, said we oughtn't to trouble ourselves for a girl not relation to any of us, but I hadn't the heart to abandon her. She meant the world to her pa and I wanted to do right by him."

"You served under her uncle? You know him for a good man?" I asked, seeking reassurance. "I don't much care for the thought of leaving Cora with folks she don't know, kin or otherwise."

"Royal is a decent man, I've no doubt. He spoke often, and with fondness, of his wife. They've five or six of their own young'uns, I can't rightly remember the exact count. And Royal is well appointed nowadays, what with cattle prices. One more child in his house won't cause too much a stir, I don't believe."

"She's grown so attached to Malcolm," I said, torturing myself. "He told me just now he'd be willing to marry her so she could stay with us," and Grady snorted a laugh.

"Aw, it's a fine heart that boy has," he acknowledged, with affection. "I admire the little feller. And Cora has taken strong to him, there's no denying. It's a shame to separate them."

"That's why I figured I'd ask Lawson if she might stay with us, return to Iowa in our company. If you'd be willing to put in a good word for me, might be that Lawson would agree."

Grady's surprise was evident as his side whiskers, but he shrugged and said, "I s'pose it's worth a try. Though, Cora ain't up for the hard riding you'll need to do to get back south before snow flies. I can't imagine Royal agreeing it would be a wise decision."

I feared this was true, but I was determined to try.

Grady persisted, "What about Malcolm? Is he up to such a long ride?"

"He'll be right as the rain. We'll rest up once we's home."

Home. The word rolled from my tongue without a thought. Home was where Rebecca was, and Sawyer and Lorie. Our home, mine and Malcolm's, was with them, I understood. They were not blood kin but our ties were every bit as strong. Perhaps even stronger. If we never made it to northern Minnesota, I finally understood I could live with that decision. It had taken a twister and hundreds of miles of separation for this truth to bore through my thick skull. My gaze roving southward, I thought, *I'd bear any hardship at this point, just to get home.*

But I should have known worlds better than to make such a bold declaration, even an unspoken one.

I<small>T'S CALLED MUMBLETY-PEG,</small>" I explained to Cora the next evening, after we set up camp at the edge of a long, bowl-shaped depression in the earth, which Grady called a buffalo wallow. This particular wallow stretched a good half-mile, ample space for Royal Lawson's cattle to gather so that we could see the entire herd at one time, allowing Virgil the leisure of spending the evening at the fire rather than horseback. The setting sun glowed in a particularly pretty fashion along the western horizon, spilling violet light over us. Clouds lay in piles, stacked high, which suggested an overnight soaking, but we'd been rightly spoiled this journey, riding along through weeks of mainly clear, dry skies.

"Mumblety-peg?" Cora repeated, faltering a little over the unfamiliar words, sitting on her heels at my left and watching as I held my pocketknife by its short blade; the girl's gaze proved steady as a hawk's. The flow of the river was pleasant in the background. She asked, "Is it a game?"

I nodded and then knelt, better to demonstrate the technique. Malcolm, munching a hunk of hard cheese, watched with amusement; well-acquainted was he with the pastime. Quill and Grady held their own knives, ready to best me once I threw down, while Virgil lounged against his saddle with a second cup of coffee. I'd been on guard since yesterday morning, paying careful attention to how Cora reacted to Virgil's presence. His routine was opposite of the rest of us; he slept through the days and was a more solitary soul than either Quill or Grady, and as such I'd never witnessed anything amiss in his interactions with Cora. In fact, he tended to avoid speaking directly to her at all. I did notice that Cora took care not to sit near him, and kept her gaze from him; but then, she was shy as a fawn and perhaps I read too much into her reticence. But, then again…

"Who found Dyer?" I had wondered aloud to Quill only this morning. I'd accompanied him on his daily scavenge for eggs, figuring I could ask a question or two without anyone else hearing the exchange. "Did Cora see her father dead?"

Moving deliberately through the waist-high grasses just ahead of me, using a walking stick taller than his person to hold aside stalks in his search for breakfast, Quill paused at my words. I felt at ease in his presence, more so than ever since the night we'd spoken of his lost Ellie, and was therefore slack-jawed around him; when he didn't answer immediately, I feared overstepping my bounds. He finally said, "Cora saw Dyer as Grady carried him to his room at the boardinghouse that night, but we kept her from any other sight, figured it would hurt her too much to see her pa so damaged. It was Grady who found Dyer in a stall at the livery barn with his head stove in, earlier that afternoon. Dyer was a fair hand with horses and it was a piece of ill luck, I figure. Horses can be unpredictable, that's for certain. He was mighty trampled. Poor mare was agitated at the blood, stomping about in her stall. But Grady hauled him out of there."

"Dyer was still alive at that point?"

"He were, for a spell. A shame the doc weren't in town. Dyer passed at the boardinghouse before dawn, with Virg at the bedside. Virg and Grady knew Dyer, along with Royal, during their time as soldiers. Both of them drove cattle up from Kansas with Dyer last spring and I figure it was a comfort to Dyer to have someone he knew at his side when he left this world. It was Virgil come to tell us the news that early morning, but when we entered Dyer's room, Cora was there ahead of us, weeping over his body."

A chill passed over the back of my neck as he spoke. Quill knelt to retrieve eggs from the shallow roosting of a prairie fowl; I could hear the fretful chirping of the hen from somewhere nearby as her nest was thusly robbed. The tint of the morning light seemed garish, hurting my eyes; the prairie fowl's distress swelled – or was I only imagining it? Hearing instead the escalation of my own misgivings?

I muttered, "That would be a comfort to any man, yessir."

In the lavender light of advancing evening, hours since our breakfast of eggs, I thought again of what Quill had told me this morning, of Cora at her daddy's deathbed; I glanced at the little girl, whose dark eyebrows drew inward in concentration as she observed my mumblety-peg lesson. I found her far too serious for a game intended for levity, and decided at once to change my hold. In the back of my mind was the picture of her daddy with his head lolling as he was carried to the room where he would die within a few hours' time; I wanted to banish the grave expression from the little one's face, to see it replaced with lightheartedness. I recalled how she'd giggled yesterday when Malcolm and I introduced her to Aces High.

"I ain't got the right stance yet," I said, pretending to be deep in thought; I scratched my head with the knife handle, twisting up my mouth, and then wrapped my right arm around my head, positioning the handle near my left ear. Next I gripped my right ear with my left hand, hold Number Four if I remembered rightly, thinking back to long summer evenings in Georgia with the Second Corps. For better effect, I crossed my eyes and stuck out my tongue.

"See here?" I tried to say, hampered by my tongue. Malcolm laughed and Cora smiled shyly, ducking her head; I grinned in response and, this time with nothing in the way, announced, "Then, you chuck your knife."

So saying, I stood, holding the throwing position, awkward though it was, and tossed the knife with a precise movement. It sank blade-first into the earth, almost dead center of the circle I'd scraped into the dust at the base of an old, lone oak tree which, based on its substantial size, had likely been growing since the previous century. Nodding at my knife, I said smugly, "I ain't gonna lie, I'm a bit of an expert."

Grady snorted and all of them laughed; Cora beamed in response.

"Scoot over, Tennessee," Grady ordered, shouldering me to the side and positioning for a throw. He bent one arm for showmanship and braced his knife on his elbow; the blade sank cleanly, only an inch or so from mine.

"That's near a tie," said Malcolm, who was keeping score. "You's up, Quill."

Quill's knife knocked mine askew, giving him the edge on me. We threw twice more each before Quill and I determined that we'd beat Grady, fair and square.

"You want to do the honors?" Quill asked, nodding at the small stick lying near the rim of the circle scratched into the dust.

"Surely do," I said, using the handle of my knife to pound the stick as far into the ground as I could; losers were forced to retrieve it from the dirt with their teeth. Just for show, I asked Quill, "Might I use yours?"

He handed over his knife, with a grin.

"All yours, Ballard," I said, with a gracious gesture; the top of the stick was barely visible in the dirt thanks to my efforts and Grady heaved a long-suffering sigh.

"What's he must do?" Cora asked, puzzled, as I wiped my hands on my thighs, folding Quill's knife back into its sheath before setting it aside.

"Fetch up the stick with my teeth, like a critter," Grady explained, giving her a wink.

"Ain't fun," Malcolm said knowingly. "I always get dirt in my mouth."

"Might I try?" Cora asked. She'd tied back her long hair with a bit of twine, her sweet, pretty face glowing with what I was gladdened to recognize as gathering determination. The last of the sun brought forth a sheen of gold in each of her different-colored eyes, in a way that lessened the strangeness of them; Malcolm had gone still and silent, and this drew my gaze his way as he leaned on his elbow a few paces away, studying her with an expression almost severe in its intensity. Despite his youth and decided lack of experience, I realized with a start that he looked just like our father. It was a look I'd observed many a time upon Daddy's face, when he settled his sights on Mama.

A twinge tightened my guts.

"Cora-bell, you don't want to pull that stick from the ground," Grady admonished. "I lost the game, hon, so it's my duty."

"Mightn't I try throwing, I meant," she corrected, indicating my pocket-knife, which I wiped clean on my trousers.

"You surely may," I said, swallowing my qualms, with some difficulty. "Grady can eat dust a bit later."

Cora practiced while the light leached from the sky, politely accepting enthusiastic suggestions. Grady, Quill, and I took our places around the fire, contenting ourselves with coffee, while Malcolm dusted his hands on his trousers and stood, demonstrating techniques; he was careful with his touch, guiding her hands as gently as he was able. Her fingers were so slight she struggled at first to position the blade and I flinched to imagine it cutting into her, but with Malcolm's help she proved a fast learner; at last we determined her to be a novice mumblety-peg player.

"One biscuit left," Quill said, lifting the lid on the small, deep-sided iron pan he used for baking. He eyed Malcolm. "Got your name on it, son, if I don't mistake."

"You wanna split it?" Malcolm asked Cora, who nodded; the two of them sat close, Malcolm cleaving the biscuit with his fingers, offering her the larger half, while Cora swept her skirts to the side and settled on the ground, smiling up at him with such trust, such naked and vulnerable loyalty, that my chest hurt.

Virgil was also watching them, the firelight casting shadows over his narrow, mustached face.

An unbidden question rose within me like acrid smoke.

Stop this. You can't go about accusing a man of something you ain't even able to put words to. Wrongly accusing blame is itself a crime.

Dyer Lawson was horse-kicked. It ain't as though Virgil could make that happen...

Unless...

As though aware of my troubled thoughts, Virgil shifted, looking my way.

"Fine evening, ain't it?" I asked, level as a tabletop; his expression remained bland, not a hint of suspicion present.

"It is pretty out here," Grady agreed, surveying the land to the west. A faint afterglow remained in the wake of the sunset, though the clouds had slowly bulked and grown, overtaking the sky to the west. "Always liked the sight of this here wallow. Violets grow in it, in the spring months. Almost like a purple carpet, then. You recall, Virg?"

"I do, indeed," Virgil said.

"I can see why Royal would choose the Territory for his home," Grady continued. "It ain't exactly in the midst of civilization, but a man can appreciate that."

"Might we sing a few songs?" Malcolm begged; I figured it was purely innocent the way he sat so near to Cora that her skirts brushed his hip and spilled onto his lap. He added, for the countless time, "I wish you had your fiddle, Boyd. I miss me the sound of it."

My fingers twitched at just the mention of the instrument. "Me, as well."

Quill possessed a harmonica, which he'd fetched from the wagon many a night, blowing out tunes of a joyful nature; Grady, Malcolm, and I sang gamely along on those occasions, my right hand aching to hold my bow, wishing for the familiar feel of the fiddle Uncle Malcolm had crafted long ago resting beneath my chin. I could sense the music in my fingertips and would play along with Quill even though my hands remained empty. Malcolm sang well, as did Grady; the rest of us were only middling, but never failed to add our voices. Virgil was always on night watch and so Cora was the only one who did not join in the singing, instead watching our faces, each in turn, as if searching for clues known only to her.

"Not tonight, little feller. We've a soaking coming our way, I do believe," and the old cook nodded at the western sky. To Cora he said, "You best climb in the wagon, little one. Where's your wool cloak?"

"Might Malcolm join me?" she implored, and the cinch strap constricted its hold around my heart.

"Get in there," I ordered my brother. The air grew increasingly chill and rain splattered the ground; he did not have to be told twice.

"Quill, you take the spot beneath tonight," I invited. The wagon was crowded with belongings, tools, and cooking implements, or I would have suggested he climb inside as well.

"Fellas, we best saddle up," Grady said, nodding westward. "Rising storm could startle them into a stampede. Tennessee, you mind joining us this night?"

"You got it," I said, settling my hat low over my ears. I saddled Fortune only to find her agitated, and rested my palms to her square jaws before mounting. I muttered, "What's the matter, girl?"

Of course I didn't expect an answer but I'd trusted my horse's instincts for a damn long time. I scratched the sides of her neck, watching her eyeball the restless sky. I saw no sign of any funnel-shaped clouds amongst those gathering and so let my shoulders relax. I led my mare by her halter as I checked the remuda, patting flanks and speaking soothingly; I was accustomed to large numbers of horses, if not cattle, and drew comfort from their presence. So very many horses had I witnessed cut down in battle, enough to spawn nightmares for the remainder of my life, horses bloody and limping, with ribs blown apart, shrill with distress; after a battle, they sprawled dead and bloated, immovable, at times diverting the flow of streams.

"You's a good boy," I said to a bay I particularly liked, a solid yearling marked with black patches; one such patch appeared to blot out his right eye and ear, and he reminded me of the first horse I'd ever called my own, back in the holler. I put the images of broken horses from my head, concentrating on the here and now, as Gus had always encouraged Sawyer and me to do, resting my forehead against the bay's warm brown neck. Three others crowded each other for my attention, as would large dogs, and I smiled at their antics.

I nudged aside long, questing noses and climbed atop Fortune before my saddle grew too wet. I muttered, "Hold tight, you-all, I don't expect it'll rain all night."

Despite my assurances, the rain increased from drizzle to shower. Having reclaimed the saddle, prepared to join Grady and Virgil, I found myself suddenly wary. Fortune snorted and tossed her head, echoing this unease.

There's no twister, it's only raining. So what the hell is wrong?

I looked at once to the wagon, roughly twenty galloping strides distant; I heeled Fortune in that direction, straining to see through the murky haze of falling rain. The mumblety-peg circle beneath the oak had washed away, the embers hissing as the rain smote them to darkness. Near to them as I now was, I could hear Malcolm murmuring to Cora; Quill's boots stuck out from beneath the wagon. Nothing appeared to be amiss, and Grady and Virgil would be expecting me to join them for this night's watch. But my blood would not quiet.

Stop this foolishness. It's only the rain, addling your senses.

"Everything all right?" Quill called in a hushed voice. He'd stretched out to sleep, though sleep seemed unlikely in the damp.

"Yessir," I responded; I knew Quill slept with his pistol nearby, nonetheless. But no sooner had I spoken when a crawling chill centered itself as squarely upon my spine as someone taking a bead.

He's here, I thought, reining Fortune in a tight circle, scanning the entire area as fast as I was able; there was no logic to the assumption, only instinct. *He's near. He followed you.*

With instant reproach, I raged, *You's crazy as a jaybird! He ain't here! We's weeks gone from Minnesota! There's no one out there!*

I slid my repeater from its scabbard and heeled Fortune in a new direction, taking her southeast, away from both the cattle and our camp. I roved in a loose half-circle, keeping the wagon in periphery as I searched the landscape for signs of someone lurking, angered at the way the rain muted my senses. I couldn't hear a thing beyond the dripping prairie grasses; there was no wind, but the deluge worked to dampen sounds the length of the landscape, as well as my spirits. I considered the conversation with Malcolm yesterday morning, regarding the events in Minnesota, and guilt thumped anew, buzzing in my skull. Surely Grady long ago deserved to know that the man he had hired for a job constituted possible danger to his entire party.

Ill luck, I heard Kristian Hagebak mutter.

You can go straight to hell, I thought viciously, not sure if I meant Kristian or the man who'd been following us, who'd shot at me in the darkness.

"I'll send you there, in fact," I muttered, peering through the wet gloom as I rode.

It was too quiet. I knew it was a harebrained notion when it was raining, but it was the sort of quietness that rose from the belly, in warning; something was wrong, something beyond my suspicions about Dyer Lawson's death or any threat of approaching storm. I sheathed my piece in its scabbard and gathered up the reins, cantering Fortune to the cattle, coming abreast of Grady and Virgil, both sitting watch to the west of the herd, chatting with mounts drawn near; despite the rain, Virg was in the process of lighting a smoke, keeping the match protected beneath his hat brim.

"Fellas," I said, drawing Fortune to a halt on Quartermain's left flank.

At the urgency in my voice both men looked my way, conversation ceasing.

"Tennessee?" Grady questioned, twitching the left rein to ease Quartermain closer to Fortune and me; the palomino gracefully sidestepped, her fair hide gleaming even in the gloom. Grady sat the saddle as well as any Southerner I'd ever known, and I admired this. I would never fail to believe that he was, above all else, a decent man.

"Something's amiss," I said, looking hard at Grady. I felt the need to confess rising up like floodwater.

"What do you mean?" Virgil demanded in a steely tone I'd never before heard from him, steering his raindrop gelding in a half-turn so he could see my face. "What are you talking about, Carter?"

Rain slipped beneath my collar. I would have told them everything, I intended to do just that, but before I could speak a word Quill bellowed, "*Ballard!*"

A discharging pistol split the air; my spine jerked, the sound drawing our attention as swiftly as would the detonation of mortar rounds. Quill, hunched near the tailgate, fired his piece to the east; I saw the spark of flame from its muzzle as it discharged a second time, near the wagon. Gunfire was returned from the darkness. I heard hostile, shouted threats, making little sense of the words.

Malcolm, I thought, single-minded with purpose, heeling Fortune with no other thought than to get to him, charging up the edge of the wallow to the wagon, fetching up my rifle as I rode. I dismounted before Fortune's hooves ceased movement, holding her lead line in one hand and racing for the oval-shaped opening in the wagon cover. I positioned myself there, backing up and holding my repeater at the ready, ignoring Malcolm's frightful questions, ordering him and Cora to stay put. Blood charged through my body; I saw things in tiniest detail, even before I could rightly make sense of them.

Quill was dead. He lay flat on his back, hat askew and rain striking his face; a bullet had taken him in the cheek. Practicality, and years of existing as a soldier, intruded and I thought, *Grab his piece before they do*, catching it up from the ground, tucking it into my trousers. Rain poured from my hat brim. Sweat burned my eyes. I swore violently, hearing men shouting and rounds cracking the air. A rumbling as of thunder trembled up from the soles of my boots; it took me seconds to understand the cattle were running. Horses and riders unknown to me converged from the east. Fortune reared, almost ripping my arm from its socket. I let go her lead line and used my body to block the entrance to the wagon, expecting at any second to be pierced dead by a round.

"Boyd!" Malcolm loomed behind me, trying to peer out into the night.

"*Get down!*" I shoved him out of sight, cursing the meager, pitiful protection the wagon offered. "And stay down!"

Despite the lack of a good shot or stationary target, I fired my repeater eastward, its shells striking my forearms. Between rounds and over the sound of the stampeding cattle, an aggressive voice ordered, "Drop that Yellow Boy, go on now!"

A Yankee, only a stone's throw from my position, made this demand. His voice was unfamiliar; *not Yancy*, I thought. Instead of obeying, I crept around the edge of the wagon, easing to a crouch behind the back wheel, and chambered a new round.

"Come an' get me!" I bellowed. Fury blazed across my vision, tinting red the entire nightmarish scene. "You sonsabitches, come an' get me!"

Malcolm, oh Jesus, my brother. I couldn't protect you...

I will die trying...

"Carter!" I heard from the right, a desperate call for my attention, and I stalled, unwilling to fire on Grady. And then I spied him and Virgil approaching on foot from the wallow, stripped of all weaponry, flanked by a man on horseback. A rifle was trained on their backs. The cattle were scattered across the prairie as effectively as if hurled by a giant's hand. Virgil had lost his hat. We were plainly outnumbered. I tightened my grip on the repeater, finger slick on the trigger. In the sudden absence of gunfire, the sound of the rain swelled in my battle-numbed ears.

From a short distance away the Yankee hollered, "Drop that piece, kick it away! And the pistol and your blades, go on now!"

The rider with the rifle centered the barrel on my chest and I had no choice but to submit, praying Malcolm and Cora stayed put in the wagon. Effectively stripped to the bone, it hurt to obey as I tossed aside pistol, rifle, and knives. I lifted my hands in surrender as another stranger rode into our camp, halting his mount only a few paces from where I stood. He had spared a moment to light and hold aloft a small lantern and so it was that I saw, and cursed myself to the lowest pit of hell; I was the sorriest goddamn fool that ever walked the soil, a field mouse in the sights of a striking hawk. Not a stranger, after all.

"Is this your man?" the Yankee inquired of his companion.

Fallon Yancy's face was slim, almost delicate beneath the brim of his hat, an oblong shape with dark holes for eyes, unblinking as they held mine. He was just a boy, and yet he was not; the hairs on my nape rose, recognizing threat as swiftly as any prey animal. Rather than answer the query directed at him, Fallon inquired, "Where is your brother?"

"I will die before I let you have him," I vowed.

Behind me, but a few steps away, Malcolm climbed from the wagon, tailgate chain jangling with his passage.

"Get. Back. *In there*," I ordered, hardly able to speak for the brace of dread in my throat.

"We'll lose the stock," said the man with the rifle, a Federal-issued Springfield, using it to gesture in the direction of the dispersed cattle. His way of speaking and his coloring both suggested a person of some mixed breeding; he was clad in the shirt, jacket, and trousers of a white man, but moccasins encased his feet rather than boots and he wore his hair in a long, fur-wrapped braid, shaved to the scalp on either side above his ears. A quiver of arrows was strapped to his back and a small crossbow, the sort folks in the holler had used for short-range hunting, was lashed to his saddle.

The Yankee said, "Hoyt's rounding up the herd. It ain't as big as we figured. He don't need our help."

"I can help you," Virgil said suddenly, addressing Fallon.

Grady stepped forward, as if uncertain concerning Virgil's intent; surely he could not have guessed what was coming. Grady lifted his chin into the rain, arms bent in a fighter's tense hold, and spoke at a heated clip. "We're delivering these cattle to my employer, Royal Lawson. We mean harm to no one. You've killed our cook. Explain yourselves."

"You're traveling with a pair of criminals, feller," the Yankee said, loading the words with sarcasm, shifting position on his saddle.

Fallon refused to break his gaze from Malcolm.

"Explain that statement," Grady demanded, as irate as I'd ever heard him.

"This here Reb and his brother," the Yankee clarified, gesturing at me with his pistol. "They shot to kill a federal marshal back in Iowa last summer, blew the man's elbow to bits. Marshal Yancy lost the arm on account of it." Indicating Fallon, he added, "This here boy is his eldest."

Grady gaped at me, speechless at these pronouncements.

Quicker to calculate his own odds, Virgil repeated, "I can help you men."

"I shot that marshal, not my brother," Malcolm announced.

"*Get back in the goddamn wagon.*" I spoke through my teeth but Malcolm stood his ground alongside me, bareheaded and with shoulders thrown back, unwavering beneath Fallon's regard.

"Help us how?" the Yankee asked, walking his horse a few steps closer; I could have closed my fist around his gelding's lead rein, but all three, Fallon and both men, kept their firearms in play, not about to be caught off guard. The half-breed slipped the crossbow over his right forearm in a gesture so effortless that in other circumstances I might have marveled.

"I am known to Royal Lawson," Virgil said, in a hurry now, avoiding Grady's eye. "I will vouch for you men. We can divide the pay. Lawson is a generous sort unless you cross him. Don't risk stealing this herd. Lawson will hunt you down like dogs, I assure you."

"Virg," Grady said, aghast.

Virgil pressed, "Do what you will with the Reb and his brother, but don't risk cattle theft. I can lead you to Lawson's, I know the way."

"You son of a bitch," I said, anger rising hot and strong, thrumming along my arms and into my fists, displacing the chill of rain and disbelief. "You fucking weasel-faced *son of a bitch*."

"Shut your trap," ordered the Yankee on horseback, and rubbed a hand over the back of his neck, as one irritated by an unexpected decision.

Fallon said, "Prove it."

"Come again?" Virgil asked, cocking his head; he'd stepped away from me, putting distance between us, perceiving my intent to cause him harm if given the slightest chance.

"Prove it," Fallon repeated, and nodded at Grady. "Shoot him. If you're willing to help us, as you claim, you'll shoot him dead, and therefore prove it."

"Jesus Christ," I uttered.

Without a hint of discomposure Virgil said, "Let me kill the Reb," and nodded my way.

"I have plans for him," Fallon said. "Shoot the other. You can use Church Talk's bow."

A beat of hellish silence hung thick in the air.

Virgil nodded curt acceptance of this condition and a jackal's grin bared Fallon's teeth.

Before I could draw my next breath, Grady lunged at Virgil, taking the slighter man to the ground. Seizing our meager advantage, I yelped at my brother, "Get down!" and dragged the Yankee from horseback before he had a hope of firing at me, using the momentum of his falling body to slam him to the earth. Malcolm scrabbled for the pistol the Yankee unwittingly released. In the confusion, Fallon's horse reared; he sawed at the reins. The half-breed heeled his mount with a vicious double kick, striking Malcolm's head with the stock of the Springfield before my brother could close his fingers around the dropped pistol; Malcolm sprawled to his belly without a sound.

"*Malcolm!*" I roared, but the Yankee rolled into a crouch as I was distracted, driving a hard shoulder into my side. I descended into a fighter's narrow focus, throwing my weight into his attack, curling my knuckles into weapons and slamming his face, aiming for nose and eyes, the weakest points. I heard a discharging shotgun. I heard bones crunching like kindling twigs. I watched as the Yankee crumpled beneath my assault, his gullet a pale, bowed arch.

"*Contain him!*" Fallon shouted.

Caught in the crush of hooves, I tried to crawl to Malcolm's side but a white-hot poker speared my lower leg; I was sure if I looked over my shoulder, I would behold a quivering iron spike driven into the ground. Before I could react a knee jabbed my spine, a cattle rope cinched my upper body. I cursed, twisting against the confinement, and the half-breed cuffed my jaw.

"Drag him," Fallon ordered, somewhere beyond my line of sight.

THE RAIN HAD stopped.

I was not dead, though I would have instigated my own death to prevent what was happening, if it could have helped.

"Her eyes are bad. I won't kill her," said the half-breed. I lay sprawled on the ground near his gelding's hooves, unable for the moment to move, the camp churned to mud around us. The half-breed was greatly bothered by Cora's eyes, holding the lantern closer to her face to steal another fascinated look but refusing to touch her.

"Don't matter. She won't last long out here," mumbled the Yankee, words distorted by his split lower lip and the pocket handkerchief stuffed up his bleeding nose.

From my position in the mud I watched Fallon Yancy approach. My wrists and ankles were bound with lengths of thick rope intended to keep horses hobbled. Blood smeared my face and my right leg was numb, a broken crossbow shaft still embedded there, my skin lacerated in a hundred places; the half-breed had dragged me along the prairie with his gelding at a canter, until I couldn't tell up from down, day from night, keeping the pace until he tired of the sport. But just now rage overpowered all physical pain, so potent I felt feverish; Grady was dead, facedown near the wagon with two bullet holes creating dark, bloody patches on his back, and Virgil was not in sight. I did not know if Virgil had been the one to kill Grady. Of my multiple wounds I felt little – no damage they inflicted upon my body could hurt as bad as harm to Malcolm.

"There ain't a place you can hide from me," I vowed to Fallon, tasting the rust of fresh blood in my mouth. "I will find you an' kill you like *the fucking vermin you are.*"

Fallon only shrugged, unconcerned. "You'll be dead," he replied. No heat in his words as there had been that morning at Charley Rawley's homestead when he and Malcolm fought over an insult; Fallon was unmoved by my wrath, considering our deaths a foregone conclusion.

The half-breed eyed me, shaking his head side to side. He said, "Big talk for a dead man. *'Vengeance is mine, and retribution. In due time, their foot will slip.'*" And then he laughed.

The Yankee muttered, "Long as it ain't *my* goddamn foot."

Malcolm remained silent. Aces High gave a quiet whicker. I turned from Fallon to speak to my brother's horse. My voice shook as I begged, "Hold up, fella."

"I'll kill her," Fallon said, and I had no doubt he would; he was not someone to dither over a decision. With unmistakable derision, he added, "If you can't."

"You won't, you young pup," barked the half-breed, all traces of good humor gone.

"Kill me," I said, changing tactic, imploring the Yankee. I'd beaten him severely and he appeared unsteady on his saddle, listing to the right. He wanted me dead as it was; I begged, "Kill me an' leave the boy. He's just a boy."

Fallon dared to step between the Yankee and me and drove a boot into my ribs. I could not stifle a gasping groan. He said, "*I* would accept that offer, Reb, except there's no more chance for suffering once you're dead. And I don't believe you have suffered enough just yet."

"Hold your tongues, all of you," the Yankee ordered through his broken mouth, with pure exasperation. At last he decided, "Leave the girl-child be, I ain't killing a white girl-child, and anyhow, she won't survive a day out here with no protection."

Fallon held his ground, face hard as February ice as he grappled with the order, and I tensed further. I was helpless. Malcolm was helpless. It seemed the magnitude of my rage should have the power to slay Fallon where he stood, even with the distance between us.

The Yankee, not about to be trifled with by a boy, let his right hand skim closer to his holstered pistol and offered a flat-eyed challenge, stern despite the swelling that made one of his eyes a slit. His impatient posture asked, *How far do you want this to go?*

Fallon clenched his jaws but was intelligent enough to relent. He muttered, "Tie him to the tree, or he could stop the horse."

"Turnbull, get up here!" hollered the Yankee, and then directed his next order at the half-breed. "Tie what's left of this goddamn Reb to the tree."

The clouds had since shredded away, allowing a grim and murky moon to beam. At this summoning, Virgil appeared on his raindrop gelding from the direction of the wallow; he'd been working with a fourth man to regroup the herd. Upon seeing Malcolm sitting atop Aces and with a noose around his neck, Virgil's lower jaw went slack with surprise, which he immediately contained. The men had resituated us beneath the lone oak tree with its limbs reaching outward like arms; the other end of the hanging rope was secured on one of its long, low branches. I could hear the Missouri as it coursed along in the nearby gloom.

"Get this Reb up and tied to that oak," ordered the Yankee. As though just deciding, he added, "And that there girl."

Virgil and the half-breed yanked me upright; I took care not to react, or to fight them, as sudden movements might startle Aces High. I could not think ahead more than a second at a time – at this second, my only concern was keeping Aces calm until I could think what to do. Blood collected in my mouth, the taste of iron creeping over my tongue. I wanted to tell Virgil that I would come for him, that I would find his traitor hide, ram a pistol down his gullet and empty the entire chamber there, but I didn't waste words, not now.

Malcolm sat stiff as a pike, wrists bound behind his back, chin lifted to accommodate the heavy rope about his slim neck. His hair was damp with rainwater and falling over his forehead; he watched as they led me to the tree's massive trunk, following with just his eyes, until we were behind him and out of his range of sight. I would rather be drawn and quartered, flayed alive, than see him hung. Anguish tore at me but I kept my voice steady as I said to my brother, "Keep still."

They'd had Malcolm trussed up and seated on Aces before the half-breed dragged me back to the camp, his right temple already discolored by a bulging bruise.

I said again, "Keep still."

Fallon took care not to come too near me, even bound like a hog as I was, as he'd rightly seen the promise of his death in my eyes. I would gut him like a carcass if allowed the slightest opportunity, and he knew this. Cora made not a sound as Virgil led her to the tree, docile as a lamb being brought to slaughter. It took both Virgil and the half-breed to hold me in position and wind a new length of rope about the oak, tying me upright against its trunk. I struggled to stay afoot, my wrists and ankles bound; my hands and feet might as well have been severed from my body. They made certain that I faced Malcolm and Aces High, whose chestnut rump twitched as I watched.

"Hold steady," I begged the animal.

"Her eyes are bad." The half-breed gestured again at Cora.

Fallon said, "Tie her like a dog," and smiled at his own order.

Finished with me, they wasted little time on Cora; the half-breed refused to touch her and so it was Virgil who latched a rope about her neck and tied her low to the ground, on the opposite side of the tree, allowing her perhaps two feet of leeway; she could not have crawled around to get Malcolm in her sights even had she wished, tied so low standing was impossible; she hunkered instead on her heels. She'd retreated into herself to a degree that she seemed unaware of what was actually happening. From the corner of my gaze I saw Virgil crouch to her level; she turned her chin away from him but he murmured, "You knew, didn't you?"

Before I could consider what he meant my attention was diverted elsewhere as Fallon approached my brother. My vision closed inward on all sides, my lungs collapsed, gurgling in my ears. I knew Fallon's intent was to quirt Aces into forward motion, thereby allowing Malcolm to drop into empty air.

"*No*," I choked. "*Jesus, please no.*"

"You shot my father," Fallon whispered, staring up at my brother; I could only see the back of Malcolm's curly head and could not begin to guess his expression. Fallon's face appeared as a death mask to my terrorized gaze, skeletal and inhuman as he continued speaking. "He lost his arm. He nearly died. He is in exile. This is because of *you*."

Malcolm lifted his chin and I imagined his dark eyes flashing with righteous fire. He leaned forward as much as the noose would allow and spoke low and clear. "Your daddy is a criminal, through an' through. An' I'll live to see him die, *I swear to you this night.*"

The throbbing in my brain redoubled. Malcolm sounded exactly like our father. For the span of several heartbeats, I was sure that he *was* our father.

Fallon stepped closer to Malcolm's left boot. He put his hand on my brother's knee and said with certainty, "Your brother is going to watch you die *this night*. I hope your horse stands here for a good long time while you wait for your neck to crack, I really do."

And then they rode out.

THE CATTLE herd faded away at last, every single one of them disappearing along the line of the western horizon, their mournful lowing drifting back to our ears. The land grew still and quiet with deepest night, and after a brief spell it was as though none of the men who'd stolen them, who'd killed Quill and Grady and left us for dead, even existed. I couldn't think about myself, or the girl tied like a dog, or that every last head of livestock was now gone, excepting Aces High, who held my brother's life on his back. I was beyond rage, beyond anything but saving Malcolm. They'd left us alive and I clung to this. Soon enough we'd likely be dead, but we were alive right now.

"Malcolm, sit tight," I said, struggling as aggressively against my bindings as I could. I bled from both wrists as they chafed against the bristling ropes and prayed the slick wetness would help ease free my hands. Aces was a good boy and dutifully remained standing with Malcolm settled on the saddle, but the horse was not likely to stay content in this stance much longer. His back hooves stomped in succession, one after the other, despite my brother's murmurings to him, encouraging him to stay put. I knew the animal could smell the blood and it distressed him.

"Boyd," Malcolm said, and his voice was small and hollow; no longer did he sound like Daddy. He wobbled over the words. "He's gonna walk..."

"Sit tight," I growled. "I am gonna get you outta this, I swear on my life."

"Mr. Boyd." Cora's urgent whisper startled me; I'd almost forgotten she was there. I couldn't see her because she was tied on the other side of the trunk. "Mr. Boyd. It's Quill's knife, here under the tree. I see it."

I hissed, "Can you reach it?"

"Yes."

"Fetch it up, quick now!" Hope gouged at me.

"He's gonna walk. I can feel it!" Malcolm moaned.

"Hold him," I ordered. "Cora's found a knife!"

Straining noises came from the little girl, sounds of struggle, and then a rhythmic scraping met my ears. She cried out, a high, pained bleat and then popped around the oak, a length of sawed-off rope dangling from her neck. Blood smeared her hands. Her strange eyes seemed to glow in the meager moonlight, rabid with purpose. Horror gullied out her features as she beheld Malcolm's precarious position.

"You gotta climb up there on Aces, real slow, an' cut him free." I stared bullets at her; there was only one shot and Cora would have to take it. She was all we had. It meant having to approach a horse, which I knew she feared, and so I said, "He's *gonna die* if we don't do something, you hear me?"

She nodded; I felt I'd never spoken so seriously in all my days.

"Go around front of the horse, nice an' slow, let him see you. Malcolm, you keep Aces steady. There's a good boy, Aces, *a good boy*."

Aces High stood only an arm's length from me. If my hands were free I could have grabbed his tail and held him in place even if my arms were wrenched off at the shoulders in the process, but I was tethered like a beast. I began grinding again at the ropes about my wrists; I'd almost eased free my right hand. Before Cora could step forward Aces whickered with increasing distress, sidestepping. Malcolm began to cry, his body pulled at a sharp angle, the rope about his neck stretched taut. I clamped through my tongue restraining a horrified shout. "Cora, *don't move*. Come here an' cut free my wrists, *hurry now!*"

She scurried to my side and began sawing, gnawing at her lips, working like a child-sized demon. She freed my hands and I shoved her aside, not intending to hurt her, but I meant to get to Malcolm. Forearms slick with blood, I used both hands to tug down the rope about my waist; it was at my knees when Aces could refrain no longer and jerked forward, unseating Malcolm.

The roaring that shredded my throat I'd heard only in battle, when death is closing fast and a man knows it, and is unable to evade any longer. My brother fell – *I watched it happen* – and it was only the ineptitude of the noose that saved him. A properly-tied knot would have broken his neck on impact but instead he was jolted by the end of the rope and began to strangle, kicking and gagging, boots no more than a dozen inches above the ground. Cora screamed as though dipped into a vat of lye, running to him and wrapping about his lower legs, trying with all her scanty strength to provide lift.

"*Malcolm!*"

I freed myself from the rope tethering me to the trunk, brutal with resolve.

My ankles remained bound but I crow-hopped forward, stumbling, dropping to my knees beneath his twitching legs with what seemed syrupy slowness, but then I had him in my grasp. I rose with a guttural, groaning sob, balancing on my bound feet by the grace of God, and lifted him up enough that the rope about his neck went slack. The choking sounds cut short and he wheezed a partial breath. Tears and sweat stung my eyes. I yelled to Cora, "Cut free my ankles!"

I could conceive of no other way than to steady myself and summarily cut free the boy. Cora fell to her knees, attacking the last of the rope hindering my movements. The second she freed my feet, allowing a full range of motion, I demanded the knife. Malcolm slumped, awkward and weighty, on my right shoulder, hindering my frantic efforts. I reached up and begged, "Help me. *Help me.*"

My brother ducked his head just enough and I sawed at the noose. The rope frayed, then split, and we three tumbled to the muddy ground.

I LOVED SAWYER like a brother, and still I hadn't wept this way over his recovery. I eased the rope over Malcolm's head and cradled him, sobbing like a child. I kept asking if he was bleeding and he kept trying to tell me that it wasn't his blood, but mine. Blood was everywhere, hot and wet on my feet, all along my lap. Malcolm's voice emerged hoarse and raw, his breath in heaving chunks; my heart slammed like a butter dash at my ribs, churning them to liquid, and would not stop. Cora wrapped about him from the other side, laying her cheek between his shoulder blades and holding fast. Malcolm took both her hands into his right, the three of us knotted together.

"Your knife saved us," I told Quill later, once I'd regained a measure of control, using my fingertips to close the old cook's eyelids; his jaw hung slack and undignified, no helping it. I whispered, "Your knife saved us and I could never be thankful enough."

I intended to bury Quill and Grady, even though I'd not yet determined the extent of the damage to my lower leg, shot at close range with a crossbow. Trouble was I didn't know how I would manage the strength required for gravedigging; already I recognized I could not walk. I crawled to the edge of the buffalo wallow as dawn overtook the prairie, staring mutely westward, having left Malcolm and Cora slack with exhaustion beneath the oak. The sky brightened, appearing whitewashed, the prairie dripping after last night's rain. The bastards had taken everything they could drive off or carry – the cattle, the horses, the mules, all of the bullets and much of the food contents from the wagon; they'd summarily smashed the front wheels, so even if one of us managed to survive there was no possibility of it hauling us to safety. The camp was divested of all but us and Aces High. I could not howl my rage to the empty sky; I was scraped raw, inside and out.

After a time I heard Malcolm approaching.

"Boyd." His voice was a low bark, rasping over the single word; the hanging rope had left a crosshatching of red marks along his throat similar to the ones on Tilson's neck. He coughed before whispering, "Your leg."

"It ain't…" But I could scarcely finish the thought, let alone the bluff. I sank to my forearms and then listed to one side, the cold damp of the ground seeping through my tattered clothing. Small whitish dots skittered like mice across my vision. Malcolm dropped to a crouch and tugged at my pant leg.

"I gotta take a look," he said, clutching my knee, keeping me steady to examine the wound; even such a gentle touch was unbearable. "C'mon now, lie still. You's beat up like I never seen."

"Lemme see it," I muttered, trying to sit but unable, smote by a familiar sensation, that of hovering apart, as though I'd become a shadow attached by only the thinnest of threads to my own body.

Malcolm ordered in his husky voice, "Hold *still*. I'm awful sorry I gotta hurt you like this, Boyd, but that shaft gotta come out. It can't stay in your leg."

"Don't pull it out…the wrong direction," I insisted, a cold sweat beading along my hairline. I pictured the field doc's tent in Georgia, a rank, blood-stained patch of ground beneath a canvas covering, humid and reeking as a swamp choked with dead critters. Grafton had died in those miserable confines, bleeding like a stuck pig from the stump they'd made of his arm. I gritted my teeth against the memory.

"I won't." He spoke with a tone of promise, pale face looming near, as white as milk skimmed of its cream. His eyes burned with purpose. I reminded myself that Grafton was dead, that this was my brother Malcolm; for a second, I'd grown confused.

"Not backward," I whispered, pinning him with my sternest stare. The arrow's pointed tip was visible, poking out beside the long bone comprising my shin; by contrast, the entry wound was a deep gash in the muscle, crusted with dark blood and in which the broken-off wooden shaft protruded a good two inches from my flesh. Now that I'd focused on it, the wound hurt so bad I was fearful I'd lose consciousness. I clenched my jaw, recognizing that Malcolm would have to force the shaft forward so the two points forming the base of the triangular arrowhead would not further destroy my leg. Dizziness forced my skull back to the ground.

As though there was a chance I might flee, Malcolm ordered, "You stay right here. I'll return directly."

I jerked a nod as he hurried away at a clip, feeling the prickle of the hard ground, my chilled body overtaken by a shuddering tremble, as if the cattle were still running. Words played through my head in the manner of a prattling drunkard as I studied the white, sullen sky.

I will kill you, Fallon Yancy. I will find you an' kill you, an' I'll make it a slow death. Slow an' painful. I know how, believe me.

Grady. Quill. I am so goddamned sorry, I couldn't be sorry enough if I lived ten lifetimes beyond this one.

Malcolm nearly died. He nearly died.

Oh Jesus, forgive me. Forgive me.

You will not live long, the next we meet, Yancy. Nor you, Virgil Turnbull. Both of you will beg me for mercy.

Fortune, my horse. My good girl. I am so sorry.

Ain't no place you can hide, Yancy. No place on this earth.

Malcolm returned carrying a small bundle of supplies and a damp cloth, Cora with him, a saddle blanket folded over her arms. They knelt, and Cora set aside the blanket and cupped my face in her hands, her flesh warm against the ice of mine. She surprised me by leaning close and bestowing a gentle kiss on my forehead, her breath soft as it skimmed my eyelids, her hair brushing like wings against my jaws. She positioned the saddle blanket beneath my head, thereby offering what meager comfort was possible.

"Run an' fetch up that blanket from the wagon, we forgot it," Malcolm instructed, briefly resting a hand on Cora's elbow; she followed this order at once and Malcolm turned my way, explaining his intentions with uncharacteristic authority. "I'm gonna pull that arrow outta your leg an' then we'll patch it up. I got a stick for you to bite. Remember the time Mama pulled the prickle-pig quills from Graf?"

"I surely do. You's smart to think of that," I whispered. My limbs shook with increasing violence and I clenched my muscles against it; the ground was so goddamn cold, I felt half-dead already. I allowed him to settle the kindling stick between my chattering jaws, the tree bark rough and bitter on my tongue.

"I love you, my brother," Malcolm whispered, leaning over me, blocking out the pasty heavens; his head appeared wreathed in light and he cupped a palm over my forehead, as though offering a benediction, or a last rite. I tried to tease him but could not manage a word. I wanted to say, *I ain't dead yet, stop that.*

Cora returned and draped the blanket over my midsection, tucking it about me as would a concerned mama.

"Thank you," I told her, and then held Malcolm's eye. "Pull that arrow forward, boy, *not back.*"

Malcolm worked as fast as could be expected and made a clean job, but no amount of care could staunch the flow of blood, nor lessen the agony. With dutiful purpose he examined my leg, concluding that rather than clutch the arrow's deadly tip with his bare fingers he would have to force it forward enough to grasp the shaft beneath the arrowhead itself. Malcolm's light touch sent stabbing pain through my leg; sweat streaked the sides of his familiar face, now gone gray as yesterday's ash pile, but he set his jaw as one determined to complete a nefarious, but necessary, task.

He muttered, "I'll do it fast, hold tight, Boyd," and caught my knee in one hand and the broken shaft in the other, driving it forward through the torn muscle. I cried out against the stick between my teeth, tears rolling down my temples as I bent my head against the ground, my throat bowed like the Yankee's from last night. Malcolm issued a moaning gasp, reaching now for the front of the shaft and, inch by agonizing inch, tugging its length free of my leg. I felt I might die before he finished the job.

At last he gasped, "*It's out...*"

He and Cora staunched the flow of hot blood, the little girl rallying her strength and assisting with all the grit of a field nurse. My gut heaved and I lurched to the side, spitting out the stick not a moment too soon. Malcolm bolstered me through the vomiting; he would not stop repeating apologies. I cursed my weakness, vision skittering and blurring, and willed myself to regroup, to understand that the worst of it was over now. My nose but inches from the contents of my innards, I bit back a cry and gasped, "You done... good work."

"We gotta stop this bleeding," Malcolm understood. "I got one of Grady's shirts to use as a bandage." Coldness leached from the ground and into my bones; wetness struck at my face and I realized the sky was shedding bits of ice. Malcolm muttered, "*Goddammit,*" fumbling in his task of tying the make-shift binding about my leg.

This accomplished, he bent to tuck his shoulder beneath my right arm. With considerable effort he hauled me upright; I refused to let my weight burden him as we hobbled at a halting pace. Cora stuck close as Malcolm led the three of us back to the oak, settling beneath its protection; Aces was tethered nearby and whickered at us, exposing his teeth. Malcolm had arranged Grady and Quill as best he could, unable to bury them without the use of shovel or trowel, but taking care to wrap their heads and shoulders in what were surely the remainders of their shirts. I tucked my arms about my brother and the girl, drawing them around the far curve of the tree and away from the sight of the dead, propping my spine against the trunk.

"It's snowing," Cora whispered, pressing close, wilting against my ribs. She reached to touch Malcolm. My brother caught her hand into his and kissed her knuckles, before tipping his face to my shoulder. My arms soon grew numb, trapped between them and the rough bark of the trunk, but their warmth eventually served to still my shaking; both dozed. I rested my jaw against Malcolm's tangled hair and drifted with eyes half-closed, unwilling to watch as the prairie took on a flour-dusted appearance. I felt detached, terror so near the surface that my heart beat too rapidly; I imagined blood pumping out of the wounds inflicted on my leg at the speed of my heart, draining my life. I floated through a haze of pain, the cold and the snowfall bringing to mind the battlefield at Murfreesboro, in January of 'sixty-three...

Riding hard around a ragged column of burning supply wagons, pushing my mount, choking on thick black smoke as I clear the line to see Ethan astride his dapple-gray gelding, Arrow. I'm no more than twenty yards away, closing fast on his position as Ethan swings his rifle like a sword, clutching the barrel, teeth bared in a snarl. I watch him unseat a mounted Federal; the man tumbles from saddle to rocky ground but Ethan has not a second to lose, as another Federal grasps for Arrow's reins.

Coming abreast, sleet slick on my face, I raise my pistol. The Federal lurches sideways as my shot takes him in the left side, falling to his knees in the fray with blood darkening the indigo of his overcoat, felted hat slipping from his head – the first man I ever kill, whose face I can't recall from a hundred others – yet I'll never forget the sight of his hat sliding askew. My first instinct is to reach to help him right it. No more than seconds after that moment Ethan's throat is shot out, from behind; I look up from the fallen soldier and it is the very next thing I see.

Ethan! I bellow. The sound carries over the battle and then echoes in the trees beyond as if Ethan's name is stuck in the low, empty branches.

My uninjured leg jerked.

I opened my eyes to the empty prairie beyond the oak, silent but for the whisper of snowfall; the white flakes sifted onto the river and became part of it, icing its rocky banks. A sickness gripped my bowels, the sense that had I opened my eyes a fraction faster I would have caught a glimpse of Death lurking close by, watching with a fixed and unblinking stare, waiting for us to succumb.

Not yet. I tightened my grip on my brother and Cora; I'd been badly damaged but I would not let Death claim the two of them. Not goddamn yet.

There ain't no hope.

You know this. You ain't half-witted.

We's a week away from any settlement.

No food, no rifle. Aces can't carry the three of you.

You got water an' nothin' else.

You ain't gonna last a night.

I woke sometime later to find Cora wrapped in my arms; the movement of her head dragged me to consciousness. At first I could not make sense of the noises I heard, those of a grunting struggle, and in the attempt to leap to my feet I sent Cora tumbling. Unable to manage standing, I crawled over a crunching layer of snow to the opposite side of the tree to spy Malcolm with a two-handed grip on the hanging rope still dangling from the oak, yanking for all he was worth. A stubborn grimness altered the set of his mouth. He worked with purpose, refusing to acknowledge my presence, winding the bristly length about his palms, tugging with renewed strength. He heaved and grunted; sweat stained his shirt. At last the limb could no longer resist the assault and cracked loose, striking the ground in a violent spray of splintering wood. Without a word, breathing heavily, my brother wound the rope about the broken branch, carried both to the riverbank and heaved the burden into the flowing water.

THERE WAS the matter of food.

We hadn't yet spoken of last night's events; as the murky afternoon advanced, Cora and Malcolm worked together in silence to lay out Quill and

Grady, hauling rocks from the riverbank and covering their bodies, attempting to offer the dead men as much dignity as possible. I remained braced against the oak, now short one of its branches; I wished to help them but I could not stand, despite my stubbornest efforts. I might have rested in the wagon but since the front wheels were smashed the entire thing was pitched at a cockeyed angle; the few remaining supplies within all lay in a pile at the front end, where they had tumbled.

You will die here, I realized. *The two of them'll be hauling stones to cover over your body, right quick.*

Aces High remained tethered near the tree. Of the supplies still in our possession there was little of immediate value to us, stranded as we were – Malcolm's saddle, Quill's throwing knife, two corncakes my brother had stashed for a snack from yesterday's breakfast, a dented tin of milled flour. As I watched Quill and Grady slowly disappear beneath layers of stones, some no bigger than pebbles, I tried for all I was worth to remember when I'd last heard Grady mention a settlement, or our proximity to the fort on the Missouri River. I figured there were other settlers and homesteaders somewhere on this expanse of prairie, but finding them would be similar to searching for a grain of salt in a bucket of sand. I recalled Grady saying the fort was built on the west side of the Missouri; he'd once wintered within its stockade walls.

Due west, Grady had said and it was a start, some small hope to cling to.

Malcolm an' Cora might be able to reach it. We can't be more'n a week's ride. Aces High won't have no trouble carrying the two of them. We's goddamn lucky to have him, there'd be no chance otherwise. You can save them.

There was no sense in resuming our original course, or of attempting to reach Royal Lawson's homestead. Besides having no history with the man, I did not know the exact location of his acreage; I could not send Malcolm across the prairie on what amounted to a wild goose chase, nor would I risk putting him in the potential path of our attackers. The devil alone knew what story Virgil would concoct to justify his lone presence when Lawson expected Grady, or how Virgil would explain the small contingent of men he now traveled with.

I hope they decide you ain't worth the trouble, Turnbull, an' slit your worthless gullet right there along the trail. Goddamn traitor.

I had not asked Malcolm if Virgil was the one to pull the trigger on Grady, and would not; Malcolm would tell me when he was able. I knew

I was a goner – no point in denying the fact – but I wouldn't let Malcolm believe this. I would instead keep up my spirits until he and Cora were safely away. Malcolm would never leave me behind if he thought I would die in the meantime, or if he thought he could save me by staying. But I would make my last act that of saving him, I vowed here and now.

West, I decided. *First thing, by mornin' light. If they ride due west, keeping the river in sight, sure as shooting they'll reach the fort settlement on its banks. Malcolm can get them there. They's sure to find help. I'll tell the boy to find men that'll come back here for me.*

A sudden onslaught of panic struck the bridge of my nose and flooded my limbs from there; I knew I'd be dead when they returned, if any men would even be willing to venture after a stranger. God willing, Cora and the boy could find shelter for the winter at the fort; they were only children, no threat to anyone, and would inspire sympathy. Malcolm would eventually realize his only option was returning to Sawyer and Lorie, and he would be able to make that journey come next spring, I had faith. He was a Carter, and Carters had constitution. Carters were stubborn as hell. But he could not think of returning eastward until next spring, and I must impress this truth upon him.

And then I could not help but wonder if he would leave my body here on the Territory prairie.

Of course he would; necessity would dictate his actions.

He ain't able to haul your carcass back to Iowa or Minnesota. Not today, not next month. He'll bury you here, along with Grady an' Quill, with this goddamn fucking oak tree the only grave marker the three of you will have.

No. Please, no.

Rebecca darlin', oh Jesus, I was coming for you and you'll never know.

I want them to see me one last time. Even in death. I want them to bury me in a place they might all visit.

In the space of a day and night, I'd grown macabre. But far worse than the fear of being laid to rest in the wilds of this place, far from any home or soul I'd ever known, was the thought of witnessing Malcolm, the last of my brothers, ride away from me. I didn't mind dying alone so much as knowing he'd be left without me. He would be the last of the Carters.

He's so young. He ain't ready for this kind of burden, or this responsibility.

Forgive me, Daddy. I pray you'll forgive me.

Maybe I'll be seein' you soon.

I HEARD Malcolm say, "We oughta say a few words, don't you s'pose?"

He and Cora had settled me in the wagon, leveling the damn thing as best they could manage, shifting the remaining tins to one side and arranging the two blankets left in our possession so I was allowed an improvised bed in its confines. The canvas covering bore roughly a dozen bullet holes, star-shaped rends in the fabric; the entire covering flapped on its wooden support bows as the wind increased. The cold was reduced inside the wagon and I demanded that they join me once they'd spoken over Grady and Quill. Evening advanced; the wagon's interior grew dim and blurred. I hurt too much to do a thing but lay my head, fixing my gaze on the arch of canvas directly above. I felt as helpless as a suckling babe. The picture of my body reduced to its bones wouldn't stray from my head.

I heard Cora say, "Grady and Quill were kind to me, and cared for my pa. I loved them. I won't ever forget them, either one."

I imagined Malcolm latching an arm about her waist. He spoke into the silence left behind by Cora's soft words. "Grady Ballard and Quill Dobbs was murdered here in this place. It's an injustice." His voice hardened with a resolve that I was thankful to hear – it was this iron which would get him and Cora to safety. Malcolm vowed, "I aim to find those men. I aim to kill them. I ask forgiveness for being unable to save good men from being kilt before my eyes."

The three of us lay huddled as the wind increased through the night. I was uncomfortable to the point of madness, gritting my teeth, finding no position that did not sear my battered flesh. The flapping canvas became a noise I could not bear; I imagined tearing it from its moorings if only to stop the constant flap. Malcolm had it in his head that by morning's light he would have formed a plan to save the three of us – he spoke of repairing the wagon wheels, of hitching Aces and hauling us to safety. I felt near the end of my ability to reason with him and loathed to fight with the boy on what was our last night in each other's company, whether he knew it or not. Any hope of rest vanished.

"You an' Cora will ride Aces to the fort due west," I said for the hundredth time.

Cora kept silent as Malcolm and I bickered, curled near my hip and appearing asleep, though I knew she lay listening. Malcolm sat facing us, bracing his heels to keep from sliding, no more than a smudged gray outline in the darkness. I felt the strength of his desire to convince me otherwise, to allow him to try to haul me along with the two of them.

"I ain't leaving you behind." No room for argument in his tone, a sound I knew well. But when it came to it, I was eldest. No matter that I could hardly sit upright, let alone walk or make good on any threat to strap his disobedient hide.

"Boy," I warned. My tongue flapped big and dry in my mouth; I needed water. I thought, *What's it matter if you take water, when you's gonna be dead by this time next week?* Knowing I could convince him best by mentioning her, I said, "Cora is your responsibility. You get her to safety an' then, *only* then, you think about comin' back for me, d'you hear me? I'll keep here in the wagon. You leave me with a fire an' water. Y'all ride for the fort on the Missouri. If you don't take Cora an' ride out, all three of us'll die here." He did not at once respond; I sensed my advantage and pressed, "You know I'm right. You get Cora to safety before anything else."

Cora lay tense as a threatened fawn. Malcolm was silent; he remained wordless for so long that at last I barked, "Did you hear me?"

He whispered, "The thought of leaving you behind near kills me, Boyd," and it was the admission of a young boy terrified beyond imagining, hesitant to admit this when he so badly longed for me to view him as a man. He did not want to ride away from me because I was all the security he had in this world. Far as we were from Sawyer and Lorie, from Rebecca, from Jacob and Hannah and any hope of family, in a wild territory not officially part of the United States, I was all he had.

I reached my hand towards him and he clutched tightly, the bones of his fingers still narrow and fragile-seeming in my grip. Malcolm's palm was warm against mine, roughened with calluses, his fingernails so ragged and dirty that Lorie would scold him from here to perdition. I squeezed with my remaining strength. I hated like poison to lie to him, but I said, "I'll be here when you return." I thought of something else. "If Virgil an' them show up at the fort, you pretend you don't know them, you hear? Don't confront the bastards. Hide from them. No one's gonna believe a boy over a group of grown men. I ain't got no reason to think they'll winter at the fort, but just in case. You hear?"

"I hear," Malcolm muttered, wiping errant tears on his shoulder. "I always hear you, Boyd, even when you think I don't, I swear."

"C'mere," I ordered, and he came near, burrowing with great care, resting his temple to my shoulder. I thought of our parents, of Daddy and Mama waiting in the beyond, of the way Mama used to stroke Malcolm's curls, her precious baby she never dreamed of leaving behind. I knew the boy's memories of Daddy and Mama were dear, cherished close to his true heart, but he was only a young'un when they passed; I'd been his sole parent for over three years, since having returned from the War. At his age I'd have shit myself many times over at the thought of being without my kin. For all my youthful blustering and bragging, I'd depended greatly upon my family; if I'd been asked to ride away from the last of them, could I have mustered the strength to do so?

I rested my free hand upon Cora; it was almost as long and wide as her back. A shudder wracked her spine; she was a child lost, flung to the mercy of strangers. If not for this outlandish little girl with her two-colored eyes, who'd found Quill's knife and sawed through my bindings, Malcolm would be dead this night, I had no doubt. She would save Malcolm twofold, I understood; if not for her presence, he would not be convinced to leave me behind. And therefore I owed Cora her own life, in exchange. Malcolm would survive because of her, and I could never be thankful enough for this instance, however unexpected, of grace.

❀

A NEW DAWN loomed on the horizon, casting out the bleak gray of night. The wind's force had died out over the course of the past hour and if I didn't mistake it, this day would shine with a fair sky. I woke, cringing with physical agony, to hear Malcolm outside saddling Aces, speaking to the chestnut in a muted voice. Cora sat straight with a start, elbow jabbing my gut, for which she apologized even as she cast about with her eyes, in search of Malcolm. Perhaps she'd dreamed he left without her, life robbing her of the one bit of happiness she could claim.

"He's just outside," I murmured, and she nodded, scrambling into her shawl, tugging tighter the laces of her battered boots.

"Mr. Boyd, I hate to leave you behind," she whispered, and her gentle fingertips fluttered over my cheeks, two small birds with white wings. She touched me as one laying hands upon a corpse, the way she'd likely touched her daddy before they took him to be buried.

I cast aside this thought and asked quietly, "What did Virgil mean when he said you seen him?"

Her movements stilled as she retreated behind a closing door in her head. Her eyes fixed on a point above my prone body as she was suddenly yanked to a moment in the past she no doubt wished to forget, were such a thing possible. Her hands fell to her sides.

Knowing it was my last chance, I pressed, "What did he mean?"

But she only shook her head.

MALCOLM BUILT a fire on the south side of the broken wagon, using matches from Quill's haversack, which I insisted he and Cora bring with them. Malcolm was not satisfied until he had gathered a substantial pile of kindling and branches, toting these and settling them under the wagon within my reach. He emptied the flour tin and filled it with water; I assured him I could fetch water when it ran dry, though my limbs were slack as empty sails. Sun lifted and stretched across the icy prairie; I prayed it would melt the thin layer of crunching snow for their journey westward. I thought, *Malcolm will get them there, I believe this to be true. The boy will come through.*

"I'm right glad I ain't got no mirror," I said, hoping to coax a smile as Cora arranged one of the two blankets over my lap.

"Are you hurting terribly?" she worried, crouching at my knees. She'd bundled into layers far too large for her slender frame, as had Malcolm, salvaging garments from the wagon. The final layer was her shawl, knotted at the seam of her ribs.

"I ain't," I lied. "Don't you worry, honey."

"Get!" I heard Malcolm holler from the far side of the oak, and he chucked a rock; a buzzard flapped but a few dozen paces before landing once more. Malcolm issued a low growling sound and chucked another rock, aiming for the ugly creature's bald head. My bowels went watery at the sight of buzzards flying in lazy circles just above; it was our misfortune that they hadn't yet flown south for winter. There wasn't a goddamn thing I could do to prevent them from going after Grady and Quill; soon enough, my own flesh would be their dinner.

"Boy!" I called, as panic began to edge aside my will. "You best get to gettin' 'fore you lose any more daylight."

Malcolm came near and stood in silence, his face solemn and set in its lines, as though he was determined not to show weakness – to convince me that he was worthy of this task. But his dark eyes burned with the agony of what was required. He crouched, slow in his movements as an old man, so our faces were on a level. He whispered, "I will return for you, my brother."

I said what I had to say. "Do not press for St. Paul until spring. We are more'n a month gone from there." When Malcolm failed to reply, eyes having clouded as though witnessing a horror visible only to him, I asked more sharply, "Do you hear me?"

He blinked, losing the fixed stare, and nodded with two curt bobs of his chin. Cora kissed my cheek and Malcolm wrapped me in his arms, holding fast, not allowing the tears I could hear in his throat to glide from his eyes. He choked, "*I love you,* Boyd."

"I know," I whispered, and caught his elbow to keep him a moment longer. His face appeared pale and wan, freckles like nutmeg sprinkled over his cheekbones. His eyes were the deep, oaken brown of all the Carter men I'd ever known; Daddy and Uncle Malcolm, Beaumont and Grafton, and my own. Flecks of lighter brown shone through, faint hints of gold. He blinked once, lashes fanning his cheeks. "You's the bravest lad I ever knew, Malcolm. You make me proud."

His lips twisted in what was meant to be a smile but tears streaked his cheeks, sliding through the dirt and grime in shiny tracks. Cora watched him with concern pinching her features.

Thank you, Malcolm tried to say, but could not. He leaned near and pressed his mouth to my forehead for the space of a breath, palms resting on my shoulders.

"Go now," I whispered. "Ride hard. Keep due west. You'll get there."

He nodded and stood, unsteady with distress, with hunger and fatigue. But he reached for Cora's hand and took it securely between both of his. "I'll return for you, I swear to you, Boyd."

Aces High kept still, allowing Cora to mount with Malcolm's help; he settled behind her on the saddle, anchoring her body to his with both arms about her waist. He caught up the reins and kept his eyes from the buzzards. Turning Aces westward, my brother vowed again, "I'll return."

He resettled his hat and then heeled the chestnut into a walk, jaws clenched, bundled into Grady's coat along with his own, appearing twice his size with the extra bulk. I watched them grow ever smaller, until they were no more than a blurry speck; Malcolm looked back three times, longer with each look, until they disappeared over the edge of the horizon.

THE BUZZARDS converged on Grady and Quill, and there wasn't a goddamn fucking thing I could do. I'd sent my brother unarmed into the Territory prairie; the bastards had taken our every armament, and now I sat equally as unprotected. If I had my pistol and a handful of rounds, I could have cleared out the death-eating creatures with their miserable bald heads and hunching wings. I shouted at them and attempted to drag myself upright but could not manage, cursing my unfortified position, the weakness in both voice and limbs.

I was no doc, but had borne witness to uncountable injuries during my time as a soldier, enough to realize that bones in my body were damaged. As the day wore on, sun straying over the pitiful remains of our camp, I was certain I'd a cracked rib or two. The realizing of it did less than no good, did nothing to ease the pain, or my helplessness. I hurt as though beaten with a hefty branch; of being dragged behind the half-breed's horse, I could recall very little, only a series of bumping and blurred images, the nighttime prairie racing past on all sides. I remembered a sense of twisting and turning, of trying to protect my face. The torn-up skin all along my back side suggested I'd spent the majority of the ride in that position.

"Dead, dead, dead," I muttered, referring to the half-breed, as if I was capable of a thing beyond talk. I was the one who'd be *dead, dead, dead* and I fooled myself thinking otherwise.

I sipped water from the dented tin, wishing to God that it was whiskey.

I stared at the crackling fire, wishing I would hurry up and die so I could stop thinking on it.

Some fucking soldier you are.

My leg is bad. It's bad as hell. The binding is already ripe.

It was Fallon following us back in Iowa, all along.

I shoulda figured. A boy seeking revenge for his father. I woulda done the same, I can't deny.

Fallon said his father lost an arm. Malcolm's shot disabled the bastard.

I wish it had killed the son of a bitch.

Did Fallon choose to follow us on his own? Or did Yancy provoke him into taking action?

The thought of what had occurred in Iowa in our absence plagued me anew, now that I knew Fallon Yancy had been the one on our tail, trailing us from Iowa City. Had his father dared to return to there? Sawyer and Tilson were more than capable of protecting the homestead, of protecting the women. But as my terror grew and my hold on the here and now waned, I imagined a hundred different scenes – I saw Yancy attacking in the night as he'd done once before, shooting them all dead and then rousing his eldest son to ride in pursuit of Malcolm and me, to carry out the last of his revenge. I thought hard, fumbling over words, watching the fire eat up the pile of oak branches, keeping the cold at bay only so long. Fallon had said to Malcolm that his father was in disgrace; he'd lost his arm on account of the shot. This meant Yancy had been in contact with his sons, who'd been…

I struggled to recall.

Staying with the Rawleys, I remembered.

For a time my eyes sank shut, against my better judgment. I drifted through a hazy mishmash of wavering images, as if I stood looking at a reflection on the surface of a windy pond. I heard Rebecca calling for me when I knew damn well this weren't possible.

Boyd! Urgency rang in her sweet, familiar voice. *Boyd Carter! Where are you? Tell me where you are!*

I'm here, darlin'. But my response was nothing more than a sigh of wind.

Feathers brushed my cheeks. I thought Malcolm had returned and jerked awake, ready to lit into him for disobeying, startled at the press of darkness against my face; fool that I was, I'd slept and let the fire burn low. It was nigh on evening, the prairie cold as a tomb. No more than a few strides distant, the flock of buzzards appeared a solid mass of blackness; no amount of rocks could keep the critters from their obscene feast. I was no stranger to birds of death, carrion-eaters; battlefield creatures. And then I yelped, thrashing at the one that had strayed near me and my low-burning fire. It lifted its wings in a menacing hunker and shuffled away mere steps. I leaned, fetching a branch from the kindling pile and taking a swipe at the loathsome thing. But I was weak as a newborn foal; even a bird didn't fear me.

"Get!" I muttered.

I built up the fire, knowing I needed to gather more wood before morning. I had no food and had not felt the need to make water all through the day, which meant I'd not been taking enough. The dented tin held about a dipper's worth of river water. I attempted to maneuver into a crouch, intending to fetch a drink, and immediately stumbled, unable to bear my own weight. The pain in my leg was intolerable; I was no squeamish boy never before hurt but this was as agonizing a wound as I'd ever sustained. I gritted my teeth, slowly bending my knee and twisting my leg to expose the raw gashes to the fire's light; I sucked a sharp breath to spy the festering. The entry point appeared the worst, red and ugly, oozing like a rabid critter's mouth, a sight that would have spurred a field doc to swipe at his sweating forehead, curse, and take up his bone saw.

Take it off, I heard someone behind me mutter. In the distance was the sound of a regiment settling in for the night, men murmuring, the clanking of tin cups, here and there a low laugh and the notes of a harmonica. The field doc insisted, *Gotta come off or you'll lose the leg, son.*

This here'll make an even thirty for the day, sir, the doc's assistant said, spitting a neat stream of tobacco. He nodded and offered me a grin, teeth smeared with brown juice. *I been keepin' a tally.*

I reached for my pistol before recalling it wasn't strapped on my hip as usual.

You ain't taking my leg. You'll have to kill me, first.

Suit yourself, soldier, the doc said, wiping his hands on a length of red-streaked toweling as he walked away, his assistant trailing like a favored dog. No more than a few steps later their outlines blurred and became part of the darkness. I squinted, straining to see where they'd gone.

After a time the pain was so bad the only way I could figure lessening it was to sing to the tune of my fiddle. Cracked, I'd become. Tetched as the old woman from Suttonville who sat on her porch smoking her corncob pipe all the livelong day, anchoring it with the stubs of her remaining teeth; we'd called her a witch, though never in our folks' hearing, and sure as hell never in hers. She'd have cursed us stone-dead we believed back then; slumped here in the Territory before a sputtering fire I wondered if perhaps the old witch had cursed us after all, my brothers and me, mayhap the entire Carter family. Likely she'd heard Beau or me snicker as we walked past her ramshackle porch, swinging the saplings we'd whittled for fishing. She'd muttered, *Alone an' in pain, that's how you's gonna die, young Carter.*

Is this my time of dying?

I always figured I'd know it.

Please God, give me the grace to bear it, if this is my time of dying.

Hymns rolled from my tongue as if no time had passed since standing near my brothers in the Suttonville church, Reverend Wheeler leading the singing. I truly believed I was playing my fiddle; my bowing arm kept smooth pace with the singing. The kindling ran out and the pain in my leg overtook all else. My awareness grew muddled. My hands seemed to swell before my eyes, fingers bloating like the exposed guts of a dead horse, cumbersome and useless; I could not grasp hold of the water tin. My bad leg went next, growing round and full as a tree trunk, heavy as Howitzer shot; I watched through a threadbare red cloak as it seemed to expand to twice the size of my other leg. I played songs of Christmastide. I spoke to my mama, begging her for a taste of water. Nearby, whiskey gurgled from a bottle as Daddy poured a glass and raised it to his nose, inhaling the fumes with heartfelt appreciation.

I need to lie down, I told my folks. *Let me rest by the hearth. I ain't been rested in so long.*

I lay on my side and the smolder of dying embers was but inches from my face. The beating of my blood seemed centered not in my chest but instead my leg; every breath was an agony. I closed my eyes and drifted. I thought I was walking, and after a spell I came to the mouth of the small cave in the holler of my youth, the one we'd played in as boys, the selfsame place where Sawyer once lost his boot. I blinked, feeling the damp chill of the familiar cave reach out and crawl wetly along my skin. I put my right hand on the edge of the opening, the rock face rough, crumbling into little grains against my palm. It was late afternoon by now – *or maybe it's tomorrow, or maybe the day after that, I ain't sure no more* – the heavens murky with clouds and the air humid; cold sweat greased my spine. Farther inside the cave, where there should have been nothing but darkness, I caught sight of a patch of light. An opening, deep in there where I knew there wasn't one. I squinted, wondering at it; I took a step inside.

No!

I hesitated at this cry, the single word resounding between my ears. The patch seemed brighter than before, and I was right curious.

Where does it lead? Why's there light back there?

I took another two steps and stood fully inside the cave.

Boyd!

Boyd Carter!

Her voice was behind me, out in the holler, and at this sharp summoning, the desperation in her tone, I knew at once I should proceed no further in the direction of that strange light. I ran my hands over the rock face on either side. *But what is it…there shouldn't be light back there…it's kinda pretty…*

Boyd Brandon Carter! You wake up, do you hear me?

Wake up!

Wake up this very minute!

I jerked to awareness, abruptly returned to the October dusk on the Territory prairie, and the fullness of pain. A sickly fear rolled across my gut.

Where in the hell had I been? My heart slammed a frightened rhythm. Rebecca's voice had been so close I expected her to be kneeling alongside me; of course she wasn't, and bitter disappointment sank its teeth.

You ain't ever gonna see her again, not if you don't get your ass up. Get up right now, you hear me? G'on now!

I can't get up. I ain't got the strength. It hurts too goddamn much.

Boyd! Rebecca's voice was in my ear, unrelenting as a buzzing hornet; I understood it was nothing more than the depth of my longing for her creating this sense that she spoke to me now, but I welcomed it. If I'd lost my mind, at least she was here with me in the losing of it. She poked my shoulder with an extended finger, persisting, *Get up, build up that fire! You shall freeze!*

There ain't no more kindling. My voice was petulant as a little boy's.

The wagon, she pressed, now shaking my shoulder as my eyes tried to close. *The wagon is made of wood. Do you hear me?*

It began to snow.

T HIS NIGHT THE sun had set upon the last day of 1868.

Boyd and Malcolm had been missing for months and we could hardly bear the daily strain, poised now on the precipice of a new year, which should have allowed for unparalleled celebration, the promise of a fulfilling set of months to come – and yet we would continue to shoulder the burden of the unknown, as this granted a certain reprieve, a chance to hope that word of their survival would still reach us.

"1868 has been a year of change," Tilson said earlier, at this evening's dinner table, directing at each of us in turn his somber gaze, stern in its desire to convey the sincerity of his words. He continued, "Let us believe 1869 will bring good news."

Tilson was correct in his statement, as 1868 proved a year of significant change for the country; November beheld the country's first presidential election since Reunification. General Ulysses Grant would now preside as the nation's leader, come his formal inauguration in March, three months from this bitter-cold December night on the last day of the old year. Back in July, Secretary of State Seward announced the Fourteenth Amendment ratified, granting citizenship to former slaves, while Congress declared the formation of Wyoming Territory. Word reached us most often in the form of newspaper articles; thusly, we had learned of the large earthquake which struck the state of California in October, and of the fierce fighting between General Custer and the Indian people in the Territories south of Kansas.

And but a week ago, on Christmas Day, President Johnson, despite apparent bitter opposition, had granted unconditional pardon to all persons involved in the Southern Rebellion.

"Our first Christmas together," Sawyer had whispered that night, as we curled together atop our feather tick clad in flannel nightclothes; the chill weather did not allow for a continuation of sleeping skin to skin. Sawyer was warm as the woodstove, his arms anchoring me to all that was good and true in the world; more than ever, the two of us had relied upon each other in these past dark months. We were together, and safe, and for that the both of us remained steadfastly grateful. I could not ask for more than the gift of my husband, the abundant reassurance of his presence, his kindness and gentle humor, however muted now that our worry flowed so close to the surface. I recognized I could bear any agony so long as Sawyer remained at my side. Wrapped together in our shanty cabin as Christmas Day faded to deepest night, Sawyer's hands formed a perfectly-molded cup about the swelling curve of our growing child.

At his quiet observation, warm tears streaked along the bridge of my nose. Unable to answer, I fit my hands over his; in the past few weeks, the child had begun moving within me, pressing outward with tiny hands and knees, elbows and feet, allowing for moments of irreplaceable joy. Sawyer was fond of pressing his lips to the small hills thusly created by our child's movements, speaking to her with his mouth upon my bare skin in the singular privacy of our cabin, firelight streaking over us, his profile casting shadows across my belly. I had dreamed of the child on more than one occasion, and though would not be proven correct until the day of her birth, believed her to be a girl.

"*Mo mhuirnín milis,*" Sawyer whispered, cradling us, our child and me, in the protection of his arms. "There will be word, I believe this." As was his habit each night, the words now imbued with the quality of a ritual, he said, "They are alive."

I nodded my unfailing agreement, turning so I was able to rest my nose to his neck, inhaling his familiar scent until I felt capable of speech. I whispered, "Yes."

The land office in St. Paul yielded no answers; Boyd had not filed for a homestead claim in either his own, Malcolm's, or Sawyer's name, leaving us no proof that they had ever reached the town. As unfathomable though it may be, all evidence we possessed suggested they had disappeared somewhere between Iowa City and St. Paul. Upon another visit in early November, Charley Rawley relayed to us that no sign of Fallon or his father had been discovered, either.

"I believe Thomas to be in hiding," Charley said on that visit. "Fannie and I surmise Fallon found him and the two of them have holed up together, awaiting God only knows what circumstance for reappearance. The marshal's office has no information, and I trust they would not attempt to keep news of relevance from me, in light of the situation at hand."

"Do you believe Fallon capable of pursuing Boyd and Malcolm over a significant distance?" Sawyer asked; we'd related to Charley our suspicions concerning the notion. "That the boy might take it upon himself to enact what he perceived as revenge?"

"Fallon is an uncommon child, far more ambitious than Dredd," Charley allowed. "As a father of five sons, I could well imagine any one of them daring to take action in my stead, as much as I would disapprove of such a bold and dangerous endeavor. It would depend upon whether young Malcolm's shot struck Yancy that night."

"Yancy was not kilt, much as I would wish otherwise," Tilson said, speaking around his pipe stem. "And since he wasn't kilt, we must suppose he was injured, perhaps grievously. A wound significant enough to keep him from public sight and to perhaps spur his eldest into some sort of action. Goddamn this mess."

"I've long since wired the telegraph office in St. Paul with Fallon's description," Charley said. "Though, the boy is unremarkable in looks, resembling a hundred other fellows his age. Unless he creates some sort of disturbance, or draws attention to himself, likely no one would take especial notice of him."

Bound to Iowa City for the time being, we chafed at the lack of action which could be taken in our present circumstances, the shortage of available resources. My mind became a breeding ground for terrible thoughts – those of Boyd and Malcolm pursued by a loathsome father and his frightening son, Fallon of the empty eyes – dispelled only by proximity to Sawyer and his capability of offering comfort. Jacob Miller's correspondence grew increasingly urgent, the last letter with a promise to ride south come spring thaw, to search for his nephews until they were found. His letters, however, ceased with the advance of winter, another maddening necessity. I found myself damning the snow and its subsequent instigating of trouble; additional nightmarish thoughts circled, of Malcolm and Boyd caught in a blizzard, ice and snow burying their bodies as effectively as any gravedigger, perhaps never to be discovered…

Such pictures plagued all of us. Though I could have wept every tear from my body, I restrained this weakness; at times, even so, the weeping came upon me without consent. Riding home from a stillbirth during early December, Tilson at my side, I'd given way to sobs with the suddenness of a gust of winter wind; Tilson remained unperturbed, simply drawing me to his side so that I might be allowed the comfort of his shoulder. I'd curled my fingers into the rough hair on the buffalo hide covering our laps that bleak afternoon, weeping abjectly, the sky overcast with a flat, unrelieved gray, unwilling to give a hint as to the actual time of day. If not for the darkening air, it might have been midmorning.

"Let it out," was all Tilson said, three or perhaps four times, planting a kiss on the top of my head.

"I can't..." I gasped, in a broken refrain. The stiff canvas of Tilson's jacket grew slick with my tears but he paid no heed, nor did he ask for clarification of what I believed I could not do.

"You can," he finally murmured, easing back and withdrawing his arm from my shoulders, resuming a two-hand grip on the reins. His Tennessee drawl further served to offer me reassurance, as it brought to mind a faint echo of my daddy's voice. He insisted, "You more than *can*, Lorie."

I scrubbed at my wet face, chilled by the December air. I hissed, "*I despise this goddamned cold weather.*"

Tilson drew the lap blanket more securely about us, flicking a light rein over Pete's gray hide; the sturdy mule obediently increased our pace, the flat-bed rumbling over the road from town. Fixing my gaze straight ahead, I saw not the grim colorlessness of the late-autumn prairie but instead Malcolm's dear face, his earnest eyes and overgrown hair, the way he burrowed into my embrace and held fast. I beheld Boyd's countenance next, observed the stubborn set of his shoulders and chin, the kindness in his dark eyes and how they lit with the joy of teasing or telling a tale, of drawing forth music from his fiddle. And then I saw again the ashen, immobile features of the dead child pushed from its mother's womb, the small, stiff boy warmed only from his passage through her body, already growing cold in Tilson's hands. The mother's wailing cry wrapped around my heart as would a binding of steel bands; I knew I would never drive it fully from my memory. The boy would have been her third child.

"It ain't any easier than the first stillbirth I witnessed. I wish I could tell you it was," Tilson said at last, maintaining honesty with me, for which I found room to be grateful. He did not spare my feelings when it came to my training, pointing out missteps with all the stringency of the sternest school-master; I would have been offended if he attempted to treat me with delicacy. His high expectations spoke of his respect for my capability. He sighed. "It's the worst lesson to be learned at the birthing bed, honey, that of dealing with the loss of the infant, or its mother."

"She was…so sad," I choked out, pressing my knuckles to my lips to hold back a sob. "How can she…bear it?"

Tilson remained silent for a time, gathering his thoughts. Finally he asked, "How do you bear the sadnesses you've encountered?"

I'd not expected him to counter my question, which had been rhetorical, with a query of his own. As he'd intended, the consideration of an answer staved off my tears and allowed my troubled mind a new path of thought. I felt my eyelids sink shut as I whispered, "There were many times when I did not want to bear my sadness a single breath longer, and would have died to end the pain of being alone."

Tilson waited, patient and somber, without further prompting.

I opened my eyes to the ashen light of stark afternoon. "But of course I did not take my life. It was only a desperate fantasy. I was so young, and had no context for suffering. And then came the War. And…Ginny's."

With a note of gentle chiding, Tilson murmured, "You are young yet, Lorie."

"I lost a child." A soft exhalation of breath accompanied the words. The admission flowed forth from deep inside my heart, the urge to speak and thereby perhaps cast out the lingering horror of miscarriage, both my own and the one from which we'd only just come; if I remained silent, the memory would take root. I was no fool ignorant to the realities of childbirth; hadn't I witnessed an expectant mother die before my eyes, my sweet Deirdre passing from life in the upper hallway of Ginny Hossiter's whorehouse? I'd bled out on the Missouri prairie in the confines of Sam Rainey's dirty tent, my body releasing the child Gus had perhaps planted within me the night we met, in my room in St. Louis. The guilt over this had indeed lessened its grip upon my soul with the passage of time but would never completely take its leave. I admitted, "I was not so far along as Mrs. McGiver. There was no body to speak of, only blood."

Tilson was unflappable, and I loved him for it; besides Sawyer, I could conceive of speaking to no other man of these things. But Tilson shared his vast collection of knowledge with me, passed along his medical expertise, trusting me with the care and administration of these techniques as he would any apprentice demonstrating a talent for the trade. I confided in him because I understood he would refrain from judgment. He would only listen. He knew I'd worked as a whore, he knew what I'd been, and yet he did not allow these truths to color his opinion of me. In his eyes, I was worthy. Despite the negative opinion harbored not-so-secretly amongst many of the town's members, I no longer believed myself disreputable; Tilson and Rebecca, and their unfailing support, were in no small way responsible for this.

"Sawyer has spoken of it," Tilson acknowledged, with quiet dignity. "I am frightful sorry this afternoon has spurred ugly memories, honey."

"I would not make much of a midwife if I allowed memories to override my sensibilities." I had regained control, suddenly concerned he would prevent me from further attendance at birthings.

Reading my thoughts, Tilson mused, "I oughtn't to bring you, for the time being. I know you for a fine, brave woman, Lorie, but you's in a family way. You must consider that."

"Please," I implored. "Don't leave me behind. I am able to handle it, I promise you."

Tilson said, "I know you can. Don't mean you *should*."

Fearful of losing the battle, I changed tactics. "What do you believe caused it?"

"The babe appeared hale, an' whole, an' she carried to term," Tilson said. "Sometimes there's a distinct deformity to the child, or the birthing rope wraps about the babe's neck. At times, like this one, there ain't a certain cause." He tucked my elbow closer to his side. "There ain't any reason to figure there's danger to your child, honey. None a'tall."

"You asked Mrs. McGiver if she'd felt the child in the past week," I remembered, shielding my belly at the mere mention of trouble. Beneath the layered garments protecting me from the cold, I formed a protective bulwark with my forearm. Despite the bite of the wind and the falling temperature, which decreased nightly, there had been little significant snowfall over Iowa City and its surrounding farms. Still, I tugged at the woolen scarf looped about my neck, drawing it over my chin, trapping the warm, repetitive clouds of my breath.

"She hadn't felt him stir, which tells me that the babe likely succumbed in the past week. It's a sadness all too common, I'm afraid. Ain't much worse for a doc to witness, unless the mama herself dies along with the child. But Grace McGiver will have plenty more children, you'll see. She's birthed two healthy young'uns afore now."

"These truths provide no comfort to her this day," I said, unduly contrary.

"That's so," Tilson acknowledged. "But I know her husband for a good man. He'll pull her through. Besides, her little ones need her attention, grief or no."

I murmured, "You're right, of course."

I thought of Rebecca's sons, Cort and Nathaniel, their boyish chatter a necessary and perhaps even welcome distraction, one which forced Rebecca to focus upon the daily tasks of washing and mending, cooking and cleaning. I helped her with these chores, offering what solace I was able, but her eyes could not lie; no matter how cheerful her tone when addressing her sons, no matter how capably she attended to the household, the expression in her eyes destroyed me. I wanted so badly to ease her misery, knowing nothing less than word of Boyd and Malcolm could.

I'd found her in the barn one evening shortly after the arrival of Jacob's letter in October, within the stall in which Boyd had stabled Fortune last summer, which she favored when seeking a moment to grieve, her skirts billowing as she sat on the bare floorboards. I joined her without a word, easing to a seat with great care; Rebecca reached a hand to assist me, the other holding fast to a page torn from her ledger, one upon which Boyd had begun a letter, last July, but had not finished.

"I've told Leverett I shall not be able to marry him," she said without preamble. Strands of hair slipped from her topknot, curving to the collar of her blouse, its top pearl button unfastened. Her eyes bore the unmistakable signs of unrelieved weeping, her nose red, and I wished I'd been considerate enough to bring her a handkerchief. She whispered, "You shall think I've taken leave of my senses. Lev surely believes this."

I shook my head, squeezing her slim fingers. "You know I do not believe you've lost your senses."

"I care deeply for Leverett, I shall not deny," she said, punishing herself with the words. "I understand he should make an ideal husband. I am foolish to cast aside the proposal of a fine, decent man, and one who loves me, this I am also unable to deny." Her eyes held fast to mine, strong with conviction. "But the arrival of Jacob's letter has made me realize, more completely than ever, that I should be living a lie were I to take Leverett as my husband. I would never forgive myself if I did not attempt to find Boyd Carter in this life, and tell him that I love him."

"Oh, my dearest," I whispered, touched beyond measure. My heart beat in gladness even as tears inundated my vision, blurring the sight of my dear friend; I could not help but hope this meant she would accompany us to Minnesota in the spring. I asked, "What did you tell the marshal?" and only dared to ask because I trusted Rebecca implicitly, as she did me; we spoke honestly to one another. She was one of a very few people to whom I'd confessed scraps of my darkest memories; in turn, she kept nothing of her feelings hidden from me.

"I believed Lev deserved the truth, as anything less would serve to insult his dignity," she said, her voice rough with strain. "Though, he had guessed. Instead of speaking harshly to me, or behaving in an accusatory manner, Lev remained a gentleman. He said only, 'I am stunned, Becky, but if this fellow Carter is your choice then I have no more say in the matter.'"

"Oh, *Becky*..."

"Please, do not offer pity, as I do not deserve it. I have offended the heart of a good man. Lev rode from here and he shall not return. I have not gathered courage enough to ask after him, and have been waiting for Clint or Uncle Edward to relay to me any news."

"I am so sorry you are hurting, dearest."

"We are all hurting," she whispered, and held Boyd's unfinished letter to her lips.

"There will be word," I said, attempting to simultaneously convince myself. "There will be word from them, I believe this. It brings me comfort to think of them together."

Rebecca nodded agreement, stroking her fingertips over the writing on the abandoned letter, Boyd's scrawling penmanship that resembled nothing so much as chicken-scratching; I had no difficulty picturing Boyd as a reluctant young pupil, casting his mischievous gaze about the Suttonville schoolroom in hopes of rousing a bit of excitement during the otherwise long, dry hours of endless lessons. He'd related many a tale of strappings meted out by exasperated instructors.

"I wish he'd signed his name, if only so that I might touch it." And then she read aloud a line, so softly her voice emerged as scarcely more than a whisper. "'A woman name of Rebecca Krage has allowed us a bed in her homestead.'" Her eyes blazed into mine, fresh tears tracking her cheeks as she confessed, "If Boyd was here this night, I would take him to my bed and everything else be damned. I longed so for him last summer, to the depths of my soul I longed for him, in spite of all the reasons I knew it was improper. I have existed as a proper woman all of my life, Lorie, and yet I would cast all of that aside, forever, for him to be returned to me." She pressed the letter to her breasts, then bent her head.

I was quick to say, "I am not shocked. If you feared I would be, please do not harbor the notion another moment." Rebecca looked up and understanding flowed anew between us; I touched her arm as I admitted, "No doubt a 'proper' lady would be scandalized. Surely my mama would never have confessed such desires, certainly not in the drawing room, but I am not my mama."

"Nor mine," Rebecca whispered, and a ghost of a smile touched her mouth. "Perhaps a stall in the barn is a more suitable location for speaking of desire." We sat encased in the dim glow of a single lantern Rebecca had hung on the iron hook above the stall. To either side of us, horses stomped and whickered, jaws grinding over their nightly hay. The milking cow issued a low bellow then fell to chewing. The stable smelled familiar and stirred feelings of security within my heart, as always. Further, it seemed a fitting spot for hushed confidences.

Rebecca continued, "I longed for Elijah before we wed, though I was brought up to understand such longings were unseemly and so attempted to quell them. I would never have contemplated speaking them aloud, not to anyone. The first night Elijah and I spent as husband and wife the two of us were so awkward and uncertain, green as sapling leaves." She issued a soft exhalation, partly laughter, partly a sigh. "It is such a gift to speak to you of these matters, and know you shall not be startled."

"You may tell me anything you wish," I said, not for the first time.

"And I would wish the same, for you," Rebecca replied. "You, dear Lorie, are the first woman with whom I have ever been able to speak freely, and the relief of this is immeasurable."

"Thank you," I whispered, and prompted, "What of your wedding night?"

"We learned together. Elijah was unfailingly gentle, considerate to his core. I loved him very much, as he loved me, but he and I shared not the depth of ease I witness between you and Sawyer." She drew a fortifying breath. "Before I met Boyd, I never imagined myself capable of falling so suddenly, so deeply, in love, falling without a hint of warning or notion of the inherent danger. The agony of it is almost unbearable, as a knife protruding from my heart. I am reasonable enough to recognize Leverett as the better choice, all around. Boyd is incorrigible and rash. He is stubborn, and immutable in his manners. And yet, I have no control over my feelings for him. They have overtaken me as surely as would a current in a springtime river."

"That is the way of it, sometimes," I whispered, clutching her free hand in mine. The heat of her was almost shocking; speaking of Boyd raised the temperature of her entire being.

"I miss him so dreadfully. The house echoes without his voice, without the physical *presence* of him." She heaved with a sharp gasp, as though stabbed between two ribs. "Oh, Lorie...what if..."

"We will find them," I vowed, interrupting. "There is a reasonable explanation for their absence. I do not, *I swear to you*, believe them dead. The waiting is dreadful, I'll not deny, but we'll find them and you will tell Boyd of your feelings, dear Becky."

"I despise waiting." Her sweet voice emerged as a growl. "Come spring, Lorie, if there has been no word, I shall wait no longer."

And I harbored no doubts of her sincerity; given what I knew of Rebecca Krage, a fine, strong woman, and the truest friend I could imagine, I expected nothing less.

THE FIRE was banked for the evening hours, Cort and Nathaniel retired to their loft bed. In light of what would have been a celebratory dinner, given the arrival of the newest year, Sawyer and I lingered in the main house after dinner, joined at the hearth by Tilson and Rebecca. I sat near Rebecca in one of two rocking chairs, a length of fine, spun wool stretched across our laps; there was always work to be done, even while stationary, and Rebecca was attempting to instruct me in the art of knitting, for which I possessed a shameful lack of skill. She proved unfailingly patient, guiding my fingers over the needles when required, exclaiming over the smallest of achievements.

Tilson smoked his pipe, chatting quietly with Sawyer, who'd not yet taken up a pipe of his own despite Tilson's continual insistence that smoking was an inevitable consequence of advancing age.

"I've only advanced to a quarter-century," Sawyer had joked the night of his twenty-fifth birthday, November the eighth. "Perhaps when I've advanced closer to the half-century mark."

"Son, that's a slight at my age, ain't it?" Tilson had fired back, jabbing at Sawyer's shoulder with the stem of his pipe. "I ain't a day over a half of a century. Well, mayhap more'n a day."

This cold night, snow having fallen steadily for the past twenty-four hours, we were reluctant to retire, remaining guarded, fearful to welcome 1869, or to dare to hope it might bring about any news – good or otherwise. The rocking chairs issued a creaking rhythm against the floorboards. The fire snapped, releasing a shower of crimson-hearted sparks. Tilson's pipe tobacco smelled pleasant, combining with the scent of dinner, biscuits and smoked pork laden with gravy. Tin cups of mulled cider for Rebecca, Sawyer, and me, while Tilson contented himself with two fingers' worth of whiskey. Despite the lull of the warm room, a restless knot near my heart worried itself ever tighter, a sensation not unfamiliar; many hours had I lay awake, stretching outward with my mind, attempting to find them.

Malcolm, I'd begged, to no avail. I could not reach him as I could Sawyer. Even still, I cried the boy's name night after night, pleading with him to re-spond. *Sweetheart, answer me. Where are you? What has happened? I know you are out there, this I will never cease to believe.*

My gaze flickered to the candles Rebecca had placed in the windowsills this night, following a custom long ago established by her mother, a way in which to tangibly welcome the incoming year as it arrived with the midnight hour. The small bright flames appeared doubled by their reflection in the panes, swaying with the breath of the air. A wreath of pine boughs hung on a nail driven into the door, which Rebecca had helped the boys to construct, attaching the slim boughs to wire she'd curved into a circle roughly a foot in diameter. At the top, she'd affixed a length of red grosgrain, a proper Christ-mas wreath to spice the house with its green scent.

The baby kicked at my belly as if delivering a message; she was prone to bouts of activity this time of evening, as though the slowing of my daily movements sparked a yearning to roll about. I often envisioned her as a tiny, precious fish, playful and gorgeously tinted, swimming about the confines of my womb. I set aside the knitting needles and rested both hands upon the commotion.

"She hears your voice," I said to Sawyer, who grinned and leaned to add his touch to mine.

"And yours," he said.

"Have you settled upon a name for the little lady?" Tilson asked. He knew we anticipated a girl; at the top of our list of possibilities were both Ellen and Felicity, in honor of our mothers.

"I would name her for you," Sawyer had said the first night I'd dreamed of holding our daughter to my breast. "I would name her Lorissa."

"I'd like her to have a name of her own," I'd responded. "Besides, if we shared one there may be confusion."

"I'd call her my little Lorie-love, as so to alleviate any confusion," Sawyer had explained.

Now, at the hearth, Sawyer gathered my fingertips into his and brought my hand to his lips, bestowing a kiss upon my knuckles. He explained to Tilson and Rebecca, "Lorie has determined it stands to reason that we first see her before choosing a name."

I cupped my husband's jaw, love for him as visible upon my face as nose or eyes, but I did not mind anyone's observation of this. It was no secret. I thought of those nights on the trail from St. Louis, the two of us running through the darkness to steal a moment away from the wagon and our camp, and therefore allowed blessed time alone together. And, with sudden and unrestrained urgency, I wanted him between my legs and held deeply in my body – my body made full with his seed, the evidence of our love growing daily. Because Sawyer's access to my thoughts, not to mention his ability to simply read my face, was so very strong, I saw the trace of brief surprise lift his brows; I'd been ill with both morning sickness and unrelieved worry for weeks now, and we'd not made love beyond holding one another close. A hint of his old, half-wicked grin lit his eye and lifted one corner of his lips.

"A reasonable determination," Tilson was saying, tamping the bowl of his pipe, and I refrained from a bout of nervous coughing, cheeks ablaze at the unreserved heat of my thoughts.

With no words, Sawyer asked, *How quickly might we excuse ourselves?*

At once, I ordered.

The door to our shanty had scarcely closed before I tore the clothing from his body, from my own, need rising within me as hissing steam from a boiling kettle, ready to explode with the force of its increasing pressure. In the orange light cast by our brazier, aglow with embers, hampered not by the trousers about his ankles, Sawyer took me to the bedding. There he spread my lips, both upper and lower, claiming my mouth, gliding to the root with the first stroke, issuing a hoarse, groaning cry as my body swallowed whole his engorged length.

I clamped my legs about his waist, blood flowing hot and feverish, the fear we'd been crushed beneath these past months subsequently bursting to fragments. I realized it would return to strangle us the moment we ceased to make love and gripped his head, angling to take deeper his questing tongue, his taste, the immediacy and necessity of him. Hungry kisses, the need for satiation, to consume one another and blot out all else in the world – no words, no sense of our earthly names for those moments – we existed as *us*, requiring nothing more.

Later, short of breath, sweat sleek along my ribs and between my breasts, gliding down Sawyer's temples and over the planes of his chest, we fell still. I lay flat upon our feather tick, ankles latched low on his spine; Sawyer's booted feet remained upon the floor as he bent over me, underskirt bunched about my hipbones, blouse crumpled beneath my elbows. My breasts appeared rounder and fuller than I'd ever beheld them; they seemed to expand a little each day, just as did my midsection.

"Lorie-love," he worshiped in a husky murmur, bending to lick the salty dampness from the hollow between my collarbones. "I could eat and drink of you and need no other sustenance, all the days of my life," and so saying, tasted my nipples, which shone with a tint as of port wine, taking me lushly between his lips, caressing with his tongue until I could not catch what little breath I retained. I slipped the eyepatch from his face, tossing it to the side, grasping fistfuls of his golden hair, feeling him again grow as hard as a split-rail fence post, still engulfed within me.

"*Yes*," I gasped as he flowed into steady motion, overcome as the rhythmic tightening I'd never known before Sawyer rendered the rest of my body motionless.

"My Lorie, *mo ghrá*," he groaned, taking my lower lip between his teeth, shuddering with the impact of release. Pressing soft kisses to my jaw, he whispered, "I would see you happy again, darlin', and cast out the worry from your eyes."

"Shhh," I soothed, caressing his hair. He rested his forehead to mine and we studied one another at close range. "I am happy, beneath everything, I promise you, my love. I long to see the strain lifted from you as well. Oh, *Sawyer...*"

"As soon as we are able, we'll resume our original course," he said, quietly adamant. "It is the immobility that is hardest to bear, being confined, however reasonably, to this place when the both of us long to continue onward. But I do not regret the decision to remain here for these winter months, Lorie-love, I would that you know this. Never would I consider bringing you through perilous weather."

"Spring thaw," I whispered. "We will make ready to travel by spring thaw."

"I would see our daughter safely delivered here, in this place."

"Rebecca and the boys will accompany us, she and I have spoken of it." With growing determination, I pressed, "I am healthy and strong, and there is no need to delay once the season for snow has passed. There is no reason I cannot –" But the familiar and unresolved argument was cut short as Sawyer's expression changed; he lifted his head as though responding to a call only he could hear, brows drawing inward.

"Rider," he said, and the faint sounds of an approaching horse met my ears in the next instant.

"Clemens?" I speculated, and a burst of fear expanded like buckshot in my center; Clemens would only be arriving so late in the night hours if there was trouble.

"I'll see what this is about," Sawyer said, hurrying into his trousers, tugging his suspenders over both shoulders, helping me into my own garments with gentle efficiency, both of us listening as a cantering horse neared. He bent to kiss me, murmuring, "I'll return directly, Lorie-love."

I fetched my shawl, draped over the back of the rocking chair near the brazier, wrapping into its warmth as Sawyer disappeared outside, wishing to be at his side but reluctant to venture into the cold night only half-dressed. Sawyer had not collected his outer garments or his eyepatch, and I gathered these from the floor – where they'd fallen or been flung in our haste to make love only an hour before – moving next to the door, attempting to derive sense from the low rumble of male voices speaking in the dooryard. A sudden burst of wind broke itself in twain around the sides of the shanty; though I could not see it through the canvas over our lone window, I envisioned the resultant chaos of falling snow swirling about my husband and the horse and rider with whom he now spoke. I thought I could discern Tilson's voice as well. My heart beat a tense and rapid refrain as I waited.

How I despise waiting, Rebecca had said. And how well I agreed. Waiting was a loathsome task, seeming the lot of womenfolk. We waited at our hearths while men left home to fight and to roam, waiting until the agony of both our imaginations and the dreadful unknown became powerful enough to peel the skin from our very bones. Until we could bear no more the increasing darkness of our thoughts, the subsequent helplessness in the face of not knowing. Left behind, abandoned to this fate unless we chose to act. I drew a slow, calming breath through my nose, as Tilson had taught me, and thought, *No more. I will wait no more. Sawyer can be convinced. We will not be kept from venturing to Minnesota, from finding Malcolm and Boyd, and completing our journey.*

I placed my palms upon the swelling of my daughter; the babe responded by returning the pressure, as though privy to the restless resolve of my thoughts. Perhaps it was foolhardy, the result of desperation, but I felt her strength inside of me in that moment, the tremendous vitality of her, and knew in my deepest heart that she would be born far from where I now stood. She would survive; her heart would beat and relay through her body blood of mine, and of Sawyer's, and she would live long past either of us, carrying forth our heritage for many subsequent generations of the Davis family.

My daughter, my precious baby, I thought, communing with her, however implausible others might find the notion – but then, was not the connection forged between her father and me of the same nature? Illogical, yes, but more real than anything ever known to me. The tremendous power of what Sawyer and I shared now seemed centered in the midpoint of my body and I promised my daughter, *You will thrive, I will make certain of this. And you will do so, we will all do so, in Minnesota. I have felt it to be true, I have dreamed of us there, you at my breast, my darling girl.*

Sawyer's footsteps were returning to the shanty and I opened the door; the sight of his face sent immediate shards of trepidation through my heart. Beyond his shoulder I beheld Tilson leading Clemens' horse to the barn, toting a lantern in his free hand; Rebecca was framed in the open door of the main house, her long dark hair hanging loose over her shawl as she stepped aside to allow her brother entrance. The wind's increase caused snow to fly sideways; the chill air darted beneath my hem, inspiring shivers.

"What is it?" I asked, as Sawyer entered our shanty and latched the door behind him.

"Yancy has resurfaced in Iowa City this very night," he said.

T HE JAILHOUSE, OUTSIDE of which we parked the wagon this early Friday morning, January first, remained a place I despised revisiting. Regardless of the passage of time between Sawyer's imprisonment within these very walls and this moment, nausea clutched at me, allowing no quarter, induced by the scents of the space and the painful remembrance of how close Sawyer had come to losing his life. I held fast to his upper arm on this overcast morning a few minutes past the hour of nine, having insisted upon accompanying him and Tilson on their errand of confronting Thomas Yancy. I refused to let my abhorrence of the man keep me from the task after Clemens had related the astounding news of Yancy's reappearance. I'd been hard-pressed to keep Sawyer from riding into town in last night's blizzard, to demand of Yancy every last scrap of information.

Snow continued to fall by midmorning's subdued light, dusting our heavy woolen outer layers, the men's coats and my cloak; I tugged with impatience at my wool bonnet, which, while snugly warm, served to act as would blinders upon a horse, limiting my view of Iowa City as the wagon crunched over the icy ruts in the road. And so it was that I did not observe Alice Doherty stationed before the jailhouse until Sawyer drew the team of mules to a halt.

"What right have you?" she demanded at once, without so much as a perfunctory greeting. Bundled in layers of dark-colored cloth, she resembled a stout barrel set atop boots; a thick scarf knotted her neck, above which her eyes blazed with contemptuous fire as she carried on. "Marshal Yancy is a man of the law! What do the likes of you know of law, a man who raised arms against the government of the United States of America and a *common whore?*"

Her words seemed powerful enough to emblazon the sky above, as though cast in flames for all to see. I was rendered immobile, shocked to silence; passersby on the street paused, footsteps faltering at the sound of her voice, its cadence calling forth a picture of a preacher at his pulpit. I reflected that Alice Doherty's late father had been a man of the cloth.

Undying hatred, I thought, the knot reforming in my center.

Sawyer moved so swiftly from the wagon seat I was scarcely aware of his passage to the ground to plant his imposing figure before the fearsome woman, who drew herself straighter as though in preparation to exchange physical blows. Sawyer, a good two heads taller than Alice, leaned close and spoke in a low voice; I strained to hear his words above the falling snow and murmurings of other people. Tilson reined Kingfisher to a halt, dismounted with haste, and stepped at once to Sawyer's side.

Backing immediately away from Tilson and my husband, gathering closer her shawl, Alice took stock of her fellow townsfolk and shouted, "These men make threats to my person!"

To my great relief, Tilson issued a barking laugh. He raised his voice to say, "Alice Doherty, you noisome busybody! The only one making threats to you is that voice within your skull!"

There was a stirring of commentary amongst those listening; I yanked the wool bonnet from my head, frustrated at the lack of peripheral vision. I could not manage to clamber from the wagon, swathed as I was in multiple layers, and increasingly ungainly, and so sat observing from above. In the absence of protection, wind swirled around my ears and snow wet my forehead, but I was too concerned to cover up, my gaze roving about the small crowd. I was shocked anew at Alice's demonstrable sangfroid, considering, as we learned last night, that she had allowed Thomas Yancy recent quarter in her very home.

Clemens had further relayed to us that Marshal Quade's testimony, in addition to ours, concerning the events of the night Zeb Crawford took Sawyer from the jail in order to burn him alive in Tilson's yard, was sufficient to create a sizeable stain on Yancy's reputation as a lawman; he had been summarily stripped of his former route in Iowa and reassigned to the newly-formed Wyoming Territory. There was a modicum of satisfaction in learning this, though I would be a liar if I did not admit I continued to wish the man dead and buried; further, it proved even more reason to appreciate Leverett

Quade's help. Quade, as Clemens told us a few weeks ago, had ridden forth from Iowa City, bound northward, but Clemens retained no new information regarding Quade's current location. I knew it hurt Rebecca to learn of his absence, especially considering how Quade rode from town in haste, with his pride and – I was honest enough to recognize – his heart both wounded.

Tilson, Clemens, Rebecca, Sawyer, and I debated long into the hours of last night, gathered at the table near the woodstove, speculating over Alice Doherty's role in harboring Yancy; had she been motivated to extend this invitation and resultant shelter because of Yancy's shared hatred of former Confederates? Or was there something perhaps deeper, a relationship of a physical nature between them? Of course Alice, being a self-appointed paragon of virtues, would hardly admit to taking a lover. She would likely cleave to her story that she offered the marshal a place in which to recover. Since last we saw him, Yancy's right arm had been removed at midpoint; the surgeon had not been able to save the elbow joint, leaving behind a stump approximately six inches in length. Clemens explained that Yancy had walked into the sheriff's office yesterday evening, for all the world as though he hadn't been missing a single day.

"Clear outta here!" Tilson ordered the small crowd in the no-nonsense tone I admired so in him. He wore his wide-brimmed duster, long gray hair hanging past his jaws. Having served as the town's physician long enough that his reputation was well established, and subsequently untarnished, people obeyed without trouble; all except Alice.

Sawyer lifted me from the wagon, murmuring against my temple as he set me upon the snowy ground, "I am sorry, love." I could feel the angry tension vibrating from him, as strings upon a fiddle when struck soundly by the bow. That someone would speak so to me infuriated him; had Alice been a man, I retained no doubts that Sawyer would have taken him to his knees for directing such insults my way.

Alice insinuated herself in my path, hissing, "Whore!"

Sawyer's ire was so heated she should have been incinerated; he ordered through his teeth, "You will not speak so to my wife, you *wretched* woman."

"Or what?" she challenged, and belligerently jutted her chin closer to my face; I refused to shy away. Sawyer's desire to smash a fist against Alice's jaw grew more potent with each heartbeat and I eased between them, as subtly as I was able.

"Or I'll set you toppling into yonder stock trough, frozen over or no," Tilson answered instead, his tone conversational. "Get yourself gone, woman, this instant." Not waiting to see if Alice followed this command, Tilson ushered Sawyer and me into the jailhouse, shutting the outer door firmly behind us.

No respite, I understood, confronted suddenly with Sheriff Billings, a gaunt, angular man whose patience was usually as thin as gauze. And, beyond his shoulder, there stood Thomas Yancy. At once encompassed by a sensation not unfamiliar, I nonetheless held my ground as the overcrowded room seemed to crush inward around our bodies, rotating on a large axis. I fought the sensations and drew a steadying breath, taking comfort in the fact that Sawyer and Tilson stood to either side, unwilling to allow any harm to me – but even their combined reassurance could not fully negate the darkness of my memories. It had been on Yancy's order last summer that I become Zeb Crawford's prisoner, a man who would have killed me within a day and a night, but not before exacting torture upon my person. Yancy had run my dying pony to ground, had witnessed my desperate struggle with Jack Barrow and my subsequent shooting of the loathsome little man.

Far worse than any of these things, Yancy's sole desire had been – and likely remained – to cause as much pain to Sawyer as he was able; despite a judge having absolved Sawyer of the charges against him, Yancy continued to wish him dead by whatever means necessary, of this I harbored no false assumptions. The air in the space melded into a hard lump of antagonism. My eyes darted over Yancy's imposing form; even short an arm, he retained a sense of arrogance afforded to him by his station as a marshal. Though, he wore not his marshal's badge this morning, cloaked instead in dour grays this snowy day, his shirtsleeve trimmed and pinned to accommodate the missing appendage; he was thinner in frame and feature, pale with winter, full beard neatly trimmed beneath the shadow of his hat. I squelched, with effort, the need to turn away from his cruel gaze.

"Where have you been?" Sawyer demanded, without hesitation. "Where are Boyd and Malcolm Carter? Did you follow them north?"

"So quick to assume," Yancy said, and his voice was all too familiar, faintly hoarse; he spoke around a sore throat. "I have no answers for you, Davis. If I'd had my way, summer past, your rotten carcass would have swung in the town square."

"God*dammit*," Billings grunted, on a sigh. "I'll not stand for wayward bickering. Davis is cleared, Thomas. And Davis, Clemens said you wished to ask a question or two and be on your way." Billings drew from his vest a pocket watch and ordered, "You've the space of five minutes, starting now."

Sawyer squared his shoulders and began afresh. "Where have you dallied these past months?"

"My whereabouts remain none of your concern," Yancy said. "I am passing through Iowa City solely to collect my youngest son from the Rawley homestead and be on our way. I've been reassigned to the Wyoming Territory but I intend first to find my eldest."

Tilson barked, "Fannie Rawley is a good woman, much aggrieved by your boy's disappearance. Charley Rawley has exerted considerable effort searching for him."

Yancy allowed, "And I remain indebted to them."

"When did you last see Fallon?" Sawyer pressed.

Yancy's nostrils narrowed with an indrawn breath and it was apparent he grappled with the desire to say nothing; conceding that we would discover the information regardless, he finally admitted, "The last I saw my son, Fallon told me he intended to track the Carters and bring them to justice, dear and loyal lad that he remains. I did not consent to these wishes of his, nor did I believe at the time that he truly intended to ride out after them. I would have prevented him, had I suspected the depth of his resolution."

"When was this?" Tilson demanded.

"'Justice?'" Sawyer repeated, tensed as though to spring forward. His words flew, clipped and fiery. "Your son is no lawman! He has less than no right! Where the hell is he this day?"

"He had every right to demand justice for the Carter boy's unlawful actions! I lost an arm for my trouble!" Yancy blustered, gesturing unnecessarily at the stump. "I've not spoken a word with my boy since August last, that is God's truth, and I'll not deny I fear for his continued safety. I would have stopped him from riding forth, had I been able, but I didn't believe he would leave Iowa. I ordered him to wait for me and he disobeyed."

"You admit that Fallon intended to pursue the Carters and now we've even more reason to believe that he has delayed their journey," Tilson said, eyeing Billings to include the sheriff in the accusation. "They've been missing these many months. By God, if we learn that Fallon had a thing to do with it –"

"Are you threatening my son?" Yancy thundered.

"If your son took unlawful actions against Boyd an' Malcolm Carter, then *yes*, I am!"

Billings all but growled, "Enough of this!"

"It was on *your* orders that Crawford attack my home, might I remind you, Yancy," Tilson went on, stepping aggressively ahead, undeterred by Billings' aggravation. "Upon two separate occasions last summer!"

"I ordered no such thing! Crawford was mad as a tick-bit hound. He acted alone, as I've recently stated before my superiors in Washington." Yancy's tone was again circumspect, controlled. "I did my best to stop Crawford that night."

"You lie," Sawyer accused, quiet and dangerous. "You told that bastard to come to the jailhouse for me, and later to Tilson's homestead. You told him to *finish it*. You hid and watched, and rode like a coward when you saw that Crawford was dead."

"I am no coward," Yancy hissed. "Nor a liar! I'll not be accused of such by the likes of you, Davis. Shameful enough that a fellow marshal speak out against me. Thanks to Leverett Quade, in my absence I've been stripped of my route in Iowa and reassigned to the Territories. I'll not be accused of further untruths, not by a *goddamn murdering Reb*."

I found my voice, facing Yancy for the first time in months, refusing to flinch away in fear, as instinct dictated. Thinking of the empty-eyed boy I'd first met at the Rawleys' homestead last summer, I said, "You admit your son spoke of following the Carters. What was his intent for them? Did his 'justice' include killing them?"

All eyes came to rest upon me as I made these queries; there was a sustained lull as Sawyer and Tilson reined in their anger. Yancy drew a breath and I imagined his thoughts whirling as he endeavored to fashion a response which would not unwittingly incriminate his offspring.

Billings spoke, this time with a marked lessening of ire. "Charley Rawley claims the boy ran away last September. Rawley has put out a great many inquiries regarding him, Thomas. The Rawley family has been greatly distressed over his welfare, this you must acknowledge."

What meager color there was in Yancy's face drained; for the first time I spied a glimpse of the man beneath the beast I'd known while existing as his captive, and found the former almost more unsettling than the latter. He appeared in that moment not a fiendish lawman bent on revenge but instead a father whose concern for his child overrode all else. He rested his remaining hand upon the top of a nearby ladderback chair, as though unbalanced both physically and mentally, and spoke with quiet despair. "Fallon was in a black rage after seeing my missing arm. I ordered him to remain on our homestead and await my return, which he did not. And now he is missing. I have only learned of this since returning to Iowa City."

"Charley Rawley has inquired after him in St. Paul, as I told you," Billings said. "But the boy has not appeared, nor have the Carter brothers reached their intended destination."

It was a strange, otherworldly sensation, each of us pinned beneath the same slab of sudden and heavy silence, Tilson, Sawyer, and I staring at Yancy; I did not in that moment believe Yancy was lying about Fallon. His desire to protect his son overruled any acknowledgement of that which his eldest was likely capable; despite having committed numerous heinous acts of his own, perhaps Yancy was unable to comprehend his son doing the same. I shied away from the memory of Fallon, whose smooth, deceptively angelic face belied what I truly believed to be a dark and twisted soul, one far worse than his father's. A boy who was not a boy, who was instead empty, devoid of some vital component; I could not articulate what I felt any more clearly. It was as Sawyer and I had first suspected, and I could sense my husband's galloping thoughts.

Boyd can handle himself. He'd protect Malcolm with his life. Yancy's son is no match for him.

I asked in unspoken response, *But what if he ambushed them? Came out of the night and fired upon them? Boyd had no way of knowing they were being trailed...*

I tightened my grip on Sawyer's arm, abruptly rushed by nausea.

"We are through here," Yancy said then, all traces of vulnerability hidden away. I understood that he despised having fleetingly appeared weak; this side of him would never again be visible to me. His eyes burned with a hatred approaching fanaticism as he regarded us anew, his voice scratching over his parting words. "My only concern is locating my son. I pray I never see the lot of you sorry Rebs again in this life."

"A notion we firmly second!" Tilson heralded, tipping his hat brim with a gesture which mocked his usual effortless courtesy.

Sawyer remained rooted, at long last facing the marshal with no qualms, no threat of Yancy's power hovering over him. All former charges against Sawyer had been absolved, allowing him the freedom to declare, "I do not believe you. So help me if I find that you or your kin caused harm to the Carters. You will never again threaten me, or those I love, do you hear me, Yancy? I have no fear of you. Ride from here in disgrace, you miserable, armless wretch. And pray we *never meet* outside the boundaries of law."

"Dammit, that's a threat, Davis, you're pushing your goddamn luck. Besides, your time is up," Billings announced, flinging open the door to the snowy morning. "Tilson! Get him out of here!"

Yancy's face was awash with fiery red, displacing his winter pallor. Sawyer's jaw was set, his expression as ferocious as I'd ever seen it; I hated that Yancy retained the power to rouse in him such powerful vengeance.

"Come, son," Tilson urged, laying a hand to Sawyer's back; I tensed, but Sawyer relented, not before stabbing an extended finger into Yancy's chest, sending the man quickstepping backward.

Tilson hustled us out, muttering at Sawyer, who allowed himself to be led summarily away. I made the mistake of looking back at Yancy, catching a final glimpse of his reddened face in the view made narrow by the closing door; his eyes glittered viciously as he mouthed a single word at me.

Whore, he said.

Part Two

S T. PAUL BENEATH the April sky was a sight to behold.

Brilliant sunshine heralded our arrival in the bustling river town, the air warm and humid, the Mississippi like an old friend, the original waterway which served to guide Sawyer and Angus, Boyd and Malcolm, from their home in Tennessee well over a year ago, its indigo length leading eventually to St. Louis, where they'd found and subsequently saved me, fate bringing together our paths. We'd left the mighty river behind for a time to cross through Iowa and now stood again along its rushing banks, at last in the state of Minnesota, marveling at the grand coursing of the water, flowing all the many thousands of miles south to Louisiana, to empty into the Gulf of Mexico.

"Much better to be standing at the headwaters than its tail end," I reflected, speaking over the energetic rush, leaning my cheek upon the hard warmth of Sawyer's upper arm. The sun dusted our heads with golden radiance, dazzled our eyes with its unceasing dance atop the water, so that we saw floating starbursts upon blinking. Its warmth seemed a benediction and despite everything I was overtaken by satisfaction, a sense of powerful accomplishment. We'd made it here to Minnesota, however diverted from our original schedule.

Sawyer marveled, "We have never been as far northward as we stand just now, darlin', can you imagine? I figured the farthest I'd ever roam from Suttonville was perhaps Nashville." He kissed my hair and proclaimed, "It is quite the most beautiful landscape I've ever imagined."

I nodded agreement. "It is far more wild than home. But gorgeous for its wildness." The past fortnight of travel, wolves had distantly serenaded our night hours. If not for the comfort of knowing Sawyer and Tilson were armed to the teeth, I would have been quite unsettled; eventually the mournful howling of the creatures grew familiar, at last becoming a sound I no longer feared but instead oddly anticipated. Spring, the season of renewal, turned the prairie into a pallet of bursting color, wildflowers overtaking the gently-undulating landscape to the horizon on all sides. Birds – prairie wrens and sparrows, hummingbirds and hawks, meadowlarks and pheasants – existed by the hundreds. I felt I could never grow tired of simply staring into the distance, imbibing the joyous rioting of bloom and trill of birdsong. Poems from my childhood lessons at Mama's knee sprang to mind as though unbidden and I recited bits of them for Sawyer as we rode together on the wagon seat; I thought, *A springtime prairie possesses the power to rouse inspiration for such lines.*

"Did they stand just here, do you suppose?" I wondered, resting one hand to the enormous curve of my belly; I expected our daughter's arrival within the month. Clad in the loosely-gathered dress, one of two which Rebecca lent me, let out to accommodate the swelling of a growing child, I pictured Malcolm and Boyd gawking at this same view last autumn.

"It is an ideal place to appreciate the river cliffs," Sawyer said, tightening his arm, drawing me closer to his side, cupping his free hand atop mine and intertwining our fingers over my belly. In response to his unspoken words, I rested my cheek on his chest.

If Boyd and Malcolm had wintered in the vicinity, as we chose to believe until evidence proved otherwise, then the logical place for them to travel with the spring thaw was St. Paul. In that regard, and for the sake of giving birth near a town, we were reluctant to ride out before mid-May. We had left word at the land office and with as many local merchants as we were able this very morning; if May waned and we'd not heard a word, the tentative plan was to resume our northward course to Jacob's homestead. Boyd and Malcolm, should they appear in town after that time, would quickly come to realize we looked for them; there was no shortage of people in St. Paul informed of our purpose. We had also sought any information regarding Fallon Yancy, thus far to no avail.

"Young Sawyer! Young lad woodcutter! Are you and Lorissa about?" yodeled a voice altogether familiar despite my very recent introduction to its owner. The man attached to it had known Sawyer from boyhood, had himself been raised in the Bledsoe holler, and the intonation of Tennessee lingered in his words, even years after leaving the state. At this lively summoning Sawyer and I turned to greet Jacob Miller, uncle to Boyd and Malcolm, younger brother to Clairee, a man of three-and-thirty years whose teeming energy seemed capable of righting any wrong. As did we, Jacob refused to believe his nephews were dead; as agreed upon through written correspondence earlier in the spring, he'd met us in St. Paul only yesterday afternoon, having himself arrived but a day past, and vowed we would determine the truth of their fate.

"I didn't want to approach from the left and startle you, Davis!" Jacob said. I was still growing accustomed to his outrageous humor, though Sawyer minded not a whit, explaining that he expected nothing less. It was just like coming home, Sawyer told me last night, after my initial introduction to Jacob; it seemed he had been known in Suttonville for his blunt-spoken nature, could be counted upon for unvarnished opinions, and seemed predisposed to tease – though I sensed in him a kind spirit; his devotion to kin proved his loyalty.

Because Boyd and Malcolm resembled their father, Bainbridge, to a marked degree and Jacob's relation was to their mother, Jacob did not look as much like them as I'd hoped, but there was a similarity in the way he moved, a set to his wide shoulders and sturdy, long-limbed frame that called Boyd to mind, especially. His hair was a pale brown, as of autumn oak leaves, grown long enough to be arranged into a thick braid, around which he had ceremoniously wrapped otter fur. His skin bore a ruddy tan from relentless exposure to sunlight, white squint lines at the outer corners of wide-set eyes, a shade of brown to match his hair. Lower face swathed in a full beard, into which were twisted many small braids, some adorned with indigo-colored trade beads shaped like tiny barrels, and clad in leather from shoulders to boots, Jacob cut an intriguing figure. He proved an incessant talker – *just like Malcolm*, I kept thinking – and smiled with affable frequency.

"My youngest favors my face decorated," he'd explained upon our first meeting, catching a bead between forefinger and thumb. "I am a gol-durned softhearted fool for my little ones. And don't they know it! Their mama is the disciplinarian in our household, mark my words."

"You'd hardly approach unannounced from right or left, the way you crash through the brush," Sawyer said in response, and Jacob laughed, tipping at the waist to direct his merriment at the sunny sky.

"Aw, young Davis, it does my heart a good turn to hear your voice, to see you married up, proper-like, with a little one on the way," Jacob said, winking amiably at me. In the tone of a conspirator, he added, "This one was a right devil as a boy, always seeking trouble with my nephews." And then to Sawyer, "Bainbridge and your daddy was as busy thrashing your hides as they was farming. That is, if they could catch the rowdy lot of you. Them days was golden as sunlight. I ain't got a bad memory from that time, I swear. You done grown a piece, might I observe, young lad. Last I saw you, you weren't rightly at my shoulder, and now look. Sweet Clairee, God rest her dear soul, always expected you'd marry the pick of the ladies, and of course she was right as the rain."

Jacob paused for breath and I managed a word. "Had you any luck this morning?"

"That's what I've come to tell the both of you," Jacob said, indicating the gradual incline which led to the town itself, a humming wasp's nest of activity this fair Saturday, the last week of April. The Mississippi provided its primary industry, and cargo flats and paddlewheels were in the process of being loaded even as we stood idle, watching from above. Docks led to anchored riverboats, barrels rolling along gangplanks and men scurrying, toting goods and pushing wheelbarrows, leading livestock. Warehouses dotted the length of the river, the levee stretching east and west, and the busiest streets were those adjacent to the water. I spied saloons and boardinghouses, a hotel, mercantile shops and dry goods; there was the livery stable, bustling with plenty of business of its own.

"You'll think me licentious for the getting of it, though I am not," Jacob continued. "A young woman employed in yonder cathouse remembers Boyd and Malcolm, both, from last fall!"

Hope pulsed at the juncture of my ribs. It was the first confirmation we'd been given that the two of them had indeed reached St. Paul. I wanted to sprint to our camp – never minding that I could hardly walk unassisted, these days – and relay this good news to Rebecca and Tilson.

"What did she say?" I begged.

"I bid her wait and let me fetch the two of you before she told me what she knew. Lorissa, your sensibilities ain't easily offended, are they? My Hannah would have a thing or two to say about my setting foot within such a place, but in this instance I do believe it was a necessary act."

While Jacob was kin to people I dearly loved, and indeed considered my own kin, I was unready to trust him with the magnitude of my past and so replied with only the briefest truth. "No, I am not easily offended."

We had departed Iowa City just after dawn on Monday the fifteenth of March, a journey since well documented in the journal with which Sawyer gifted me before we left. Our first week proved arduous, as my comfort was Sawyer's primary concern and our resultant pace was suitably slow; however, as the weeks progressed and I showed no signs of overt fatigue, or ill health, and in fact felt more spirited than ever at the prospect of at last moving onward, we made better headway. In our company were Tilson, Rebecca, Cort and Nathaniel, and Malcolm's gray cat, Stormy; the house and shanty cabin, the barn and surrounding land existed now in the sole possession and care of Clemens, who did not wish to leave Iowa with us. Rebecca parted tearfully from her brother, with whom she'd lived since her husband's death, and promised to write frequently; Tilson told him there would never fail to be a place for him if ever he chose to join us in Minnesota.

Tilson's decision to venture from home was one he made only after careful deliberation; his final say on the matter was, "I can't rightly let my niece and great-nephews roam so far without me. Nor can I allow an expectant young pair, a pair I love as dearly as any daughter or son of my own, to travel without a physician. And beyond that, the picture of myself without you-all is more than I can bear."

We had passed the dreary winter with preparations for the journey, which helped to ease the restless agitation of necessary immobility, and at last set forth with two covered wagons, one with a pallet made up for my use – Sawyer would not allow me to sleep upon the ground – a contingent of livestock, including Whistler, Admiral, and Juniper, and Tilson's Kingfisher. Pete and Penelope, the mules, pulled Tilson's wagon, which Rebecca and Tilson took turns driving, while Juniper and Admiral pulled ours, loaded with all of the supplies Boyd and Malcolm had been unable to carry with them last summer. Food, tools, crates and tins, equipment and tack, all stowed neatly; we would build what furniture we needed upon arrival. Tucked carefully into the bundle of Clairee's silk wedding dress, which I had worn for mine and Sawyer's handfasting, were my mama's ivory hairbrush and my wedding ring, awaiting a time when, post-birth, my finger could again accommodate it. The dress itself was folded into Sawyer's old leather trunk, the one which contained the pieces of his past he had recovered from his family's burned-out home after the War.

Occasionally I drove our wagon so that Sawyer might ride Whistler, an act once as familiar to him as breathing; since the loss of his eye he had resumed riding with subsequent difficulties, but his determination eventually won out. He used the hours of daily travel to grow accustomed to sitting the saddle with the altered perspective of one-sided vision; with the same concern in mind, he and Tilson spent many an evening hour target-shooting, or hunting if we set up camp early enough. His noticeable pleasure at taking the saddle, of cantering our dear Whistler over the prairie, filled my heart with quiet joy.

"Look there, little one, there's your daddy," I would speak aloud to my bulging belly, watching as they raced along, as swift as water over rocks in a creek bed. Whistler's legs appeared a flowing blur of motion while Sawyer bent low over her head, effortless and beautiful, as though they were a single entity instead of two. He would circle her back to the wagons, drawing near just slightly out of breath, Whistler prancing in her delight at once again carrying him upon her back, and grin at me in the way he had – a grin belonging to me alone, that spoke of happiness and contentment, and of promises yet to be fulfilled.

"How I love to see you sitting there in the sun, *mo mhuirnín milis*," he would say, without fail. "A simple pleasure I am eternally grateful for."

"How I wish I was riding alongside you."

"I wish the same," he said, Whistler at a graceful walk beside the wagon; she whickered her agreement and Sawyer angled close enough to reach and grasp my outstretched hand. As he asked every day, multiple times, "The ride isn't too rough, is it?"

I felt each and every rut; it was difficult to sit upon the hard wagon seat for hours on end, even with a blanket tucked beneath, and the discomfort banded my lower back by day's end. I admitted, "A little. But I am well, love, don't fret."

"I'll rub the knots away this evening," he promised, and he had, without fail, every night of our journey as we lay together in the cramped quarters of the wagon, Sawyer cradling me through the night, listening to the spring wind as March gave way to a mild and sunny April. Tilson's pipe smoke often drifted into the wagon, as he preferred to sit near the fire just as he had back in Iowa, long after everyone else retired. Many a night Sawyer joined him, the two of them speaking in low, comforting tones.

"So Fallon has more gumption than we'd figured," Tilson had said shortly after the confrontation in the jailhouse. Yancy had departed Iowa City the very winter morning we'd spoken to him, presumably bound to retrieve Dredd from the Rawleys' homestead; from there it seemed he would not rest until finding Fallon – and, God willing, then make haste to Wyoming Territory, our paths never to cross again.

If only it were that uncomplicated, I thought, too distrustful to assume we'd heard the last of them.

"I feared such a thing from the start," Sawyer said, quiet and adamant, his hand resting upon my thigh as we sat at the table with Rebecca and Tilson that same January night. "Boyd and Malcolm are alive out there. I'll believe this until it is confirmed otherwise. Circumstances beyond their control have caused them delay, and we must find them. I do not believe that a boy, even an ambitious boy, killed them. Boyd lived as a soldier for nearly three years and there are few other than he that I would trust with my life. There are foul dealings to which we are not privy and I will not relent until we have learned the truth."

The picture of Malcolm or Boyd harmed burned into my heart as would branches tipped in flame; I wanted so badly to believe they were safe. Clenching my elbows closer to my sides to contain any errant trembling, I'd whispered, "Fallon is not to be underestimated. They could not have known he was trailing them."

Listening closely, watching our faces with all the scrutiny of a hawk, Rebecca said, "You have spoken of this boy, Fallon, I recall well. He is dangerous."

I nodded even as Sawyer attempted to reassure her. "Lorie is right, the boy's capabilities should not be undervalued. But I cleave to my belief that no boy is a match for Boyd. Few *men* are a match for him."

Her lovely face seemed carved of ice but Rebecca at last nodded silent agreement; I so strongly sensed her yearning to find solace in Sawyer's words that she might have been screaming.

"As soon as the snow clears and the weather warms, we'll continue onward," I said, leaning forward over the tabletop as though this action might spur the arrival of springtime. "We'll reach St. Paul and ask after them, in every shop and saloon."

Hearing the fervor in my tone, Sawyer did not contradict or suggest he would rather we remain stationary in Iowa City until our child's arrival. He gathered my hand into his, braiding our fingers. "We'll imagine them safely wintering in the Northland. We'll think of them planning just now, as are we, to reach St. Paul by fair weather."

And now the weather was fair as the moon in a cloudless night sky, the spring season in full flush upon the lively river town, and we followed Jacob as he led the way through the noisy dust of a street adjacent to the Mississippi, choked with buggies and carriages, riders and those on foot, dotted by small blooms of ladies' parasols held cockeyed to shield their skin from the noon beams. Sawyer kept our pace slow to accommodate me, an arm latched about my waist. I recognized that a woman in my condition was a rarity walking the streets of a town; a proper lady would remain confined in her home when her pregnancy had reached such a visible state. I reminded myself that no one in St. Paul had read Horace Parmley's self-aggrandizing articles, as they had in Iowa City, and that here I was safely anonymous, with no shadow of the past hovering over me; Alice Doherty was not poised to block our path with her hateful words.

"Yonder, the saloon called Dolly Belle," said Jacob. "A woman, name of Mary, recalls speaking to them."

Noontide had not slowed the gaiety of the place; a piano player was accompanied by a man with a harmonica, sending forth a rousing tune, the long counter crowded with workers from the riverboats, seeking to whet their appetites for drink and women. With monumental effort I cast aside the panicked swell of excruciating memories the interior of such a place provoked, the sounds and scents of a whorehouse bar, women painted with rouge and kohl, men exuberant at the prospect of an afternoon's revelry, with more chaotic carousing to follow as night rolled over the town. Jacob nodded surreptitiously at the painted canvas just opposite the entrance, featuring a nude woman sprawled amongst flowers, and his eyebrows cocked in a half-appreciative, half-shocked angle; I imagined Malcolm's response to such risqué artwork. Sawyer kissed my temple, keeping me close to his warmth.

I placed a shielding hand over my belly. *I cannot change what I was, my daughter, but know that I would die before letting you near such a place. I would die any death, would pay any price.*

"*Bonjour,*" heralded a woman approaching from the gaming tables, taking especial notice of my belling skirts, eyes widening. As she walked in our direction she earned the immediate attention of another woman, who extracted herself from a table of men and joined us without further ado. I took stock of these women as I would have any others in their line of work, unable to resist drawing upon my past. Any whore worth her salt understood her survival depended upon earnings, always at the mercy of coin or gold dust, and the madam's whim. The best earners were allowed first picks and prime positions on the floor; jealousy ran rife, even in the best of times. I squelched the thought of Eva, the meanest of Ginny's whores; neither of the women now standing before us brought Eva distinctly to mind but their speculative, calculating expressions were all too familiar.

"I am Cecilia," said the curvaceous French woman who had initially addressed us. Her errant gaze roved with unapologetic appreciation over both Sawyer and Jacob and I watched the way she angled her ample hips and breasts for greatest display; it was pure business, part of a perilous game learned by necessity to play, this I understood well. My memory snagged upon the final night of my employ at Ginny's whorehouse, when Angus had paid for my services, when I'd approached him with just such an inviting jut to particular parts of my body.

Sawyer sensed my growing discomfort and thought, *I am here, darlin', don't fear.* His protectiveness warmed my heart, as always, though I had nothing to fear in this place – only my memories, which even Sawyer hadn't the power to fully banish.

"And I am Mary," the taller woman said, and her voice held no trace of nasal French. She was long of leg and fair of skin, while Cecilia was plump and olive-complexioned; both possessed the hooded, observant eyes of longtime whores. Mary offered her hand to each of us in turn and her grip was as firm as any man's. She shouldered around Cecilia and acknowledged of Jacob, "Mr. Miller. You asked after the Carter brothers."

My heart took up an erratic thumping at her casual reference to them, as though Boyd and Malcolm were perhaps just the length of the room away, seated at a table beyond our line of sight. Though Mary maintained a guarded mien I ascertained a depth of information beyond it, if she was willing to trust us. Cecilia's sleek, dark brows lifted as she studied us anew; there was unmistakable, if subtle, tension in her expression before she controlled its presence.

"I did indeed," Jacob agreed. "If you would be so kind, Miss Mary, we'd appreciate any word. These here are my friends, Sawyer Davis and his wife, Lorissa. The Carters are my nephews, as I've stated, and the three of us are indeed anxious for any news, any a'tall."

"I spoke with them last autumn," Mary said. "And so did Isobel."

Cecilia said, *"Excusez-moi,"* and skirted Mary, effectively interrupting her explanation. The jet comb entwined in Cecilia's hair and the pearled fastenings along the back of her pale satin gown caught the sunlight as she hastened away. Mary and I watched her go, Mary biting her lower lip.

Sawyer prompted, "Did they mention where they might be headed? Did they seem troubled?"

When Mary did not appear disposed to answer I turned my full attention upon her, ignoring Cecilia's abrupt departure. "Please. Any detail you can recall."

Mary seemed to regain her resolve and leaned nearer to me, speaking quickly. "I must tell you –"

Before she was able to finish this statement a male voice, loud and officious, speaking rapid French, claimed her attention as absolutely as would a bolt of lightning sizzling down from the punched-tin ceiling. I saw the way her teeth came together on their edges, the tightening of her jaws. Mary eased straight as the man approached and the memory of Ginny Hossiter so forcefully intruded my thoughts I could hardly swallow. I'd long ago accepted that my fear of the despicable madam would never let me completely from its clutches.

"Qu'elle se passe-t-il ici ? Je ne vais pas avoir cela!"

Mary stepped aside, with obvious deference, as her employer swept to a halt and stood with fists to hips, trailed by Cecilia, who had clearly fetched him. An oiled beard, shaped to a point, first claimed my eye, along with the brilliant-blue scarf swathing his head, trimmed by small, cone-shaped embellishments that jangled with each movement. Earrings of polished silver gleamed, several hoops dangling from each earlobe; pale, narrowed eyes took stock even as he offered what was meant to be a charming smile. In thickly-accented English he inquired, "Who have we here?"

"I am Jacob Justin Miller and I seek my kin," Jacob explained with thinning patience, wasting no time upon trifling small talk. "They passed through St. Paul last autumn and visited this place, perhaps you'll recall? Boyd and Malcolm Carter?"

"These men were my guests for an evening's meal," the Frenchman said with a remarkably even tone. "I do recall this man and boy." He disregarded Mary, Cecilia, and me; womenfolk, no threat to him. By contrast, his dissembling gaze moved with deliberation between Sawyer and Jacob. Eyebrows lifting in an expression of calculated innocence, he asked, "You have not heard? Then, I dearly regret to inform you I received word of their passing, last winter."

The shock of these casually-spoken words was that of scalding water to the skin, a knife blade to the gullet. The room seemed to list before my eyes.

"Who gave you this information?" Sawyer demanded, hollow-voiced.

Rather than answer, the Frenchman's grin stretched farther across his too-animated face. He said grandly, "Might I inquire as to your name, good sir? And to your lovely woman's? Or perhaps I assume too much? Is this lovely woman not yours?"

Sawyer's muscles bunched with tension. "I'll thank you to keep a civil tone when addressing my wife. And I ask again, who gave you this information?"

The Frenchman's grin slipped not an inch. "I fear I am no help to you in this matter," he said, and shrugged, palms lifted. "You see, despite my many talents, I cannot bring dead men from their graves. I am sorry for your loss but there is nothing to be done. Perhaps a drink, before you depart?"

I could not take my eyes from the Frenchman's face; he was the sort with dominion over his expression, giving away nothing.

Jacob advanced a pace, as of yet not hostile but entering into the man's space all the same. "You claim my nephews have been killed and yet you refuse to explain this statement? What do you take us for?"

The Frenchman shrugged, this time conveying irritation. "Word of their deaths reached town last autumn, as of the deaths of many others who ventured into the Territory. Traveling outside the bounds of established law is a dangerous endeavor, in the best of times."

Sawyer demanded, "Where in the Territory? How were they killed? I will not leave this place until you tell me how you came to possess this information."

"You will leave my établissement when I request," the Frenchman said evenly. "And not a moment later."

"Their party was attacked," the woman named Mary offered, with the sense of a child speaking out of turn, and our attention snapped to her as swiftly as a bowstring releasing an arrow.

Mary pressed together her lips as if to contain further information; her gaze fluttered to the Frenchman's and he picked up the dropped rein of the explanation, with a sigh. "The man and boy you seek were visited with misfortune, you see, having lost their supplies and cash money in a storm. They signed on to drive cattle through the Territory the very night I made their acquaintance, but their party was attacked along the route by Sioux raiders, who proceeded to kill the party and steal the cattle." His sardonic gaze came to rest on me; as though he felt I did not comprehend his meaning, he clarified, "Red men, you see. *Savages.*"

I could not conceive of Boyd and Malcolm as dead and gone – it was not possible. Thoughts whirled in the confines of my head. *Misfortune. A storm. Lost their supplies and cash money. Red men. Oh Boyd, Malcolm, oh God…*

Sawyer grappled with similar notions, unwilling to simply accept. "What of their remains? What of their mounts? Where did this attack occur and how came you to know of it?"

"The Sioux attacked a cattle operation?" Jacob scoffed, standing in an unmistakably confrontational pose, knuckles to hips; his wife and children were Indians, and the Frenchman had just referred to Indians as savages. He declared, "No *such.* Even had Sioux warriors wished to lift the cattle they would have done so in the dead of night, alerting no one. They's near experts at such."

"I only relate to you what I have heard. Word trickles in from the Territory," the Frenchman said, shrugging a third time. "No bodies were recovered. There is nothing more I am able to tell you."

The woman named Mary, standing just behind his shoulder, caught my attention with a small jutting of her chin; her blue eyes dug into mine but a second, perhaps two, but it was enough. I did not dare nod understanding and instead looked away from her.

I said, "Then we will take our leave. Thank you, sir."

Consternation rolled from Jacob but Sawyer understood what I did not say; he tipped his hat brim and forced himself to abandon further questioning. "Good day."

"This ain't over!" Jacob declared, furious.

"You are most pale, ma'am. Do come along, you need a bit of air." Mary had adopted a kindly, maternal tone in the hubbub of Jacob exchanging words with the Frenchman. She gathered close my elbow, feigning concern over my appearance, ushering me towards the swinging doors. Aware that we were observed, she did not linger; I scarcely heard her murmured promise of "Look for me at sunset," before she turned away, retreating into the depths of The Dolly Belle.

S HE MET THEM? She spoke with them?" Rebecca asked, all but wringing her hands. The picture of calm serenity for the entirety of the journey
from Iowa City, Rebecca appeared near the end of her emotional endurance.
I hugged her as closely as I was capable with my bulging midsection, rubbing
her back; she rested her cheek to my hair and simply clung. I could feel a
trembling way down deep in her body.

Summoning all of my resolve, I whispered, "Mary was unable to converse
with us in that moment, with her employer present, but implored me to look
for her at sunset. I have made up my mind to hear what she has to say before
I believe a thing."

We had set up camp near a low rise less than a half-mile south of town;
from our current position, St. Paul itself was not visible, though in the absence of wind the rush of the Mississippi could still be heard. Jacob's horse,
a stocky gelding named Sundog, was tethered with our stock; Jacob traveled
light, having left home with a bedroll and his saddlebags, including provisions and a pouch of tobacco. He intended to help us seek any possible answers, but all subsequent plans were indefinite; Jacob would ride for home by
early next week but whether we would accompany him was another matter.
Sawyer had filed for a homestead claim only this morning, he and Tilson
paying for and submitting another claim by proxy, for Boyd, upon acreages
adjacent to Jacob and Hannah's land, near Flickertail Lake. But now, after the
devastating news at The Dolly Belle, our plans had been dreadfully upended.

We spent the afternoon discussing what we had learned at The Dolly
Belle; Tilson and Jacob rode back to town to further inquire over the matter,
returning to our camp with grim faces. It seemed that deaths in the Territory

were so very common they caused little to no stir on any given day; although
the news of Indian violence provoked a ripple last autumn, few even recalled
the story now that spring lay blithely upon the land. Apparently one man
had survived the attack of which the Frenchman spoke, and this man, whose
name, Tilson said, was something along the order of 'Trundle,' had appeared
in St. Paul in late October to tell the tale; he'd not been seen since.

"This means perhaps Fallon Yancy never found them at all," I speculated,
and imagined the boy lying dead on the prairie somewhere between Iowa
City and St. Paul, with no guilt over my hope that this picture proved true.

"Were Indian folk truly responsible for such an assault, it seems highly
unlikely Fallon was also involved," Tilson agreed.

"I don't buy the story of a Sioux attack, not for a bleedin' minute. They'd
signed on to drive *cattle*," Jacob mused yet again, mystified. "I just can't figure
why Boyd didn't come straight to me. They's my kin, I'd have taken them in
with nothin' to their names, though if Boyd is as prideful as his daddy, I s'pose
I can see why he'd not wish that. But why didn't he write of his intentions?"

"Did this woman Mary speak of how they appeared? Were they well?"
Rebecca asked for perhaps the fourth time, dissatisfied with my lack of answers; if Mary did indeed appear this eve, Rebecca may well tear her apart
to glean what information she was able. Pale and distraught, Rebecca could
scarcely remain still. Cort and Nathaniel – who, from the first, had regarded
the journey to Minnesota as a stupendously grand adventure – offered her
some small distraction, chasing each other in the rich sunset glow as afternoon passed slowly into lengthening evening. We were gathered near the
crackling dinner fire, Tilson and Jacob smoking their pipes; the two of them
had taken to one another as peas in a single pod, both appreciating the com-
monality of their state of origin. The Tennessee in Jacob's voice had resurged
in our company.

"She did not," I told Rebecca. "I pray she'll have more to tell us."

Sawyer's face appeared gilded, the stark lines of his eyepatch tempered by
the fading light, his soft mouth uncharacteristically dour at the nature of our
conversation. I sat at his side, settled as comfortably as possible on a folded
quilt, and found room to notice that Sawyer sat in his usual pose, the one
with which I'd first become accustomed in the days along the trail in Missouri, after I'd joined him, Angus, Boyd and Malcolm – both legs bent and
arms wrapped about his knees, left wrist caught in the opposite hand.

I was angled to keep watch for Mary approaching from the direction of town, still uncertain if she would be able to manage such a potentially dangerous feat; I recalled all too vividly the night I'd crept from Ginny's on an errand of some magnitude, imperiling myself to help my sweet Deirdre. I would not have dared to leave the whorehouse, which kept us as effectively imprisoned as any jail, for a lesser reason. All of us remained strangers to Mary and I would not blame her for reconsidering such personal risk to deliver a message to people unknown to her. Would the threat of punishment change Mary's mind? I prayed it would not but my heart was sinking along with the sun; the road into town had quieted with the dinner hour, no more than a rider or two, there a lone buckboard drawn by a team of mismatched mules. When a man appeared at the crest of the rise, backlit by the magenta sky and headed our direction, my spine stiffened in instant alarm.

I thought, *The Frenchman...*

"Yonder fellow." Jacob indicated with his pipe. All three men shifted, hands moving to their armaments; when it became apparent this individual was indeed bound for our camp, we stood, Sawyer assisting me, then angling so I was behind him.

"Boys!" Rebecca heralded, but as she called to them I realized the man striding our way was none other than Mary from the saloon, clad in boots and trousers, and a heavy jacket too large for her frame, long hair concealed beneath a wide-brimmed duster similar to Tilson's.

The men, reaching this same conclusion, swept the hats from their heads as she came near; Mary, with a note of irony in the movement, executed a small, formal bow but refrained from doffing her own headwear. She said, "Good evening. No need for alarm, it simply proves easier to navigate the town when dressed as a man."

"Please, do sit," I invited at once, indicating our fire. "Thank you ever so much for coming. We'd begun to fear you would not."

Mary settled on her haunches with the ease afforded to her by men's clothing, folding her long legs and resting wrists to knees, a masculine pose which would prove impossible had she been clad in customary skirts. As tall and lean as she was, her femininity was neatly disguised by the bulk of the leather garments.

"To bed," Rebecca told the boys, kissing their foreheads, nodding at the wagon. "I'll join you shortly."

"Mary Henriksen, late of Ohio," she said, leaning to offer her hand to Tilson, nodding at Jacob as she affirmed their acquaintance. And then to Sawyer and me, "Beg pardon. We exchanged introductions earlier this day, but please do remind me of your given names."

"Sawyer and Lorie Davis," I said. "Might you care for food, or drink?"

"Thank you, no, Mrs. Davis," Mary said. "I mustn't linger long or my presence on the main floor will be missed."

If only she knew how well I understood.

"I am Edward Tilson, my dear, and this is my niece, Rebecca Krage," Tilson said, as Rebecca knelt at Mary's side; the two women regarded each other, Rebecca with the scarcely-concealed desire to beg for answers, Mary with outright surprise.

"Rebecca, you say?" Mary asked. "Why, I've heard of you. Might you be known to young Malcolm Carter as *Mrs.* Rebecca?"

"I am," she breathed, hands clasped at her breasts. "Please, what news have you?"

Mary's jaw squared; her manly garb and the darkening air would have fooled any onlooker. She said, "I best back up," and sighed deeply. Not without sympathy, she continued, "Word reached us last autumn that both of them were killed. Though he is a born liar, Jean Luc was not lying about that particular detail." So saying, she regarded each of us with an expression both wary and watchful. I did not believe I imagined the note of regret buried in her tone.

Jacob prompted, "What can you tell us about my nephew signing on to drive cattle into the Western Territories? Was that the truth?"

There was no mistaking Mary's tension, the brief downward flicker of her eyes, the subtle lifting of her shoulders with the inhalation of a deep breath. But her voice was steady as she said, "That is also true. The night I met the Carters, they had only just arrived in St. Paul. The elder brother spoke of a storm which destroyed their possessions. He appeared at the end of his rope, hiding this for the sake of the boy, I could tell plain. It was me who suggested…" Her throat bobbed as she swallowed and I was stunned to observe moisture in her eyes. She roughly thumbed aside any telltale tears. "You see, I knew of a party that needed a wrangler because one of their men, Dyer Lawson, was killed before they could ride out from St. Paul. The man heading that drive was my…my friend. His name was Grady Ballard."

I met Sawyer's gaze; he saw, as did I, that this man's name held great meaning for Mary. She cared for him, perhaps even loved him, even though loving someone was the worst thing a whore could do to herself.

I asked quietly, "What of this Mr. Ballard?"

Mary ground her teeth. "I knew Grady well. I thought not to see him, or any of his party, until this spring, but one of them arrived late last October, intending to return to his home in Kansas before winter struck, or so he claimed. It was he who brought us news of the attack, and of Grady's passing." She drew a small, tight breath before her words tumbled as debris over a falls. "Grady was familiar with that route, never had trouble before. Virgil's tale didn't set well with me from the first, I'll not lie. I knew Virgil for Grady's friend, but I never took to him as Grady and Isobel did. Virgil is a weasely sort, always made me nervous. He made Emilia nervous, too, and I always believed it was why she left The Belle last summer."

"Who is this Virgil?" Sawyer asked.

"Virgil Turnbull," Mary said, with discernible fire in her tone. "He and Grady were raised up together, back in Kansas. Was Grady who got Virgil a job driving cattle when no one else would take him, one-handed as he is since the War. They'd driven cattle together a dozen times in the past few years. Grady was no one's fool, I swear this to be true."

"*Turnbull*," Tilson muttered in acknowledgment, elbowing Jacob. "That's the 'Trundle' we heard of, earlier," and Jacob nodded immediate agreement.

"Do you believe Grady is dead?" I asked, and the pulsing swell of Mary's desire to believe he was not was tangible in the air around her. "Do you believe the tale that this man Virgil told, of an attack by Indians?"

What it cost Mary to answer, I could not accurately guess; my heart clenched as she whispered, "I could not stomach Virgil's tale, I'll not deny, but I no longer believe Grady is alive somewhere out there. He would have returned to St. Paul by now."

Rebecca's face was pale enough to resemble a bare skull. Her hand shook as she pressed a fist to her lips.

"Why would this man Turnbull lie about being attacked?" Jacob pressed. One question atop the next, just like Malcolm, he added, "Why would my nephews travel so far off course without leaving word?"

Mary explained, "Mr. Carter was in a fix when he arrived in St. Paul, as I said. He was seeking work at The Belle, but Jean Luc had no positions for a man to fill. Jean Luc needed a woman to take Emilia's place, since she ran off. That very night I told Mr. Carter of Grady's need for another wrangler and Grady appeared not a quarter-hour later. He and Mr. Carter spoke, and struck a bargain. As I said, Mr. Carter was desperate. He needed money and agreed to take the job. Grady was in my company that night, later, and he always talked to me, trusted me with matters important to him. I am no green young thing, fool enough to think he loved me, but he cared for me, on this I'd bet my last dollar, and I cared for him, a great deal. The news of his passing pains me yet."

I reached and took one of her hands; rather than drawing away, she curled her long, tense fingers about mine.

"What else?" Jacob asked, solemn and intent as he studied Mary, seated directly across the fire from him; red light gleamed along the facets of the beads braided into his beard.

Mary wiped her nose with the back of her free hand. "I don't know why you received no word from Mr. Carter. Grady gave to me two letters that night, written by Mr. Carter's hand. In turn, I gave them to Cecilia and she promised to deliver them to the post office by morning's light."

"The woman we saw today?" I asked, thinking of the way Cecilia had fetched her employer once we started asking questions.

Mary nodded affirmation.

"Where is this woman? Might we speak to her?" Tilson asked; he had placed his comforting touch upon Rebecca's back. "Or would this Jean Luc prevent it?"

Mary's knowing gaze flashed to Tilson. "I will ask Cecilia, in your stead. She never spoke of failing to deliver the letters, but I feel responsible. Grady trusted me with them and I should have seen them delivered with my own eyes."

"Did you see Boyd or Malcolm again before they left?" Sawyer asked. "What occurred that night?"

"I did not see them again after they left The Belle. Neither had eaten in a good few days, I'd have wagered. Mr. Carter appeared haggard, and the boy could scarce keep from gobbling. I played a round or two of cards with the little feller."

"Was he well?" I begged.

"He was a sprightly little thing, sweet as honey. It was plain to me that

Mr. Carter looked after him. The first thing he said to Grady that night, after Grady offered the job, was that he wouldn't take his brother through any territory that wasn't safe."

My breath was short and Sawyer rested a calming hand between my shoulder blades. I prompted, "You said Malcolm spoke of Rebecca?"

"Yes, the boy claimed his brother was in love with a Mrs. Rebecca and his words brought Mr. Carter pain, if you don't mind my saying."

Tears washed over Rebecca's face; she pressed hard against her mouth as Mary continued bluntly, "Mr. Carter refused two separate offers that very night, of girls ripe for him. But hardly did he flicker an eyelash. Handsome devil, he could have had the both at once. Izzy didn't care but Cecilia was in offense at the refusal."

"The same woman who was entrusted to deliver his letters?" Tilson asked; I'd been about to ask the same, increasingly wary. Jealousy and offense amongst that lot – the lot of which I'd been a part for nearly three years – was dangerous as a dose of poison.

Mary nodded again.

Sawyer asked, "What of when Virgil Turnbull returned to St. Paul in October? What was his story at that time?"

Mary eyed the heavens, deep with nightfall, the advent of darkness forcing her to take her leave. I restrained the urge to grasp her arms, to make her stay. Speaking hastily, she said, "Virgil claimed that In'juns drove off the stock and killed all of them in the party, which would have been Grady, Quill, the Carters, and the little Lawson girl. I hate to give you folks false hope, I do, but I ain't survived being a whore without learning to notice things, little things, and something about Virgil's tale was off. For a long time I expected Grady to show up here, but enough time has passed that I no longer believe he will, as I said." She closed her eyes for the space of a breath. "Virgil rode into St. Paul in the company of two other men that day. The three of them was gaming and drinking at The Steam House, not but a stone's throw from The Belle when I spied him. Wasn't Virgil surprised when I appeared at his table." She released a small, humorless huff of laughter. "He didn't seem to realize a whore can walk across the street same as any old person, that it ain't against the rules."

"You say he was gaming and drinking? Seems cold for a man who'd lost his entire party to a murderous attack," Jacob observed.

"That's his way. I asked him straightaway where was Grady and the others, and Virgil pulled off his hat and told me they were killed, calm as a summer afternoon," Mary said, the muscles in her cheeks tightening. "I asked him why he hadn't seen fit to find me first thing, as he knows well Grady was my friend. I asked what happened to them and he said they were set upon in the night hours, but that he managed to escape and was lucky enough to meet up with these new fellers."

"Who were these men he was with?" Tilson asked.

Mary said, "One I knew from around, a half-breed name of Church Talk. He's never been a customer of mine, I don't take on half-breeds unless Jean Luc says I must."

Jacob said, "I have heard of this Church Talk. Ojibwe. He was given the handle for his fondness of quoting Scripture."

"What of the other fellow?" Tilson pressed.

"He was a stranger to me, and hardly more than a boy. Light of hair, slender." As Mary spoke, a bootheel seemed to increase its pressure on my heart. I saw understanding dawn upon Sawyer's face, and Tilson's –

"What was this boy's name?" Sawyer spoke so intently that Mary leaned slightly away from him, startled.

"Yancy," she whispered. "He wore a blouse with frilled cuffs and in my head I nicknamed him 'Fancy Yancy' even as I stood there at the table."

"Oh, dear God…" Rebecca breathed, and I feared she would faint; Tilson bolstered her with an arm about the waist.

"You know him?" Mary asked, her bewildered gaze flowing over each of us in turn, perceiving our evident shock.

"Are any of them about St. Paul now?" Sawyer asked, and his thoughts were racing, making ferocious leaps, as a horse pursued by starving wolves.

Mary's too-large hat listed to one side. Straightening it, she said, "No. I would tell you if I'd seen any of them, I swear. Virgil tends to visit The Belle when he is in town, though perhaps he won't in Emilia's absence, as he favored her. But Isobel would tell me if she'd spied him, as she's fond of him, God knows why. I know you folks ain't got a reason in this world to trust me, and to be honest I am here now mainly for Grady's sake."

She bowed her head; when she lifted it her face had softened, grown somehow younger in the firelight. It was the face of a girl who'd never spent hundreds of nights spreading her thighs for an onslaught of men, who'd never been forced to feign enjoyment or learn to observe her employer's mercurial moods, down to the smallest gesture, in order to avoid punishment or blame. She whispered, "Grady would want me to get to the bottom of this sorry situation. If I can be of help to you folks I will, this I vow."

"Thank you," I said, and she squeezed my hand.

"I'd best return," she whispered. "I don't dare visit your camp again, but I will get word to you, if there is any to be had. It does not do to anger Jean Luc, please know this. I will get word to you if I hear anything."

"Come, lass, I'll accompany you back to the edge of town," Tilson said. "I don't much like the thought of a lady walking alone."

The momentary vulnerability that had shone through Mary's countenance promptly vanished, replaced by the hardness which she'd adopted to survive. "I thank you, Mr. Tilson. It's been a long while since anyone's mistaken me for a *lady*, especially in this get-up, but I appreciate it all the same."

Later, alone in the wagon, I lay in Sawyer's arms, tears pouring brokenly forth, inundating his shirt. He murmured, stroking my hair, understanding I could no more contain these tears than I could beams from the sun in my cupped hands. He let me speak without interruption, understanding without being told my need to release tears and words, both at once; I could feel the tension emanating from his body, his internal battle to accept that Boyd and Malcolm may truly be dead, no matter how we fought the notion, no matter how we longed otherwise.

"Mary spoke to them, Sawyer…she *saw* them, saw my sweet Malcolm. How can Rebecca bear it?" I could hear the choked, muffled sobs coming from her wagon; worse, somehow, than had she been outright wailing. "Fallon was *here*, he must have found them somewhere out there on the prairie… what if Mary is right, what if they are dead? Traveling here eased my worry… allowed me to think of other things, but now that we are here and they are not, I cannot bear it, oh Sawyer, oh God, *hold me…*"

At last he spoke, whispering against the tangles of my hair. "I will hold you always, my Lorie. I will never let you go."

I gave over to the tears I'd kept at bay as we traveled, burying my face against the familiar scent of him. His arms were of iron, banded about me, keeping me whole. Our daughter pressed her heels into my ribs, as though concerned at the storming of emotion to which she was unwittingly privy. After a spell, when the moon had set and the camp was dark and still, I calmed, cradled between husband and daughter, thusly secure; Sawyer glided his palm in small, soothing circles over the crest of my distended belly, finally succeeding in settling the babe to quietude. I whispered, "Being in that place today…"

"I saw how you went pale," he murmured in response, pressing a kiss to my jaw.

"It is strange to feel brave in many regards but so vulnerable in others," I whispered, shifting so that I could rest my nose to his neck, feeling the steady beat of his pulse against my cheek and his breath upon my forehead. I elaborated, "Before Mary arrived, I was thinking of the night I dared to sneak from Ginny's, to the docks, for Deirdre's sake."

Sawyer knew the story and cupped the nape of my neck, kissing my right eye.

I sensed his concern, his willingness to do battle with anything that caused me harm, even my memories. I whispered, "I stole from the saloon because I knew Deirdre needed me, no other reason. I cared not for my own worries that night, I cared only for helping her. For Mary to venture forth, even in a clever disguise, means she cared more for Grady than she willingly admitted. She loved him, or she would not have risked herself to help strangers such as we are to her."

"I believe what she told us was the truth," Sawyer said.

"Do you believe…" But I could not finish the question. Clinging to hope that Boyd and Malcolm had survived was the worst sort of delusion; a desperate wish, a pipe dream with no more substance than exhaled smoke. Tucked close to Sawyer's warmth in our wagon, I rebelled at the thought of continuing on without them, of reconciling ourselves to the acceptance of never again seeing their faces or hearing their voices in this life. And then I thought of something else Mary had related to us.

"Mary spoke of a little girl traveling with them. How little, I wonder? Old enough to journey such a distance, I suppose." Thinking of the boy's tender nature, I whispered, "She would have taken to Malcolm."

A FTER A STRETCH it seemed Cora and me had been traveling the prairie since the time of Jesus and Mary.

"Do you think we'll die out here?" Cora asked. Her voice was a small speck in the big old bare prairie, a place bigger and emptier than anything I ever saw. Its exact middle was where we rode along on Aces High, his ears twitching at our voices, waiting for me to tell him it was all right. But I wouldn't lie to my boy, my good boy who'd carried me all the way from Tennessee, who held his ground firm even when that piss-ant varmint coward Fallon Yancy meant for him to bolt and snap my neck.

"I do not," I said, and tried with all my might to sound like I meant it. Cora was under my protection and Boyd said a man's job was to do anything he must to keep those under his protection safe. I was scared enough to blubber like a pint-sized tagalong, scared enough that my innards was tangled up in knotted ropes so I couldn't move them, even when I squatted to try. But I weren't about to let Cora see how frightful scared I was. It would be shirking my duty.

For the longest time I didn't think I could ever love any girl but Lorie. From the moment I first saw Lorie-Lorie, months back on the prairie outside St. Louis, my heart near stopped a-beating. I stared at her in a way that would have made my daddy slap the back of my head, as it was so rude. Stared until I thought my eyes might pop right out and roll along the prickly ground like plums shook from a tree. It was just that never had I seen a girl so pretty in all my livin' life. Prettier than an angel from heaven. Gus, good old Gus, who was still alive then, had lifted her down from Admiral's back as careful as you'd lift a child. I was setting on a stump at our fire, yards away; all

I could see was the outline of a long-haired girl and so I galloped over fast as my feet could carry me.

When I drew near I caught sight of her face and felt like someone had kicked me in the chest with a booted foot. Her eyes were scared, I could tell, roving from one to the other of us, and Sawyer had been yelling at Gus as Lorie stood between them, acting like he hadn't been taught his manners, even though I knew he had. I looked at once to my brother, but Boyd weren't worried and when I saw he weren't, I weren't neither. Boyd's eyebrows was set in lines that meant he found the whole thing a titch humorous; reassured, I turned my gaze back to Lorie's sweet angel face, seeing her eyes as bright as jewels set in a necklace, blue and green mixed together. From that moment forth I made it my most treasured goal in life, along with owning a dozen horses and as many pistols as I could get my hands on, to one day make Lorie my wife.

I aim to marry her, I told my brother the second night after Lorie joined us.

Boyd had chuckled, half-asleep. He muttered, *You always was a dreamer, boy.*

It seemed stupider than stupid now. Of course I still loved Lorie-Lorie so much my heart felt near to busting apart, like an August melon split with ripeness, but I knew I could not marry her; it was a fool's dream. Before long it was plain as raindrops on an uplifted face that Lorie's eyes was for Sawyer, and Sawyer alone, just as his was for her, and she couldn't belong to me as well as to him. Thinking of them all just now, of Boyd and Sawyer and Lorie, as Aces High walked over the hard-packed crust of snow, his hooves crunching it until my ears jangled, hurt worse than a rawhide strapping.

I closed my eyes to the sun's glare and saw the same endless bright snow, but now colored purple-blue, like a new bruise against the back of my eyelids. And then I saw Boyd the way we'd left him, sitting against the base of the broken wagon. He looked so much like Daddy, their voices with the selfsame note, that sometimes when I was especial tired I confused the two of them.

I thought again, *I'll get Cora to safety an' return for him, fast as I am able.* There weren't no question. Riding away from my brother was worse than being nearly hung to death. Boyd had been struck many times, and he'd been dragged behind the In'jun man's horse. He'd taken a crossbow arrow in the leg. And still he'd saved me. I'd never seen him look so rough; his blood had left dark patches all over my clothes. I loved him with ever'thing in me but I knew it still weren't as much as he loved me; Boyd might die so that I might live, I knew this.

Cora whispered, "Are you cold?"

She huddled against me, feeling small as the gray kitten I'd left behind with Cort and Natty, all the miles back in Iowa. Stormy, we named the little critter. The boys promised to keep watch of him for me, and Lorie promised to bring him with in the spring. I imagined Stormy grown fat and sassy, riding snug upon her lap, where I'd rested my head many a time so she'd pet my hair. I longed for Lorie so awful my heart stung like I'd dragged it through a clump of itchweed. I wanted her more than my own mama, whose face sometimes turned into Lorie's face in my mind. Lorie would take me and Cora in her arms, and hold us safe.

I put my chin against Cora's soft cheek, finding it chilled. My heart beat hard against the back of her borrowed coat. I said, "I ain't cold," and kissed her cheek. Our air made clouds when we talked or breathed, puffs of clouds that melted together so our breath was combined. I knew that someday I would marry Cora and together we would have children. It was different than the way I thought I'd marry Lorie. I knew I would marry Cora because my bones knew it. My bones felt the same truth in her bones, like a bridge built between our two selves. One we could walk across and then into the other. Cora's eyes looked at my eyes and I understood things without any words at all. Cora lay beside me at night, beneath the wagon, and it seemed like her body might just become a part of mine and there'd be no space between us anymore, like butter stirred into cream.

"Are you hurting, Malcolm?" she asked, worried for me, as always.

"I am not," I said, and I wasn't just now. Later, once the sun sank over the edge of the big prairie ahead of us, due west, the cold, and hurt, would come. I had to get us as far as Aces was able, before then. Boyd thought we were less than a week from the fort on the Missouri River and I aimed to keep riding until we got there. Aces could do it. He was the best horse I knew. He was strong and he loved me, just as I loved him. I knew he wouldn't let me down. I was a-counting on it. On we rode, over the prairie that weren't near as flat as it seemed from a distance; Aces would walk up a little, low hill and down its other side, the land shaped like waves on stirred-up water.

Cora said, "You might not tell me the truth because you think I'd worry."

"I wouldn't neither," I said, contrary now. Cora's words often made me contrary. "I tell you true."

"It's bright," she murmured next, shading her eyes with both hands, long sleeves dangling into her face. She wore Grady's heavy wool shirt, which swallowed her frame. At the thought of Grady, my teeth came together with a clack I felt deep in my skull. I'd watched as Virgil rose from the ground and shot through Grady's spine with the pistol I'd tried to grab before the In'jun man struck my head. Grady was dragging himself across the grass and kept going even after Virgil shot him. Virgil's wrist stump flapped about like a startled bird but his left hand, holding the pistol, shot two more times, until Grady stopped moving. I'd watched while the In'jun man secured his rope around Boyd, who cursed and fought him.

Fallon Yancy had kept his pistol pointed at me and I couldn't stop any of it, Grady being shot or Boyd being dragged, and I felt the sickness of these truths staked out way inside my heart, where I couldn't reach it. Boyd was the bonniest fighter I ever saw, a walloping good puncher, and he'd near killed the Yankee on the roan gelding, with just his fists. I thought the In'jun man would drag Boyd to death. I was so ill at this notion I'd hardly cared when Fallon and the beat-to-hell Yankee got me up on Aces and meant to stretch my neck. But I'd thought, *I can't die. I'd leave Cora without me.*

Boyd needed me to be strong, there in that clearing beneath the oak tree, and now, riding Cora to safety across this damnable empty prairie, he needed me even more. My brother needed me to stop being a boy and be a man. I kept the thought of Boyd's strength in my mind. Boyd took care of me and always traveled without complaint. I thought of Sawyer, who had ridden without letup, hard across the miles to find Lorie. Like Boyd, Sawyer never complained. I remembered the night back in the state of Missouri when our horses was stole by men intending to kill us, and saw again the burning fury in Sawyer's eyes as he mounted Whistler to ride hell-for-leather. To get to Lorie, to do what needed to be done, no matter the cost.

Sawyer! Boyd had yelled at him, grabbing for Whistler's bridle. *You'll be killed. You got no one to watch your back.*

If I don't get to Lorie, I am already dead, Sawyer had said. His face was grim, set as carved wood. No compromise was in his voice. He gripped Boyd's hand, holding fast for a final second, and then heeled Whistler, taking her into a breakneck canter, leaving Boyd and me alone on the Missouri prairie – but that had been summer, not late autumn, and Missouri was a state with law in it, not a territory where there was no law. Sawyer always did what needed doing. And Boyd did what needed doing. That was a man's job, and I was now a man. Even if I didn't feel much like one, scared as a stupid old hen with a winter-starved fox nearby. Cora would understand if I admitted to this, but I didn't want her feeling any more fearful than she was already.

When first we'd met, she was fearful near all the time. She'd kept her chin down and didn't raise her voice. I learned that her eyes embarrassed her with their two different colors, because people always seen fit to comment on them as though she couldn't hear their words. She told me about it, quiet and low, while we rode on the wagon seat with Quill, who sometimes passed the reins to me and dozed for a spell. I knew Cora was right fond of Quill but I liked when he dozed so her and me could talk. I learned how she loved her daddy, the only kin she ever knew.

In turn, I told her of waking from the typhoid sickness, having been brought to Mrs. Elmira's house across the holler, to find that Mama and Daddy was gone, that they'd passed while I lay in fever dreams. I wouldn't have believed Mrs. Elmira's words if not for seeing my folks later that same day, laid out proper-like for burial by Mrs. Elmira and her eldest daughter, Mrs. Beulah. Mama's lips were gray and stiff, her honey hair arranged into a coronet of braids. Daddy's closed eyes looked sunken but when I touched his beard it was still soft. They were dreadful thin, their bones close to the surface. We'd been near to starving.

I told Cora of how I'd wanted to be dead along with my folks and wondered why I was spared; I felt my body should be carried with theirs to the Carter plot on our farm, out near the blackgum grove, to be laid to rest alongside Beaumont and Grafton, and Granny Rose. Back then, late in the War, there'd been no word from Boyd for many months. Cora asked if I remembered the sound of Mama's and Daddy's voices, and I explained to her what Lorie said, about the singing. Lorie and me sang to remember our mamas' voices, and so I'd sung for Cora on the wagon seat, while Quill laughed, or snorted in his sleep, or sometimes played his harmonica.

And all those times, riding along on the wagon since September, Virgil had been sleeping in the pallet bed, no more than a few feet away. He never yelled at us, or told us to pipe down because he needed his rest. He lay quiet. All that time I never figured he was capable of turning so terrible against us. Of shooting Grady, a man who'd been his friend. Of riding away to let us die. Had Virgil reached the Lawsons' ranch? I had trouble thinking of the Lawsons as Cora's kin. Would Virgil and Fallon, and their party, ride back this way to be certain we was dead? A coldness that had nothing to do with weather gripped me – what if they came upon Boyd before I got back to him? He hadn't a weapon besides firewood. Not even a blade. And them buzzards had swarmed.

"We shouldn't a-left," I said over the snow crunching under Aces' hooves, and I couldn't find room to be shamed that my voice sounded high as a little girl's. If Aces threw a shoe we was good as dead, but I couldn't think on that now.

"We can turn back," Cora said. Her hands were curled into Aces' thick mane, for warmth, but she slipped them free and gripped my knees, as if to make certain I knew she meant her words.

Instead of answering I put my face against the back of Cora's head, only just lightly, for comfort. Her curly hair was full of snarls and smelled like wood smoke, warm on my cold mouth. I wanted to be a man, to make my daddy and my brothers proud, but there was a secret part of me, close to where my heart beat, that wanted to be watched over. That felt safest when Boyd and Sawyer was near, knowing the two of them would make the decisions and would let no harm come to me. I'd seen Boyd get almost killed to stop harm from coming to me, but I knew not even he could stop all harm. I knew I had to depend on myself, that this was part of becoming a man. I thought of the drizzling day Boyd and Sawyer rode up to Mrs. Elmira's house in the holler, riding through the rain to come for me. Gladness just about burst apart my ribs that day.

I had no gladness now. I wanted to cry. I was thirsty as the devil in a dry spell. I wanted Sawyer and Whistler to ride up and save us. I wanted to be back in Iowa, in Mrs. Rebecca's dooryard with Cort and Natty, who were my friends. I wanted Boyd, my bold brother who clamped me into headlocks and knuckled my scalp. Who liked best to laugh, who wouldn't let me curse and scolded me six ways from Sunday on any given day, who played games with me, games like trying to sweet-talk Mrs. Rebecca into making fried chicken, or walnut cake with whipped cream frosting. Boyd meant to ride back to her before Fallon found us. Boyd wanted Mrs. Rebecca for his wife. He loved her dearly, I knew this to be true. He'd always looked at her like she was a meal he intended to lick his plate over. But he wasn't here; he was left behind, waiting on me, and all decisions sat on my shoulders.

"We can't turn back," I muttered, in despair. "Boyd would be angered."

"Then we must get to the fort," Cora said.

BOYD'S ESTIMATION was off by a few days; we reached a settlement on a late afternoon only four days after leaving him behind. I was ragged-tired, ready to fall headlong out of the saddle. Aces was limping. His back and belly were saddle-sore and I was sick over it, but we couldn't stop. Cora hadn't spoken since yesterday, her head lolling against me. Neither of us had been able to move our bowels since before the attack on our camp. It had sleeted like the dickens since noon, hard ice collecting on our shoulders and sticking to Aces' mane in thick clumps, but a rising wind tore apart the clouds and let the sun break through as we came upon the settlement, winking red in Cora's hair. Tall bluffs stood high at the edges of the Missouri River, a flat, dark blue mirror in the distance; the sudden sun speckled its surface. My hands were raw around the reins, but we'd made it here.

I thought, *You done a man's work.*

From a distance we saw the tidy line of a stockade wall, and hide structures that looked like cones set on their flat ends, long poles jutting from the top along with smoke, all clustered together, dozens strong. Curious faces of the few who'd ventured out in the storm, each and every one In'jun, dressed head to toe in leather, some with bear-hide robes, peered from behind hoods lined in thick fur. The scent of roasting meat on the air made my stomach cramp into knots too tight to be untied.

Our passage towards their camp caused the sort of gossip-like flutter that strangers in Suttonville had occasioned; Cora and me hardly looked a threat but we were unknown to them, all the same. Two men with long braids and rifles in the crooks of their elbows rode out to greet us. I drew Aces to a halt when their horses were twenty strides distant and lifted my hands to show I had no weapons. I was no danger to them. But just as quick I had to grab Cora about the waist, as she almost fell without my arms holding her in place.

"We need help!" I tried to call out, but my throat felt as dry and rough as if I'd been eating sand. The two men heeled their mounts and cantered to us, talking to each other in their own language. Tired and half-witted as I felt at present, their words flowed like sap from a tapped tree, warm and thick around my head. I whispered to them, "Please help us."

Up close I saw their bold and impressive faces, broad and red-brown, quick black eyes missing nothing. Noses like knife blades jutting. One of them was tattooed across his cheekbones so detailed I wanted to stare at the pattern made of little black shapes, circles and arrows and such, but I did not wish to be rude. They bristled with armaments – Springfield rifles, pistols in cross holsters, hatchets and neck knives stowed in pouches decorated with beads. They wore leather moccasins beneath leather breeches, fringed and also brightly beaded, the beads painted with colors to dazzle my eyes. After I spoke, one leaned near and asked plain as day in English, "Who are you?"

"My name is Malcolm Carter, sir." I tipped my hat brim, holding Cora steady with my other arm. She did not stir and I felt the heat of fear. "This here is Cora Lawson an' she's near froze through. We rode a piece to get here, mister, please help us."

"Wagon?" asked the other, motioning back the way we'd come. He lifted a hand to his mouth and then mimed eating something.

I nodded. "We did leave a wagon behind. We ain't had no food in days."

"Come," he said, gesturing with his head.

Within short order, Cora and I were guests behind the stockade wall, a small, timbered square surrounding a cluster of cabins built of stacked logs, with thick gray-white chinking between each log. More of the In'jun structures was pitched inside the stockade, which had a heavy gate that was not latched. People, white and red, moved freely between the inside and the out. There were plenty of In'jun women with crow-black braids and I wondered if they looked like my Aunt Hannah would look, when I finally saw her. A flagpole with a flapping United States flag was positioned near the front gate and the cabins inside had been built with their doors facing to the middle. I was so cold I could not climb down from Aces after one of the In'jun men lifted Cora, holding her the way Mama would have held a newborn babe. People gathered around like we was a carnival come to town, all a-chatter and a-flutter.

"Come, lad," and another man, and he sounded like I remembered Jean Luc from The Dolly Belle. "Let me help you."

"I don't need no…" But the words stuck in my mouth like a stubborn frog leg, one that wouldn't be swallowed because the frog still wanted to jump out, even after Mama fried it up in a pan. I lowered my eyebrows so the world wouldn't look so strange – like I'd ducked under muddy creek water. And then I slid headfirst down a long and icy hill.

"TAKE MORE water," said a low voice, a woman's voice that felt so good in my ears I shivered. I was warm, tucked beneath blankets. I could feel all my fingers and toes. A fire crackled, throwing red, leaping light.

"Lorie?" I whispered. "Is that you?"

"Hush," she soothed, and the outline of a woman leaned close and helped me to sit upright. I smelled her and knew right away she weren't Lorie, re-membering that Lorie was far away. I put my hands around the tin cup the woman offered and brought it to my lips, taking water.

"Where is Cora?"

"She rests," the woman said.

My eyes could see better now, into the edges of a room with no edges. The room wasn't inside of a house but instead a round In'jun structure, animal-hide walls pitched like a tall canvas tent, slanting up to a point at the top, where smoke curled and escaped. A fire burned low in the center, near to em-bers. I saw Cora tucked beneath a blanket, curled into a ball like she always slept, both hands under her cheek. The fire showed me her face and I could take a full breath again.

"Thank you kindly, ma'am," I whispered, keeping my voice low because there was a-plenty of sleeping bodies around the fire. I needed to explain about Boyd, about going back for him, but it was the dead of night. Fear and worry gnawed inside me like mice in the grain bin.

"Rest," she murmured, taking the cup.

I lay down, afraid to disobey, curling into the blessed warmth of the blan-ket. But I could not return to sleep. My thoughts held fast to my brother, back there on the prairie. He needed me and I was doing nothing in this moment but worrying. I was lying here and he was hurting.

What if he passed? What if he's gone?!

I pressed my knuckles hard against my forehead, driving out such bad thoughts. But they stayed, hanging on like molasses in a cold jar. I did not sleep again before gray light began trickling through the smoke hole. Lying on my side and facing her, I saw Cora wake. She sat upright with a jerk, eyes searching for me; I reached a hand and she crawled to my side, dragging her blanket along the ground. I tucked her close and smoothed a hand over her head, and she burrowed into my blanket, tangling up our arms. Her movements woke others, a bearded man wearing a union suit and three children who looked more In'jun than white, two girls and a boy.

The man was the one I'd thought sounded like Jean Luc. He sat and scratched his chest, swiping at his eyes with both fists. His hair was in disarray but he tugged a knitted cap with a long tassel over his head before scooting closer to the fire and stirring it, shifting the iron grate and the coffee pot into better position. The woman who gave me water in the night hours was not in sight. The three children spoke to the man in a language I couldn't understand and he answered back in the same, grinning and gesturing at Cora and me. I sat up as all three scrambled our way on hands and knees, giggling and speaking over top of one another. I did not understand their fast-moving words but I understood their curiosity; I wasn't a-feared of them but I lifted a forearm and blocked my head when one of the girls reached to pet my hair.

The man laughed and spoke in English this time. "Albie! Introduce yourself, girl."

Cora ducked beneath the blanket as the In'jun children knelt beside us, three in a row, mouths smiling, eyes snapping with excitement. Their hair was long and black, arranged in shiny braids, even the boy's. They wore leather garments and their hands fluttered around like slender brown birds, wanting to poke and prod. Even so, I could tell they wanted to be friends, to know us. The oldest girl was of an age with me, the boy in the middle, the littlest sister no bigger than Natty, just a sprite. With a strange lilt to the words, the oldest girl said, "My name is Albertine Darvell." She gestured to the others. "This is Emeline and Pierpont. What name is yours?"

"I am Malcolm Alastair Carter," I said with my best manners and offered a hand, which Albertine accepted and shook. Her grip was strong as a boy's and she grinned so big I saw all her teeth. She giggled and pointed at the blankets and so I explained, "This here is Cora Lawson. She's right shy," but I drew aside the top edge so Cora could see they meant no harm. She didn't want them to see her eyes, I knew without her speaking of it. These three might laugh, or poke fun.

Cora blinked as the light fell across her face, slow, like a fawn who didn't know where it was, or if it was safe; her green eye shone like clear creek water, her dark eye with bits of gold, like treasure beneath the creek water. Her hair

was tangled over with curls so messy a comb would have a terrible time dragging through. My heart made a feeling like a hand squeezing into a tight fist.

Cora was so pretty.

The three of them leaned closer and peered, exclaiming to each other in
their own language and trying their best to touch her face; Emeline crawled
right over my lap to get closer and I shifted my whole body and made a fence
with my arms, sheltering Cora so they couldn't pester her. I wanted to keep
her safe so bad my chest hurt. The entrance flap shuddered with a sudden
movement as someone tugged it aside, sending white morning light scatter-
ing all through the smoky space. A woman came inside, dressed snug in a fur
wrap, and spoke sharply to the children. They retreated to the fire in a noisy
clamber, still murmuring.

The man said, "Pleased to meet you, young lad Malcolm and Miss Cora. I
am Xavier Darvell. This is Fern, my dear wife, and you have met my inquisitive youngsters. We do not often receive unexpected guests, please forgive
them. You have ridden far to reach the fort, yes? I too am most curious." He
sat at the fire the same way Sawyer always did, knees bent and arms about
them, fingers latched. He did not sound upset but the woman was scolding
her children just like I remembered Mama scolding me when I was naughty,
talking fast and low, shaking a pointed finger. All three sat with downcast
eyes and chins, but Pierpont peeked sideways at us and a smile pulled at his
mouth. I knew he and me could be fast friends, if only I weren't on so desperate an errand. I thought of the Sauk boys my friends, Grant and Miles Rawley, spoke of back in Iowa. Sauk boys got to choose their own names when
they was of an age, and could claim three or four horses each. I bet Pierpont
had him at least two fine horses.

I waited till the woman was done scolding before I said, "Sir, thank you
kindly for helping us. We traveled far to get here an' left my brother behind.
He was hurt bad when our camp was attacked less than a week ago, on the
prairie." Words tumbled like rocks from an upturned wheelbarrow as I tried
to explain. "We was on a cattle drive, headed for a spread owned by a man
name of Royal Lawson. We was attacked an' the cattle stole. Two men in our
company was kilt. My brother was wounded. Please, I must ride back for
him. I must have help. I'll do anything you ask, in return." Tears filled up my
eyes, stinging and raw as skinned knuckles. I didn't care if they all saw me cry.

At my words, they stared at me like I'd sprouted a corn crop from my head.

"Please. I can't leave him there, he'll die."

"Son," Xavier said, kind and serious, the voice of someone who means to deliver bad news and is sorry to deliver it. "An ice storm has roared for the past forty-eight hours. The landscape is slick as a frozen pond, and just as treacherous."

"I must go." I was sick with frustration. I stood, dragging Cora with me. "I can't delay no more. He *needs* me."

"You have a most brave soul," Xavier said. He stayed sitting and they all kept watching me like I was putting on a fine show, dancing and singing and the like. "But there can be no travel this day, young sir. You would not get far, even with such a fine horse as you rode into the fort with."

"I must," I said again, and my throat felt slit with pain.

But Xavier only shook his head.

I *cain't lift you alone, you see. Can you hear me?*

You gotta give me a hand, young feller, I ain't as strong as I used ta be.

How'd your wagon come to catch fire? Your horseflesh musta run off.

C'mon now, this here storm is gonna let loose any second and that leg of yours looks right poorly.

I came to, flat on my spine. I blinked, taking stock, stretching out with my senses as I'd learned to do as a soldier, gauging threat. A fire burned a few paces from my head; I could see its embers and smell an acrid, unpleasant scent. Not a wood fire, then, but manure-chip. I was no longer outside. I wore no boots – a feeling so strange my legs jerked, toes curling. My right hand twitched for my firearms but I possessed no defenses, not even my smallest blade, and my palm ached at the emptiness, no comforting, solid pistol grip or knife handle. My mind bumped along, trying to grasp any sense, to bring forth the last thing I recalled before this small, dank space. I blinked again, easing to my left side, which ached a little less, peering into the gloom; I could hear wind, a whistling howl that made me grateful I was not within it.

Malcolm, I thought at once, determination welling like groundwater. He might be in that howling wind, searching for me. And though I didn't know where I was just now, I knew goddamn well I wasn't where my brother had left me. I pushed free of a single blanket, groaning as I rolled to a sitting position, struggling to draw a full breath. I reached to probe at the wound on my damaged leg, encountering a lumpy bandage tied there, my trousers rolled up to the knee on that side; the wounds hurt, but not as bad as when I'd last been conscious. And then, as my eyes adjusted, I spied a figure sharing the space with me, bundled into a blanket closer to the embers. I edged that direction, not wishing to startle him, understanding it was night and whoever had hauled me here was sleeping.

"Mister," I whispered, and coughed when the word scratched my dry palette. I tried again, louder this time, "Mister!"

Not a breath of response. Both of us lay on the ground, a cold, hard-packed dirt floor. I scooted closer, hissing in pain, cursing the damage done to my body. I reached the other fellow, his form long and bulky beneath a thick woolen quilt, a man who lay atop a fur hide facing the embers. I reached and shook his shoulder, careful at first and then with more vigor. The realization was slow in coming; he was unnaturally chilled under my grip and his head lolled with my shaking. Bewildered, I rolled him to his back and beheld a bearded and bespectacled face, a man old enough to be my grandsire. His beard was grizzled and white in the faint glow of the banked fire, mouth hanging slack, eyes open a slit behind the round wire of the spectacles.

"Jesus," I muttered, releasing my hold. "Jesus *Christ.*"

Panic stormed my blood, hot and fearsome. I looked for a door, any potential exit from this small, cramped space I shared with a dead man. What if I was in hell? What if that's what this place truly was, the hell for which I'd known I was bound for a long time now? I lumbered to hands and knees and crawled towards the metallic glint waist-high on the wall to my left. A doorknob, as I'd hoped, set in a door constructed of crude wooden planks. The shriek of the wind increased as I opened the door and was met by its stinging bite. Hard pellets of freezing rain struck my face; it was deep night and the storm raged only the length of my arms away. The sky appeared dense and blue-gray, the sleet swirling like a cloud of locusts bent on destruction. I gasped at the cold, shutting the door and sitting with my spine braced against it.

"God help me," I whispered, shaking with one part cold, all other parts uncontrolled fear. I clutched my bent knees and cried for my mother, my father. I begged to see Rebecca. I begged for Sawyer and my brothers to rescue me. This was hell. I'd been cast out of all favor, barred from any pitiful hope of grace. Even in wartime I'd never been so abandoned. My wild eyes darted to and fro, like a spooked horse, like a boy afraid of the darkness. My heart seemed to explode in endless bursts; I could not breathe. Sweat flowed down my face and along my ribs. And at long last there was simply nothing left within me and I quieted, easing to the floor and wrapping both arms around my head. The air in the small space seemed fragile as eggshells, cracked all apart with my distress.

I closed my eyes and breathed in and out, in and out.

THE WIND had died by morning.

I was ashamed of my actions during the night hours, of losing control in such a way. I must have slept for a time, waking after dawn in a physical state not unlike that which resulted in partaking of too much whiskey, head aching, cheek stuck to the floor and mouth dry as a bundle of tinder rags. Determined to take stock, I examined myself with calmer sensibilities. My skin was welted with burns and scrapes from being dragged and scabs from the rope bindings ringed my wrists and chafed my waist; my ankles had been protected by my boots, both of which were waiting, patient as old dogs, near the door. My ribs ached with a dull pain, mainly on the right side; there was nothing to be done but wait for the cracked bones to heal. I needn't be a doc to understand I was lucky; had the ribs busted into separate pieces to poke through my skin or innards, I would already be dead. And as for my leg – I could only figure the old man had patched it up at some point between getting me here and dying.

More than a dozen times I found the need to repeat, *This isn't hell. You are not in hell.*

Next I examined my surroundings by the light of a circular, canvas-covered window beside the door, carved into the dirt of a structure roughly the shape of a small cave, a roundish hole dug in the side of an earthen hill. *A dugout*, I realized, managing to stand so that I might trace my fingers over the walls and the low ceiling. The floor beneath my stockinged foot was cold and smooth, dark gray in color; I stood on one leg, favoring my wound. I shared the single room with the dead old man, multiple bundles of fur hides stacked as high as the ceiling along the wall opposite the door, two stumps for sitting, a barrel, and two wooden trunks.

Atop the barrel sat a tin cup, a tin plate, and a glass bottle containing a finger's worth of corn liquor. A shallow hearth had been dug, its chimney no doubt sticking up from the earthen roof like a gopher's inquisitive head. There was a pile of dried dung to be used as fuel; the fire was out, thanks to my carelessness. Near the hearth a crude shelf was held up by two wooden pegs lodged into the dirt. Atop this shelf I found a tin match holder, a striker, and boxes of bullets; a Springfield rifle was placed nice and neat on nearby hooks.

I had no explanation for my presence here. I knelt near the man whose dugout this surely was, examining him by morning's light. He was elderly, but tall and broad; with careful movements I tugged free the quilt covering his body, searching for any signs of harm, wounds or indications of illness, finding none. He wore boots, and dirty garments fashioned of leather over a yellowing union suit; his spectacles were hooked behind his ears and a Henry rifle lay near his side. Nothing to identify his personage, no hint of what his name might have been or why he had died, and so I figured old age had claimed him, as there were no signs otherwise. No blood stained his clothing, no pustules or pox dotted his skin; he was not oddly discolored, instead tinted by the usual yellow-gray pallor of recent death. I sat beside him and thought hard, unable to recall anything more than lying cold and alone at the base of the broken wagon, watching the swarming buzzards. And after that, nothing.

How long ago? How much time since Malcolm rode away from me that morning? How far was this dugout from the oak tree with Quill's and Grady's bodies and our broken wagon lying beneath? Had this old man found me at the oak? I had to assume so, and I was goddamn luckier than I probably deserved. He'd treated my leg. I bent my knee and again examined the bandage, a tattered length of nubbled linen, reddish with dried blood. Upon closer inspection, I found that he'd applied a thick paste the color of moss, smelling of herbs that reminded me of Mama's medicine store in the root cellar back home. He'd applied something to counteract the swelling infection; I was no longer out of my head with pain. I was not scared of the dead man; I'd seen too many dead to truly fear them. This man was elderly and had not been struck down in battle, bore no gruesome wounds. No, he was an old trapper – if the hides stacked against the wall told me anything, it was that – and he'd found me on the prairie. He'd helped me and now he was dead, and I would never know his name or exactly what had happened.

I put my hand on his shoulder and patted him twice. I whispered, "You saved me and I thank you, sir. I will care properly for your body, I promise you."

It was no eulogy but it would have to do for now, and I covered his form with the quilt before looking through his supplies, searching first for food and secondarily for a hint as to his name or history. There was a store of salted pork and corn dodgers, bundles of dried onions hanging from the ceiling, and a bucket for water, which I filled with ice chips and hung over the fire; unwilling as I was at first to kindle a blaze with dried dung, it was a source of warmth and I knew I could not afford to be particular just now. I ate onions until I thought I might burst, unable to stop once I started; the tang of them proved irresistible and I ate until my stomach cramped something fierce, bending me double until the stabbing pains passed. I finished this uncouth meal with the last of the corn liquor, which burned its way down my gullet.

One trunk contained tools and additional armaments; I found both a shovel and a hoe propped beside the hearth. Sun shone today, the air flat calm, sparkling atop the ice-covered world in a way I'd never before seen, inches-thick ice the likes of which Uncle Jacob wrote about, as far as the eye could see. In such a deplorable weakened condition, it took all my effort to navigate over the deadly-slick ground to a nearby stone structure, slightly larger than the dugout and built of stacked rock; I guessed correctly that animals were sheltered here, a mule and a goat, the goat with udders so swollen she bleated in pain upon seeing me. Sweating and exhausted from the exertion of staying upright, I had to pause to catch my breath before dragging a low, three-legged stool to her side and milking her.

"There's a girl," I murmured, the task so familiar to my fingers I found it calming, a spell for my mind to simply drift without thinking, smelling the stacked hay and the scent of animal hides, hearing the hushed, repetitive whirring of milk striking the sides of the tin bucket. I drank straight from the rim, proceeding to spill and soak my ragged beard, but the goat's milk was warm and flavorful, and I felt as though I'd not eaten in weeks. The mule, tethered near the goat with no stalls to separate them, nosed at my ribs, snuffling for a bite of food. He was a big, sturdy mule and I wondered if he'd been the one to carry me back here, along with the old trapper; I saw no sign of wagon or flatbed. I patted his neck and muttered, "Thanks, fella."

I fed them and then stirred the stock trough with the shovel handle, clearing away the thin crackle of ice that formed along the top. The trapper's supply of hay looked substantial, perhaps enough to last the winter. Noon sun by now, glittering on the ice to blind my eyes, though it was dim in the little stone barn. Chores accomplished, I thought of my brother, praying he was well and that he and Cora had reached the settlement before the storm.

I would be fit enough to sit the saddle within a few days' time, I'd pray this ice would melt some, and then I would ride out. I would find Malcolm in this damnable enormous prairie.

I'd been gifted with food, with firearms and ammunition. I would care for the old trapper's body, I would butcher the goat – rather than allow her to starve slowly to death in my absence – and then the mule and I would ride out. I patted the mule's jaw, plagued by the memory of Fortune, my beautiful, prized mare who'd carried me all the way from Tennessee. I understood I would never see her again and my heart ached at this knowledge, I was not too proud to admit; I'd dearly loved my horse. But come hell or high water, I would find my brother and Cora.

I muttered to the mule, "I believe I'll call you Trapper."

HAVING LOST my own hat, my clothing in tatters, I felt justified in borrowing replacements from the old trapper. Though I would never know his given name, I called him Josiah because he brought to mind someone of the same name, a man I remembered from my boyhood. Old Josiah Fuller whittled all the livelong day as he sat on his front porch in Suttonville, stoop-shouldered and, like most of the elderly folks who daily partook of their tobacco pipes, with a perfect circle worn between his yellowed front teeth, so that his pipe stem could be neatly inserted between without requiring Josiah to open his mouth. He spoke around his pipe, calling in a hoary voice to Beau and Graf and me as we made our way to fetch up the Davis boys from the livery stable. That sun-warm Tennessee earth, dust swirling rust-red over our bare toes, the heat of the noontide sky pressing on our shoulders, was strong in my memory as I wrapped the old trapper into his blankets, my movements careful with respect.

I spoke to him as I worked, telling him of Josiah Fuller, and of the Bledsoe holler, and my brothers and me fighting over the best fish hook. Of helping Sawyer and the twins with cleaning the stalls so they could come play all the sooner. The seven of us running for the creek with a stone jar of lemon water slung on a rope over one of our shoulders; once at the creek, the jar would be kept cold by resting it in the water after tying the rope to nearby scrub brush. Old Josiah would holler at us to catch him a trout or two, that he'd pay us for a bit of fresh fish; he was a widower long before I was born, never remarried.

We'd always bring him a couple of fillets and he'd pay us with a pinch of chewing tobacco, warning us not to tell our mamas, or a piece of fruit tart if one of his many daughters had come to bake for him that afternoon.

He had been graced with seven daughters, no sons, and enjoyed our rowdy company, I'd sensed even then. Often he'd say, *Boys, tell yer daddy I'd like me a snort of that hooch he's so fond of distillin'. I got me a right hankerin'.* And Daddy would walk over to Josiah's after the day's work was done, with me tagging along, and sometimes Uncle Malcolm and one or two of my cousins, to gift old Josiah with a jug. We'd sit on Josiah's porch in the dusty-gold balm of a summer evening, the men sipping while the first stars rose above the eastern ridge. I'd get real quiet then, listening to Daddy's low, laughing voice and Josiah's gruff responses, resting my cheek on my bent forearms atop the porch rail, swiping at moths. Nightingales would call, bats would start to flutter. The air was scented so thick with honeysuckle and camellia I could almost taste the blossoms. And I'd been happy as a boy has a right to be. Josiah always said to Daddy, *Bless you, Bainbridge.*

I buried the old trapper in the stacked-stone barn, where the ground was not ice-covered and where I could sink the blade of the shovel into dirt not yet frozen over. I dug a hole at the edge of the structure, well away from the animals, though both watched, chewing their hay, the mule swishing his tail, whistling between my teeth as I did so, a tuneless refrain. I sweat like the dickens, lightheaded and resting often, and drank water from the bucket, wishing to Christ that the liquor bottle had been full. Wishing I was sitting on Josiah's porch, old enough now to sip 'shine along with the men. Like my folks, Josiah had passed during the War; we'd learned this upon returning home in 'sixty-five. Though he'd been long-lived and his death expected, it seemed more a symbol of the death of the old way of life, that which could never be again. A death of boyhood things, like innocence, and belief in the older generation – that they were invincible, and possessed all the answers. I swiped at my brow, leaning on the shovel handle, thinking, *If I am lucky enough to return to those I love, I will never travel more'n a mile from our home the rest of my life.*

And on the heels of that, *But where is home, now?*

A coldness settled low in my gut as I recognized I would never reach Rebecca before she married Marshal Quade, not now. I damned Fallon Yancy for many reasons, and would kill him were he ever unlucky enough to be again in my sights – not the least of which because he'd prevented me from riding to Iowa as Malcolm and I had intended. I wondered where Fallon's sorry hide existed just now, if he and his party had reached the Lawsons' spread and sold Royal Lawson their story; having no experience with the man himself, I could not gauge whether Royal was a reasonable enough soul to question such a tale. Of course, he knew Virgil, and Virgil's presence would give the entire episode credibility. I vowed I would kill the one-handed bastard slowly if I ever found him again, I would make him pay. He would curse the day our paths ever crossed.

I waited until the next morning to haul the trapper's rigid body to the hole I'd prepared, unwilling to risk dropping him if I slipped on the ice. Though it was by no means warm, yesterday's unrelieved sun had done a fair job of softening the ice, allowing me to walk without fear of falling. I'd shrouded his body, now gone stiff as a pike, and placed him into the grave with care, as though he was my own kin. I had no lengths of wood for which to make a cross or grave marker; I buried him with his liquor bottle and the small bible I'd found in a trunk; though old and much-worn, it contained no identification, not even a name penciled upon the inside cover. I looked down at him before covering over the body with dirt, unable to stop from shivering; likely I'd buried as many souls as any gravedigger, and me not yet five-and-twenty years. I felt my jaw bulge and knew I could not stand here woolgathering over a dead stranger, much as I owed him.

I reached to remove my hat before recalling it had been lost; instead I bent my head and said, "Sir, I thank you. I do not know your given name an' for that I am truly sorry. I hope you's been reacquainted with your kin in the afterlife. I hope you know how grateful I am for your help an' supplies, an' that you don't begrudge me the use of your firearms an' your fine mule. Nor your saddle." I paused and drew a deep breath, before whispering, "Amen."

THE GOAT meat, though stringy, provided a feast the likes of which I'd not consumed in weeks; I ate my fill and then wrapped up the leftover meat in a scrap of linen, to haul along. Early the fourth morning, when I could set weight on my leg with tolerable pain, I packed the saddle bags with salt pork, corn dodgers, matches and striker, and all of the ammunition I could carry; I strapped the trapper's gun belt about my hips, along with a boning knife in a small scabbard, settled the pistol in a cross holster (what a goddamn comforting heft its wooden grip was in my hand) and secured the big Henry to the back of the saddle. I bundled up the one quilt I'd not used to bury the old man, binding it with twine; at last, ready to depart, I pressed a palm to the earthen wall of the home he'd built here in the Territory, and said again, "I thank you, sir, more than you could ever know."

I did not look back. I could not afford to look back – I must keep my gaze forward now, must determine first my position to the Missouri River. To my great surprise, I did not ride more than five miles southwest before encountering the sight of both the river and the giant oak on its banks. I heeled the mule with a hard thrust and rode near, eyes roving wildly over the scene – there was Grady and Quill, the rocks meant to protect them now scattered, their flesh picked to the bone. Upon seeing the burned-out husk of the wagon, I could guess what had occurred; the trapper, spying the thick smoke such a blaze would have occasioned, rode near and discovered my sorry carcass. None other than me could have set fire to the wagon, though I did not recall doing so.

I dismounted, leading Trapper, and crouched between Grady and Quill, forcing myself to look upon their distorted forms. "I will do my best to avenge you, I swear. You was done a rotten turn here. I'll have you know that I blame myself. Yancy was looking for me an' Malcolm. You didn't deserve this, none of this, an' I am so sorry." I bent my head, clutching the lower half of my face, momentarily overwhelmed. But then I thought of my brother and the picture of him sustained me. I rested my fingertips to Grady's torn shoulder, then Quill's forehead, whispering, "Farewell," and left behind the oak, the wagon, and the men who had been my friends.

"To think a homestead was but an hour's ride from here," I muttered to Trapper as we rode due west, at a clip, like I'd instructed Malcolm, though how many days had passed since he and Cora rode away was unknown to me; I estimated less than two weeks had elapsed. Ice still clung to the tall prairie grass, creating the illusion of thousands of spyglasses trained upon me, the sun glinting from their metallic casings. The stalks bent with the burden of ice and the going was cold but not unduly treacherous; I made good time despite the aching in my leg. I imagined I looked a sight worse for the wear, but damned if that was the least of my concerns. I kept the river to my right, stopping to chip ice from the ground to allow Trapper a greater range upon which to graze – not that the remaining grass was tender or green, but it was enough to sustain him.

I rode until dusk each night and then only dared to sleep for a few hours at a time, Trapper's reins gripped tightly in my fist, huddled into my single blanket near a low-burning blaze. I was hard-pressed to find kindling and spent two freezing nights, waking so stiff and chilled I could scarcely take the saddle, my body dusted with snow. My toes went numb, my fingers cramped; I passed the hours curling and uncurling them around the reins. Trapper was of sturdy stock and I thanked God for him many times a day. And then, at long last, as the sun ascended on the third day since leaving the dugout, I spied a wooden stockade wall in the distance.

E MELINE AND ALBIE was teaching Cora how to work the corn grinder. The three of them sat in the bright, cold sunshine near the Darvells' wigwam, on a mat woven of rush that they'd dragged over to the grinding rock. The girls and Cora took a keen liking to each other. Since being their guests, we'd learned all manner of things about the Darvell family, which was part French and the other part Ojibwe, or *Anishinabeg*, as Fern said, the long and graceful word rolling from her tongue smooth as butter. It took me many a try to say it proper. Xavier was Fern's second husband and she was his second wife – Xavier liked his drink and was fond of a-rambling when in a bottle, same as my daddy had been. Xavier also had him two grown children, these two all parts white. Their mama had been a French lady from Ontario, same as him.

Not quite a week had passed by since Cora and me arrived at the fort. Fern and Xavier wanted to know what had happened, why we'd ridden so far alone without food or armaments, or someone to look after us. Cora let me do the talking and I knew without her saying so that she would go along with anything I told them about how we'd come to be at this fort. Though me and Boyd had not discussed it, I figured he would wish for me to tell the truth as best I could. I hardly knew where to start and therefore told a story much shorter than the whole – I said our company of cattle drivers was attacked and our livestock stolen. I said two men was killed and my brother wounded. I did not say a word about Fallon, eldest son of a man I'd shot, following us from Minnesota. When Fern asked after the red crosshatch marks on my gullet, I said one of the men roped my neck and tugged me down, but they'd tired of the sport and ridden away.

Xavier wanted to know what men, and what they'd looked like, but I said it was too dark for me to get a good look, which was an outright lie. Xavier asked, "Why were you with a cattle-driving party this late in the season?"

I explained about the storm that cleaned out me and Boyd, which seemed about a hundred years ago now, and our need for money, and how we hoped to reach Uncle Jacob's homestead by next summer. That hope seemed as tiny as a speck of dust dancing in a sunbeam; I felt as if Minnesota was as far away as the sliver of moon peering down like a pale, whitewashed eye, open only a slit. I felt we'd never get there and despair ate away at my insides. Even after my explanations Xavier would not let me ride after Boyd, as the ice stayed heavy enough to require chipping, and then it snowed atop this bright sparkle of ice.

I hurt so at being unable to ride for him, at being so weak and helpless, I could scarce walk upright. The hurt was centered in my heart and my stomach, spreading thick between the two like spilled gravy. Cora knew how I hurt and curled up next to me to sleep as was her habit, even after Emeline begged Cora to sleep between her and Albie instead. I felt Cora's heart fluttering against my forearm as she lay on it, fluttering along like that even after she slept, so it seemed it would take wing and fly away. The thought scared me and I pulled the blankets more secure around her at night, to keep her from rising right up into the sky.

I thought about running away and going after Boyd, no matter what harm might come to me. I thought about it all the time, even when Pierpont and me played. Pierpont was a great talker, same as me, and I liked him right fine. He could talk in three languages instead of just one – French, English, and his mother's Anishinabeg, which I liked hearing him speak. The words sounded like a creek flowing along, swift and cheerful. He taught me the Anishinabeg words for *friend*, *snow*, *brother*, *horse*, and *fire*. He had a butternut-colored pony name of Otter, a small, bristly-haired fellow with short sturdy legs. Otter was shorter at the withers than Aces High by a good two hands, but I could tell the little pony had him a feisty spirit. Pierpont insisted Otter could outrun Aces, an offense I would have straightaway set out to correct if I wasn't so worried and we wasn't so stuck here in the fort.

I said, "He could not," and Pierpont said, "He could, too."

The two of us was outside the fort gate, around back, on the side facing away from the river, skipping pebbles over the ice. I crouched down as Pierpont took aim, bending sideways over his throwing arm. He wore beaded moccasins and a tasseled woolen cap like his father's, and carried a small wooden crossbow fashioned for him by his mother's brother. It was right bonny, and could be strapped over his midsection the way Boyd carried his rifle on its big chest holster. Boyd's rifle that was now in Fallon's possession or one of the cur-dogs he rode with. I tried to find the room to be grateful that mine and Cora's bellies were full and we slept near a fire in a warm, safe shelter with dozens of others nearby, friendly folks both red and white – the same folks who asked a hundred-some questions the first day but shortly after paid us little attention. But I mostly felt shame that I was safe and Boyd was not.

Forgive me, I told my brother, day and night. *Forgive me. I will come for you as soon as I can.*

French people, mostly trappers and prospectors, and In'jun people from many different In'jun groups wintered in and near the fort, groups Albie named for me, her being able to tell what sort of In'jun was which just by looking. Albie seemed to giggle an awful lot, even for a girl, when I tried to repeat the names she taught me: Mandan and Hidatsa, Arapaho and Cheyenne, Lakota and Crow. I liked *Crow*, thinking of the name I'd picked for myself when in the company of the Rawley boys last summer. When I'd told Albie about the name, she plucked at my hair and crinkled up her mouth. Then she said in a contrary voice, "*Non.* Your hair is too light and curly for a crow."

"Ain't neither," I grumbled, slouching away from her teasing touch. Of course she just giggled more and ruffled my hair the way a big bossy sister would. And so when I heard her voice calling for me and Pierpont, coming around the stockade wall just now, I turned so that I wouldn't have to see the laughing in her eyes. Albie thought I was about the funniest thing she ever did see.

But "A dead man is here!" was what she said and my chin jerked around.

"What dead man?" I cried, but I was already running, Pierpont and Albie on my bootheels. One word slammed and slammed around my head.

Boyd...

Just inside the gate a group stood in a shifting cluster around a man on horseback, who was leading a second horse with a man draped over it, tied belly-down. Without a word I weaseled between elbows. I had to see. And then my breath lodged in my craw and I fell still. The horse carrying the dead man was a roan gelding and I knew it. I'd seen it before. The dead man was the Yankee that Boyd had beat beneath the oak tree. The Yankee's skin had gone slack and gray, arms and legs dangling. I shrank away, easing backward, keeping my face hidden from the other man, but when I stole a look I saw that he and his horse were unfamiliar. The man was big and bearded, waving one arm about as he spoke. His words sounded like gibberish to my frightened ears.

I turned and ran, leaving Pierpont and Albie in the crowd; I had to find Cora. She was inside the wigwam, sitting on a woven mat in its warm, smoky interior, playing beads with Emmeline. Without saying a word I told Cora I must speak with her and she came to my side at once. Emmeline sat humming, sorting her beads, and no one else was about. I bent close to Cora's ear and said, "A man just arrived here with another man, a dead one." At the fearful question which sprang from her eyes, I hurried to say, "It ain't Boyd, I made certain." I drew a breath and whispered, "But it's a man from that night, Cora, the one Boyd beat upon. I don't know how he died but it weren't from Boyd's beating."

She whispered, "Who brought him here?"

"It ain't someone who seen us that night," I answered, knowing what she meant, and Cora nodded, her thin shoulders drooping in pure relief. My thoughts went leaping like jackrabbits. "But there was another man we never seen that night, remember? He was with the cattle, roundin' them up. Do you recall his name? The Yankee spoke it…"

Cora whispered, "Hoyt. They called him Hoyt."

"Yes, that's it." I nodded, struggling to push aside the horror of that rainy night and remember it for what really happened.

"He never saw us because he never rode into camp," Cora whispered. Her eyes looked wild and scared, and I hugged her close. Emmeline peeked our way, still humming, the beads making little clicking noises as she dropped them in the cup of her palm.

I tried to think what Boyd would do, was he here with us. But I knew what Boyd would do and I wasn't big or strong enough, or armed enough, to do any of them things. On its long jackrabbit legs, my mind kept leaping. I thought, *Do we tell Xavier and Fern? Do we keep quiet? Who would believe us? I can't rightly blame this man Hoyt for killing Grady or Quill…not when it was Virgil an' the Yankee who done it, on Fallon's orders…*

If the man who'd entered the fort just now was Hoyt, he would have answers. If only I knew how to get them. I could hardly tug on his coat hem and
beg. I was a mosquito of a boy, buzzing 'round with questions a man wouldn't
trouble himself over. But he would know about Virgil and Fallon, and their
whereabouts, and he'd know what happened in the meantime since riding
away from Boyd and Cora and me. He would know what had happened at
Royal Lawson's homestead. Finally I decided, "We ain't gonna say a thing for
now," and I felt Cora nod against my fast-thudding heart.

XAVIER TOLD the story over dinner, around the hearth fire in the wigwam that had sheltered us for days. Cora ate without lifting her eyes but I
knew she listened as careful as me for any scrap of information Xavier might
let slide. Xavier was acquainted with both men who'd appeared today; he said
the dead man's name was Byron Johnston, a Yank from Ohio, once a soldier
and then a trapper. The man who'd brought him to the fort was named Hoyt
Little, another soldier-turned-trapper who claimed Johnston died of wounds
after being shot during an argument with a Hidatsa man. Xavier and Fern
did not seem to question this story but I did, and I knew Cora did. Who had
really shot the Yank? Had the two ridden from Cora's uncle's homestead?
Had they delivered the cattle Virgil helped them steal? What if Virgil or
Fallon or the half-breed rode next into the fort? I was loose in the bowels
over the worry of it.

I saw how Fern listened hard, leaning forward to watch Xavier as he
spoke. Albie and Emmeline never failed to pantomime their mama's actions,
even if they didn't know they was doing it, and kept their black eyes fixed on
their daddy, food forgotten. Pierpont was too busy scraping his plate to pay
much attention to the conversation; I figured that out here in the Territory,
so far from any law, a dead body wasn't so unusual. When Xavier paused to
sip from his bottle Fern asked her husband a question in her own language.
Xavier shook his head in response and I might not have thought about it
again except that he said, "My dear, your brother did indeed ride with them
for a spell. You might ask after him in the morning. Once Johnston's body is
properly cared for, Little would surely have a moment to converse."

My eyes locked with Cora's.

Later, Pierpont and me went outside to make water, away from the wigwam in the cold dark night. Standing with our backs to each other, our breath making big clouds of steam, I tried to sound like I was just asking any old question. "Your mama's worried about her brother, huh?"

"He worries *Maman* often," Pierpont said in his strange English, each word emerging like he'd swallowed part of it. I figured he spoke English least of all three languages he *could* speak; the common tongue here was mostly French. "He carved for me my crossbow and a quiver for all the arrows I can make."

"What's his name?" I wondered, hunching up as I waited for Pierpont's answer.

"Animkii," he said over his shoulder.

I closed my eyes against the night. I felt a bolt of relief at this news; behind me, Pierpont continued, "But Papa calls him *Celui Qui Cite des Saintes Écritures.*"

"That seems a right mouthful," I said. The French language was too wordy for its own damn good.

Pierpont explained, "Other white folks call him Church Talk, but *Maman* does not like that, either. She believes he should not make quotation from the white eyes' religious book, not when he was raised Anishinabeg."

It took me a fair amount to pull in a full breath.

At last I whispered, "I would think not."

HOYT LITTLE remained at the fort in a wall tent he erected outside the gate. I had no contact with him, nor did I seek out any even though I felt I should. I told Cora of what I'd learned from Pierpont, that Fern was likely kin to the half-breed who'd shot Boyd with his crossbow and dragged him behind his horse, who'd been part of the attack and would have seen us all killed under that oak. And I was all the more tangled up inside. Fern was a kind and gracious woman. She'd braided up Cora's hair and sometimes rested her hands on Cora's head, just like a mama. Fern cared for us, two strangers in her home, fed us and provided woolen blankets. She figured we'd spend the winter at the fort, she had said so many a time. And yet her brother was a killer, a criminal a dozen times over. What would Fern say if I dared to tell her the truth, like I wanted to a hundred times a day? Would she believe me? Or would she cast us out like dirty water from a washtub?

As the days rolled by I knew I must return for Boyd. I could no longer delay no matter what the weather. My heart was tore all the more in two; I couldn't bring Cora on such a ride across the prairie, not for a second time. And neither did I wish to leave her behind; I could not do that to her, it would destroy her. But I had to ride for my brother and understood I would have to go alone, without telling Xavier. He would not allow me to leave, nor was anyone willing to ride out into the open prairie with winter on the advance. I would have to go without help. If I died, I would at least die trying to rescue my kin. I was a coward staying here where I was warm and safe, when Boyd was not.

Lying in my blanket before everyone rose, the dawning air as gray as sadness, I saw Boyd's face as it looked when he bade me farewell. I knew he thought he would be dead before I could return for him, that he'd done his best to be brave for me. He was the bravest man I'd ever know. Great, choking sobs tore a hole right through me. I scrambled up and outside, running past the fort wall and falling to my knees, alone but for the wind and snow pellets hurling from the sky. I wanted to curse a blue streak, to scream at the sky, angry enough to break something apart with my hands or slam my own head against the fort wall. I bent forward, resting my hands to the frozen ground, and thought, *Quit being a suckling coward. You gotta leave today.*

I HEELED TRAPPER at the sight of the fort on the horizon, seeing smoke lifting from the hide huts of Indian people, praying with everything in me I would find my brother and Cora safe within this place. I'd scoured the land as I traveled westward along the Missouri, hawk-eyed for any hint of Malcolm's passage through it; finding none, I allowed myself to be reassured. I'd been in dread of spying the bloated carcass of Aces High, the boy and Cora curled alongside the horse's cooling body. All manner of terrible visions plagued me as I traveled. I kept sane by fixing on the next horizon and what fortune I'd gleaned, determined to take nothing for granted – I had food, I was armed. I'd been in far worse straits only a week ago. I came across not a soul as I rode, cantering and walking the mule in intervals, fearful to push him too hard, though he was sound stock.

Think only on the next hour. Then the next. There ain't no other way, not just now, you'll go crazy as a jaybird.

Despite the early morning there was plenty of activity around the stockade wall, fires from many hearths sending out the scents of frying meat and coffee. My progress towards the gate was stopped by a small contingent of men, clad in furs and armed to the teeth; they were Indian, imposing but not unfriendly; they spoke in English and I explained my presence as best I could, not wasting time on anything but basic facts, answering their numerous rapid-fire questions. Yes, I was alone. Yes, I'd been traveling for days. No, I bore no furs or other trade goods. No, I was not a trapper. When they seemed satisfied, snow dusting our shoulders, making Trapper's long ears twitch, I said, "I seek a boy riding a chestnut gelding. He woulda ridden in with a girl, perhaps two weeks gone."

One of the men, whose cheeks were finely etched with a tracery of black tattooing, widened his eyes and nodded with a single bob of his head. He reined his gelding about and invited, "Come."

It was all I could do not to gallop abreast, to grasp at his sleeve and beg for answers. Instead, Trapper and I followed this man and his horse at a sedate walk, into the fort and past small, log-constructed cabins and more of the Indian structures. At last he halted his gelding, dismounted, and tugged a small bell-pull at the entrance of one of these. I all but tumbled to the ground in my haste and on my weakened leg, tugging the knitted cap I'd taken from the trapper's dugout from my head. My beard was coated with ice but I hadn't the energy to be ashamed of my ragged appearance as an Indian woman lifted aside the opening, hunched over to peer outside, her black eyes roving over me with plain curiosity.

I clutched the hat to my chest and said, "Ma'am, my name is Boyd Carter –" but got out not another word, as I heard a wild exclamation from within, a heart's cry. I scarce had time to brace myself before Malcolm hurtled forth and into the morning's light, leaping at me. I caught close the boy and buried my face to his neck, tears hot as blood on my face.

Malcolm wasted no time telling me everything he knew, and I wasted none telling the Darvell family exactly what had transpired on the prairie. I knew there weren't a thing to be gained by hiding the truth; for only seconds did I consider telling Malcolm to hold his tongue, allowing me the chance to find this Hoyt Little in the dead of night and get a knife point to his gullet. Little would tell me the truth then, I had no doubt, but I was not in any position to be on the run or to enact vengeance without minding the consequences. I had Malcolm and Cora to consider, foremost, and the memory of Lorie ripped apart by a judge's questions in Iowa City, the both of us defending Sawyer's actions, rang in my head. I could not risk being carted to jail and rotting away for an action I'd not thought through. Was I furious enough to kill Little with one deft sweep of a knife? Quiet, no one alerted by the action, no one the wiser? I was, and would, if not for the threat of consequences. And so I made short work of explaining what had occurred that night.

Somewhere in the back of my mind I was thinking, *Little…why do I feel like I know the bastard…*

I could hardly miss the looks passed between husband and wife; the woman, Fern, struggled to believe her brother was capable of such harm, naming her doubts in halting English the moment she'd sent her children on errands. Only Cora and Malcolm remained inside, Cora tucked beneath my arm as she'd been since I set foot within the hide structure, as though I was her own daddy returned from the grave. The Darvells were kind and generous; I thawed before their fire, had been given food and drink, and the mule cared for with a few brief orders from Xavier to his son. Still, it was no secret Fern wished me and my story gone from her home; her dark, eloquent eyes worried over my face and then back to her husband's, in an endless circle. Xavier was less sentimental; he waited until I was done eating before catching up his tasseled woolen cap and saying, "Come along, *Monsieur* Carter, let us pay a call. Little is not an early riser, likely still abed this morning."

As Xavier and I approached the wall tent outside the stockade I saw at once the roan upon which the Yankee had been mounted staked alongside a second gelding. My heart increased its speed, the wound on my leg throbbing. Now that selfsame Yankee was dead and the man within the tent had answers. My right hand twitched; I could not help but trace my thumb over the smooth reassurance of the pistol tucked into its holster. Xavier Darvell was a stranger to me but he'd cared for my brother and Cora, had offered all of us shelter and food, and therefore I owed him a debt beyond gratitude. I followed just a step behind his confident stride, over crunching snow, watchful and trying not to allow anger any firmer a handhold; this Little might not have taken direct part in the violence, but neither had he stopped it. He'd ridden with Fallon.

Xavier paused at the entrance and bent down; there was no bell-pull on this tent and he addressed the man within, inquiring through the canvas, "Little? Are you about?"

A grunt met our ears, then a snuffling snore. I eyed the empty bottle half-sunk into the snow near the entrance, its cork missing. Xavier's breath emerged in an exasperated cloud as he heaved a sigh and said, "I would like a word."

A snort this time, and a gruff, drowsing voice responded, "It ain't even the noon hour, Darvell. Bugger off."

I gripped the edge of the tent, where its sides met in a long seam; I'd slept in just such a tent in my soldiering years, its canvas stained with filth. I fought the urge to jerk the structure from its stakes. With no patience for pleasantries, I demanded, "Where did you meet Fallon Yancy?"

In the following silence I heard Little slide a piece from its leather holster. Xavier lifted a hand, silently shaking his head as I reached at once for my own pistol.

Little ordered, "Tell me who's asking."

"Come out so I can see your face," I said.

"What in the goddamn hell? Who are you?"

"Gentlemen," said Xavier, in the tone of a longtime father. "I have no wish to be shot to death this early morning."

"My name is Boyd Carter," I said, grim with impatience. "We ain't been properly introduced but I know you. An' I ask again, when an' where did you meet Fallon Yancy?"

Little did not answer and I sensed him calculating.

My teeth met at their edges. "Tell me."

He finally spoke. "I ain't acquainted with a man of that name."

"That is a goddamn *lie*. You rode with him but weeks ago. You stole cattle with him. Did Royal Lawson swallow the story you cooked up? Does he know your men left his niece to die on the prairie?"

The interior of the structure shuddered as Little rose and stormed to the entrance. I tensed and stepped away, holding steady with my piece; the barrel of his pistol appeared first. I could see one eye peering out behind it. He barked, "Stand down, for Christ's sake."

Seconds later I stood facing him in the gray morning light, our barrels directed at the ground, ready to spring into play at the least suggestion of hostility; Little was older than me, closer to the age Angus had been, heavyset and stone-faced. His eyes were cold and hard as he took stock; I understood he would defend himself against any accusation I could throw his way, that he was known here at this fort while I was not, and there was nothing but my word against his at this point.

I kept my voice level. "The corpse you rode in here with, how did you know him?"

"We done some hunting together these years since the War. We met up a week past, at the Hidatsa camp near Fall Creek."

"How did he come to die?" And it was as I asked this question I heard Grady's voice, the very first night we'd made acquaintance; Grady had said, *The Littles take money where they can get it, you take my meaning?* I gave no sign I'd made this connection; it could be that this man Hoyt was no relation to the scarred buffalo hunter named Bill Little. *Clannish*, I heard Grady say.

Little lifted his chin and refused to answer my question. "I brung him here for a proper burial." He looked to Xavier and asked, "What is this young firebrand about?"

Rather than letting Xavier answer, I leaned farther into Little's space. "The party I rode with was attacked near the Missouri, east of here, on our way to deliver cattle to a man named Royal Lawson. Our livestock was stole an' two of my party shot to death. What do you know of this?"

"I don't know a goddamn thing, boy," Little said, unshaken by my words. I could tell nothing I said would rattle him. "I been on my hunting route since August."

Xavier asked, "Have you seen my wife's brother this autumn? I know he rode with Johnston for a spell. I know you've ridden with him in the past."

"I ain't seen him this season. Church Talk is awful fond of the whores in St. Paul. 'Course they make him pay extra, him being red, but he's willing to pay for them saucy white gals. I figure he's wintering there." Little maintained his stone face. He was a good liar, I'd give him that; and I knew, to my very bones, that he was lying.

"What of Fallon Yancy, Virgil Turnbull?" I pressed. "Where are they just now? Where are they wintering?"

Little was not intimidated by me. His upper lip curled as he ordered, "I'll thank you to leave me be, boy."

I wanted to shoot him dead. I wanted to pistol-whip him until he spoke the truth. I knew I could do neither of these things; further, I knew I could not prove his deceit, not without fault, and that I must admit momentary defeat. I muttered, "I ain't got another word for you," and turned on my heel, boots grinding over the thin layer of ice on the fresh snow as I stalked away.

Xavier followed close behind; before we reached the stockade wall he said, "I believe you speak the truth, *Monsieur* Carter."

I stopped and looked at him. People moved about between their lodges; it seemed a hundred different languages drifted around my head, none familiar in my ears. I had no solid reason to trust Xavier but I saw no guile in his eyes, only the hints of a night spent drinking. Xavier said quietly, "My wife means more to me than all else. She is my second wife and the mother of three of my children, and I will not have shame or dishonor come to her because of her brother."

His gaze shifted away, seeing into the past perhaps, eyes narrowing as he considered his next words. I waited without speaking. At last Xavier said in the tone of a confession, "Animkii is Fern's younger brother, this is true. They share the same mother and before the poor woman passed from life, Fern swore to care for Animkii. He has already caused Fern much shame, I will not lie, but she loved their mother and will honor her wishes. You claim Animkii rode in a group that left you for dead, that stole and killed, and I am unsurprised at these things. But I will not allow you to upset my wife. I do not believe Animkii will appear here at the fort. He has never wintered with us. Likely he is in Minnesota, as Little has said. You will never reach Minnesota before the blizzards arrive, please trust my experience in such matters. You are welcome to spend the months of winter here and make plans to ride out in the early spring, but you will not speak again of these matters, do you understand?"

Xavier's voice was somber, unthreatening, but I understood how very much he meant his words. Though he did not strike me as a violent man, any man that considered his loved ones threatened had tremendous power to become dangerous, and to become so very quickly. I looked back the way I'd come, thinking of riding Trapper over the ice of the wide, empty prairie and risking a cold, lonely death for the both of us. I knew Xavier was right; if I dared to bring Malcolm and Cora east before spring all of us would perish out there. This fort must be our home until then and it took all my strength not to grit my teeth, to beat my fists on the earth. Despite Little's demeaning words, I was no boy. I was a man who must think of others first; I must not heed my wish to stride back to Little's wall tent and fire two rounds through his gut. I returned at last to Xavier's steady, expectant gaze. I had no quarrel with Xavier Darvell and finally nodded brusque agreement.

Hoyt Little, his mount, his trappings, and the dead Yankee's roan all disappeared that afternoon.

J ACOB WAS PACKED to ride forth by morning's light, his gelding loaded with supplies for the journey back to his homestead. April had drifted to May and Jacob could no longer delay returning to his family and the necessity of spring planting. By now I knew his beloved children by name and had been graced with so many stories I felt well acquainted with them. Jacob and Hannah were blessed with three sons, Daniel, Harlow, and Jesse, and a daughter, Elizabeth. Elizabeth was the youngest at nine years and seemed the unspoken apple of her father's eye; he called her Libby and though it was endearingly apparent that Jacob doted on each of his children, Libby held sway in his heart. He spoke with such fondness of his family and the beauty of the lake country in which he'd made a home I could scarcely wait to lay eyes upon the place.

If only...

Our despair only grew as spring advanced with no sign of Boyd and Malcolm. Mary had not reappeared with any word, and indeed likely would not, as she'd offered all she knew. Sawyer, Jacob, and Tilson spent the days in St. Paul, inquiring discreetly after Virgil, Fallon, or the man called Church Talk. We kept constant watch; because our camp was erected south of town I found my gaze roving time and again to the western skyline, aching for the first glimpse of Fortune and Aces High carrying Boyd and Malcolm back to us. Rebecca sought the horizon with similar frequency; she was torn apart by the ever-increasing necessity of resuming our northward course before any word.

I knew she believed if we were to move on without them it was akin to relinquishing hope once and for all, tantamount to an acceptance of their deaths. I attempted to prepare myself for exactly this possibility, to shield my heart with a layer of armor; I acknowledged that we may never know for certain, recognizing this sort of deceptive hope might linger as would a poison in the soul and prevent Rebecca from the ability to wholly recover.

Her eyes were raw with pain. I sensed she retained control with great effort; only the presence of her boys kept her from abject anguish. Cort and Nathaniel had thrived on the journey, the two of them browned by the constant sun, delighted to run wild through the prairie grass, chasing gophers and collecting rocks near the riverbank after suffering the morning lessons Rebecca insisted upon and with which I assisted, thinking with fondness of the copy of *Roget's Thesaurus* open atop Mama's lap. Rebecca's sons were young enough that neither comprehended the full extent of their mother's pain. Of course they understood she was concerned over Boyd's and Malcolm's whereabouts, as were they, but did not dwell on matters over which they had no control.

Both boys chose to demonstrate their love with simple gestures, such as bringing her armloads of flowers they spent afternoons collecting; Nathaniel had a habit of resting his cheek to her upper arm that made my eyes prickle with unshed tears. As the birth of my own child grew ever eminent, I found myself imagining her as she might look at Nathaniel's age, of how she might behave. With this notion in mind, I rested a palm upon the most immense of the swelling curves comprising my entire front side; my body had become a sight at which I marveled when I undressed in the dim evening confines of the wagon.

"Soon they'll not fit in my grasp," Sawyer had whispered only a few nights past, cupping my breasts, resting his face between as I twined my fingers into his silken hair; we'd not made love in a month, as I'd grown far too rotund and unwieldy. Sawyer gently shifted position, holding me close with both hands curved about my backside, tucking his chin atop my hair while I clung to him, wrapping my legs around his thigh, letting its solid strength press against the juncture of my thighs.

Resting my lips against his heartbeat, I'd whispered, "There is not a task in this world your hands cannot accomplish."

Now, we surrounded our evening fire, the western horizon blazing with bright orange light, bisected by thin, horizontal stripes of indigo clouds. I sat near Sawyer, his right hand resting on my knee, mine upon the hillock of my stomach. I had not ventured far from the wagon since morning and though I'd not spoken a word to indicate my growing distress, Tilson's practiced eye alighted upon me. He sat alongside Jacob, just opposite, the two of them smoking their pipes; speaking around the slender wooden stem, Tilson observed, "Lorie, you's having pains, ain't you?"

His calm words occasioned an excited bustle at the fire; all eyes sprang to my face.

"It's time?" Sawyer's words were tinged with both reverence and caution; at once his hand moved from my knee to cup my belly.

I'd felt the first stirring in my womb in the early morning hours, initially no more than intermittent shivers. Uncertain whether these indicated advancing labor I'd not spoken of them; with the passing daylight hours, however, the ache across my lower belly grew increasingly difficult to ignore. Troubled by the gathering knots of apprehension, I simply nodded in response to Tilson's question; beneath the layers of shift and skirts, my knees began to tremble. I reprimanded, *You must be braver than this, Lorie. You are no coward.*

"When did they begin?" Tilson was already rising.

"Before dawn," I whispered, clinging to Sawyer's forearm; he felt the trembling in my grip and kissed the side of my forehead. I admitted, "But they've grown in strength in the past hour."

Rebecca's eyes shone with understanding. "Sweet Lorie, do not fear."

Tilson knelt beside his niece and peered at me. I withstood his perusal, watching his face, on the alert for any signs of alarm. Upon our arrival in April, Sawyer and Tilson had inquired at the boardinghouse near the river and the owners promised a room so that I might be allowed to give birth within a bed; Tilson scolded gently, "Honey, I wish you'd have bent my ear before now. If you's too far along I'd rather not risk carting you into town." He pressed, "How far apart?"

"Perhaps two minutes." I clenched my teeth as another contraction advanced.

"There ain't a thing to match the joy of holding your firstborn, young woodcutter," Jacob said. "I remember your mama and daddy well and good, Sawyer. I know how dearly they'd welcome this grandchild."

Powerful emotion overtook Sawyer's expression as he said in his familiar throaty voice, "I believe they'll know, Jacob, I truly do."

"Mrs. Lorie, shall the baby come tonight?" asked Nathaniel, kneeling beside me.

"I dearly hope so," I said, cupping a fond hand about the boy's head.

"How does the baby get out?" Nathaniel further wondered, blue eyes gone wide as he considered this perplexing dilemma perhaps for the first time. His gaze bounced between my belly and my face.

"Through a rather difficult but exceedingly natural process, young nephew," Tilson said, saving me from any sort of explanation. "Lorie, are you able to travel into town? Tell me true."

I knew Sawyer would choose for me to give birth upon a bed rather than within the confines of the wagon or one of our wall tents, but would honor my wishes before all else; if I chose to remain here, on the prairie, then remain here we would. Though the open sky offered me comfort and the evening was calm and lovely, I told Tilson, "I am able to travel."

"Come then, let us hasten." Tilson rose, casting orders about. "Nathaniel, run to fetch my satchel. Cort, hitch up Sawyer's wagon, g'on now!"

Nathaniel returned from their wagon, satchel in hand; I knew well what it contained, having grown quite accustomed to utilizing its contents since last summer. Tucked neatly within, each item stowed in its proper place, were folded lengths of linen, vials of chamomile oil, witch hazel, vinegar, and laudanum, two small wooden bowls, three precisely-edged cutting tools, an iron clamp and iron forceps, these instruments practical but unmistakably menacing in appearance; the shaking in my knees increased twofold. The controlled violence my body must experience was unavoidable now in a way it had not been even a scant week past. I'd understood plainly the time for birth would eventually come, and harbored no delusions concerning my role in the process; it was simply that the buffer of months, and then weeks, between speculation and reality had served to calm my nerves up to this point. The eminence of labor pressed upon me, smothering my sensibilities; for the very first time, wild thoughts I'd kept at bay assaulted.

What if I die in the process? What if I am dead before morning's light? What if this is the last time I'll look upon Sawyer's face?

My insides heated with pure fear. Sawyer, carrying me to the wagon, felt my agitation. His gaze was steady, his breath upon my cheek as he held me in the shelter of his arms. "I am here. I will not leave your side."

I managed a small, tight nod, hearing Rebecca and Jacob and Tilson, all of them talking, determining that Rebecca accompany us while the boys remain behind in Jacob's care. Though I already possessed his full attention, I clutched Sawyer's ears and admitted, "I am so frightened."

"Lorissa Anne Davis," he said sternly, intent upon shattering my distress. His single eye held mine, unwavering. "You are the bravest soul I have ever known. My sweet love, you are fathoms braver than you even acknowledge. All will be well, *I swear to you.*"

Rebecca sat with us on the wagon seat while Tilson rode Kingfisher, flanking us to the right as we rode the half mile into town, a route that had never seemed so riddled with deep ruts and jolting bumps. Tucked between Sawyer and Rebecca, a new surge of panic strove to destroy my composure and I demanded, "What is today's date?" Though I'd written an entry in my journal only yesterday morning and had of course recorded the date at the top of the page I could not at the moment recall. My child was on her way into the world and I could not name the day of the week.

Rebecca, holding fast to my right hand, brought it to her lips and kissed my knuckles. In the gloaming she appeared young as a girl, her dark hair trailing over one shoulder in an unpinned braid, lovely eyes aglow with joy for me, no matter how deep our collective pain. She intoned, "It is Sunday, the second of May. And before May third, I'd venture to suppose, you shall hold your daughter in your arms."

Her words of comfort intertwined with those of Sawyer's, and perhaps something even beyond, an understanding that rose up out of the ground beneath the wagon wheels, the scent of new grass and turned earth, the quality of the westerly light reaching to touch our faces – and with that orange radiance came a stirring in the deeps of my being, an awareness of forces outside our control. A similar notion had overtaken me the evening of my handfasting to Sawyer, and in the fireglow of sunset I recognized the strength of my connection to them, to Sawyer and Rebecca, to Tilson and Boyd and Malcolm, to Jacob Miller, our souls fitting together as necessary pieces of a larger entity, linked in ways I could not begin to fathom.

Necessary…and yet unbearably tenuous.

Smote by the sensation, I closed my eyes and beheld our existence in a great and immeasurable context – a blink of sunlight in an otherwise vast darkness. I curled my fingers through Sawyer's and Rebecca's, on either side, quelling the urge to gather them as close as I was able, to override the strange perception that our bodies retained less substance than soap bubbles, with the ability to lift free of the confines of what kept us anchored to solid ground and drift away.

Sawyer felt it too, I knew he did; he squeezed my fingers in his warm, strong grasp, sending the thought directly into my mind, *I am here and you are safe. I will let nothing harm you, this you know.*

But I knew even Sawyer could not prevent all harm, could not prevent our eventual separation.

At last I whispered, "I venture you're right, Becky."

The boardinghouse was situated a block from the river, the town in typical high spirits in the pleasant evening air; chatter and laughter rolled from all directions, the clatter of buggy wheels along the streets, the scent of pipe smoke and dust and roasting meat, the glint of candles flaring to life in the window lanterns of nearby saloons and shops. As Sawyer jumped from the wagon seat and reached to lift me down, the entrance to The Dolly Belle caught my eye amongst the other establishments, with its ostentatious red globes and steady crowd; the building sat catty-corner across the street, angled so that a woman on its upper balcony was allowed plain sight of us. I watched her grasp the railing, leaning over it to peer our way; she lifted a slender arm, beckoning to us without calling out.

"It's Mary," Rebecca recognized, clasping my elbow with a fervor belying the quiet statement.

Mary gestured again, indicating her fervent wish for us to approach; perched a floor above the street and cast in the gloaming light she appeared ethereal, swathed in white garments, her arms long and pale, fragile-seeming. Her movements were minimal enough not to garner overt notice but she clearly desired a word. Sawyer turned to look over his shoulder at what had claimed our attention as Tilson tethered Kingfisher to the hitching rail.

"She has news for us," Rebecca understood, and sudden tension flowed from her body. All of her passionate energy, so long repressed, rose to the surface, no longer able to be contained; I almost expected to see her skin split with the subsequent force. She said, "I shall speak to her and return directly," and grasped her skirts, lifting them just enough to hop from the wagon seat without assistance, every bit as nimble as her sons. She paused to speak with Tilson, who bade her return quickly, before hurrying towards The Dolly Belle, her long, dark braid bisecting the back of her pale dress. The entire town was suspended in the distinctive light of dusk, all objects leached of color, tinted by ash; Rebecca disappeared into the crowd.

Despite the tension aroused by Mary's request for a word, Sawyer wasted no time carrying me into the boardinghouse; one of the five available rooms was fortunately unoccupied and at our appearance, Mrs. Jeffries, the owner's wife, sent her daughters running with sharp commands in order to make it ready for us. A winding staircase with a carved banister led the way to the second floor. Following Mrs. Jeffries, who clutched her ample skirts to navigate the steep steps, trailed by Tilson, Sawyer carried me straightaway to the room designated for our use. He placed me atop a four-poster bed stripped of its fancy bedding and outfitted with a layer of plain ticking by the younger of the Jeffries girls; I hunched around the clenching pain in my abdomen, seeking to center and perhaps contain it. The young girl hovered to the side, asking, "What else might I fetch?"

Tilson placed his satchel on a rocking chair near the bed and began rolling back his sleeves. He told her, "A basin of water, if you would, little one."

Mrs. Jeffries left behind the lantern, with promises to bring another. She offered kind congratulations and then invited Sawyer to come downstairs for a bite to eat; when he politely refused, she pressed, "Mr. Davis, surely you do not intend to remain here while your wife labors?"

"I do indeed, ma'am," he said, tipping his hat brim before removing it altogether.

Mrs. Jeffries inhaled through both nostrils and pressed a fist to her midsection in a manner conveying her disapproval of this statement; I was reminded at once of my mother. Clucking her words, she scolded, "It is most unseemly for a husband to witness such a thing, Mr. Davis."

Tilson chuckled. "Dear lady, you couldn't force this man from the room at gunpoint."

Mrs. Jeffries blinked several times before regaining her composure. She pursed her lips but conceded, "I'll send Meggie with the basin," and motioned for her daughter to accompany her from the room. The girl, Meggie, offered a shy smile before following her mother.

Sawyer sat atop the bed and gathered my feet upon his lap, unlacing and removing my boots. His lips lifted in a half-rueful grin as he murmured, "Seems we cause a stir wherever we go."

The ache encircling my belly tightened its grip, the pains so evenly spaced I could have set a timepiece by them, and Sawyer took my knees into his grasp, gently stilling their incessant trembling.

"Darlin'," he murmured.

Tilson approached to rest a hand upon my shoulder. "I'll wait to examine you until the basin arrives and I've a chance to wash up. How are you feeling, honey?"

"They are still perhaps two minutes apart," I said, anticipating his next question.

Tilson's eyes crinkled at the corners as he smiled. His lined and craggy face remained so very dear to me; I loved him as much as I remembered loving my own daddy, long ago in another life, and wasted no time feeling guilt over this fact. He murmured, "For certain before morning, then, we'll meet her."

A rapping on the door indicated Meggie returning with the basin. She handed this to Tilson and left with obvious reluctance, peeking over her shoulder as the door closed, and Tilson washed his hands; the droplets stirred by the motion created tiny, wet plops of muted sound in the little room. I clenched my jaw and closed my eyes, bracing against another onslaught, and was suddenly beset by an image of Rebecca – the picture of her disappearing into the crowd materialized like a still photograph on the backs of my eyelids; I was troubled by the fact that she'd not looked back at us as she crossed the street. To my flustered mind it seemed ominous, a sign I may never see her again.

Stop this, I admonished, opening my eyes and willing away the frightening thoughts. *You are in a state of nerves. Rebecca is not in danger.*

Sawyer moved to sit near my hip and braced my lower back with his forearm, holding steady. He kissed my temple, which was already slippery with sweat, gathering my hair and drawing its heavy, braided length away from my face. Tilson took up the customary position at the foot of the bed; on any other birthing occasion, I would be at his side at this point in the proceedings. My knees began to shake anew and Tilson cupped one warm hand over the right, patting me, reassuring with no words, before lifting my skirts to examine my body's progression.

"All feels well. You're far along, as I figured," he mused, eyes fixed on the wall above mine and Sawyer's heads as he explored my swollen flesh; his physician's gaze, I'd always thought, one which saw inward, using hands and fingers for sight rather than eyes. He lowered my skirts. "I do hope you two have settled upon a name for the youngster, as you'll likely be meeting her within the hour."

The pace of my heart increased another notch, not only at the prospect of holding my daughter after dreaming of her all these many months, but at the knowledge of what my body must do in order to produce her forth into the world.

Tilson saw my agitation as he dried his hands on a length of linen. Adopting the brusque tone he knew would best rescind my fears, he said, "Lorie, there ain't a reason to worry. You are healthy as a mare. You oughta be up and walking, at least for a spell. Sawyer, you help her about the room. I aim to hurry over to yonder saloon and collect Becky." His wrinkled face creased into a smile. "If you've a mind to allow it, that is, honey."

"Of course, please do," I said, reassured; no harm would come to Rebecca as long as Tilson was there.

"Mind your wife's every order, do you hear me, son?" Tilson instructed Sawyer, before resting his gentle touch upon my cheek. "You'll be right as the rain, Lorie. I'll return shortly."

Tilson collected his hat and tightened his holster belt; his footfalls sounded on the steps and in his absence Sawyer flowed into motion, arranging his holster within easy reach on the bedside table, placing my boots on the floor, worrying over the pillows situated behind me. He stroked my hair, bundling it at my nape, recognizing, "The pains are coming faster."

I nodded acknowledgment of this truth, gnawing at my lower lip.

Sawyer cupped my jaw. "For this moment, we must put aside thoughts of all else."

For all that he'd witnessed dozens of foalings at his family's livery stable I realized afresh this would be his first time at a birthing bed. I reached for his hand. "The pain will only escalate, love. You must prepare to see me hurting. She is our first, and may therefore take time –" The next word broke around a hard and inadvertent gasp as a contraction seized my innards, this one stronger than any prior. Sawyer held fast and I thought of Letty Dawes, whose twins were the first birth with which I'd assisted Tilson. The strength of Letty's grip had startled me that July afternoon nearly a year ago.

Sawyer said, "Tilson has spoken to me of what to expect. He warned me that watching you suffer through it would be most difficult of all." He gathered me close, bending his face to my unkempt hair. "I would bear any pain for you, my Lorie, and would bear this pain in your place, were I able."

"I know it," I whispered, sheltering in his embrace before another pain surged. I hissed a sharp breath; the contractions ebbed as swiftly as they overtook. In the momentary lull I requested, "I'll walk a spell, as Tilson suggested. Will you help me up?"

Sawyer kept me tucked close to his side, allowing me to set the pace about the small room. I felt less vulnerable walking rather than prone upon the stripped bed; there was a quality to the muffled sounds in the rooms adjacent, the rise and fall of murmured voices and the knowledge that others lingered nearby along a shared hallway, which allowed a crack in the heavy boards I kept nailed over the memories of my time at Ginny Hossiter's – the gaping pit containing ugly and hated remembrance. I would not allow those memories to intrude; would that I could banish them for all time.

As we walked, Sawyer recognized my need for distraction and spoke in his storytelling voice. "Have I ever told you about the day Whistler was born? I was late for a picnic at the Carters' farm and I knew it was an insult to Clairee to arrive so late, especially since I was well beyond boyhood, but I couldn't leave before my horse came into the world. Her dame was a beautiful bay mare, bred with Piney Chapman's stock, the finest in Suttonville. Daddy promised me the foal…"

Sawyer paused in this beloved and oft-told tale as I cringed forward, rubbing the base of my spine with his knuckles. Though I'd never been inside the Suttonville livery which his family owned in the old days, I suddenly beheld the picture in his thoughts, seeing plainly that summer afternoon in 1860, dust motes twirling in the sun slanting between the slats of the stall in which Whistler's dame labored. I witnessed Sawyer crouched as near as he dared, a much younger Sawyer than the man I knew now, a sunburned boy slender with gangly youth, forearms resting on thighs, surrounded by the scents of hay and horse. Anticipation lit his boyishly handsome face; I accepted the sweetness of this vision as a gift.

"Her forelegs emerged first, as I'd expected," Sawyer continued when I'd straightened, the ache of the contraction receding, though not for long. Already I tensed, dreading the next, as he said, "And I saw at once that she was a paint—"

I interrupted the tale to add, "As was her sire."

Though my gaze was directed at the floorboards I felt the warmth of his grin. He murmured, "You've heard this story before, it seems…"

I pressed my face to his ribs, unable to answer. The intensity of the pain had grown shocking and I could not help but groan.

Sawyer cupped the back of my neck. "Lorie. Do you want to lie down? It seems a brutality to keep you walking."

I shook my head in immediate response. The night unfolding outside the rippled glass of the east-facing window appeared clear and fine. Curtains covered the lower half of the pane but stars spangled the darkening sky in the upper, having winked into existence without my noticing; Rebecca and Tilson remained absent despite the advancing night. Sawyer obliged my request, leading me about the room in an endless circle, stopping when I required it, murmuring in his low voice, telling me stories of his boyhood days in the holler, neither of us openly acknowledging our growing concern over Tilson's and Rebecca's whereabouts. Sweat eventually drenched my dress and Sawyer helped me from it so that I wore only a shift, a now-soiled garment let out to accommodate my girth. We'd just resumed the cumbersome pacing when there was an excited rapping on the door and young Meggie Jeffries called from the hallway, "Mother wonders do you need her assistance, Mr. Davis?"

Sawyer asked, "Has Tilson returned?"

"Mr. Tilson has not," Meggie said, with plain apology in her tone. "Please do call if you need a thing, Mother said."

Her footfalls danced back down the wooden steps, leaving us in bewilderment, but I could dwell upon little other than the contractions flowing one atop the next, in a successive wave of agony; just as I was about to tell Sawyer I needed to lie down an entirely new ache heaved across my lower abdomen. Sudden wetness streaked my thighs, hot beneath the sweat-dampened shift, and I felt in that moment the wetness was my heart, liquefied and draining away – I thought I was losing our baby.

"Is it blood?"

I'd lost a child before and I would die before losing this child. Sawyer carried me at once to the bed, baring my lower body with movements simultaneously urgent and deft. Grasping my knees, stilling their violent shaking, his voice cut through my panic; he said, "No, Lorie, *no*. It is but your birth water."

Gasping with fearful breath I attempted to sit, to achieve the impossible task of glimpsing the flesh between my thighs. Sawyer eased me back against the stacked pillows and braced above. He looked deeply into my distraught eyes. "Lorie, it is all right. I will help you, but you must focus. Can you do that, love?" At my jerking nod, he smiled sweetly, hiding away all of his worry, any hint of trepidation. He whispered, "Good."

Sawyer left my side only to wash his hands in the basin and reposition the lantern, bringing it closer. He rolled back his sleeves, fair hair trailing the sides of his forehead. He removed his eyepatch and took up a position at the foot of the bed, easing the damp shift out of the way and drawing my hips closer to him; my legs bent and splayed wide, my head fell back as stabbing pain attacked my belly, lowering into my bowels. I felt an almost complete loss of control over the workings of my body and reached blindly above my head, panting, to clamp hold of the bedposts, gripping with both fists.

And then, half-choked with the wonder of it, Sawyer cried, "I see her, I see the top of her head! She's right here!"

I knew what I must do, instinct overriding all else. My teeth ground together in my skull as I strained through the gouging pain of a crowning head. I gulped for each breath, struggling to push again, and again, and yet again.

Sawyer said, "Once more!"

I can't...

I tried to speak the words but they would not emerge. 'Once more' became a hundred more. A groaning sob bulged in my chest; I felt as though I would push myself inside out, undulating pain so intense it seemed I would never be free of it. Stinging heat seared the flesh between my legs. Bursts of light flashed behind my closed eyes, as though I'd been struck at the bridge of my nose.

I can't do this...

Sawyer cried, "Her head is out! Once more, Lorie!"

Surely I would snap the bedposts with the force of my gripping. I heaved and experienced a tremendous gushing; unable to see past the swell of my belly, I pictured a broiling waterfall bursting from my nether region.

Sawyer's grin split his face as our daughter emerged from between my parted thighs. For there she was, our girl, held up and cradled in her daddy's long, lithe hands, slippery-pink and streaked with blood. A cap of wet golden hair covered her scalp.

"She's here!" he rejoiced, wiping tears upon his right shoulder, and I struggled to my elbows, tasting the salt of tears as I cried and laughed at once, enraptured at the sight of her in Sawyer's tender grasp. Her fists and feet appeared blue-tinted and churned with energy; a chuffing squall parted her tiny lips, both eyes clenched tight. A long, crinkled rope, pulsing with blood, trailed over her tiny stomach, the last link between our two bodies. Sawyer bent and pressed his lips to her forehead, worshipful.

"She's here," I whispered, laying my hands upon her at long last, swiping fluids from her tiny mouth with one practiced sweep of my littlest finger. Sawyer placed her in my arms and leaned to kiss my lips, with utmost care. Blood covered his familiar hands as he proceeded to knuckle my belly, ordering softly, "Once more, darlin', push once more."

The delivery of the afterbirth was messy but swift; Sawyer, at my instructions, snipped the birthing cord two fingers above our daughter's belly and tied the end with a length of twine from Tilson's satchel.

"You're bleeding still, but not an alarming amount," Sawyer said, bundling a length of linen to tuck between my aching legs as I cuddled our daughter to my breasts, marveling at the perfection of her little face, unable to keep from pressing my lips to her cheeks, her forehead, her crinkly closed eyes. Sawyer helped to tidy both our daughter and me as best he could, using a linen he'd dampened in the basin; he restacked the pillows and at last knelt and wrapped the two of us in his embrace.

"*Mo mhuirnín milis*," he whispered. "My Lorie, how I love you. The both of you."

"She's here," I repeated, tears streaming. My body felt as though a team of draft horses had trampled over it but all of the pain summarily receded into the distance, straight through the walls of the boardinghouse room and into the night, eradicated by the intensity of what we'd accomplished. I looked from our child to Sawyer, who'd delivered her into the world, this man I loved so fiercely it was akin to pain. I traced my fingertips over his face, whispering, "You did marvelous work."

Tears streaked his right cheek and he disagreed, "The work was yours, Lorie-love." He cupped a hand about our daughter's head, his wide palm bracketing the fragile curve of her skull. "*Mo iníon milis*, welcome to our family. We love you so."

"I've imagined so many times what she would look like." I kissed her again; I could not cease kissing her sweet face, already fathoms-deep in love. I recalled, "You didn't name Whistler until later that first night."

"That is indeed true," Sawyer agreed, and I tugged him closer, our mouths joining with a soft suckling sound. His nose brushed my cheek, his taste was upon my tongue, the sweat of my skin combining with the salt of his. I held fast to my husband, our child between us as she'd been in the womb, recognizing and imbibing the blessing of them without speaking, as if to do so would be to somehow negate it. Sawyer nuzzled my jaw, my ear, resting his lips to my temple; he murmured, "I would name her for you, my sweet love. Lorissa Rose, if that suits you, darlin', and we'll call her by her second name, as to avoid confusion."

"Yes, that's the way of it." As I spoke there was a swelling of voices from the lobby below. Hurried feet ascended the stairs, more than one pair, surely Rebecca and Tilson at last returning. Wouldn't they be surprised to see what Sawyer and I had achieved in their absence, wouldn't they delight in meeting our daughter? I intended to scold them for arriving so late; it did not occur to me in that moment of joyful wonder over my baby that such rapidly-approaching footsteps could mean danger –

Sawyer was steps ahead, rising swiftly, collecting and buckling his holster, his entire frame taut with sudden tension; positioning near the closed door, he called sharply, "Edward?"

But the reply was not Tilson's.

Sawyer flung open the door.

*L*ife changes most when you least expect it, Papa had always been fond of saying.

But what if you always expect it? I'd contradicted the summer of my ninth or tenth year, intending not to be impertinent; rather, I enjoyed discussing things Papa, who never failed to speak to me in a scholarly fashion, who perpetually sought ways to challenge my intellect.

You shan't, dear heart. Constant expectation would prove a tiresome path.

I shall make up my mind to always expect it, from this moment forth, had been my final say on the matter.

I believed him now.

Lifting my hem to hurry across the street towards a saloon called The Dolly Belle, I heeded Papa's words. I was no coward, and sustained no false modesty; I had weathered the loss of my father and mother, my husband and marriage, the content and quiet life I had once called my own – all vanished as permanently as smoke in the rising wind of War. I bore two sons to a man I dearly loved, and with whom I believed I would grow old, only to learn of Elijah's death in the blistering summer of 1863, while Nathaniel was yet three months from being born.

Each of these changes indeed struck without warning, serving to pierce ragged holes through any security I hoped to claim; I remained grateful beyond words for the presence of my brother and, later, my uncle, both of whom rearranged their lives in order to help me with Cort and Nathaniel. Though as a little girl I'd anticipated change as a tremendous potential adventure, I'd grown into a woman who neglected to expect and instead despised it, with its startling nature and resultant agony. And yet, here I stood on a dirty street having chosen to undertake the most significant change of my life, that of leaving Iowa and journeying into unknown territory –

As I had a thousand and more times since he rode away from me that wretched August morning, I held his face in my mind and silently prayed, *Come back to me.*

Leaning over the elaborate upper balcony a floor above the ground, watching my uncertain approach, Mary was visible from the waist up; as I neared, she hissed, "Around back!" and promptly disappeared. I paused and pressed both hands to my belly, drawing a slow breath, fighting the smothering sensation which had crept behind me ever since word reached us that Boyd and Malcolm were missing; if I let down my carefully-constructed rampart, the terrible feeling would ambush. The sense of hovering menace was heightened by the lack of color as gray twilight rolled across the town, creating the illusory sense that all objects retained no substance. I needed to discover what Mary wished to tell me but I was simultaneously terrified; as long as I believed Boyd alive, as long as the hope existed of seeing his face once more in this life, I found it possible to continue moving forward.

Come, Rebecca, I thought, gathering strength.

I hurried along the alley between The Dolly Belle and the adjacent business establishment, both whitewashed buildings looming over me in a fashion to which I was not accustomed; the home wherein I'd spent most of my life had been a much smaller structure, with a low-pitched roofline. The alleyway was narrow and dotted with patches of mud, sucking at my bootheels as I hastened, my passage garnering little attention, just as I had hoped. Of course most patrons would enter the saloon through its front doors rather than skulking about the rear of the building, and there was no one here about, save myself; I emerged from the alley to find a small back porch adorned with a pair of rocking chairs and a single lantern, currently unlit. The river was visible down the long slope of a grassy incline, the purring rush of its water filling my ears just as the musky, but not unpleasant, scent of its banks saturated my nose.

I waited, tense with uncertainty; though I could hear the sounds of gaiety and carousing from the front of the saloon, they were muted, distant-seeming. One could hope for a modicum of privacy in this spot, and sure enough, Mary appeared momentarily at the screen door with its decorative oval frame, easing it open with a lengthy creak and stepping at last outside. She was clad in garments far more feminine than the last I'd beholden, a long skirt and draped shawl of white silk, paste brilliants glimmering in her fair hair, pinned up for the evening. Her lips were a dark slash in the gloom and her eyes sought mine at once; she tread the porch boards with care, as so not to create undue noise, and grasped my wrist.

"Come," she implored in a whisper. "I ain't got but a minute," and so saying, led us closer to the river, keeping the roofline of The Dolly Belle in sight. Once satisfied with our isolated location, Mary leaned close. "I intended to slip away this very evening. It's pure good fortune you've appeared in town. Is Mrs. Davis delivering?"

"She is," I affirmed, clasping my hands and pressing them to my breastbone as though to sustain my heartbeat. Lorie was the sister for whom I had always longed and I loved her dearly; only one thing could tear me from her side in her time of need. I pleaded, "What news have you?"

"Mrs. Rebecca," Mary said, and my heart became solid, unmoving as a boulder, with pure trepidation; her tone could indicate nothing but news of magnitude. She promptly grasped my shoulders and peered into my eyes. "Boyd Carter is *alive*. Do you hear me? I could scarce believe my ears, but he is alive!"

There was a roaring in my head to rival the river. My knees gave way as though kicked from behind; Mary issued a muffled exclamation and bent to retrieve me from the ground. The world pitched and swayed, and only my grasp on Mary's wrists kept me steady. Tears swarmed my eyes as I choked and gasped over the words. "Boyd is...*alive?* Oh dear God...he's alive?" Heaven had opened its gates to me, here on the damp and muddy earth behind a saloon called The Dolly Belle.

Mary released my elbows and promptly enfolded me in a robust embrace. The lace of her costume scratched my cheek; the scent of her oiled perfume was syrupy and overpowering but I stood trembling in her arms, weeping even as I recognized the need to gather my wits, to find out how she came to possess this knowledge. Mary murmured into my ear. "I know what you're feeling, I do. If I'd learned Grady was alive I would rejoice, too. I wouldn't ask for another goddamn thing in this life."

"Where is he?" I begged, drawing abruptly away, resonating with the need to see him, to lay my eyes and hands upon him, in that order. My gaze darted wildly about, as though Mary was keeping him hidden from me. "Is he here? Is he nearby?"

Mary clamped my shoulders and rattled me with two quick shakes, rife with the desire for me to pay attention. She ordered, "*Listen to me.* I got no real proof but I believe Mr. Carter is in harm's way. Virgil Turnbull rode into town yesterday evening, from the north and in the company of three other men, one of them that half-breed feller I spoke of. The others are a pair of brothers named Little. Do you hear me?"

My chin jerked like a marionette's as I nodded, assuring her I did indeed hear.

Mary continued, "Virgil spoke with Jean Luc, and Cecilia overhead them talking about the Carters. Virgil was demanding to know if they'd appeared in St. Paul this month. Virgil seemed riled up, Cecilia said. If I hadn't been with a customer just then, I'd have skewered his worthless little hide to the wall and questioned him like a criminal on the stand. He disappeared right after and I ain't seen him yet with my own eyes. But Cecilia wouldn't lie. She feels badly that she never delivered Mr. Carter's letters to the post, seeing as how she was put out he'd rejected her that night."

My mind floundered over these breathless explanations, attempting to piece together sense. Thinking as rapidly as I was capable, I said, "Boyd must be riding this way from the Territory, as we first suspected. We must warn him." I battled the urge to lift my hem and run for the edge of town, knocking aside anything in my way. What if I was already too late? Nothing would prevent Virgil and the others from drawing the same conclusion and riding promptly westward upon discovering Boyd was not in St. Paul. He would be outnumbered. He could not possibly realize they were coming for him. Panic grew tenfold in my heart. "I shall fetch my uncle and Jacob Miller this instant."

"Yes, warn your people," Mary encouraged. "Likely Virgil already knows that other folks have been asking after him. I'll round up Isobel just as soon as she's free. Might be that she knows more. She's likely seen Virgil already. Isobel always had a soft spot for him."

"And the sheriff must be told, I must go to him – "

Mary shook her head. "Mrs. Rebecca, there ain't a sheriff alive who'd ride out for the Territories because we claimed a feller was in danger out there. There's nothing but my word, a *whore's* word, to go on, don't you see? I wish I knew more. I wish I could help you, for Grady's sake."

"You *have* helped, in every way possible." I clasped her forearms and rose to my toes to kiss her cheek, finding it cool and smooth as porcelain beneath my lips. "Thank you, Mary. For the rest of my life I shall be grateful to you."

"Come," she urged. "Find your uncle and Mr. Miller, don't bother with the sheriff. Slip around that-a-way, behind The Steam House. I don't want Jean Luc to –" But she was not allowed to finish the statement because a man strode into view, emerging from the alley in my footsteps. Mary looked over her shoulder as this man snared my attention; I caught a brief glimpse of an imposing figure with a long braid before Mary inhaled a sharp breath and hissed, "Run!"

I saw the knife clenched in his fist and obeyed without question, lifting my skirts and aiming for the river, tall grass slapping at my thighs. I did not have to understand what was happening to perceive the danger. I heard the man give chase even over the sound of my churning breath and Mary's attempt to stop him – there was a small, thin cry – then silence. I stumbled and slid a dozen feet on the thick mud, realizing there was nowhere I could run that he could possibly fail to overtake me. My experience with being chased or roughhousing amounted to playing with Clint in the summers of our youths; no one had ever purposely struck me and therefore the jouncing blow between my shoulder blades caught me all the more unaware. I went to my knees like a hamstrung horse, skidding down the bank with hands splayed. The breath was so thoroughly knocked from my lungs I could not make a sound as I was grabbed by the hair and yanked upright no more than a few steps from the black, coursing river, its water robbed of all color by the night sky.

"Keep still, beautiful woman," cajoled a deep voice at my ear, an unforgiving arm clamped beneath my breasts. "*Like a gold ring in a pig's snout is a beautiful woman without discretion.*"

I expected the blade and my vision narrowed to pinpricks, but the knife I feared did not slice my skin. From behind, he deftly gagged me with a strip of cloth, making short work of knotting this at the base of my skull before hefting me over his shoulder; a hard ridge of bone and muscle dug into my belly as I hung upside-down, helpless to fight him, struggling to breathe, the taste of the dirty cloth bitter on my tongue. He was sizeable and solid, and his stride took us quickly away; he followed the riverbank, one arm clamped over my hips, my skirts encumbering my legs as effectively as shackles. I watched the ground bounce along beneath his leather-clad feet, so frightened my mind flashed in bursts like that of heat lightning.

Cry out, scream for help, fight him!
He'll hurt you! He'll kill you!

What of Mary?

Oh dear God –

I could not gauge the amount of time which passed before he came to a sudden halt, dumping me to the earth where I crumpled to hands and knees, aching and overcome with shock. We were well away from the town and night sounds teemed in my ears, crickets and bullfrogs, mosquitoes and the unending gush of the river itself, flowing along through the darkness, flush with spring thaw. I lifted my head and stared about in wide-eyed horror, my eyes lighting between the man who'd carried me here and another man who crouched on the riverbank, holding a lantern fitted with a guttering candle and smoking a pipe; its scarlet embers glowed as he drew on it and then blew a stream of acrid smoke. In the darkness behind me, away from the river, I heard the sounds of several horses.

"You brung a whore?" the smoking man asked, rising to his feet, gesturing at me with the stem of his pipe.

This query was ignored; my captor demanded, "Where's Yancy?"

"Having a shit," was the reply; still in disbelief, he muttered, "You brung a whore."

The man who'd hauled me here made a derisive sound and I sheltered my head as he approached with a single stride. He knocked aside my hands as he would gnats and gripped my chin, immobilizing my head, tilting it so he could study my face. He said, "Better than a whore. Keep her bound until I return, there's rope in the saddlebag. I want a good, long taste of this one."

"For *Christ's sake*," grumbled the smoking man. "This ain't the time."

From the darkness came a new voice, flat and lethal. "Talk to me, Church."

My spine went colder still. I thought, *Yancy.*

The man called Church released his hold on my chin. "Lawson's dead. I got him in the street but a half-hour ago, just in time. He didn't talk to nobody yet."

"What about the Carters?"

"Bill's waiting for them to show in town. Lawson must have ridden ahead," was Church's reply. "We ought to have found them on the trail, as I said. We could have killed the entire lot with one sweep."

"That would have happened, as you fucking know, if Turnbull weren't such a coward. He's useless as hell. I'm done with him."

"Bill's tetchy as a mother hen. He won't kill them in town." Church spoke with unmistakable contempt.

"All the more reason for you to *get back there*," Yancy said through clenched teeth.

The smoking man spoke up. "Bill does what needs doing, don't you accuse my brother of being tetchy!"

My disjointed gaze darted between them as they bickered, noticing minute details in the strange manner of heightened fear; the man called Church wore a leather chest plate over his shirt, its entire surface decorated with intricate beadwork; Yancy was slender as a willow switch and possessed no visible musculature, his features almost feminine in their fair delicacy. His eyes, lit from below by the guttering flame, appeared empty sockets. When he suddenly trained them upon me, I could not restrain a gulp; in that moment I understood without words why a person would obey this slim, terrifying youth. The gag scraped my tongue as I tried to swallow, but could not.

"What is this, Church?" he whispered.

"I followed her and the others from their camp. This one crept over to The Belle and out of my sight. Found her talking with one of the whores."

"Goddamn gossiping harlots," grumbled the smoking man. He spat into the river, swiping at his mouth with the back of one hand, pulling Yancy's focus back to him.

"Shut the hell up and get downriver, keep watch," Yancy ordered, indicating with an outstretched arm, and the man tamped out the remainder of his cigar, tugged lower his hat brim, and slouched away.

"This one'll do for me," Church said, again clutching my chin, forcing my regard; I had not dared to rise from the ground. My insides curled over on themselves. His face was sharp-edged, his eyes black as char. He appeared to be of mixed breeding, the long-bladed knife strapped to his hip winking with the promise of an excruciating death. But no brutality enacted my physical person could be as painful as what he'd just said.

My boys – he spoke of our camp. Cort, Nathaniel!

Boyd, oh dear God, Boyd, you're riding into danger!

Before I could comprehend the threat, Yancy grabbed my hair, yanking me from Church's grasp. He raged, "I will cut off your goddamn pecker before I let you *waste time fucking.*"

Church loomed in Yancy's space and I hunkered low, shielding my head. Yancy released my hair and his seething voice belied no lack of composure despite the decided physical disadvantage of his narrow build. "Get back to town and *finish it.*"

"And let you ride away? No way in hell."

"Where is Turnbull now?"

Church gritted his teeth, staring bullets at Yancy. At last he muttered, "He's holed up in the whorehouse with that little whore what owes him a favor."

"And there he can stay. Useless one-handed bastard."

I peered at the boy who had run away from the Rawleys' homestead in Iowa, whose father's intent had been to kill Sawyer and Lorie, the boy who had tried his best to kill Boyd and Malcolm. The Yancys had perpetuated such violence, had been the cause of such anguish for those I loved, that undiluted hatred welled in my center, so forceful it overrode all else. I entertained the notion of lunging at Yancy's midsection, knocking him to the ground and gripping his pale throat, thinking of Lorie's bravery on the prairies of Iowa, of the way she had shot an attacker in the gut. I must cling to a shred of valor. I was surely stronger than this slender boy, and neither my hands nor feet were bound.

As though ascertaining the direction of my thoughts, Yancy crouched down so his face was on a level with mine; I struggled to compose my expression. I could not restrain a flinch as he reached for me and slipped the gag from my mouth, leaving it dangling about my neck.

He whispered, "You want to hurt me?" I was too stunned to attempt a reply and he cajoled, "Do it. *Hurt me.*"

I made no sound, no movement, sickened by what I heard in his voice, what I witnessed in the holes of his eyes. The silence grew first thick and then oppressive, and he belted my mouth so effortlessly I did not see his fist before it made contact. The blow sent me sprawling to the side. I tasted blood. He was upon me at once, standing now, planting a boot between my breasts. Applying pressure, he bent low. His tone was that of someone conversing pleasantly as he remarked, "As you can see, I will not hesitate to hurt you."

Church snorted. "I get her first, you young pup."

"You get nothing! We can't linger here." Yancy peered down at me, tilting his head to one side in the fashion of a schoolmaster puzzling over the best presentation of a particular lesson. My breath was shallow; each inhalation was a struggle. He murmured, "Shoot her between the eyes and strip her to the skin. That's what you savages prefer, isn't it? Leave her on the path." His lips curved upward and my blood turned to ice. "On her back."

From a short distance the smoking man bellowed, "Rider!"

Yancy and Church sprang to immediate alert, cursing, drawing sidearms. Instinct overrode both pain and sensibility and I scrambled to my feet, seizing this opportunity before the thought fully formed. Though I'd never learned to swim, it was the lesser of two evils in my current state; I lifted my hem and raced for the springtime rush of the Mississippi. A pistol discharged a shot, then another, and I jolted forward, as helpless as a kitten tossed to drown.

Y OU BEEN A good traveling companion," I told Trapper, scratching beneath his square jaws, patting his long face with both hands. The mule twitched his rabbity ears and blew a breath against my side and I smiled, lifting my hat to swipe at my sweating forehead. The air was warm and dry on this second morning of May, the sun's heat a downright blessing on my shoulders. We were but a day's ride from St. Paul for the first time since last September and I had a plan, and reasonable hope of it succeeding. I could not deny the restless energy flowing in my blood, the bitterness of the knowledge that we were also closer to Iowa City than we'd been since riding forth from it; I did not let the aching despair that Rebecca was lost to me gain any firmer a handhold than it had already claimed – and I thought for the countless time, *We are alive. I ain't come this far, been through this much, to lose sight now.*

Malcolm, Cora, and I had marked the passing of the winter months at Fort Pierre with beads strung on a length of sinew, gifted to us by little Emeline Darvell. One bead for each day, which Malcolm or Cora slipped into place at the evening's fire, the clack of a bead coming to rest beside the one representing the day before allowing for a small sense of satisfaction. By now we'd amassed a proper necklace, adorned with beads in a variety of bright colors, indigo and crimson and sunny yellow, greens to rival a cedar forest. Some were painted with fine white lines, others were chipped or cracked; the necklace had become a sort of talisman, which Cora kept tucked in a soft leather pouch she'd made with Fern's help. We remained indebted to the Darvell family; Malcolm and Cora had spent every day in the company of Albie, Pierpont, and Emeline, and now understood more French and Anishinabeg than a year's worth of schooling could have provided.

Folks wintering at the fort were a gregarious lot, as a whole, the predominant blood French or Indian, or a mixture of the two, trappers and traders, or families intending to stake homestead claims come spring. I respected Xavier's wishes and did not again speak of the events on the prairie, except with Malcolm and Cora in the privacy of the wigwam erected for our use during the winter months. The lodge was much smaller than the one in which Xavier and Fern lived but it proved warm and snug, and I was in no position to utter a thought, let alone a word, of complaint. As the weeks ticked by I forced myself to rest and therefore finish healing, helping the Darvells as I was able; after a spell, my full strength returned. I accompanied Xavier to the river bottoms, where trees grew in greater profusion and we chopped the week's wood supply. I hunted with the Henry rifle, bagging rabbits and the occasional deer, and spent hours under the chilly morning sun, learning to use a crossbow.

Pierpont was an expert, delighted to teach Malcolm and me; the irony of shooting lessons given by the nephew of the man who'd fired his crossbow into my leg was not lost on me. And when I envisioned Church Talk's face as I grew ever more accurate in aim, firing upon a target tied to a hay bale, I refused to feel guilty. The desire to kill those who'd harmed my brother and Cora, who'd tried their best to kill all three of us, hibernated within me; I lay awake at night, listening to Malcolm's snoring and Cora's soft breathing, studying the cone-shaped peak above us in the red glow of the embers, and allowed the dark thoughts sway. I would find Fallon and Virgil, Church Talk and Hoyt Little. I would make them pay for what they'd done to us, whether I took their lives or saw them carted to their hangings. None of these men appeared at the fort during the long winter months and so I understood that justice must occur in a different place, and on my terms this time around; I would not hesitate to kill any of them, but only if there was no other choice, or if I could do so without being caught. I could not risk being hung or spending the rest of my life in jail.

I was no fool. I knew what slim chance I'd had at finding Rebecca unmarried and waiting for me in Iowa City had passed as surely as any yesterday – never to return no matter how goddamn hard I wished it – and I wished hard enough to turn my body inside out, torturing myself and further fueling the desire to kill those whose actions kept me from her. How I hated letting such dark thoughts have free reign; I'd believed the time for such darkness had

passed with the War. I was afraid to let these thoughts mix with the sweetness of my memories of Rebecca, which sustained me in ways she would of
course never know. Brutally honest with my pitiful self, I knew I must acknowledge that the hope of her ever being mine was surely lost – I'd ridden
away from her, I'd left her behind – and the agony of this mistake coursed
like poison through my body. Even had I been fortunate enough to return to
Iowa last autumn and find her still waiting, all such prospect was destroyed
with the passing of the winter months.

And yet I could not, *would* not, release hold on my precious store of memories of her, letting them overtake me as I lay there through those cold nights
no matter how it tormented my heart, so goddamn lonely, missing her so bad
it hurt to inhale. I recalled Granny Rose speaking of a woman in the holler who'd died of a broken heart; I could hear my granny's voice clucking in
concern over the matter.

Undone in sorrow, that's what. Poor, poor girl.

Sending out the plea the same way I believed Sawyer sent words to Lorie,
I would think, *Rebecca, if you can somehow hear me please know that I pray to see
your face one last time. I am alive out here and what keeps me alive is the thought
of seeing you once more. Even if it's just to hear you say you already wed Marshal
Quade, I pray to see your face one last time.*

And my hands would crush into fists at the thought of the wedding which
had surely taken place, at Rebecca becoming the wife of another.

*But it's nothing less than you deserve, Carter. You rode away. Sawyer an' Lorie
warned you not to, an' yet you rode away.*

There was no answer but the wail of the wind, the whisper of snowfall.

With the arrival of spring, and warmer weather, the need to move rose
within everyone in the fort as palpably as the sound of voices lifted in song.
Xavier and Fern, and their children, left the fort each April to travel to Fern's
family in Indian Territory, eastward and then due north as Xavier explained
their annual route, and they would accompany us as far as they were able.
Other than Malcolm and Cora, and the Darvells, I kept mainly to myself at
the fort, even as the ground thawed and the sap rose, and the anticipation of
traveling onward from the confines of the wooden walls sparked ever more
rowdy nightly drinking and cavorting. I withstood Malcolm's teasing that I
looked like a black bear; I'd not trimmed my hair or shaved my face since
last summer. In turn, I was fond of perusing his smooth jaws for any trace

of a beard, teasing him that at this rate he'd never require a shaving brush or straight razor.

In the company of gentle Fern and her lively daughters, Cora thrived; while she'd once allowed Malcolm to do all of the talking, she now spoke and laughed with ease. I'd grown accustomed to the oddity of her eyes, seeing instead the sweetness of her entire face; it was plain she would not be separated from Malcolm, nor he from her, and I outright dreaded the attempting of it – but I had also decided I would seek out Royal Lawson on our return journey to Minnesota, even if this meant a detour from our intended route. Lawson deserved to know that his niece was alive and I was finally capable of delivering this knowledge to his homestead.

Further, Lawson deserved to know that his brother, Cora's father, had been murdered.

Cora finally told us the story when a March snowstorm was shrieking over the fort, the three of us clustered around our nightly fire, Cora threading the day-bead necklace through her delicate fingers, Malcolm gnawing a deer rib. I sat on my haunches, painstakingly sewing together two lengths of canvas with a heavy leather needle, intent on finishing repairs to the flatbed wagon I'd been given thanks to the generosity of a family no longer requiring its service. I'd repaired its broken axle and missing bed boards, and now only the rending in the canvas cover remained. When Cora said, "I must tell you something," I glanced up without yet interpreting the serious nature of what she meant to tell us.

Malcolm, much more attuned to her, paused in his eating and invited, "Go on."

And so we learned of how Cora had crept from her bed in the boarding-house the night her daddy had been horse-kicked, knowing he was in grave condition, disobeying Grady's orders in order to see him. Quiet as a field mouse she slipped along the hallway to his room; he lay alone in the gut-tering glow of a single candle when Cora arrived and curled beside him on the bed, resting her head to his chest, feeling the labored rise and fall of his breathing. He could not move his arms to hold her and his eyes were covered in a length of bandage blotted by dark blood, but he knew she was there, and spoke her name. When the creak of the doorknob alerted her to another's presence Cora slipped beneath the bed, and it was from this hiding spot she observed Virgil Turnbull enter the room. Seconds later the entire bedframe pressed upon her as she stayed hidden beneath.

"I do not know for certain but I believe he smothered Papa," Cora whispered, her gaze entangled in the flames. Her fingers, clutching the necklace, had stilled.

Virgil left the room immediately after his grisly errand was completed, the door closing behind him with a click. Cora, too terrified to move, remained under the bed; it was not until dawn, when Grady appeared in the room, discovered Dyer was no longer breathing, and hurried to rouse the others that she dared to slip from her hiding spot. She saw her daddy's slack face and knew he was gone. When Grady returned, Quill and Virgil along with him, they found Cora bent over Dyer, her face pressed to his neck. She did not tell them what she had seen, or what she suspected, and in fact refused to speak at all, until the morning she met Malcolm.

"I should have told Grady," Cora said, and it was clear that no matter what we said, she would punish herself with these notions. "I was a coward to hide and to keep it a secret."

Scooting closer and curving an arm about her shoulders, Malcolm said, "You are no coward."

"You have one of the bravest souls I know, honey," I said to her, my mind leaping as I wondered at Virgil's motive. No point in smothering a man already half-dead unless you'd brought him to that state in the first place, or he knew something you intended to keep quiet. Quill and Grady had believed Dyer was horse-kicked, his head crushed by the blow of a hoof. I'd considered the thought back on the trail, when Grady and Quill were still alive, that Virgil had been the one to smash Dyer's skull and arranged it to appear as though a mare had done it, instead. But why? What sparked such a violent action? And to what end? What had Dyer, or Virgil, known and therefore had to lose?

Cora rested her cheek to Malcolm's shoulder, her long and wild hair floating about his face and into which he sank his free hand, caressing her in a gesture far too intimate for two as young as they; and yet the tenderness of it, the depth of love it conveyed, tore at my heart. I could not help but imagine plunging my hands into Rebecca's loose hair with no restraints, of her head against my chest, indicating a much greater need – a need for my love and comfort, for the security of my touch. I covered my face with both hands, pressing hard, damning myself for so many mistakes I'd lost all count.

MY HEART quickened its pace now, months later, on the prairie just west of St. Paul. The journey had proved muddy, the going slow, but we'd encountered little other trouble. Malcolm and I were armed to our fullest capacity, with a modest store of food packed in the flatbed I'd spent the winter repairing; Trapper and Aces High took turns pulling us along the rolling prairie. Not long after parting ways with the Darvells we'd ridden for Royal Lawson's homestead, following the directions as I remembered Grady speaking them.

We found the sprawling ranch in isolated country, situated at the base of a towering ridge; we spent a night there, welcomed by Cora's family – Royal and his wife, and their five children. By then it was mid-April and Royal was distressed enough at learning the truth – he explained how Virgil Turnbull had delivered his cattle, as Royal expected, but with a contingent of men he did not – that he left his ranch under the temporary care of his foreman and accompanied us to St. Paul in order to enact what justice he could manage.

Royal explained how he had paid out wages to Virgil, who arrived with men introducing themselves as Fallon Yancy, Hoyt Little, and Byron Johnston – no mention of Church Talk the half-breed – and that Virgil's party collected wages and rode out before evening, refusing the offer of a night's rest at the ranch. Virgil had lamented to Royal of the bad luck which stalked him on the journey, relating the news of Dyer's death in St. Paul, and the subsequent deaths of Grady and Quill, and indeed Dyer's girl-child, along the way. Virgil spoke of 'others' being killed as well, a man and boy Grady had hired; of course, Virgil failed to mention he'd done his best to kill these others, and had never expected us to arrive in Royal's dooryard months after the fact.

"Turnbull had an answer for everything," Royal told me. "And I had no reason to distrust him. For Christ's sake, we served together. Had you been killed as intended, likely I would never have questioned the sad tale. But this changes everything."

For all their kind offering and then outright pleading, Cora would not be convinced to remain at the ranch with her kin. Malcolm's tension over the matter rendered him as rigid as a fresh-strung rope bed; he was terrified they might convince her to stay. I insisted that we loved the girl as our own kin and would provide for her a home with us in Minnesota. For all that she was his niece, Royal had not seen Cora since she was a tiny babe in Kansas, and his love for her was motivated chiefly by the fact that her father had been his younger brother.

Though Royal was plainly a successful rancher, with a wood-framed house grand in scale, there was limited space in his busy home, and at last he consented to allow Cora to remain with Malcolm and me for the time being; he did, however, insist upon accompanying us to Minnesota, and saddled a solid bay yearling in order to make the journey with the dual intent, he explained, of speaking to the law and secondarily inquiring about disinterring Dyer's body for return to his homestead and a proper burial. I sensed he would insist at that time upon Cora returning along with him but figured we'd cross that particular bridge when we came to it, and not an ever-lovin' moment before.

I found Royal's presence a pleasant one in the following weeks as we traveled towards Minnesota; he was a rather solitary fellow, courteous, solemn of demeanor and prone to riding restlessly ahead of the wagon as though scouting, returning in the late afternoon. He made real effort to speak with Cora and she seemed to welcome his company. Following the same route, now in the opposite direction, we eventually came to the oak tree on the Missouri beneath which we'd played mumblety-peg that terrible night; the winter had taken a toll on the burned-out frame of the wagon, and critters upon Grady and Quill's bodies. Royal dismounted along with me and together we collected up what bones were left behind, burying them with all vestiges of dignity we could offer. The last of the day's fading light struck our faces as we stood four abreast at the fresh-dug graves, Cora between Malcolm and me, her arms about Malcolm's waist; my brother rested his chin atop her head.

Hat held to his chest, Royal spoke with solemn dignity. "Grady Ballard and Quill Dobbins were good and decent men, and I aim to see justice served in their stead."

I thought of what Grady had once said about the violets in the buffalo wallow and what Quill told me about Ellie, the woman he'd left behind, the one he'd loved to his final breath, I had no doubt. I said aloud, "We don't know just when our life will be taken, but if I learned anything from these two men it was to value what we have in this life, while we's living it."

Malcolm reached for my hand and I threaded together our fingers.

"Boyd, do you think we might find Sawyer an' Lorie-Lorie? Do you think they might be there in town?" Malcolm rode near on Aces High to direct his question my way; saddled and ready to ride, the boy had been up and about camp since dawn on this May morning. I was too cautious to allow for as much eagerness but felt a spike of hope pierce my heart nonetheless at the idea that my oldest friend and dear Lorie had perhaps arrived ahead of us. I prayed they'd received my letter last fall and expected us to be in St. Paul as planned; I felt as though two hundred winters had passed since last I'd seen them.

All I would say was, "Soon enough, we'll find out."

Malcolm's sweet-talking had finally worked its wiles on Cora; she sat in front of him atop Aces High, clad in buckskin trousers once belonging to Pierpont, with which he'd gifted her before we parted ways. The Darvell children promised Malcolm and Cora their paths would cross again, and all five had plied one another with gifts, raiding their own belongings in order to provide these offerings. Cora's leather pouch, tied to her waist with a length of ribbon, was plumb full of beads, a coiled length of sinew, pretty pebbles, and snail shells she and Malcolm plucked from the banks of creeks we forded. She also collected feathers she found, crow and hawk, mainly, as these were large and stood out against the green of the spring prairie. Malcolm picked flowers for her as the days lengthened and blossoms grew in abundance; a week or so ago, Royal, observing this, had muttered to me, "I don't know that I presented my wife so many flowers even when courting her. I suppose I'm not above learning a few lessons from the boy."

Sitting near the evening's fire we'd watched with wry amusement as Malcolm helped Cora to bundle the stems with a bit of sinew from her pouch, the two of them sitting on the grass near the wagon, as content in each other's presence as any two people I ever saw. I looked then to Royal, whose stately and expensive garments seemed hardly worse for the wear even after weeks of travel. He kept his beard and mustaches trimmed, using a small handheld mirror which reminded me of the one Sawyer and I had once shared. I intended to take care of shaving once we reached St. Paul; my hair was unruly with curls all over my body – head and beard and torso. I'd almost forgotten what my chin felt like.

I said to Royal, "The two of them's kindred spirits, I reckon."

Royal sighed and sipped from his coffee, a tin of which he'd stowed in the wagon. "Your brother is blessed with a kind soul, that's evident. My brother was a similar sort. Dyer cared for Cora's mother, Millie, very tenderly. I see Millie in Cora, though I do hope the girl is possessed of a stronger constitution."

I thought of the way Cora had wrapped about Malcolm's kicking legs, attempting to save him from strangling, her hands bloody and a length of rope still tied about her neck. I gritted my teeth before saying, "I've known few stronger."

"Dyer would wish for the girl to live with kin," Royal said quietly, and I met his somber gaze. There was no challenge present in either his eyes or tone; he simply spoke the truth.

I said, on a sigh, "Any daddy would."

"I would like for you to know I have given the matter much thought. Young Malcolm may court her when she's of an age," Royal said. "He strikes me as the sort destined to roam before settling. Might be that he'll ride westward again, once a few years have passed."

I felt like a right traitor as I murmured, "I figure you's right."

I'd not yet spoken of this conversation to Malcolm.

"A fine morning," Royal commented just now, taking up the reins of his bay.

We'd been plagued by poor weather the past two days. Though not heavy, the misting rain served to dampen clothes and spirits, both. I tried to see the fair morning and the promise of sunlight as a sign that all would be well.

"It is indeed," I agreed, resting my forehead briefly against Trapper's warm neck, an age-old habit, a seeking of comfort in the familiar scent of animal hide. I dearly missed my Fortune but had grown fond of the mule in his own right, a creature I'd found to be far less stubborn than most horses I'd ever known.

"Let's ride!" Malcolm enthused, heeling Aces, his arms secure about Cora, tucked before him on the saddle.

I climbed atop the wagon seat, disengaged the brake, and slapped the reins over Trapper's rump. Malcolm and Cora rode ahead, keen-eyed under the gold dust of the morning sun, but for a spell Royal stayed abreast of the wagon.

"I intend to wire the Turnbull family in Kansas, inquiring after Virgil's current location, first thing," Royal said as though thinking aloud; we'd spoken often of our plans upon arrival in St. Paul and I was well aware of his intentions, but he was the sort that preferred to mull aloud in this fashion. "We know the man named Johnston was killed but the others remain unfortunately at large. Further, we must suppose they have been made aware of the fact that you and your brother, and indeed my niece, remain alive. That is, if Hoyt Little has made contact with them."

We figured this for a certainty; Royal and I had taken turns with guard detail, trading off each night of our journey, and we both remained armed at all hours. I remembered all too clear the day I'd first crossed paths with one of the Littles, Bill with his scarred face, and the words were bitter in my mouth as I acknowledged, "The Littles are bad seeds all around, I reckon. Grady said as much the first night I met him, back in St. Paul. I knew I shoulda taken it upon myself to kill Hoyt at the fort, I knew it that very morning."

"Now, Carter, let us refrain from such violence if possible. Justice will be served, and served well, I will see to it. I am a man of no small reputation and wealth, and I refuse to be ignored in any matter, let alone one as criminal as this." Royal adjusted his hat, shoulders lifting with a sigh. "Though I would never confess such in the presence of my wife, I am not above admitting I would glean a fair amount of satisfaction from firing upon Turnbull, watching the light go from his eyes. The puny, one-handed bastard, daring to tell such lies to my face when he is but a murdering coward of the lowest order."

I thought of everything I had to lose as I admitted, "I wouldn't mind seeing him die, myself. Let's hope it ain't at our hands."

We did not stop to build a fire or take a meal, impatient to reach our destination before nightfall. A quickening in my blood made it insufferable to remain stationary as the hours of the day burned past; I longed to jump to the ground, knowing I could run much faster than the ponderous flatbed. I yelled after Malcolm to take a turn driving Trapper but the boy pretended not to hear and heeled Aces, he and Cora racing for the horizon. I rolled my eyes heavenward, muttering about how I would thrash his misbehaving hide. Royal too had deserted the wagon, riding ahead, every inch as twitchy as me; at least he was able to travel faster than a plodding walk. As the evening advanced I peered over my shoulder at the western horizon, taking a moment's pleasure in the blaze of bright orange present there, letting the auburn rays bathe my face.

I heard approaching hoofbeats seconds before Malcolm shouted, "We seen the town!" Aces reached the wagon and Malcolm turned the chestnut in a neat circle, bringing them abreast. Excitement rolled from him as he extended his right arm to indicate. "Just beyond yonder rise, Boyd!"

"Where's Royal?" I asked, arching to stretch my back, ordering Trapper, "C'mon, boy, *gidd*-up!"

"He rode ahead at a clip now that we's so close, said to tell you he'd meet us at the sheriff's office." Malcolm squeezed Cora with his left arm, kissing her cheek. "We made it. We made it here!"

"Stick near." I fixed the boy with my sternest eyebrows.

My heart took up a swift thumping as the first structures came into view on the horizon. We approached from a southwesterly angle while twilight claimed the landscape by inches; I heard the river and thought I must be imagining the sound of a harmonica tinkling through the gray light to my ears. A few hundred yards ahead I spied the glint of a cookfire to the right of the trail; the music seemed to be coming from this camp. As we neared I made out the shapes of two covered wagons and a few head of horse, one with a paint hide; a man and two children were seated around the fire's warmth and all three, roused by the rumbling sound of our approach, turned to look.

"Hallo there!" Malcolm crowed, waving with typical enthusiasm, perhaps ten yards ahead.

The man stood. "Good evening, young fellow!"

My heart lurched. I squinted into the dimness. Surely I'd heard wrong...

And then my brother yelped, "*Boyd!*"

Relying on instinct, I yanked Trapper to a halt and jumped from the wagon, watching as though from an impassable distance as my brother dismounted and two little boys leaped at him. My boots seemed mired in mud even as I ran full-bore, arms churning.

"*Jesus Christ*," I gasped, realizing that what I was seeing was actually real, that I was not in the midst of a vision. Wild with disbelief, with an ardent hope the likes of which I'd never experienced, I choked, "Cort, Nathaniel! What...*how*...Uncle Jacob?"

My mama's younger brother, whose face I'd not looked upon since I was a boy in the holler, stood before me. Steeped in the shock of it, the stun mirrored on Jacob's bearded countenance, I fell into his arms as though I was no older than the boy I'd been when last in his company.

"*Boyd*," Jacob acknowledged, thumping my back, rocking us side to side. "You're alive! Thanks be to Jesus, you're alive!" He drew back, gripping my shoulders, and regarded me with an expression of such abiding joy that tears bled into my eyes; Jacob looked next to Malcolm, hauling him into an embrace, knuckling his scalp, kissing the boy's cheeks as he proclaimed, "And young Malcolm! Glory be! Near about everyone in these parts has tried their best to convince us you two was dead!"

Cort and Nathaniel pounced at me and I hugged them close, delirious with exultation at what their presence meant. My voice gone hoarse and shaking, I begged, "Where is your mama?" I set them gently aside and flew for the wagons, certain she must be within them. "*Rebecca!*"

The boys chased me; I all but ripped the canvas coverings from their moorings, hollering for her, finding both wagons empty of all but belongings.

"Where is she? Oh Jesus, where is she?" I begged again, falling to my knees. The boys clambered into my arms, climbing all over me as they'd always done. I gathered them to my sides, Rebecca's beloved sons, kissing their cheeks and cupping their heads. My heart thundered so hard my vision was blurry, blood roaring in my ears.

"Mama rode to town on the wagon with Mrs. Lorie," Cort explained.

Nathaniel tugged on my beard to gain my attention, his round face alight with the excitement of it all. He announced, "Mrs. Lorie's having her baby!"

One shock atop the next, I tried to draw a full breath, utterly unable. Jacob caught up with us and stood with fists to hips, grinning wide enough to crack his jaws, shaking his head. "I'll be a monkey's uncle, young nephew. If you ain't the *spittin' image* of your daddy."

"Uncle Jacob," I pleaded. "Where are they?"

"Town, dear boy. Sawyer's Lorie is delivering their young'un likely as we speak. Tilson and Becky accompanied them."

Knowing they were so close was almost more than I could bear. Again I hugged the boys, their faces against my neck; I was tear-stricken and unashamed.

His voice tickling my ear, Cort said, "Mama's been missing you something fierce, Mr. Carter."

ONCE I REGAINED a sliver of sense, I realized all of our livestock was present and wasted no time saddling Admiral, while Nathaniel and Cort crowded my elbows and Jacob did his best to offer a bare-bones explanation for what had occurred since we'd gone missing last autumn.

"My letters never reached you?" I repeated, tightening the cinch, so eager to ride to town that my hands shook.

"For whatever reason, they did not. I am more grateful than I can say to see you in one piece, Boyd. I couldn't bear thinking I'd lost Clairee's last two sons. You've a hell of a fine friend in Sawyer, and his Lorie, and a damn fine woman pining over you, I do not believe Becky would mind me saying. She's been much aggrieved thinking you and young Malcolm dead."

"Mama's been crying every night," Nathaniel said, tugging at my pant leg, and my gaze flew to the rise in the earth that hid the town. Rebecca was there – just over that ridge. She had cried for me. She cared for *me*, Boyd Carter. She had not married Quade and done her best to forget my name; by the grace of God she had waited for me and I would never ride away from her again. I would catch her in my arms and never let go, not for a blessed thing.

Jacob laid his hand upon my shoulder, just like Daddy would have done, and I put mine atop his; I'd not beheld an elder member of my family in many years. I'd been the eldest, the one responsible, for so damn long. "Young nephew, you ride after your woman. They's at the Jeffries' boardinghouse, a block east of the river. I'll keep watch of the young'uns."

"Thank you kindly," I whispered.

Polite enough to have retrieved Trapper, guiding the mule by his bridle with the wagon grinding along behind, Malcolm hollered, "Not without me,

you ain't, Boyd!" To Cora, who hovered near him as though attached by a
string, he said, "Cora-bell, you warm by the fire with Uncle Jacob an' the
boys, have somethin' to eat. I know you's hungry. And Stormy needs holding."
Malcolm had already draped the big gray cat over his shoulders like a fancy
fur stole; I could hear the critter purring.

Cora nodded acceptance and reached to take Stormy into her slender arms.

Jacob looked between Malcolm and Cora with eyebrows curled in question, and I promised, "I'll explain everything once we's returned."

I took the saddle and yelled to my brother, "Hurry if you's coming!"

I heeled Admiral, bending low over his familiar neck, knowing Malcolm
would catch up with us; sure enough, I heard him and Aces gaining ground
within fifteen seconds. Admiral responded by increasing his speed, powerful
legs a blur beneath us, fine mount that he was; he'd seen Gus through the
entirety of the War. I grinned, stunned by the level of my joy; it had been so
long. Such unfettered happiness left me almost fearful, and decidedly lightheaded. My heart seemed to be repeating *Rebecca* in a wild, three-beat clip.

"Can you believe it?" my brother cried as Aces nosed abreast. We rode as
if racing each other at the county fair, laughing and hollering, startling those
folks camped along the edge of town; parked wagons, settled in for the night,
increased in number as we drew closer to the outskirts of St. Paul. A man
crouching at his cook fire yelled after us, hollering, "Pipe down, you dern
fools!" but we only laughed all the more, giddy with relief and anticipation.

The main road into town, which Malcolm and I had traversed so gravely
last fall, was once again beneath our horses' hooves. The river bluffs loomed
into immediate view, the water a rushing artery tinted black with evening, its
many docks like the rungs of a ladder laid atop the river. Forced to rein to a
slower pace or risk trampling an unsuspecting soul, I scanned the busy street
for the boardinghouse of which Uncle Jacob spoke, damning the bustling,
lively crowds. The rush of the river seemed to crash through my skull and
pour out my ears; sudden tension kept straight my spine.

Out of breath, Malcolm puffed, "They ain't gonna…believe their eyes, Boyd!"

"We gotta find them first," I said, rabid to do so. My eyes roved over the
hanging shingle of each business we passed, scarce a drop of daylight left to
help; the street lanterns set at the corner of every block cast golden light over
faces of passersby, all unknown to me. I eased Admiral closer to my brother
and Aces and reminded, "Keep a lookout for the Jeffries' boardinghouse."

"I know, I know. I am!" Malcolm sent me a grin. "Uncle Jacob said Lorie's having a baby! Aw, I can't wait to see it. I'll bet Sawyer is beside himself."

"Them two'll have a half-dozen…in as many years," I predicted. I'd not caught my breath, not with the promise of seeing Rebecca this night, maybe within this quarter-hour. It was all I could do to sit the saddle without falling, to keep my shaking grip firm about the reins. We angled north, Admiral and Aces forced to walk as we navigated the busy route bordering the river. Sweat gathered on my spine and along my hairline as we drew closer to the far side of town, my tension growing; I despised admitting that I felt something was wrong, but something was –

"Look there!" Malcolm pointed.

Just ahead, a knot of bodies gathered around the swinging doors of a saloon. Excited voices lifted from the group like birds taking wing. Without waiting for my response, Malcolm heeled Aces, drawing to a halt and angling so he could peer over the shoulders of those standing; coming abreast, I saw the assembled crowd was bent over a man crumpled on the edge of the road, his boots lolling.

"He's been stabbed!" someone hollered, and the cacophony swelled. "This man's been stabbed!"

My gut jumped. I dismounted, handing Admiral's lead to Malcolm, and elbowed without apology through the gathered, rumbling men. It took no more than a second to realize that the man whose left side bloomed with a growing red stain was no other than Royal Lawson. I fell to my knees and grabbed for his arm, desperate to believe he was not yet dead, that he would be able to tell me who'd done this to him. His face was stark in the lantern light, lips gaping; I could see the bottom row of his teeth and the arch forming the upper curve of his mouth. His eyes had rolled back into his skull and whoever administered the knife to Royal's side knew what he was doing – grab the victim's left shoulder, aim for the heart by angling the blade downward between the ribs beneath the armpit, a swift, sure kill. Even if I'd never served three years of my life as a soldier, I'd have known he was a goner.

"*Royal,*" I implored, leaning close. I didn't believe he saw me, headed as he was for what lay beyond. I shook his arm, cupping a hand under his head, witnessing as this man in whose company I'd ridden hundreds of miles bled out. "Royal!"

He issued a low gurgling and then was still.

"Who is this man?" asked someone at my shoulder. "Do you know him?"

I looked up into a gaggle of male faces, all curious, all strangers. Malcolm remained astride Aces at the back of the crowd, watching with lips compressed, his earlier gaiety having dissipated like dew beneath an unrelenting sun. I demanded, "What happened here? Who saw it?"

A thousand thoughts tried to gain purchase in my head, fighting for the strongest hold.

If Royal's dead, then Fallon's nearby.

They'll be looking next for you, if they ain't already.

May be that you're in their sights just now, Carter.

The darkening air seemed thick, my vision rippling with dizzy revulsion. The busy street listed and I fought the sensation, voices growing hushed, distorted; words made no sense, becoming instead a rushing stream of sound. My eyes darted about like those of a prey animal seized by the steel teeth of a sprung trap, knowing the hounds approached and there was nothing to be done. The first thing I saw was the gaping mouth of an alleyway, next the upper-floor windows of a nearby saloon, where a sniper could easily position to strike. Coldness clawed my nape.

Hold up. They stabbed him, kept it quiet. They didn't risk shooting in the crowd. One of them is near, hidin' until it's safe to emerge.

"Sheriff's been sent for," someone behind me said. "This here feller got himself killed not but five minutes past."

"Did anyone see who done it?" I asked again, but more than one man answered and I understood plainly I would get no reliable information. I squared my jaw and ordered, "Help me!" sliding my arms beneath Royal's dead weight, hooking my hold about his torso, a rush of furious energy allowing me no time to grieve, or to consider what Cora would feel to know her uncle was gone just as surely as her daddy. Two men assisted and we carried Royal's body into the nearest saloon, where men surged anew, babbling with anxious questions.

"What the devil?"

"What's happened?"

"Is he dead?"

I couldn't linger, but promised, "I'll return as soon as I am able. I rode with this man from the Territory. His name is Royal Lawson and I believe the man who killed him is named Virgil Turnbull." And then I asked, "Where is

Jeffries' boardinghouse?"

Malcolm had remained in the saddle, waiting for my instruction; I hurried to him, ordering, "C'mon," as I put my boot in the stirrup.

"Royal's dead?" Malcolm was breathless and fearful, and trying not to let me see it.

"Yes," I muttered grimly.

"You think Fallon's near, don't you?"

I looked over at my brother, the two of us exchanging words without speaking. At last I nodded, just a fraction.

"How will I tell her?" he whispered.

I had no good answer; with renewed desire to reach our destination, I heeled Admiral. We rode up to a deep front porch at a clip, dust swirling. I dismounted before Malcolm and saw a small flatbed wagon, with Juniper hitched to it, parked in the alley between the buildings. I tethered Admiral fast as my fingers could fly and took wide steps leading to the front entrance at a dead run; fortunately the door was propped open to the evening air. A plump woman and a young girl were stationed behind the long, chest-high counter and I startled them as I broke my run with both palms against its wooden length and rasped, "Davis!"

The woman reeled away from my wild appearance, grabbing for the girl's elbow, calling urgently, "Harold!"

The girl's eyes snapped with excitement and she squirreled free of her mother, declaring, "They're right up these steps, come along, mister!"

"*Meggie!*" the woman cried, but the girl was already clattering up the stairs leading to the second floor; I followed, hearing commotion in the wake of my uninvited passage, not caring. Voices rose behind me, Malcolm's included, but I was single-minded with purpose now, too close to the promise of Rebecca to pay heed to anything else.

The girl skittered to a halt before a closed door on the right side of the hallway and from behind it Sawyer demanded, "Edward?"

"Sawyer!" I hollered and just that fast, the door was thrown wide.

My oldest friend scarce had time to holster his piece before I clutched him in an embrace fit to smother his breath. Past his shoulder I beheld Lorie upon a rumpled bed, holding a tiny babe to her breast. Her lips dropped open and she began weeping at the sight of me, reaching with her free hand – and then, like a long-lost fledgling to its dear mama, Malcolm streaked past Saw-

yer and me and dove for Lorie. He fell to his knees, burying his face against
her side and holding for all he was worth as she curled over him and kissed
his cheek, his ear, his forehead, issuing choking sobs.

"*Malcolm*," she wept. "My boy, *my sweet boy.*"

"Boyd, you're alive! Jesus Christ, we all but gave up hope!" Sawyer drew
away, smucked with stun at the sight of me before him. "What...*how...*"

"Where is she?" I begged, interrupting him, clutching his shoulders. "I
swear I'll explain everything, but first tell me where Rebecca is."

"But where have you –"

"Sawyer! Where is Rebecca?"

Behind us, in the hallway, a man demanded, "Davis! Do you know this
fellow? Scared my wife half to death!"

Lorie implored, "Boyd, come here, *please come here,*" and I reached the
bedside in two long strides, there gently clasping the back of her head and
pressing a kiss to her forehead, leaning over Malcolm's huddled form to do
so. Lorie smelled like sweetness itself and I inhaled of her, struck anew with
love for this woman I considered a sister, who'd given Sawyer a reason to live.
Tears glistened on her face as she stared up at me.

"Lorie-girl," I whispered, and stroked a fingertip over the baby's silken
cheek. "Who you got here?"

"Oh, *Boyd,*" she said again, using one shoulder to nudge aside flowing tears;
both her hands were pinned beneath Malcolm and the child. "Becky will be
exultant! She and Tilson are across the way, at The Dolly Belle. They promised
to return before Rose was born but they have not, and I am so worried."

"The Belle?" I repeated, confused. "But why..."

Sawyer was there, cupping Malcolm's head as he explained, "A woman
named Mary, there employed, wanted a word with Becky." He studied me
and understood, "You know this woman Mary."

"I do," I confirmed, tight in the chest, my mind galloping like a cavalry
charge. I thought, *Virgil.* Fast, not to be contradicted, I said, "I'll return directly. Malcolm, stay here with Sawyer an' Lorie. Don't leave this room, you hear?"

Sawyer's one-sided gaze drove into mine, the two of us exchanging messages in the way of longtime friends; he was not wearing his eyepatch and
the healed wound appeared rigid with scarring. Before he could speak, I said,
"No. I thank you, I know you would, but no. You stay here with them. Malcolm can tell you where we been." I heaved a breath, overcome, gripping

Sawyer's upper arm, seeking reassurance in his familiarity. "I aim to hold that baby when I return."

And then I ran, down the stairs and out into the dark night, across the street and through the swinging doors of The Dolly Belle, garish red lanterns swaying in the slight breeze. It was a despicable place I'd hoped never again in my life to enter, but Lorie had said Rebecca was here. I threw my gaze about the bustling, noisy space. Blood beat at the interior of my skull; Rebecca was not in sight, nor was Tilson. Though I didn't believe Virgil, Fallon, Church Talk, or even Hoyt Little would be careless, or fool, enough to slay Royal Lawson and then blithely enter a saloon for a drink, I looked for them. My eyes darted with desperate movements, pinwheeling in their sockets in the glow of the many-colored lights thrown by the mullioned glass in Jean Luc's lanterns.

I saw the proprietor himself, seated at a table near the painting of the nude woman; though he was angled away from my position I recognized the ostentatious Frenchman with his blue scarf and earbobs, as though no time had passed since last autumn. The men seated at his table all fell silent as I strode their way, wary but not yet fearful. Jean Luc did not rise to greet me, only leaned back in his chair like a show-off youngster daring his daddy to reprimand. If he seemed surprised to see me alive and well, he displayed none of that.

"I am seeking a woman named Rebecca Krage," I said, glowering into his objectionable face with its oiled mustaches and greasy grin. If he knew where she was and would not tell me, I would not be responsible for what I did to him next.

"If it is not *Monsieur* Carter, returned from the dead!" Jean Luc pronounced in the grand fashion I remembered. "Mayhap *Monsieur* should seek a bath before all else, *non?*"

I hauled him from the chair, toppling it to the floor, grabbing him by the shirtfront and bringing his simpering face close to mine. "Tell me where she is."

"There is no woman by that name in my employ!" he yelped, affronted.

Through clenched teeth I demanded, "Has Virgil Turnbull been here this night?"

Jean Luc shoved at my hold and I let him free, setting him roughly upon his feet. He dusted at his garments, cursing in both English and French, but at least I'd wiped that simper from his expression. He declared, "I will have the law on you, Carter, see if I will not!"

"The law?" I rasped, driving a hard finger into his chest. "*There is a dead man* just across the fucking street from your *establishment*." I drew out the final word into four or so parts, mocking him. "You go right ahead an' get the law in here! Where is Turnbull? Where is Mary? I need a word with her!"

"*Monsieur* Carter!" The voice approaching from the left was not unfamiliar, though far more sincere than the last time I'd heard it. I turned to see the woman named Cecilia headed our direction, her eyes fixed on me with unmistakable alarm. Without preamble, ignoring Jean Luc's sputtering, she said, "The man you seek was seeking *you*, just yesterday."

"Virgil was here?" I demanded, and Cecilia nodded at once. Afraid she would hustle from sight and I'd get no more straight answers, I grabbed her arm. "I'm looking for a woman named Rebecca. I was told she was here. Has she been here tonight?"

"*Non*, I have not seen any such woman, but..." Cecilia's nasal voice trailed to a halt and I watched the way her eyes roved to the stairs leading to the second floor, a telltale sign if there was any. I didn't wait to hear what else she might say, clearing the saloon floor before I knew I'd moved, taking the stairs two at a time.

"Rebecca!" I hollered, pounding upon the first door I saw; there were four down a long hallway, two on either side and all closed. At the far end was a second staircase, narrow and enclosed, which allowed passage to the rear of the building. "*Rebecca!*"

The piano music from the ground floor seemed too loud, fit to bust apart my sanity. Cecilia, red-faced and short of breath, had followed me up the steps, clutching her skirts. High-pitched with fright, she called, "Isobel! It is Ceci!" She swept past me, to the second door on the left, and rattled the knob. "It is locked!"

I set her to the side and drove a shoulder into the wood. It sprang open and struck the opposite wall with a bang.

"Get in here and *shut that door!*" Virgil hissed.

He was positioned in the corner farthest from the entrance and I could do nothing but obey, Cecilia on my heels. The door closed with a click, muffling the sounds from the floor below, and the edges of the room receded like I remembered things receding in the hot, dark heart of battle, time slowing to a crawl in that lull before it charged, full-force, and propelled me to action.

"You will let her go," I ordered, low and calm, even as I envisioned placing a bullet between Virgil's eyes. But I did not dare to reach for my pistol, not yet. "You will let her go *now*."

Virgil's eyes were feral, a rat in a trap. He had the small woman named Isobel on her knees before him, her spine to his front, the side of his wrist stump shoved between her lips in place of a gag. His remaining hand held a pistol to her head and she dared not move. A man lay sprawled on the floorboards near the edge of the room and I risked a glance at him, only to see that it was Edward Tilson; the dread in my center doubled, swelling like slippery elm in a hard rain.

At my side, Cecilia seethed, "Virgil Turnbull, you beast! *You coward!*"

I risked a step forward; the floorboards creaked and I held my ground.

"Stay back," Virgil whispered. He was gaunt and clean-shaven, nearly unrecognizable. His pistol hand shook and I fought the urge to lunge at him.

"Let the woman go."

"Stay put!" Virgil redirected the barrel at Cecilia. My muscles ached with violence held in check as Virgil spat at her, "You will not leave this room, whore. I will kill the lot of you, see if I won't." He was close to losing control; I could hear it in his voice. It was a sound I knew from my soldiering days, the sound of a recruit about to start shooting to kill, no matter who was in the path of the rounds.

"Let her go. You can leave this place, I won't stop you," I said.

Isobel's wide, fearful eyes were fixed on my face; she did not attempt to speak, nor did she struggle against his hold.

"*Carter*," Virgil sneered, as though we'd only just parted ways on the trail, as though the horror of that night was only hours past. With no little curiosity, he wondered, "How'd you get out of it?"

"Cora saved us." I eased another step closer, taking a small amount of pleasure in delivering this news to him. "Cora found Quill's knife. She sawed through the bindings."

Virgil's eyes glittered as bayonet points catching the sun. I knew I must keep him level, stall him; my thoughts fled in all directions, as a herd of deer scattered by a bounding catamount, determining what choices were available, what course of action I could take. Above all else, one thought sliced repeatedly across my mind, screaming for attention – *Where was Rebecca?*

"You can ride away from this place, Virgil, I give you my word. Just let her go."

"I let her go, you kill me. I'm no fool."

"You are a fool, and a coward!" Cecilia pronounced again, just beyond my shoulder. "Isobel has done nothing to you, *you small, one-handed bastard!* You pitiful excuse for a man!"

"You will shut your *whore mouth*," Virgil ordered in no uncertain terms. His upper lip curled as he regarded Cecilia as one would an ant crawling along a window ledge, a nuisance easily crushed from existence with a single thumb.

There was a sudden shout from the floor below, the sound of alarm rather than merriment; I thought I heard Malcolm hollering for me just as Virgil wheezed an anxious breath, his attention redirected, but it was enough –

I charged, grabbing his pistol in both hands, using our momentum to take him to the floor. Isobel was thrown aside but I could pay her no mind, concentrating all effort on disabling Virgil. He fought savagely against my hold, desperation affording him strength. Our legs scrabbled, boots scraping the wooden floor planks. He bit my wrist, sinking his teeth. I yelped and slammed my forehead into his nose. His head lolled as the blow dazed him and I yanked the pistol from his grip, overcompensating and sending it skittering across the floorboards.

"You...*son of a bitch*," Virgil groaned. I pinned him at the collar and chest, one forearm over each. Blood ran down my left hand and onto his shirt.

"Where's Rebecca?" I growled, holding him flat. I failed to notice Isobel. I would have stopped her, Virgil had information I needed, but she was small and slight, rabid with intent. The pistol intruded into my line of sight a moment too late. She'd fetched it from the floor and shot him pointblank, the bullet's report crashing through the room, stripping my ears of all sound but that of ringing. I reeled away, Virgil's blood hot on my face. Cecilia sank to the floor screaming, open-mouthed.

Isobel sat back on her heels, the barrel now trained downward. She blinked rapidly, staring at Virgil's limp form as though bewildered by what she'd done. I floundered to my knees, only a pace or two away from her, but I did not fear the pistol in Isobel's hands and scrambled over the floor to Tilson's side. As I did so a man burst into the room, his mouth flapping; I heard nothing except the roaring in my head. I bent over Rebecca's uncle, rolling him to his back, seeking the pulse at the base of his throat, finding it. He'd been struck at the back of the head but he was alive.

"Tilson!" I cried, shaking his arm, heartened to hear him groan. His eyes opened a crack. "Tilson! Where's Rebecca?"

"On your feet!" A repeating rifle was trained upon me and I was forced to obey, rising, stepping away so Tilson was not in the line of fire. The man holding the repeater was dressed to ride hard, a deputy badge pinned to his leathers. Gesturing at Virgil, he demanded, "What in the goddamn hell happened here? Who killed that man?"

"I did," Isobel said.

"Drop that piece, go on now!" The deputy barked and Isobel complied, with no hesitation. Cecilia huddled near the door, clutching her head in both hands.

"Isobel," I said sharply. "Where is Rebecca? Was she here this night?"

"There's a dead woman out back of the building," the deputy said before Isobel could respond and I ran from the room, pounding down the back staircase and through a screen door, out into the night. I saw Malcolm first thing – he'd disobeyed my orders, it *had* been him calling for me from the main floor – along with Jean Luc and another deputy, both of them holding lanterns aloft. Near senseless with dread, the scene before my eyes swayed and blurred. A woman, the deputy had said, *a dead woman* –

I saw then, and clenched my teeth, sickened at the sight even as a deep and primal relief entered into me; the dead woman was not Rebecca. The tall, lean girl Grady had favored lay on the porch at Jean Luc's feet, for all the world as though she was but sleeping, pale garments stained with blood. Malcolm knelt at Mary's side while Jean Luc and the deputy argued heatedly, gesturing so that the lantern light wobbled all about. Isobel was on my heels. She screamed, "Mary!" and fell to all fours, weeping in high, heaving bursts. Malcolm looked from Mary to me and back again, his brows flattened with horror.

I crouched beside Isobel and clamped hold of her elbow, disregarding everything, even Malcolm's distress. "Where is Rebecca Krage? Tell me."

Isobel's eyes were red-rimmed and distraught, reflecting the quivering flames. She did not reply and I restrained the urge to shake answers from her.

"I beg of you, Isobel, please tell me what you know."

She blinked and at last spoke, almost too quietly for me to hear. "They are camped north of here, two miles, along the east side of the river. I do not know if your woman is with them, but it is likely. She was here earlier, to speak to Mary."

I was already on my feet.

NIGHTFALL HAD SETTLED, dark and weighty. Malcolm ran for Aces before I could stop him, cantering after me even as I heeled Admiral into a full-out gallop, following the east bank of the river, riding with my pistol at the ready. The big Henry hung in its saddle scabbard on Admiral's left flank and I handed it over to Malcolm as we rode; an understanding was likewise exchanged in the gesture. He was determined to help me and I could not lose time stopping him; I recognized that allowing him to ride with me when I intended to kill amounted to accepting him as an equal, from this night forth no longer man to boy but man to man. Riding to my right, bent low over Aces and clutching the Henry, I knew Malcolm understood this, too.

My brother. I've known few braver than you. I am goddamn proud to ride with you.

My focus narrowed as it had when fighting Yanks, as it had when I'd first been aware of Fallon the evening we crossed the border into Minnesota, when we ate at Kristian Hagebak's fire. If only I'd killed Fallon that very night, if only I'd given chase and taken him out. If only I'd done so many goddamn things. I trusted that Isobel had told me true – that Fallon was encamped somewhere ahead, with Church Talk or Hoyt Little, or both, in his company. I must figure both, which meant at least three armed men. Four, if Bill Little had joined up with the bunch. I would find them. They had killed people I cared greatly for and I would kill them, no question now. I could not allow myself to imagine beyond that.

"C'mon, boy," I urged Admiral, Gus's warhorse, leaning farther forward and tightening my knees to urge him faster; Malcolm responded and Aces kept steady pace. Together Malcolm and me, and our mounts, rode hard through a strange, dreamlike lull, a temporary peace which existed before unrestrained violence – and violence was coming, I could sense it to the pit of my soul. I kept my gaze fixed upon the darkness ahead. In my mind I saw the way Rebecca appeared when I'd looked back at her as I rode away from her homestead. I saw Malcolm's face as he bid me farewell on the Territory prairie. I saw the tears in my mama's eyes as she kissed me one last time before Beau, Grafton, and I left Tennessee to join the War. I saw my daddy playing his fiddle, sending notes out over the holler of my youth and into time eternal. I understood that what happened this night would shape the rest of my life beyond.

There would be no fire to give away their presence, I knew, and kept a sharp eye trained for the sight of horses, the pale blur of animal hide. We'd cleared roughly a mile and a half and I drew on Admiral's reins, bringing him to a trot, listening hard, hearing nothing but the river. Malcolm slowed Aces and kept near; I leaned closer and muttered, "Keep quiet, we'll go slow from here," and he nodded assent, holding the Henry by its receiver, barrel pointed heavenward.

I didn't dare risk shouting for Rebecca. The only advantage we possessed was surprise.

"Ought we to dismount an' walk?" Malcolm whispered.

"No. We might need to ride hard. When we find them don't fire unless I say. Rebecca could be there."

We crept forward, straining to peer through the darkness and hear over the river. I cursed the lack of trees, struggling hard to stay calm. Pictures of what might have occurred thundered through my skull in increasing intervals.

It occurred to me seconds too late; just as I realized someone would be keeping watch a man bellowed, "Rider!"

"Follow me, get down low!" I ordered Malcolm, cutting Admiral to the right, heeling his flanks, not giving them a chance to take aim on us; Malcolm obeyed immediately. Men shouted and I bent low over Admiral's neck, circling wide, coming about straight out from the small cluster of people assembled near the river. Two men had taken to their horses, the third running for his mount. I could not tell if Rebecca was among them and my dread increased. I was perhaps five dozen paces away, Malcolm and Aces on my left flank. And then a flurry of movement caught my eye, someone rising from the ground and running for the river. *A woman.* One of the men on horseback gave immediate chase, discharging his firearm in her direction. She fell forward and he grabbed her by the arm, yanking her onto the saddle before him.

"*Rebecca!*"

My throat bulged with roaring fury; Admiral's haunches bunched as I heeled him with all my strength, rushing them, taking aim upon the man running along the bank, discharging rounds as I rode. *Aim for his torso. No quarter.* He crumpled and fell hard, arms flailing, and I wasted no time racing after the horse over which Rebecca had been thrown, burning with a fury that turned the entire world red. I could not risk firing upon the rider, not when he had Rebecca braced over the saddle in front of him. Aces galloped at a right angle to my position, Malcolm unable to aim the Henry at a gallop but risking a charge all the same.

"Shoot him!" my brother yelped, hoarse with raw determination. "He's right there!"

I was dimly aware of the second horse fleeing due east, a slender rider leaning forward, using the horse's head for cover.

"*Malcolm!*" I roared as he and Aces flew past in pursuit of Fallon Yancy, vanishing into the night.

I had to let them go.

I spurred Admiral anew, vicious with purpose. Eyes focused on the horse galloping some fifty paces ahead. Blood churning. It was Church Talk who had Rebecca; I spied his long braid.

I'll gut him. I'll cut out his heart and crush it in my fist.

Admiral's legs churned beneath me in a full-out gallop and we gained ground. Church Talk was slowing his mount's pace.

What the hell...

The half-breed had been taking stock while I plotted his torturous death and I failed to recognize his intent. He let me close the gap between us just enough that when he let Rebecca slide from horseback to earth, I took Admiral to the ground to avoid riding over her. I sawed the reins with every ounce of strength I possessed as Admiral issued a frenzied whinny, his head yanked to a severe and unnatural angle. Instinct saved me in that moment; years of soldiering graced me with the ability to haul my leg out of the way before the gelding went down hard. I rolled left as he fell right, protecting my head. Admiral thrashed in an effort to regain his footing before my own momentum had ceased – but I couldn't spare him a second, not just now.

I scrabbled through the grass on all fours, stricken with the hot sickness of fear.

"Oh Jesus, *oh Jesus*...I'm here, Rebecca, *I'm here*..."

The world had gone numb, as if I'd been dropped into a nightmare of crawling up steep, rocky hills, unable to reach her. Rebecca lay silent, crumpled on her left side, and despair rammed its claws down my gullet as I fumbled, seeking evidence of her pulse –

I choked a gulping, almost inhuman cry; the purest relief I'd ever known as Rebecca's heartbeat fluttered against my fingertips in the soft hollow between her collarbones. "I'm here, darlin'. You're safe. I won't let you go."

Tears poured from my eyes and clogged up my throat. I eased her to her back as if handling a newborn babe, cradling her head in the crook of my left elbow as I glided my right hand along her body, everywhere at once, checking for damage. Her face was before my eyes at long last – the face which had haunted my dreams and sustained me in ways she couldn't begin to imagine. Her long dark hair fell across my arm. And then I saw blood at her waist. Dark blood in a widening circle upon the pale material of her dress.

"No, oh Jesus, *no*."

Get up. Now. Hurry.

Admiral was but paces away; I knew he required care, he was hurt from his fall, but he was on his feet and nothing mattered except getting Rebecca to town. I shut out all else, focusing my will. I carried her to him, clenching Admiral's lead rein, taking the saddle with Rebecca braced in my arms; she felt slight, unbearably fragile, but I knew her for a brave, resilient woman, the woman I would give my life for.

"I got you, darlin', stay with me, do you hear me? Stay with me, Rebecca." I tucked her as close as I could manage and heeled Admiral, cantering back the way we'd come.

Boyd. I tried to speak his name but was unable. *Boyd.*

Is it really you? Am I in a dream?

I could not focus my senses to understand what was occurring.

Green, he'd once said by the fair morning light. *Your eyes. I can't rightly decide if they're green or brown or gold, exactly. But so very green, this morning.*

You came for me. Oh, Boyd, you came for me.

Floating somewhere distant, I was visited by a series of soundless pictures, images flickering across the backs of my closed eyelids. Sunshine dusted our hair as Boyd carried me in his arms in this vision of another place, somewhere far from here, lit by the radiance of late afternoon rather than blackest night. In this golden light I retained the strength to latch my arms about his neck as he grinned at me with all of the love for which I had longed so deeply that only its utter satiation could ease the gaping wounds in my heart. His dark eyes held mine, blazing with need and desire, dimple flashing at the promise of what was to come.

Rebecca, he said, and I watched his sensual lips speak my name, the lips I wanted upon my flesh until the anguish of missing him, of believing he was dead, was banished forever. And still I would beg for need of his touch, his mouth, his hands, his tongue. The needing would never cease; not even dying could destroy it. I opened to him, the soundless pictures dancing faster still, blurring and flowing as he entered me, grasping my hips, sleek with sweat as we winged together beyond all words, warm sunlight lambent upon my naked belly – *but why is there so much blood* – and his wide shoulders, his bare back. On and on, into an eternity of living and loving, our babies at my breast and his kisses upon my skin. Boyd playing his fiddle on long summer evenings, a love of music passed from father to child just as dark eyes and a certain tilt of the head, beautiful memories of love and laughter and happiness taking root, sustaining generations long past our deaths.

I knew I was dying even as Boyd carried me through all of it, the images of the life we could have had.

I RODE as fast as I dared push Admiral over the prairie, shielding Rebecca as best I could over the uneven terrain, fearful to cause her more harm. The Jeffries' boardinghouse might as well have been on the far side of the goddamn Territory, a thousand fucking miles away. I reached the outskirts of town, keeping Admiral at a clip over the dusty streets; my shirt had grown wet with the warmth of Rebecca's spilling blood and I prayed Tilson was well enough to attend to her. In the light of the lanterns on street corners she appeared so pale my heart was slashed anew; she had not yet returned to consciousness. Terror numbed my perception; if I acknowledged its presence I would lose all control. The boardinghouse loomed in sight.

"Clear a room! Sawyer! *Tilson!*" I entered bellowing, sending Mrs. Jeffries into a new set of nervous convulsions. A small crowd had assembled in the boardinghouse, folks gathered to chaw over the evening's events. Sawyer appeared from an adjacent room, Tilson on his heels, a strip of folded linen tied about his wounded head. I could have wept with relief.

"Dear Lord, what's happened to her?" asked Mrs. Jeffries, dogging my elbow, but I paid her no heed.

"*Help her*," I begged Tilson, my voice coming loose at the seams. "Rebecca's been shot."

I WAS aware of being placed upon a bed. Pain sliced me in two at the waist. Sudden brightness gouged the seams of my eyelids; a lantern had been brought near my face. I meant to speak but a groaning sob emerged instead.

"She's hurting! Goddammit, help her! Please, help her!"

I tried to reach for the man attached to this voice, this warm, husky, drawling voice. *I wanted him, I needed him –*

His next words were much softer, delivered closer to my ear. "I'm right here, darlin', I ain't gonna leave your side. Can you hear me, Rebecca? Can you hear me?"

Light haloed his head. His hands were upon me, gentle as those cradling a fledgling bird. It was truly him; he was here, not a figment of my imagination. Joy burst through the pain as my eyelids parted and I beheld him at last.

"*Boyd...*"

His face, the selfsame face I longed for every moment of our separation, bearded and wet with tears, split with a grin as I spoke his name. The dark intensity of his eyes beat into mine. His hands formed a cradle around my head, his thumbs tracing my chin.

"I'm here, I'm right here, an' you're safe, darlin', you're safe now."

"Stay with me," I begged. I wanted to enclose him in my arms but I was no longer in control of my limbs; I could not keep my eyes open. I was so cold. My fingers jerked, curling inward.

"I will never leave you again, darlin', I swear on my life."

"She's in shock, get her out of these clothes, hurry now!" Uncle Edward, brusque and forceful, his physician's tone I'd jumped to obey a hundred thousand times. I sensed him alongside the bed and he bent close to say, "Becky, we're here, honey."

Uncle Edward barked additional orders, calling for what he needed. *My satchel! Basin! Vinegar! Stoke that fire and fetch another blanket!* Boyd gathered my hands into his and kissed the back of each, his lips warmer than life itself, his thick beard soft against my chilled skin. I knew I'd been shot and recognized that blood drained freely from the wound. The shaking in my limbs increased and hampered their efforts to free me from my garments. Boyd stretched full length on the bed, enveloping me in his blessed heat.

He spoke at my temple. "We got laudanum comin' for you, sweetheart, I'll help you take it so you won't hurt so bad. Oh, darlin', I am so sorry. I'll warm you. *You stay with me, Rebecca, stay with me.*"

I wanted nothing more than to stay with him. I wanted to tell him, I *needed* to tell him, but I could not make anything work. I hurt so much. The shaking would not cease.

"We must stop that bleeding," Uncle Edward commanded, and proceeded to press a bundled cloth to my stomach; moaning cries burst from my mouth, I could not contain them.

The bedding beneath me was soaked with blood.

I PUT from my mind all but what must be accomplished. There was no other way.

But I felt as though my skin was peeled back at the sight of the blood, at the damage a bullet had inflicted upon Rebecca. The fury that this had been done to her burned through me like acid as Sawyer and Mrs. Jeffries ran to retrieve what supplies Tilson required. Tilson and I worked feverishly, removing Rebecca's clothing so Tilson could examine the extent of the wound; that she was first bared before my eyes in this fashion tore at my heart as I lay on the bed at her side, as careful as if she was spun from glass, afraid to hurt her.

Once Rebecca was devoid of all garments I kept her as close as I dared to my warmth. I wanted to crack apart my body and take her within it so we'd never again be separated, that I'd never know another day or night without her; I spoke these words aloud to her. The need to protect was primal and overpowering. Blood leaked over her hips and down the curve of her right leg, collecting where her thigh bent against her body. Tilson hurried to bundle a cloth.

"Oh Jesus, help her, *help her.*" I could not bear Rebecca hurting this way, not when I was so goddamn helpless to stop it.

Tilson snapped, "If you can't handle this, you get yourself out of here!"

"I ain't leaving this room."

Tilson nodded curtly; his face seemed gray as his hair as he ordered, "Hold her steady, keep on talking to her like you been."

And I did, keeping my gaze trained upon her face as Tilson bent over her lower body, sheltering her as best I could. Someone had struck her mouth and she breathed shallowly between panting cries while Tilson made a dart of his fingertips and probed the flesh on her belly. I bit through the side of my tongue as I watched, terrified to hear what he would say; if he believed she would not make it, he may as well put a bullet in my heart.

"Carter, help me ease her over," Tilson instructed, gesturing, and I understood he needed to see the extent of the wound on her back; he seemed to have aged a dozen years in the past five minutes. He examined the damage while I stared at him, wild-eyed, and at last he explained, "There's one entry point, one exit. I don't feel any protrusions. The round passed clean through but she's sustained broken ribs and blood loss. I must clean and stitch that wound."

"Tell me what to do," I insisted.

I WAS aware of Boyd helping me to take the laudanum, its bitter-syrup taste coating my tongue. The room slowly retreated, replaced by an empty and peaceful prairie lit with an amber tint both strange and fetching. For a time I hovered there, listening to a great and distant commotion happening somewhere beyond the undisturbed scene before my eyes.

Later, I stood at the entrance to a covered bridge, a long, narrow bridge common to the Iowa countryside, and peered towards the opposite end; my head and shoulders were in shadow but wildflowers brushed the sides of my long skirt, a sunny afternoon blooming just outside. I stood rooted, waiting. At the far end of the tunnel a small window of white light winked into existence, steadily growing in size, until I squinted against the radiance. Bees hummed. The air was motionless – indeed, here upon the bridge my entire body was warm and still – the scene quietly benign, scented by summer blossoms, bergamot and columbine, cinquefoil and daisy.

The brightness seemed to beckon, inviting me. I lifted a hand to shade my eyes and took a single step forward.

B OYD HOLLERED AFTER me but I could not stop.
The truth was I didn't want to stop, not for nothing. The only thing I cared about in that black moment was catching Fallon. He was closer to me than he'd been since he ordered me set up on Aces to be hung. He'd got pleasure out of that. He'd played with me, for nothing but sport. Fallon wanted me to suffer, just like his daddy wanted Sawyer and Lorie to suffer. He could have shot me dead with his pistol that very rainy night back in the Territory but he'd trussed me up on Aces so my own horse would be forced to do the deed for him.

Fallon was a yellow coward, slimy and yellow as fish eggs. I'd missed shooting his daddy dead the night Zeb Crawford tried to burn Sawyer in the dooryard, but I did not mean to miss this time. The Henry was heavier than any firearm I'd ever handled but I held fast to its solid receiver, keeping Aces' reins in my left hand, bending low over his neck so my head wouldn't stall us none. Fallon was in sight and we were gaining on him, little by little; it was my good fortune Fallon rode a horse with a hide like the pale canvas of a wall tent, easier to follow by night.

"C'mon!" I urged, tightening my right knee on Aces' flank as Fallon angled that direction. I could hear his horse's hooves now, we was that close together. He dared a look back and I yelped blood and guts at him, no words, only fury. There was a terrible feeling of joy in the thought of killing him. I hated it and reveled in it, both at once.

Green as I was, I didn't expect him to risk slowing his pace to fire at us, but the bastard did. Almost too late I saw him twist and aim his sidearm. I yelped again, dodging Aces to the side, losing ground. Fallon squeezed off a shot and the screaming whine of the round passed through the air on my left. More fortune there – he fired a pistol, a far less accurate piece. My thoughts stormed like bolt lightning as he dared another shot, forcing me to slow and lose more ground.

Do I halt and take aim?
What if he gets away?
Can I ride with no hands an' fire the Henry?
It's dangerous as hell to ride this hard at night.
He'll get away!

I knew then what I must do and my thoughts settled. I positioned the rifle crosswise over my lap, gripping it with my left hand, and heeled Aces like we was running in the Fourth of July race back home in Suttonville. I was Ethan Davis in the old days, riding full-tilt, strong and cocksure, knowing there weren't a faster horse than mine. I stared ahead, eyes burning, focusing on Fallon's mount, hearing my breath beating in time with the thud of Aces' hooves, like we was one creature. Narrow, and narrower still, was the space between our galloping horses –

Aces came abreast. Fallon took his horse sharply left, away from me, unable to use his firearm. I'd counted on that, following directly after him. My jaws rumbled with our thundering passage over the nighttime prairie. I gripped the Henry by the barrel, palm wet with sweat, and jabbed the stock towards Fallon with all my strength. I was Boyd then, mighty as a team of oxen, with shoulders wide as a splitting-axe handle. I aimed for Fallon's ribs and the blow struck him, but not as forceful as I'd hoped. Fallon grabbed Aces' left rein, caught hold of the leather strap and jerked my horse's head straight at the ground. It was all I could do to stay in the saddle, paddling my hands for a solid hold as Aces wheeled in a tight circle, kicking his back legs and braying like a devil-horse. Fallon's hand was stuck in the strap and he fell, pulling me with.

The world made no sense for them split seconds. The ground rushed my face and I lost my grip on the Henry. I landed so hard I didn't know up from down as I rolled like spilled beans. A shadowy figure blotted out the stars and I came back to myself in a snap, twisting just in time to dodge the downward arch of his pistol grip, aimed for my head. Maybe it was play-fighting Sawyer and Boyd all them years that saved me then, but my body knew what to do, even if my head stayed stunned. From flat on my back I caught Fallon's swinging forearm, curling my knees to my stomach at the same instant, kicking like a donkey, targeting his gut. Startled air whooshed from his mouth. The pistol went flying and I slammed him sideways to the earth, panting now, scrabbling to keep him pinned. My ankle struck something hard – the stock of the Henry. But I couldn't release Fallon long enough to fetch up the rifle.

We grappled. I hated the feeling of his body fighting mine, writhing and grunting. Fallon bucked and broke my hold, striking me in the chin with a closed fist. I reeled, a loosened tooth rolling like a chipped marble over my tongue. I spat before I swallowed it, digging in my heels, steadying myself so I could punch with both fists, one then the other, like Boyd. The world became a narrow line; nothing existed but the need to overpower. It didn't matter that I was hurting another person. It only mattered that I hurt him more than he hurt me. Strange sounds burst from my bleeding mouth; my knuckles split meeting his flesh. I wrestled him to his back and there was his face, white as a slice of moon, an ill-wish doll come to life. Black night. Pale face with its mouth flapping open. I straddled him at midsection, my knees on his elbows, and grabbed for his neck.

There were tears on my cheeks and I hated myself for it. I cried, "You tried to *kill my brother*…"

Fallon could not answer; my thumbs cut off his air. His Adam's apple bulged under my fingers – it felt softer than jelly – and I hated that softness worse than my weakling tears. It made me sick and hollow across the guts. His legs jerked along the ground, up and down, behind me. I clenched with all my strength but the jelly-softness made me want to stop hurting him. A terrible thought bayed in my head. *You's murdering someone, Malcolm.* Fallon laughed then, I could tell it was a laugh even half-smothered as it was, and the back of my neck prickled so hard I shuddered; had he read my mind? My grip loosened.

Able to suck a sudden breath, Fallon hissed, "*Coward.*"

I smashed his nose before I knew my fist had moved and his frame went slack. I dared releasing him just long enough to close a hand around the stock of the rifle I'd dropped, then scrambled to my knees and adjusted my aim square at Fallon's middle. I ordered, "Get up!"

He coughed another laugh. "Or what?"

I stood, keeping the barrel trained on him, out of breath. "Or I kill you dead…right here."

"You won't," he whispered, rolling to an elbow. Blood leaked from his nostrils and painted stripes on the bottom half of his white face. "You already would have."

I couldn't let him bait me. Speaking through my teeth, I repeated, "Get up."

Aces had circled back and pawed the ground not ten paces away, reins dangling; Fallon's horse had disappeared. I tried to think fast enough to form a plan. My hair hung in my eyes, sweat greased my skin. I knew I should fire the rifle. The round would split apart his ribcage. Maybe he was right, maybe I was a yellow coward, because the thought sickened me. The trigger was smooth and tempting beneath my finger but I found I could not squeeze it. I could not shoot someone with no defenses, not even Fallon Yancy.

He eased to hands and knees, staring right at me as he said, "Bill Little likely killed everyone in your camp by now. Bill's crazy, and your brother shot Bill's brother, just back there at the river." Fallon's teeth appeared as he smiled and I felt revulsion like I'd never known; my throat clogged up. Hunched there on the ground, he bragged, "He'll have killed your uncle, and your cousins, and that little freak with the different-colored eyes."

His words shook me, as he'd intended, and he lunged, grabbing for the rifle. The barrel swung in a wide arc and the shot I fired too late went stray, booming out into the emptiness behind Fallon, sending me quickstepping backwards. The rifle was caught lengthwise between us next I knew, barrel listing cockeyed at the night sky, both of us with two-handed grips on it. His face was so close I could smell the blood on it; I could smell his breath as we struggled. He tried to slam his forehead to mine but I dodged the blow. My palms slipped along the metal barrel. Our strength was an even match.

And then I saw how Fallon's feet was planted wide, one leg angled forward, and seized this advantage, planting the sole of my boot as hard as I could into his forward knee. It snapped the wrong way and he dropped fast, with a wheezing cry. I gained control of the Henry and this time drove the end of the wooden stock straight between his eyes, grasping the rifle like it was a butter churn. I heard a crunching sound and heaved onto the grass in an explosion I could not control. My vomit struck his lolling head.

I was sure Fallon was dead. He lay still as death, white face blackened with patches of blood, a piecework quilt of doom. Only later did I realize I should have shot him, I should have made certain. But all I could think of was getting to my family. I must get to them. I could not let myself believe it was too late. I wiped my mouth, scrabbled through the grass to find Fallon's dropped pistol, tucking it into my trousers as I ran for Aces; in my blind fear it took seconds to gain my bearings.

I thought, *River. Follow the river to town.* And we did, racing back over the miles I'd chased Fallon, gripping the Henry. My first thought should have been to find the deputy who'd been at The Dolly Belle, who'd been in a consternation over the dead woman, the poor girl I remembered from last autumn. Mary had been her name, and she'd been sweet on Grady. But I headed straight for our camp. All I could think of was Fallon saying, *That little freak with the different-colored eyes.*

Cora, I prayed as I rode, skirting the town. *I'm coming.*

Aces galloped past folks settled in for the night, startling those seated around their fires; several men hollered after me but I paid no mind. From a distance, riding hard, I saw my uncle and Cora, both of them like figures drawn in black ink against the fire's glow, and relief wilted over my entire body; I near fell from the saddle. Uncle Jacob was standing, talking with a man in leathers, but spied me and shouted, "Malcolm Alastair! Thank God!"

In short order I had my arms around Cora, felt her heart beating against mine. I pressed my face to her loose hair and she clung to my waist fit to slice her arms through it. She looked up and I saw the firelight reflected in the center of her eyes as she cried, "You're hurt!"

Uncle Jacob and the man – another lawman, I saw – surrounded me and I told them fast what Fallon had said about the man called Bill Little.

"Bill Little?" the sheriff repeated, and his voice said he didn't believe me. "I know him. He ain't in town. It's rare he's seen outside the Territory this time of year. He ain't responsible for the killings tonight. It was a half-breed that done it, according to Isobel Faucon." He sharpened his gaze. "How'd you come to be so roughed up, young feller? Did you see who shot at the woman?"

I thought he meant Mary and shook my head. I hadn't said a word about the bodies out there by the river and I didn't mean to, not before I talked to my brother.

I begged my uncle, "Have you seen Boyd?"

Uncle Jacob cupped the back of my head with his big palm, squeezing me close. He spoke low and grim. "Young Malcolm, Boyd is yonder at the boardinghouse with Becky. She's been shot, as Sheriff Tate here has informed us."

"No. Oh, *no.*" My heart clenched up like a bug beneath a needle point. My mind flapped back, trying to remember the events before Aces and me gave Fallon chase. I could not piece the bits back together, could not remember Rebecca being there in that river camp. I prayed, *Not now, not when Boyd's been waiting to find her for so long. Please don't let her die. Please, God, don't let Rebecca die. Boyd ain't gonna be able to bear it.*

"She's alive, Tilson's working over her as we speak. The boys are in the wagon, we didn't tell them yet," Uncle Jacob explained, keeping his voice quiet. He bent and pressed a kiss to the top of my head. "You need care, boy." He spoke next to the sheriff. "I'll bring my nephew to town once I've a chance to clean up his bruises."

The sheriff gave a nod and tipped his hat. I watched him walk with Uncle Jacob to the horses. I knew I had to tell the sheriff what I'd done to Fallon. I must tell him, I couldn't wait to talk to Boyd. I was coward enough to wonder, *Will I go to jail?*

Tears made wet sheets on Cora's face, falling faster. She put her hands to my jaws, soft as bird wings, and I shivered at her touch, it felt so good. She whispered, "Malcolm, you're bleeding."

"I'm all right. C'mere," I muttered, and gathered her close. I did not know Bill Little or where he might be just now; he hadn't threatened Uncle Jacob's camp this evening but I believed he was still about. I did not believe Fallon had been lying about Bill watching my family, even if he hadn't made a move on them. Fallon's body was out there by the river. I'd killed him. I'd killed someone, had smashed his knee with my boot and his face with a rifle stock, and I clung to Cora all the tighter, my guts aching. The sheriff hadn't yet mounted his horse, still talking quiet-like with Uncle Jacob.

Tell him, I thought.

"What happened?" Cora whispered. Her face was so worried for me and I studied it as if I'd never seen it before. Her cheeks made soft curves like the sides of a heart whose point was her chin. There was a little white line of a scar near her mouth, just at her top lip, where she'd once fallen against the edge of a woodstove. Her hair was messy with snarls, made red by the firelight. And in her eyes was so much love I felt swept clean by it, like a good dunking in Reverend Wheeler's baptism creek, down the hill from the church back home. I knew her face. I knew her eyes, and I had always known them, even before I met her. I didn't know how that could be rightly so, I just knew it *was*.

"I love you." I had never spoken it aloud before. My heart swelled something powerful. "I love you *so*."

Cora's lips trembled. My words stole all her words, I could tell, and so I said, "I know you love me too, you don't have to say a thing."

Tears shone fresh in her eyes as she nodded. She said *yes*, but with no sound.

And I knew I could not be a coward, not ever again. Tonight I had ridden with Boyd as a man. A man did not shirk his duties, did not shy away from his responsibilities. I took Cora's hands into mine and kissed the back of each, never taking my eyes from hers. Only then did I find the strength to draw a full breath and call over to the sheriff.

"Sir, don't go yet. I got more to tell you."

T HE LAUDANUM SERVED its purpose, stilling the trembling in Rebecca's limbs; her breathing evened but I agonized in the space between each new inhalation, strung with tension as I waited to hear the next. Tilson was solid as a stone fortress and I loved him fiercely for it, recognizing the depth of his strength as he worked over his niece, a woman he loved dearly; a woman who was almost the last of his kin. His lips made a grim line, his brow furrowed deep as plow ruts in turned earth, but he was resolute.

Tilson kept a quiet commentary as he worked; Sawyer assisted him while I kept Rebecca warm with the heat of my body alongside hers. Tilson, stern as a regimental taskmaster, ordered that I was not to watch his and Sawyer's ministrations, and so I did not. I murmured to Rebecca, cradling her as best I could, and did not let my gaze venture below her waist. The cleansing scent of vinegar finally overpowered that of blood. Their hushed words met my ears from a distance.

The round missed her spine and stomach both, thank God, but we must staunch that blood.

Tell me what to do.

Bring that lantern closer, Sawyer, hurry now. Be ready with the witch hazel.

Got it right here. What else?

Run that needle through the flame, back and forth. Just like that. Now handle only the end! Don't touch the point!

Rebecca's collarbones appeared delicate as slender willow stalks; the hollow at the base of her throat was beaded with sweat and beat with each pulse of her heart. Her head rested against the pillow, tipped to the left and therefore towards me, the lantern light glinting along the hollow of her cheek. I

studied her without letup, glutting myself on the sight. Her skin was fine as a
rose leaf, made all the more pale with blood loss. Her lips retained the bluish
tint of a chilled body and I tucked her closer, close as I dared.

Her eyes sometimes moved beneath their closed lids, back and forth – was
she dreaming? Did she continue to know I was here with her? I prayed so,
and prayed she would remain blessedly unconscious while Tilson cleaned
both entry and exit wounds and then stitched her torn flesh. She'd bled so
much upon the bed that fear rendered me dizzy. I refused to think of holding
Grafton's hand while the surgeon worked over him in a sweltering field tent
in Georgia.

*I will not think of that. I will not remember the smell of blood or the rasping
sound of the bone saw, or the way his arm jerked with each pass of the blade...*

Rebecca's hands lay palm-up upon the bedding, the underside of her arms
pale as swansdown in the lantern light, blue veins like small rivers along her
wrists. I rubbed a thumb over her fine skin, following those rivers. I traced the
curve of her jaw; my skin was rough as a bison's hide, far too rough to deserve
the feeling of such softness. I felt that my heart lay there on the bed along
with her, vulnerable as a soap bubble, able to be destroyed by a single touch.

Do not let her die, oh Jesus, please. Do not let her die. Again and again I prayed
these words, in a litany of desperation.

I sensed Sawyer's concern though he spoke not a word to me as he followed Tilson's blunt instructions. And I understood fully, and for the first
time, what my oldest friend had been through when Lorie was in harm's
way. I understood why he had ridden after her against all odds, had risked
everything and faced death on more than one occasion to ensure Lorie's
survival. That without her, his life was nothing more than a bitter day-to-day
existence, a dry husk of what it could have been. I could have tortured myself
nigh unto death with recriminations – why had I ridden away from Rebecca's
dooryard? Why had I been so goddamn stubborn, so blind? But I kept those
thoughts at bay by murmuring to her, brushing aside strands of her damp
dark hair to speak into her ear.

"I'm here with you. I will not leave your side. I love you to your very soul,
Rebecca, I have been in love with you from the moment I first saw you there
in your uncle's office in Iowa City, when you nudged me with your elbow."

When Tilson said gruffly, "Boyd, hold her steady now. I'm about to stitch,
she'll feel it even through the drug," I nodded immediate acceptance and

curled my right arm in a protective half-circle over Rebecca's shoulders, keeping all my weight braced on my own hand; if she struggled, I would apply only what pressure was required to keep her still. I made the mistake of looking at their work and my stomach fell to the floor. Tilson's hands were stained red, the stitching needle poised to do its work; Rebecca's legs were splayed apart. Sawyer held a cloth, this also soaked in Rebecca's blood; beyond them, the basin water was tinted crimson. I gulped and Sawyer said sharply, "*Boyd.*" There was no mistaking his tone and I ground my teeth, nodding again.

I rested my lips upon Rebecca's hair, inhaling of her as I whispered, "You are my life, darlin', *you*. I ain't got no life without you. I won't leave your side again, I swear to you. Hear me, *please hear me.*"

"Steady now," Tilson said.

He bent to begin his work, I saw from the corner of my gaze, Sawyer clasping hold of Rebecca's knees so that her inadvertent movements wouldn't inhibit Tilson's stitching. I felt flayed alive. Tilson plied the needle and Sawyer held firm. Rebecca jerked and moaned, eyes opening a slit, dulled by the drug. Her shoulders twitched, her head rolled side to side. She cried out and sweat ran down my face as she struggled. Blood loss rendered her weak, but she fought against our hold.

"She's bleedin' afresh," Tilson said, terse with tension. "Quick now, staunch that flow!"

Oh Jesus, Jesus…

My trousers were soaked in her blood.

SHADOWS ENVELOPED my skirts as I stepped fully onto the boards of the bridge. The scent of summer wildflowers remained strong, the hum of bees pleasant in the background. The brightness at the end of the tunnel glinted with the allure of unexpected colors, gleaming blues and bewitching greens, as facets of a prism twisting in the sunlight. It was very beautiful, captivating my attention. Time passed; how much I was not certain, too occupied with marveling that such light could exist in an otherwise unremarkable bridge.

After a time I stepped closer and then closer still, now encased in cool dimness. Only a few paces more and I would be near enough to reach my hands into its brilliance. Quietude reigned here beneath the covered tunnel.

Surely my ears had misled me; I thought, for the faintest of seconds, that I'd heard Elijah's voice out there, somewhere beyond that light. I blinked, faltering. My mouth went so dry I could not manage to swallow.

I thought, *How can that be? Elijah is…why, he's…*

Pain seeped into this peaceful scene where I stood rooted, cutting across my waist, and I was elementally frightened. More than I'd ever known anything, I knew I did not want to cross to the far side of that covered bridge. A name rose from my heart and I summoned it forth, clinging to the promise of it with all my strength.

Boyd, I whispered. And again, praying he would hear. *Boyd.*

His response, his presence, was heated and immediate, and the covered bridge and its otherworldly light rippled as the surface of a creek when disturbed by a thrown stone. Relief expanded throughout my body.

"I'm here, I'm right here," he said, and he was indeed next to me, so close I could feel his solid length, strong as an oak.

I could not open my eyes, nor could I summon my arms to move. My chin tilted towards the heat of him. *Don't let me go.*

Boyd cupped the side of my neck, restraining his passionate touch to its gentlest measures, and the image of the bridge shattered and then disappeared. He rested his lips to my temple. "I will never let you go again. This I swear to you. You stay here with me, darlin', I'll hold you through this. I'll hold you, you hear?"

I hear. I hear you, Boyd Carter.

T HE NIGHT HAD grown deep and quiet. I lingered in a rocking chair positioned near the bed, Rose in my arms; I had sat at a bedside thus vigilantly before, and in the same company. The thought of sleep was repulsive. I kept the chair in a gentle, creaking rhythm, my anxious gaze flitting between Rebecca and Boyd, who sat in the dimness with his head bowed over his forearms at Rebecca's hip, his protective hands interlocked about one of hers. I had not been allowed to witness the stitching of the bullet wound, the exit point of which had torn apart the flesh near the lowest rib on the right side of her abdomen, leaving a ragged tunnel in her body, though I had heard the process through the thin walls of the Jeffries' boardinghouse, crawling from my skin in agony at the sounds of her cries.

Sawyer had assisted Tilson – dear Tilson, who'd first proceeded to bandage his own injured head with a hastily-tied length of linen. "No time, I'll tell the story later," was all he would say on the matter, worrying not a whit over the state of his injury. Fiendish with purpose, Tilson had cleansed the bullet wound with a tincture of vinegar, crushed garlic, and witch hazel, and had then sewn closed both entry and exit points with the precise stitches at which he'd long since grown expert. Despite his outward unflappability, however, I knew Tilson well enough to see the strain that performing surgery upon his niece had taken on him, the tremble in his sturdy frame when he came to check on Rose and me, afterward.

I had but one question, a husk in my throat as I whispered, "Will she…"

Tilson studied my face and I knew he would not lie to me. His voice, already made hoarse by an injury sustained in the War, was scarcely audible. "I pray so."

Sawyer, himself drawn and pale, a toll exacted upon each of us this long night, sat without words upon the bed and collected both Rose and me close, holding fast, resting his face upon my hair, bending farther to kiss our daughter's rounded cheek as Tilson offered a rudimentary explanation of how he and Sawyer had treated Rebecca's wounds; as his student, he knew I would wish to know.

"Aw, Lorie," Sawyer whispered, and I heard the ancient ache in his voice, that of his desire to protect those he loved and his subsequent understanding that harm came creeping no matter what safeguards he placed between it and us, with no regard for the resultant damage. I thought, sending the words straight to his mind, *I am here. I love you, and I am here.*

"Boyd is with her," Tilson said, sinking to the foot of the bed, wrapping his grip about one of the posts. His shoulders sagged but his voice held a note of tenderness, and acceptance, as he added gruffly, "He won't leave her side."

"Is he all right? Where's Malcolm?" I persisted, aggravated at my lack of knowledge. I'd not seen him since he had, after a hasty explanation, chased after Boyd; I could only imagine the torture Boyd had endured this night.

"Malcolm is at our camp," Tilson assured. "And Sheriff Tate is downstairs, he's come direct from speaking with Jacob." Tilson shifted, passing a hand over his craggy face. The bandage he'd tied about his head was askew, exhaustion weighting his frame as he said to Sawyer, "Son, we best meet with him. Tate's got a few questions and I figure Boyd ain't up to it, not just now."

I clutched at Sawyer's elbow. "Let me go to her."

He tucked a loose strand of hair behind my ear. "Lorie-love, I would that you rest."

"Sawyer," I implored. "Please, I cannot sleep. I will only lie here awake and wondering." He knew me well, realizing I would persist until he relented, and gathered my shawl and tucked it about me with the sweet and husbandly gestures so natural to him. And so I came to sit in a rocking chair at Rebecca's bedside, Rose a soft, weighted bundle in my arms.

Rebecca lay now in drug-induced slumber, paler still than the sheet drawn modestly to her shoulders. Her slender arms were bare, the delicate contours of her bones appearing almost unbearably fragile beneath her skin, bandages swathing her torso; Tilson ascertained that at least two of her ribs sustained fractures, and I had assisted him long enough to realize, without being told, there was very little to be done in the way of setting broken ribs. Even bound tightly, one could do scant more than allow them to heal, and endure the subsequent weeks of painful waiting.

Rebecca's blood loss was significant, evidenced by the bruise-colored shadows beneath her eyes, her ashen appearance. Doses of laudanum had not proved enough to completely dull her pain and I found room to be thankful that Cort and Nathaniel, kept at camp with Jacob, had been unable to hear their mother's distress. Too much had occurred this day and I struggled to make sense of it, finding meager comfort in the repetitive, mind-numbing rhythm of the rocker, the gentle heft of my sleeping daughter in my arms. Rose stirred and I murmured to her, and Boyd's wide shoulders shifted as he straightened incrementally, refusing to release his hold on Rebecca.

"Boyd," I whispered. I wanted so badly to tell him Rebecca would be all right, that she would wake with morning's light and restore to him his reason for living, but I remained hesitant to speak in absolutes. Tilson's prognosis was cautious, at best, which Boyd well knew. Tilson explained Rebecca's stomach had not been compromised, a fact which offered a measure of relief; had the stomach lining been punctured by a bullet's flight, not even Tilson could have saved her from a septic death. He'd done his damnedest and Rebecca was now, as Mrs. Jeffries had said, in the care of the angels.

Boyd acknowledged my speaking of his name with a slight movement of his head. I'd never heard him in such a state as that which he'd been upon carrying Rebecca into the boardinghouse earlier this evening, and prayed I'd never witness him in such torment again. I'd gleaned only incremental information since; Tilson and Sawyer continued to speak with the sheriff, downstairs in the Jeffries' lobby. I knew poor Mary had been killed, and a man named Royal Lawson, who had ridden in from the Territories along with Boyd; Virgil Turnbull was also dead this night. Boyd, assured that Malcolm was safe at camp with Jacob, refused to otherwise acknowledge the sheriff's presence.

"This is my fault," Boyd said, so quietly the words were almost lost in the thick air of the little room. His back was to me, shoulders hunched. His hair and beard were at riotous lengths but his deep voice retained its familiar Tennessee drawl. I recalled the gaping, jagged-edged rending in my heart when it had been Sawyer unconscious upon a bed; seeing Rebecca in a similar state was nearly as agonizing. I knew Boyd well enough to realize that any word I spoke to the contrary would provoke his adamant ire. And so I waited.

"I rode away from her," he whispered, rife with the desire to punish himself. "I left her behind. I should have listened to you, Lorie-girl, and to Sawyer, oh dear God, I should not have left. It's the worst mistake I've ever made."

I risked saying, "You are here now."

He looked over his shoulder and his eyes were raw and red, his voice cleaving around a dense husk. "Fallon was after the boy an' me, from the beginning."

"You are not to blame." Tears stung the bridge of my nose and flowed over my cheeks; so recently he and Malcolm had yet been missing and I'd believed I would never see them again. "You are *not to blame*. Rebecca understood why you must go, last summer. She blamed herself for not confessing the truth of her feelings for you before you left." My voice gained in intensity and I leaned forward. "She is the dearest friend I have ever known and I mean to have her for a true sister, which she will be as soon as the two of you are wed. Do you hear me? I mean to see our children raised up together, Boyd Brandon Carter, as you yourself spoke of the night Sawyer and I wed, when the four of us saw the shooting star. Y'all will recall." Swiping at my tears, I badgered, "Do you recall?"

"I recall," Boyd whispered at last.

"Good." I drew a deep breath. My lips trembled as I whispered, "We thought we'd never see you again." Rose twitched, issuing a chuffing squawk; Boyd's gaze dropped to her and a ghost of a smile touched his mouth. His upper lip was all but obscured by the tangle of a full black beard. I thought of the myriad and often ribald stories I'd heard of his father, Bainbridge Carter, and understood I was looking upon that very man's face, here in his son. A man whose love for his family overrode all else.

"Might I…" Boyd nodded at Rose, his voice hardly more than a breath, and I nodded, smiling through my tears. He stood, slowly as an old man, first bending over the bed to kiss Rebecca's lips with utmost care, caressing hair from her brow, trailing tender kisses along her neck, her shoulder, her bare arm. Rather than a flush of embarrassment that I was witness to such intimate ministrations, I instead felt blessed, buoyed with simple gladness; how I wished Rebecca was awake. Boyd ended with his face at her upturned palm, which he cradled to his cheek. Addressing her, he whispered, "I aim to give you a daughter first thing, darlin'."

"*Many* daughters," I amended for him as he lifted Rose from my arms and reclaimed the low footstool beside the bed, holding her to his powerful chest.

"She's a right beautiful little thing, Lorie-girl," he murmured, cradling Rose in the crook of his elbow. "I can't rightly recall the last time I held a little one. Fact is I don't know that I ever held one this small. She ain't but a sprite." He looked up and met my solemn gaze. His shoulders lifted with a half-sighing shudder as he whispered, "By God, it's good to be back. You can't know how much we've missed you-all."

I wanted to demand answers, to understand what they'd seen and where they'd been, for Boyd to elaborate, with far greater depth, Malcolm's hastily-told tale, which had most tenderly focused its primary attention upon a little girl named Cora Lawson. Further, I wanted to lay eyes again upon Malcolm; I'd not come close to satisfying my need to hug my sweet boy. On the heels of the thought bounded another – *he is hardly a boy any longer.* As much as I might rebel against the idea, I must acknowledge this truth. Before I could speak there was a soft rap on the door and Sawyer entered, followed by Tilson. Sawyer crouched beside my chair and Tilson went at once to the bed, leaning over Rebecca; I studied his back with a wary eye, on guard for any hint of concern in the set of his shoulders. Boyd was also rendered motionless, watching as Tilson rested the back of his left hand to Rebecca's brow.

"No fever, she's breathing well," Tilson murmured. He turned to us and his stern gaze fell upon me. "I would that you rest a spell, honey."

I shook my head, unable to relent to this request. Exhaustion dragged at me but I could not sleep, not yet. Sawyer stroked his thumb up and down along the nape of my neck, wordlessly telling me he agreed with Tilson, but he understood why I would remain here rather than retreat to bed.

"Is he gone?" I asked, referring to the sheriff.

"He is," Sawyer affirmed, and then addressed Boyd, saying in a hushed tone of concern, "Tate said they recovered one body near the river. No mounts."

Boyd's dark eyebrows knit, his spine straightened. He cast his gaze about the room as though to search for unseen intruders. I rose from the rocking chair, not without difficulty, and fetched Rose from his grasp, lest he forget he held a newborn. "Do they know who he is?"

"Hoyt Little, the sheriff said," Tilson explained, as Sawyer helped me to sit, adjusting my shawl. Beneath a linen dressing gown my nether regions were bound with cloths similar to those I used during my monthly bleeding, my entire lower body beset by a dull, lingering ache, however unwilling I was to acknowledge my discomfort in the face of Rebecca's.

Boyd plunged both hands through his overgrown hair – under happier circumstances, I would have poked good-natured fun at him, my surrogate brother, for this copious mop of curls as luxurious as any locks I'd ever beheld – and further stood its length on end. He all but growled, "What about Fallon? Malcolm said he was dead."

Tilson said, "Jacob's bringing the young'uns to town just now, Tate told us, as he figured it's better to be safe than sorry. Tate and his deputy are both on the alert, I reckon, after three killings in their town, four if you count the fella by the river."

Sawyer was watching Boyd; speaking low, Sawyer said, "I'll sit watch with you."

Boyd's agitated movements stilled as he gained a measure of calm from Sawyer's words. He nodded, looking at Sawyer with gratitude carved upon his strong features. "I don't believe them bastards'll chance a rush this night, even if they did survive to regroup, but I feel better knowing you's here, old friend, I can't tell you."

"What else?" I asked of Sawyer, studying the planes his angular cheekbones created upon his familiar face, sensing there was far more; his eye held mine for a heartbeat as he acknowledged this.

Sawyer continued, "The woman named Isobel told Sheriff Tate what she knew. Last August Virgil Turnbull strangled a woman named Emilia, who was employed at The Dolly Belle. Isobel knew he'd done it and kept his secret, for a price."

Tilson picked up the gruesome account. "The proprietor, Jean Luc Beaupré, was also privy to this sorry secret but rather than cause a scandal the likes of which could run him out of business for good, he ordered Virgil to get rid of the poor girl's body and then put out word that Emilia had run off for greener pastures."

Boyd drew an elongated breath through his nose, staring into the middle distance, dark gaze directed at the floorboards; at last he muttered, "It makes sense. Virgil fancied a girl who didn't fancy him, this Emilia. And I recall Grady once saying that Isobel was sweet on Virgil but he didn't return the affection. I s'pose a secret like that, a murdering, gave her something to hold over him." His gaze sharpened. "What of Dyer Lawson?"

"Cora's father?" I clarified. I'd not yet met Cora for all that Malcolm had

spoken of her earlier this evening. The poor girl had lost her father, and now
her uncle this very night; Malcolm had been in dread to tell her.

"Dyer must have known what Virgil did, that he murdered a woman,"
Boyd mused. "It would explain so goddamn much. Cora knew Virgil for a
killer long before I ever suspected." He blinked, abruptly returned from his
speculation. "Does Cora know her uncle is gone? Christ, I've not seen her
since we left her with Jacob what seems like a hundred years past."

As though summoned by this mentioning, footsteps sounded on the stairs;
from down the hall a hushed voice queried, "Boyd? Lorie? You-all in there?"

Tears sprang to my eyes; Tilson swung open the door to reveal Malcolm,
his expression graced by a solemn formality I was unaccustomed to seeing.
His lips parted as though to speak, his gaze fastening upon Rebecca, then
jerking to Boyd. He whispered, "Is she…"

"She is doing as well as can be expected," Tilson was quick to say.

Malcolm entered the room, dropping to his knees at his brother's side,
and Boyd engulfed him in a hug, pressing his face to Malcolm's shaggy hair.
I thought of my first days in their company, of gaining a tentative confidence,
enough to suggest that Malcolm required a haircut which I would be happy
to provide. I thought of his dusty toes, a result of a daily reluctance to wear
his boots, his keen interest in every matter large or small; his sweet, boyish
wonderment I could not bear to imagine the past year dashing to nonexis-
tence. I thought of the exultation of Boyd playing his fiddle along the trail
back in Missouri, of him making a kind gift of a soapstone bear to ward off
the nightmares that plagued me in those early days. Of what the Carters
had done to help me when Sawyer was endangered, jailed in Iowa City and
threatened with a hanging.

Further, I considered what my existence would be today if these men –
Sawyer, Boyd and Malcolm, Tilson, and dear Angus Warfield, who'd died so
that I might live – had not entered into it; I who had not so very long ago
come to believe all men were brutal and loathsome creatures bent on one
desire alone. I was so overwhelmed by the strength of these thoughts my
vision wavered.

"C'mere," Boyd gruffly requested, stretching an arm towards us, tears
staining his dirty face. Though I did not believe he could read my mind, it
was nonetheless exactly what I'd been about to request of them.

Sawyer helped me to rise; Boyd and Malcolm stood so that we might all six, Tilson and tiny Rose included, braid together in a hug. Malcolm's breath touched my neck as he rested his head to my shoulder. I sagged against Tilson's side, his muslin shirt scratching over my cheek, his big, gnarled palm smoothing my hair in a repetitive and bolstering motion; I felt as cherished as a beloved daughter. Rose kicked and fussed; Sawyer cupped her head, all of us simultaneously giving and seeking reassurance in the lantern-lit space, deep with night and quietude.

And I reflected for the countless time that the truest of loves requires not a single word to convey meaning, not one single word.

I WOKE from a dream of a feather brushing my ear. The light of a silvering dawn poked into my eyes, my mind muddy with lingering fear and tired confusion. It took me seconds to realize Rebecca's fingertips were the feather and that she was caressing my hair, her face tipped towards me on the pillow. Tears burst from my chest and into my eyes like a dam cracked by a spring flood – I sprang straight, staring at the wondrous sight of her open eyes. The bruise alongside her lips had purpled to the color of a plum and renewed my need to kill the man who'd left it there.

"Rebecca," I breathed, choked and rough-voiced, dirty and blood-stained and bedraggled as I was, hardly fit to be in her presence. I took her hand between mine, bringing it to my cheek, absorbing this gift of her, thankful beyond all earthly measure. "Thank God, oh thank God, sweetheart. I was so scared. Are you hurting? Let me get you water…" Tripping over myself, I scrambled to the porcelain pitcher Sawyer had filled with water and fetched up the matching cup.

Her face was wan and impossibly delicate; violet shadows encircled her exhausted eyes but she managed a smile. Her pale lips parted to whisper, "Boyd."

"I'm here, darlin'," I said, shaking with relief, quelling this trembling with all my might. I cupped her head as gently as I'd cupped little Rose's last night and helped her to take water, of which she managed half the cup. I set it aside and took her left hand back into mine, lifting her fingertips to my mouth and kissing them one by one, tears falling to the bedding over which I leaned. I pressed my lips to her knuckles, her palm, the inner curve of her wrist. She twined her fingers around my hand. I shivered at the depth of relief offered by her touch.

"Oh holy Jesus, Rebecca, *I have missed you,*" I whispered, studying her eyes with their wealth of color, green and gold and the brown of sunlit earth, open at last and shining with love for me. *Me,* Boyd Carter. Joy struck from all sides.

She swallowed with difficulty, and whispered, "I have been in agony, missing you."

"All I want is you. Tell me you know this, darlin', tell me you know."

Her tears welled. "I know. I truly do, Boyd. I fell in love with you the very night we met. I was so afraid you would never know."

I leaned farther over the bed, taking care not to put any weight upon her, and kissed her flush upon the lips, tender and worshipful, wanting to claim her sweet mouth and drink of her until the day I died, content in this moment to simply be near, to hear her voice. Afraid she was hurting I drew a breath away and cupped her face, avoiding the bruised spot.

She took my wrists in her hands, her grip weak but determined. "Where are the boys? Is Lorie delivered? What has happened?"

"The boys are downstairs with Tilson an' Jacob just now, don't you worry. Tilson brought them up here last night to kiss you, while you was sleeping." My eyes stung at the memory of Nathaniel and Cort bending over the bed to rest their faces to their mama's cheek. "Lorie an' Sawyer have a beautiful baby girl this morning. They named her Lorissa Rose."

Rebecca's shoulders drooped with relief. She breathed, "Oh, thank the Lord. The boys must have been so frightened. Were they..."

"No," I assured, looking deep into her eyes. "Jacob kept them away so's they didn't hear a thing."

"But you..."

Again I knew what she meant even though she did not finish. "I was. I didn't leave your side."

She studied my eyes with such intensity I longed to beg her to tell me what she was thinking. Allowed the blessing of looking so closely upon her in the morning light, I soaked up tiny details: the sweep of her dark lashes, the gold and brown flecks upon the deep moss-green of her eyes, the faint, nutmeg-colored freckles that decorated her pale skin. Before I knew I'd moved, I brushed my lips over these, following their path along her cheeks. A sweet, soft sound issued from her throat as I tenderly kissed her jaw, her chin, the side of her neck, tasting the warm, salty sweat of her skin, before my senses were restored like a blow to the head – she was wounded and hurting, had only just awakened – but she tightened her hold on me, flushing crimson as she whispered, "How I have longed for you."

A richness of contentment swelled from my heart, my nose resting against her warm temple. "Sweet woman. How I love to hear you say so." I shifted so I could see her eyes, and my smile faded as I whispered, "Forgive me for leaving, Rebecca. I should never have ridden away. I will never ride away from you again, if you've a mind to allow that."

She smiled then, slowly, and there was a glint in her eyes I remembered well; digging her fingers into my hair with a distinct air of possessiveness, she murmured, "It is so very curly."

"I must look a sight. Forgive my ragged appearance, darlin'."

She caressed the sides of my face, sending spasms of shivers along my flesh, continuing her course over the unkempt hair growing from temples to jawline, coming to rest along the edges of my thick beard, the likes of which belonged on a billy goat. She whispered, "How I love to hear you call me 'darling.'"

I grinned anew, one happiness atop the next. I gathered her hands in mine and whispered, "If I am the luckiest man alive, you will let me call you my wife." As though she hadn't understood, I hurried to say, "What I mean is, will you do me the honor, sweet Rebecca?"

Rebecca grasped my ears as though to make certain she had my full attention – and she did – before saying in the proper way of speaking I so cherished, "Boyd Brandon Carter, I thought you would never ask."

W E WERE QUITE a sight in the sunset glow, July the first in the year of 1869.

The month of June had unfolded as sweltering and humid as any Tennessee summer I recalled, and July promised more of the same, but I didn't mind. Truly, I felt as though I'd never mind a thing again; a foolish presumption, I knew, but I let my happiness soak into my soul and tried not to fear its presence, but instead to welcome and acknowledge it as our collective due – mine and Rebecca's, Malcolm's, Sawyer's and Lorie's. All eleven of us, from Jacob to tiny Rose, had ventured north over the course of the past five days, leaving behind St. Paul during the last week of June, once Tilson deemed Rebecca fit for travel. We traveled in a caravan of wagons and livestock, creaking over a trail created by years of hooves and wheels carving through the sweet-scented prairie grass.

The prairie itself was flush with blooms whose wavering stalks surpassed Cora, Cort, and Nathaniel in height. In the dusty-gold sunglow of late afternoon, the three of them liked to chase striped pocket gophers and the plump, flitting birds that trilled until the entire landscape rang with their songs. Tilson told them he'd pay out a silver dollar if they managed to catch one for our supper. Cora had taken at once to Tilson, curling up on his lap at the nightly fire. Malcolm, always close by, would hold her hand as she rested, braiding together their fingers in a way that made me glad I'd not been forced to endure their separation.

Just now, a half-hour from dusk on this first evening of July, I stretched the twinge in my back, twisting at the waist as Sawyer and I watered Whistler, Admiral, and Trapper; fifty paces up the bank, Jacob was teaching the boys a song about a wolf named Bardolf.

I leaned my forearms over Trapper's gray hide as the mule sloshed his nose in the river, drinking his fill, hunching my shoulders and rolling my head side to side. Sitting atop a hard-edged wagon seat for hours on end had never been my favorite of tasks, but on this journey it was pure heaven, with Rebecca at my side. Merely the thought of her, just up there in our camp, and the promise of coming nightfall, when I would kiss every blessed inch of her skin, measuring my way with stroking touches, made me weak in the knees. I grinned, my gaze straying towards the top curve of the wagon I shared with my wife, just visible from where we stood, and Sawyer kicked at my ankle, a knowing grin stretching across his face.

"It's a grand sunset, ain't it?" he asked, teasing me with his tone.

"It is, indeed," I murmured, rubbing a thumb along my chin – which, despite a thorough shaving back in St. Paul and the daily scraping of a razor over my jaws, still retained prickling black stubble by each day's end. My hair had also been trimmed; I'd appeared as proper and gentlemanly as was possible for my wedding service.

Sawyer and Malcolm had rustled up a preacher for Rebecca and I the very day I'd proposed; we did not want another night to pass without being wed and the little boardinghouse room split its seams that evening. Sawyer and Lorie had attended as our witnesses, the ceremony further celebrated by the presence of Malcolm and Cora, baby Rose, Tilson, Jacob, Cort and Nathaniel, and little Meggie Jeffries, who crept in and would not allow her mother to persuade her to leave. Rose fussed and fretted in Lorie's arms, and Nathaniel kept sneezing; the preacher had a slight and unfortunate stutter, which made Meggie and then Cort giggle, muffling their naughtiness behind cupped hands.

But all I saw and heard in those sacred moments was Rebecca becoming mine in every sense of the word. I sat on the bed at her side, our hands clasped and my heart full to bursting. I'd thought, *Daddy, if you can hear me I want you to know I have found my woman. I aim to make a life with her. I've assumed care of her boys, and Malcolm, and a girl he loves, named Cora. I pray that you know these truths, Daddy. I won't let them down. Not ever again.*

I played my fiddle after our vows, lifting the instrument from its hardback, velvet-lined case with a reverence borne of ancestral love. Its familiar heft felt so damn good in my hands I'd been reluctant to tuck it away; the music

I'd not been able to make all through the long, preceding winter thrummed in my blood and quickened my fingertips, and waltzes flowed from my bow. Later, alone with Rebecca in the little room, the two of us whispered as so not to wake Nathaniel, who was curled like a beloved kitten on the bed near her feet.

"Good-night," I told her, husky with love. Her eyelids were heavy from the laudanum she required to dull the pain.

"Good-night, sweetheart," she murmured, and I squeezed our intertwined fingers; the endearment flew straight to my already-besotted heart. So soft it was hardly more than a breath, she whispered, "I love watching you play. It seems an outward expression…of your passionate soul."

"I love when you talk so fine, my sweet Rebecca Carter." I kissed her forehead, her nose, her cheeks, lingering over her lips; I stroked her hair as sleep claimed her, drawing the bedding to her shoulders and lifting Nathaniel to the pallet I'd made up on the floorboards so neither of us would jostle her in our sleep.

The days directly following our wedding existed now as a blur in my memory; overwhelmed by the necessity of explaining to everyone the past year's events, dealing with the sheriff and the details of Hoyt Little's death; Hoyt Little, the man I'd conversed so unpleasantly with at Fort Pierre last winter. No doubt he had been the one to ride across the Territory to inform the others that we'd survived, and Malcolm's account of his grapple with Fallon suggested Hoyt Little's brother, Bill, had also been a part of Fallon's plan. Neither Fallon, Bill Little, nor Church Talk resurfaced before we resumed our journey northward, but my guard would never completely resettle, not concerning the Yancys or anyone associated with their thieving, rotten lot.

"I shoulda shot Fallon dead, Boyd," my brother whispered in the restless midnight hour of a night beset by thunderstorms, before we left St. Paul. "I shoulda shot him with the Henry, but I was too much a coward. I thought he was dead, I swear. He *looked* dead."

I mustered the sternest tone I possessed. "Malcolm, I should have given chase and killed the bastard the night we shared a fire with the Hagebaks. You are one of the bravest souls I know. You *ain't* to blame. Don't let me catch you thinking so, you hear?"

There was a part of me, deep down where I understood things without knowing exactly how or why – what Mama would have called a *notion* – that recognized I should waste no time in riding out after Fallon and his party, track them to the ground and kill them, no matter what it took. This belief was so strong I felt it in my gut like a fiddle string snapped by an overzealous bow; it was the same way I felt that night back in 1865, when Sawyer had stabbed to death Corbin Yancy in the clearing on our march home after the Surrender. We hadn't known the man's name at the time, but I'd insisted to Sawyer and Gus that we ought to ride after the two survivors and make certain they didn't live to tell the tale.

Look what trouble you could have stopped, had you pursued and killed them fellas that night in the clearing.

And yet, had we killed Thomas Yancy in 1865, he would never have later hunted us through Iowa to enact his vengeance; Sawyer would still possess both eyes. We would have ridden straight through Iowa City that hot afternoon last summer, had we not been delayed by Yancy and Jack Barrow – and I would never have met Rebecca. Our paths would have run near one another's that day, but not crossed. Cold and sick at the idea, I realized, *I would not have found her in this life.* The thought left me feeling removed from my physical self, struggling to understand something too profound to put into words.

"You ain't under arrest, Mr. Carter, it was an incident of self-defense from all I can gather," Sheriff Tate had told me in St. Paul. "But someone's got to answer for the dead folk. See to their burial. I understood you rode from the Territories with Royal Lawson."

Cora's uncle had been laid out in an icehouse, the best as could be managed under the circumstances; until someone could ride the many hundreds of miles to his homestead, there would be no way for Royal's poor wife to know he was dead. Time would pass and she would wonder at his continued absence, but as no mail service reached that far west, she wouldn't know for certain. Someone would make the journey, eventually, but it would not be me or mine, not this time. I thought of Grady saying, *Some four hundred and fifty miles from where we sit tonight.*

And then I thought, *Aw, Grady. I should have hauled your bones back here. I would have buried you proper, and Mary beside you. Quill, too. I am so goddamn sorry.* And somewhere in Pennsylvania was a woman named Eleanor, who'd married another and would never know that the old man who'd loved her, even after all these years, was now dead. *Quill, if you can hear me wherever you are now, please know I found my woman.*

I despised letting Fallon go free but I refused to ride away from Rebecca, or to endanger my brother and those under my protection. The life I intended to make for us would be far from St. Paul. We would never return this direction, not once we settled near Flickertail Lake. I believed we would be safe there, with Jacob and Hannah, Sawyer and Lorie, on nearby homesteads.

There won't be any reason to fear, not once you get there. You'll be ready next time, if there is ever a next time. Fallon Yancy won't take you by surprise again.

I recognized that the Yancys were connected to us, their path linked to ours by some strange quirk of fate, but I would be ready if they ever came looking for us. This time, I would be ready.

"I'd like to see to it that the woman Mary is properly buried," I'd told the sheriff.

Rebecca's recovery during the months of May and June was slow but steady; she was healthy and strong, and under Tilson's watchful eye and our collective care, she reclaimed the ability to sit, then stand, and at last walk about the room, my arm secure about her waist. Lorie sat with her for a spell every day, bringing little Rose, a plump, pink-cheeked cherub of a babe with the ability to rouse the entire boardinghouse with her nightly wailing cries. *Colic*, Tilson called it, and the blue smudges beneath Lorie's eyes attested to her lack of sleep.

"Cort was every bit as fractious for the first four months of his life," Rebecca assured Lorie during one of their talks. "It is a trial, I'll not deny, but just you wait. Rose shall grow out of it as sure as the sun shall rise tomorrow."

"Sawyer is so very patient," Lorie murmured, twining a strand of Rose's golden hair about the tip of her index finger as she spoke. Dismay gathered in her eyes as she confessed, "All while I've done little but weep and fret, and worry him. Oh Becky…" No sooner had the words been spoken when Lorie began crying.

"That is entirely natural and shall also pass, sweet Lorie, never you fear," Rebecca assured, squeezing Lorie's hand, cupping her cheek. "Let it all out, dearest. You must take these early days of motherhood one at a time."

Sawyer was endlessly patient, as Lorie said, gathering Rose into the crook of his arm and making a habit of walking about the town as dusk fell, allowing his wife to steal an hour's sleep. He spoke to Rose in a low and murmuring voice, telling her stories in both Irish and English, walking until her cries quieted. My oldest friend, who'd longed for a family of his own since I could

remember, would return to the boardinghouse with a smile of contented satisfaction, cradling his sleeping daughter, whose eyes shone gold and green
just like his, and his father's before him.

"It takes a right toll on a body," I said to Rebecca the night Lorie had
cried. "Being a mama, I mean. I can't say I'd ever rightly realized."

"Most especially with the first," Rebecca whispered, nuzzling her nose to
my chest, bared by my unbuttoned shirt. She rested her lips there, her hands
warm upon my ribs, and thoughts of anything but her fled my mind as swiftly
as clouds chased by a high wind.

I lay so my body bracketed hers, continuing to take great care with each
and every movement I made. The necessity of her healing overrode all else
– most especially the adamant blaze of desire to make love to her rising to
ever-frantic heights within me, but that I must resolutely deny for now; and
the truth was, I was so happy to simply lay talking into the night hours with
her, her voice like a caress along my skin, that were this all I was ever allowed,
I would content myself with it. Alone in our room each night I kissed her
until we were breathless, the taste of her sweet, pliant mouth helping to sustain me through the nights, and held her close as she slept; the pain-dulling
laudanum remained necessary and exhaustion was quick to claim her. Before
I fell asleep, I dutifully returned to the pallet on the floor, afraid to crowd her
on that narrow bed.

After the first fortnight, once she'd been able to sit, and with the bandages
swathing her ribs freshly replaced, she had not required a nightly dose of
laudanum.

"To feel clear-headed is worth the lingering ache," she had said after Tilson checked on her before retiring to bed, after Cort and Nathaniel came
to say good-night. Uncle Jacob was a godsend, remaining in St. Paul long
after he was due home, to help with the care of the boys, entertaining them
all through the lengthening days, regaling them with tales of the lake, and
his Hannah, and the cousins they would soon meet there. Jacob, along with
Malcolm, Cora, and Tilson, kept the boys in camp with them at night, allowing us precious time alone.

"You tell me what you need an' I'll make it happen," I promised, kneeling
at my wife's bedside and stroking the dark silk of her loose hair, tucking it
behind her ears, valiantly keeping my eyes and hands from the curving swells
of her lithe, lovely body, a task I found increasingly difficult, if not to say

downright impossible. The fresh bandages beneath her muslin shift were less inhibiting, no longer covering her breasts; I was lightheaded at the sight of them beneath her shift. But I was responsible for taking care of her, for protecting her, and I knew damn well this meant refusing to relent to my lustful desires when she was far from recovered. I whispered, "Are you hurting?"

"Not unduly so," she responded, grasping my forearms, bared by my rolled-back shirtsleeves. Our eyes held as she stroked the hair on my arms and my heartbeat increased in power and speed. She whispered, "Boyd," and there was something in her tone that had not yet been allowed release. My hands in her hair fell still and I all but gulped. Calm as a summer day, she whispered, "I want to see you. All of you. I want that so very much."

My heart seemed to explode in a burst of heat, taking up a thunderous clatter. I could scarcely swallow, even as I grew hard as a whetting stone, my trousers doing little to hold events in check. She lifted to an elbow, with care, hair falling over her shoulder, the lines of her collarbones delicate as finely-carved etchings, her breasts so full they stretched taut the material over them. I slipped my hands from her hair and cupped her breasts for the first time, letting my thumbs graze their peaks.

"You are so very beautiful," I said, a husk in my voice. "Holy Jesus, darlin', you are the most beautiful sight I've ever seen."

I could feel her hard-pounding heart. She began unfastening the buttons along my chest, sweat as fine as mist decorating her temples. She'd requested to see me, all of me, and I stood to honor this request, removing my suspenders, my shirt, my trousers, with no self-consciousness, no compunctions, aching to be fully joined as husband and wife.

"Come here," she implored, her breath shallow, the pulse thrumming in her neck. In nothing but the lower half of my union suit, a tattered garment well beyond its life span and which did nothing to hide my swelling need, I knelt again and claimed her mouth, reveling in the taste of her, in the rousing hunger which overpowered all else. Rebecca's hands were everywhere upon me; soft, urgent sounds rose, caught between our tongues. She unfastened the button low on my belly, the final restraint between her touch and my body. I took her lower lip in my teeth, shuddering at the wealth of such pleasure, afraid to move; I was but a second from spilling over.

She drew away just enough so we could look upon each other; her eyes shone with such heat I felt the sizzle of it down to my tailbone, cradling her precious face in my hands. She whispered, "I love you so, oh Boyd, let me touch you," and with no further hesitation curled her fingers about my rigid flesh. Her first stroke sent me bending forward, afraid I would lose control right there. It wasn't long – I was so far gone I came in her hand in less than a dozen frenzied heartbeats, but she held fast, keeping me in her grip as I cried out, low and hoarse, against her neck.

After a time I lifted my face to her sweetly-satisfied smile, and felt a grin just about crack my skull. I eased to both elbows and kissed her parted lips. Just for the joy of watching her flush deepen – and because I sincerely meant it – I whispered, "Thank you, my wife. Oh holy Jesus, thank you for that."

"You shall think me wanton," she whispered, and the merry glint in her eyes showed me that she teased.

"No *such*," I scoffed, fetching a damp linen towel from the edge of the basin and cleaning her hand, then bending to kiss her neck and her breasts, taking her nipples lightly between my teeth through the thin shift, delighting in her soft exhalations. Just that fast I was ready again. I knew I could not dare make love to her just now, but I meant to bring her pleasure nonetheless. Shifting to cup her thighs, caressing her hipbones with both thumbs, I said, "I want to tell you something that my old friend Ethan Davis once told me."

"Sawyer's brother?" she questioned, her hands resting like a benediction upon my collarbones. The lantern light played over the contours of her face and neck, outlining her breasts with rims of angelic gold. Her legs were bent in my direction, her bare feet crossed one atop the other; like her fingers, her toes were long and slim, and I'd learned she was fond of crossing her feet. I loved these small details only a husband would have the privilege of knowing.

"Yes, indeed," I said, relishing the telling of a story, as always. "He was a twin to Jeremiah. They looked just alike 'til you heard them talk. Jere was polite, shy as a kitten, but Eth was a true ladies' man. Lord how he loved attention from girls, and he knew how to get it. Mama once said that she was glad she had no daughters for Ethan to get into trouble with." I smiled at the memory. "Girls doted upon him, you never *saw* the likes. We was all jealous as hell and of course he loved every minute of it."

"I would imagine." Rebecca smiled, gliding her palms along the muscles of my upper arms. She was so flushed she appeared sunburnt and I delighted in it; she looked as though she wanted to eat me up in one bite. She whispered, "What did he tell you, my handsome husband?"

"He told me," and I slowly unfastened the lacing between her breasts as I spoke, letting my knuckles brush her skin, "that ladies like to be touched just as much as we like to touch them, and we'd do well to remember it." Rebecca shivered as I slipped the shift to either side, letting the soft material glide across her flesh. I could hardly speak for the stampeding blood in my body. "And you, my darlin', are every bit a lady."

Her nipples were a dusky pink, her breasts with a sifting of tiny freckles that continued from the skin of her chest. I trailed my lips over each freckle, lingering, wishing to prolong her pleasure and loving every blessed second. She twined her fingers in my hair, lifting towards my mouth, and I grinned anew, rubbing my chin between her breasts.

"This may be my favorite one of all," I murmured, grazing a small, cinnamon-colored freckle on her nipple with my tongue.

"*Boyd…*"

"Aw, darlin', there ain't nothin' sweeter than hearing you speak my name…"

Her neck was arched on the pillow, her breath coming in gasps, and I waited no longer, taking her nipples in my mouth one after the other, the puckered sweetness of them swelling against my tongue. I slid my left hand beneath her hem, cupping her knee, moving upwards along her thigh. I kept my touch unhurried but came close to seeing stars as I reached the delicate folds of skin between her bare, parted legs. *Gentle, keep gentle*, I thought, no more than a thimbleful of blood left in my head as I stroked the sleek, heated center of her.

Later, both of us sweating, I lay beside her on the bed, fathoms-deep in love and equally met; I felt whole. Rebecca assured me her ribs were not in pain despite my overwhelming concern. She eased my fears, resting her cheek upon my chest, plying her touch through the hair there. In time she whispered, "I knew it would be this way with you, a consecration. I imagined moments such as these as early as the night we met."

I cupped her nape, my chest rumbling with my words. "The way I feel with you is sacred and beautiful both, darlin'. I would never have guessed you imagined this, not that first night." I thought back to that dark time, Lorie missing and Sawyer out of his mind. If not for Rebecca's help, God only knew what might have happened to us. I recalled the surprise I'd felt when Rebecca had pulled me aside after Quade marched Sawyer to the Iowa City jailhouse, and her hushed insistence as she ordered, *Saddle your horses,*

yours and Mr. Davis's, and meet me beyond the jail once the town settles to quiet.
She had still referred to me as 'Mr. Carter' back then; I hadn't possessed any
reason to trust her, there in Iowa City, and yet I had done so. She'd been a
stranger who was not truly a stranger at all; I'd been too worried to realize.

I traced the line of her fine jaw, studying the eyes that saw to the depths
of me. I rested my thumb upon her lips, her skin flushed and damp with the
pleasure we'd just shared. I pictured the high-necked dress she'd worn that
first night; the color of it was lost to my memory but I remembered well the
pearl buttons fastened so properly to her delicate chin, the notches of her
waist, the shining dark hair pinned up so neat. And I rejoiced afresh at the
naked woman in my arms, her loose, tangled hair spilling all about us.

"You helped us so very much, chasing me into that alley, finding those keys,
bustin' Sawyer out of jail. You risked yourself, sweetheart. You're stubborn, and
brave as a warrior. There's few traits I admire more, I'll have you know."

"From the moment I heard Lorie was missing I *knew* I must help all of
you, more than I've ever known anything," she murmured, nuzzling closer,
rubbing her chin against my chest in a tender way that strove to cave-in my
heart. It was the gesture of wife to husband, a gift of cherishment that made
my throat ache, it was so damn beautiful. "When you rode out with Sawyer,
the two of you in search of her, you took my heart with you, though I would
not admit it to myself for a long time. I worried every second you were absent
from me, realizing I had less than no right. I scanned the horizon a hundred
times a day, even more than did dear Malcolm. I had to believe you would
return to me. I prayed for your return."

And I'd returned only to leave again. I buried my face in her hair. "Forgive
me. Forgive my stupid pride, for refusing to listen to my heart. Last winter,
apart from you, I was as sorry and lonely as I ever been, Rebecca. I figured
you'd have married the marshal and done your best to forget my sorry hide. I
thank God you did not."

"I understood why you must go, I truly did. There was a time when I tried
to forget you." She slipped her arms about my neck, kissing my chin. "But
I could not. My thoughts of you were constant, by day and night. I recalled
every word you spoke to me. I lay awake, hearing your voice, longing for you."

I recalled all the nights I'd done the same, never suspecting. I kissed her
eyes, one by one, her brow, her cheeks, saving her lips for last, lingering there
to savor her, a slow kiss that spoke of forgiveness. We'd spoken of many

things, but there were so many more I wanted to tell her and these all at once, I hardly knew where to begin.

"Before we were attacked that night along the Missouri, I was intending to ride for Iowa, to come back to you. But then – " My innards grew tight. The image of the solitary oak on the Missouri River struck me at unusual times, often unbidden, forcing a pause in whatever task the thought intruded upon; I'd grit my teeth until the darkness of remembrance passed over. That goddamn tree still existed out there in the Territories, no matter how I wished I could forget it.

"Then what, love?" she whispered, caressing the damp hair at my temples.

It stabbed at me to remember, let alone give words to what had occurred that night. But I opened my eyes to the eloquence of Rebecca's and was able to begin.

"You see, they meant to hang Malcolm…"

I FOUND GREAT joy in being a daddy to Cort and Nathaniel. The two
of them dogged my steps as we journeyed slowly northward, chattering
like jaybirds and trying so hard to outdo one another that they could have
been Beau and me in the holler, long ago. Cort was a thinker, whose steady
gaze could often be found fixed on the horizon towards which we traveled;
he spoke as polite as Rebecca even when begging to have his own horse, or
to fire a rifle. Natty was still young enough to relish his mama's lap come
evening, deprived as the little boy had been while Rebecca lay healing in St.
Paul, and curled at her side at the nightly fire, poking a thumb in his mouth
as she feathered his hair until his eyelids fluttered shut. I loved them because
they were Rebecca's boys, for being a part of the woman I loved, but also
because they were now my sons and I intended to see them grow into good
and honorable men.

But, damn my infernal selfish hide, if I didn't wish to God that they had
their own space to sleep, come nightfall.

The covered wagons didn't provide much room as it was, chock-full as
they were with our belongings, from cook pots to rocking chairs to seed bags
and blacksmithing tools, trunks and candles and blankets and food, enough
to sustain our first winter in northern Minnesota. Before we left town I'd
made up a thick pallet for Rebecca within our wagon, arranging a feather
tick and two pillows so she would be able to rest as she required in the day
and sleep well at night, and reminded myself with all the severity I could rally
that my need to make love with her could not overpower all else, including
her healing body and the presence of two little boys who wanted to sleep near
their mama at night. Her sons loved her and would protect her to their last

breath, I knew, and I loved them for it, but...*damnation.*

I was truly grateful for our large contingent, with Sawyer, Jacob, Tilson, and Malcolm armed to the gills at any given moment, same as me, and for the security their presence afforded at night. I found deep contentment in teaching little Nathaniel how to hold the reins steady over Trapper and Admiral as they pulled the wagon, or instructing Cort in the skinning of a rabbit. I loved the hours I spent hunting with Sawyer, and sometimes Tilson or Jacob, by turns, ranging out front with our squirrel rifles, Sawyer now more accustomed to his one-sided vision and adapting his aim to the difference. I relished talking with him about our women, and the lives we would all build together; listening to Jacob describe farming practices along the water, growing wild rice on the frigid-cold lakes of his wife's homeland, and its delicate harvest, and of his own knowledge of flax and corn and buckwheat. I imagined the cabin I would build for Rebecca and the boys, and the children that would join our family, and my heart would ache with the joy of it.

And I'd think, *Our cabin will have a separate room for Becky and me, where I can make love to her day and night, lavish her for hours on end, until I can hardly walk straight...oh holy God...*

It was so damn hard to withhold, even as I realized I was a grown man with self-control and a duty to be respectable; but my unruly mind ran wild, spurred on by the beautiful, hushed lovemaking Rebecca and I managed to steal in the night hours of our crowded camp, the two of us as wayward as any newlywed folks have a right to be...

The first night along the trail out of St. Paul, I'd settled Rebecca and the boys within the wagon come evening and then claimed the ground beneath; not my first choice of sleeping conditions, but one I accepted as the most dutiful and responsible. Besides, I'd known Rebecca was just above me, safe and warm and so very close. I lay flat on my spine on the cold ground, allowing myself to feel the relief of that blessed knowledge. I'd tucked a forearm beneath my head, reaching to press my other hand to the underside of the wooden structure, and had smiled so wide it would have stretched from one end of the holler to the other. We'd undertaken the final stretch of our journey, we were all alive, and I lay there warm with happiness, listening as my uncle and Rebecca's uncle chatted over their pipes at the fire, as Lorie soothed little Rose with a hushed song, as Malcolm murmured to Cora in the wagon where the two of them, plus Tilson, slept. I dozed for a spell, waking at some point after midnight to the rustle of a rising breeze, and to the soft sound of my name.

"Boyd," she whispered again, and I realized Rebecca was crouched near my legs, which stuck out past the side of the wagon, and wrapped in her shawl.

"Rebecca," I uttered. I would have squirreled out from under and gathered her close in less than a heartbeat, but she ducked beneath to join me before I could move.

"I missed you. I've grown so accustomed to sharing a bed with you," she whispered, aligning herself against my side, pressing kisses to my face, and just that fast the cramped space beneath the wagon became heaven. I tucked her to my warmth, keeping her from the ground, returning kiss for hungry kiss. Her hair was loose, spilling over the both of us, her breath upon my neck and her breasts against my chest.

"Aw, honey, come here, I'm so glad you're here," I rejoiced, rocking her closer. Though the darkness robbed her of color, I filled in the tints of her eyes and skin, lips and lashes. I felt wetness upon her cheeks and asked at once, "What's wrong? Are you hurting?"

She shook her head, adamant as she whispered, "I'm not hurting. I'm so very happy." She grasped my ears, as she was wont to do when demanding my full attention. Her voice was very soft as she confessed, "I cannot do without you, Boyd."

"Sweetheart. Oh God, I can't do without you." I kissed her again, this time with less restraint.

Mindful of Rebecca's healing, we'd not come fully together as husband and wife before leaving St. Paul but I sensed it was time, here beneath the wagon on our first night on the trail. Never mind that we were not enthroned within a proper bed. Never mind that it was a chilly night on the prairie and there was scarcely room to roll over, or that our families were near enough to suspect, had they been awake. Nothing mattered but our need for each other. Her tongue circled mine, our heads tilting to deepen each kiss. I inhaled against her neck, kissed her eyes and forehead and ears, burying my hands in the luxury of her thick hair, kissing her breasts through the layers of cotton separating them from my tongue, finding the rounded swells of her nipples.

"I love you, oh Boyd, *I love you so*," she whispered, rolling atop me, her hair silken as it fell over my face. My shoulder blades touched the earth. I tucked hair behind her ears, gently shifting my thighs so that they better cradled her hips.

"All I want to think of ever again is you," I whispered. "Aw, darlin', you feel so good in my arms." I drew her closer and kissed the soft indentation between her collarbones, inhaling deeply, feeling her pulse beneath my lips. She curved a hand about my jaw and our kisses were deep, a reclaiming of one another, her soft moans caught between our tongues. I ran both hands carefully down her ribs to anchor about her backside, hauling her full-length against me.

"I want – I want you to…" The love and desire in her voice was a divine, two-part harmony.

"You tell me what you want, darlin', just what you need," I said against her warm neck, clutching her hips, and she made another small sound, her mouth at my ear.

She murmured, "I need you inside of me," and issued a hushed laugh, latching her arms about my neck and hiding her face. "You are not shocked?"

"*Holy God*, woman, there ain't a thing you could do to shock me." I grinned at her teasing, my heart galloping like a runaway horse. "I want you to tell me what you need, always. Rebecca, *honey*…oh God, we're on the ground… under the wagon…"

She laughed again, muffling the sound against me. She murmured, "*Shh!*" before reaching upwards, fingers flying as she began unfastening the row of buttons running in a straight line down her center. I rolled us to the side, tasting each inch of flesh as she bared it, so goddamn grateful for the gift of this pocket in time that found us here – not so very long ago I thought I'd never see her again, that she was lost to me. Her skin was pale as moonlight. Her nipples swelled like heated pearls against my tongue. I lifted her skirts as she tugged at my trousers, freeing me from them; my union suit shackled my knees as I felt her thighs spread about my hips.

"*Rebecca*," I gasped, shuddering as I slid fully within her at long last. She clung, lifting to meet each deep thrust, and I lost all sense of time, flowing into her body, devouring her kisses, heady with joy and pleasure…when a sudden and plaintive cry sounded from the wagon just above, little Nathaniel awake and calling for his mama.

"*No*," I despaired, a groaning whisper only half in jest. We ceased all motion, breathless and sweating and knotted together, Rebecca giggling in hushed whispers against my neck; I growled into hers, teasing – though I would almost rather have died than stop just then – but I would not be as selfish as to keep her from Nathaniel when he needed her. We hurried to help each other straighten our clothes; I fastened her blouse, holding her close for a last, greedy instant.

"I promise –" she began.

"I know," I assured. "I'll be right here, darlin', you go to Natty."

As she climbed atop the wagon above me, shushing the little one, I wrapped into my own embrace, squeezing fit to displace my insides; her scent was on my skin, her sweet taste on my tongue. I turned to the side but this position proved uncomfortable, as another part of me, unwilling to relent so quickly, was quite in the way.

I thought, still with a sense of wonderment, *You're a husband.*

SUMMER MORNINGS on the prairie were a sight to behold; waking to the first glimmerings of light on the eastern horizon, the deep blue of night fading to yellow-gold, hearing birdsong, and the stirrings of those I loved as they woke and readied for the day. I felt blessed, beyond fortunate. All of the paths I'd traveled to get here had not been in vain. I would take a moment there beneath our wagon to thank God for what was mine, and with each new day the stain of ugly memories – the War, the Territory, loss and despair – faded a little more. I could almost believe there would come a time when I was no longer plagued by any remembrance. I would never forget those things, of course, but perhaps I would no longer suffer from their presence in my mind.

"I think all the birds in the world are here, singing," I heard Malcolm grumble from inside his wagon, and Tilson's rumbling laugh. Tuesday, July the sixth it was; according to Jacob, we were close enough now that we would reach Flickertail Lake by mid-afternoon tomorrow and the anticipation in our camp grew with each revolution of the wheels. My uncle could scarce contain his excitement. The wagon above me rustled and creaked as one of the boys climbed to the opening in the canvas; Natty, I saw, as he hopped to the ground and crawled on hands and knees, never minding the dewy grass, to give me a hug. I curled close to the sleep-tumbled little boy; Natty cuddled against me like a pup and whispered, "Morning, Pa."

A man's heart could hurt with the force of love. I'd been instructing the boys on how to tighten a cinch strap on a warm June evening, along with patient, docile Trapper – I was fonder of the mule than I'd been of any of the horses I'd ever known, save my dear, lost Fortune – when Cort, at my right elbow, had asked out of the clear blue sky, "Mr. Carter, mightn't we call you 'Pa?' You shan't mind, shall you?"

I stalled in my task, throat closing as swift as if tugged by a drawstring, and bracketed the back of Cort's head. "I wouldn't mind one bit, son."

Natty knuckled sand from his eyes here in the early morning light and murmured, "Rose sure can make a squall, can't she?"

I smiled, resting my chin on his downy hair. "She can, at that." The baby had roused everyone before dawn; Sawyer had climbed from the wagon to saddle Whistler, before gathering his daughter from Lorie's arms and taking her for a ride.

"Cort, Natty, you two about?" Malcolm called, and appeared from the tail end of his wagon, followed by Cora; he helped her down and collected her hand in his before they continued on their way. My brother crouched near my ankles, his grinning face popping into view. "Morning, you twos."

"Get that coffee going, would you?" I said. To Cora, I added, "Good morning, honey." I was overjoyed that she appeared to be further thriving in our company; no more threat of hers and Malcolm's separation loomed before us. We would care for her, and keep her as our kin, for always; there was not a doubt in my mind that someday she and Malcolm would marry. His devotion to her was evident as his freckles, well as I knew that there would come a time all too soon when it would no longer be seemly for them to share a sleeping space. But for today, I put those thoughts aside.

"Good morning, Boyd," Cora said, cheerful and beaming. Her hair hung in two long, neat braids, courtesy of Rebecca's efforts, her clothing mended and a new dress in progress, again at my wife's capable hands. Cora's face was browned from the sun, her two-colored eyes shining at the promise of a day spent at Malcolm's side. She was worlds different than the terrified little girl we'd first known on the Territory prairie.

"Me an' Cora are out to collect eggs," Malcolm informed. "Natty, you wanna join us?" He raised his voice to call, "Cort, you up? C'mon!"

I scooted out behind Nathaniel as Cort leaped from the wagon to join the egg hunt, anxious to get my arms around Rebecca. She was still tucked beneath the quilt, already reaching for me as I stumbled in my haste to clamber into the narrow wagon. I squeezed beside her on the rumpled pallet, groaning with pure happiness to gather her close, nuzzling her warm skin, resting my lips to her temple as she burrowed against me.

"Good morning," I murmured into her ear, loving the way she shivered at my tone. I had to be careful or I would be full-sprung, with no hope of making love just now, everyone awake and milling about, but my body responded at the merest suggestion of touching. She didn't help matters any, sliding one hand down my belly and grasping me through my trousers, as I growled against her neck. I muttered, "*Dammit*, woman."

She responded by taking my chin between her teeth and I was about to damn it all and roll her beneath me when Jacob called, "Nephew! You about?"

Rebecca giggled as I groaned, stealing one last kiss before facing the day. I tugged my suspenders into place as I joined my uncle in the dawning light; he winked at me, the beads in his long beard catching the first rays of sun. I was reminded afresh that he'd been parted from his wife and children for many weeks now. I would have understood if he were to saddle Sundog, his gelding, and ride hard for the northern horizon, leaving us to our own devices. But I knew him better than that; his grin was wide and jovial in the morning light. Sometimes, but most especially when he smiled, I caught a glimpse of my mama in his features.

"By tomorrow evening we'll be dining at my hearth," Jacob said. "I can hardly contain myself. Hannah will be jubilant. Lord above, I've missed her so."

"I am fair excited to meet her. Since reading all your letters, I feel I already know her and your little ones."

"Ain't so little these days," Jacob said, as we fell into step; so many chores to begin the day, livestock to water and wagons to hitch, the fire to be tended and breakfast made. Tilson was up, hunkered by the embers to set out the coffee pot to catch the small flame beneath the iron grate. Lorie sat on a small quilt near him, bundled in her shawl, the two of them talking quietly. Tilson's wounds – he'd taken a blow to the back of the head, delivered by Virgil that terrible night – had healed nice and neat. I watered Admiral, Trapper, Juniper, and Aces High, while Jacob cared for Sundog, Kingfisher, and the mules that pulled Tilson's wagon; by the time I returned to the fire, Lorie was the only one sitting near it.

Clouds on the horizon tinted the air a gauzy yellow. I claimed a seat beside her and settled to sip my coffee. In the distance were the cheerful sounds of Malcolm, Cora, and the boys collecting eggs; Rebecca had joined them, bucket in hand to gather their findings, while Tilson had ambled to the river to speak with Jacob. Birds trilled; the wolves we heard by night were quiet now, returned to their dens. I saw that Lorie appeared exhausted, the skin beneath her eyes smudged with sleepless shadows, and leaned to knuckle her scalp. I observed, "You's tuckered, Lorie-girl."

She nodded in response and I thought of the afternoon Malcolm and I had helped her prepare for her handfasting to Sawyer. We'd adorned her in Mama's wedding dress and tucked flowers in her pretty hair. Hoping to coax a smile, I said, "I was a-thinking of the evening you an' Sawyer wed."

Her face blossomed. "It was exactly a year ago this day, Boyd. We were whispering about that this morning, before the sun rose."

"I'll be." I hadn't realized. "Well, happy anniversary, sis."

"Thank you." She smiled anew.

"Sawyer and the little one still out riding?"

"They are. I am dearly blessed with a patient husband."

"Rose has herself a pair of pipes, that's for damn sure," I said, and Lorie made a small sound, half of a laugh, slapping at my shoulder.

Rubbing at her eyes, she muttered, "I've never heard the likes, truly, Boyd."

"You know what my granny would have said? Come to think of it," I reflected, slapping my knee, "your little one shares her name. Granny would have rubbed the babe's gums with a little hooch an' she'd be right as the rain. Likely sleep the night through."

"I understood whiskey to be a remedy for teething rather than crying," Lorie countered.

I shrugged. "Granny was fair liberal in her use of it. I s'pose that would explain Daddy an' Uncle Malcolm's fondness for the stuff."

Lorie giggled. "And *yours*, I would imagine."

"Ain't a doubt," I agreed, giving her a wink.

"I am ever so happy for you and Rebecca, Boyd. You can't know how happy I am."

I thought afresh of everything Lorie and I had been through together, of how she'd cared so immediately for Malcolm all the way back in Missouri when we'd first found her. Later, the two of us had been forced to leave Sawyer in the company of Thomas Yancy and Zeb Crawford on the Iowa prairie, and to endure a hard ride from the Rawleys' homestead to get back to Iowa City; I thought of the way we talked as openly as any two friends. I couldn't imagine my life without Lorie any more than I could imagine it without Rebecca, Sawyer, or Malcolm.

"I do know," I said quietly. "I count my blessings every day."

Lorie's expression brightened as would the sky when the sun burst from behind a cloud bank, her gaze lighting past my right shoulder. I looked that way to see Sawyer riding near with Rose tucked in his right arm, the lead rein held expertly as always in his left hand. He grinned at us, taking Whistler in a graceful walk, making a loose circle about the camp. In a hushed voice, he called, "She's asleep, I don't dare stop!"

"We've been discussing the benefits of whiskey for a good night's rest," I explained.

Rose, bundled in a small blanket, fit as neatly in her daddy's arm as a dovetailed drawer fits to a dresser. Lorie rose and shook out her skirts, setting aside her shawl; Whistler nickered at the sight of Lorie's approach and came to a halt, nuzzling her mistress's waist. Lorie kissed Whistler's rusty-red face and then moved around the mare's left side to rest her folded hands, and then her chin, on Sawyer's knee. She said, "Bless you, *mo ghrá*."

Sawyer let go the rein to cup Lorie's face; the tenderness present upon his was overpowering. I'd grown so used to his eyepatch it seemed strange to imagine him without it; *how quickly we become accustomed to things, even dire things.*

"Whiskey," I suggested again.

The temperature swelled as the day progressed, all of us traveling in our usual fashion, the wagons strung in a loose line with ours at the forefront, Rebecca at my side as I drove it, busy with her knitting; she grasped the edge of the seat beneath us whenever we struck a particularly rough patch of earth. The landscape had altered as we traveled, becoming rockier; lakes and creeks and ponds would appear around bends as though by magic, the sun sheeting over the surface of these waterways, glistening blue promises at our sweating skin.

The trees were thick, all manner of pines and cedars to spice the air with their scent; pinecones crunched beneath the wagon wheels. The way the trees hemmed in the horizons reminded me of the hollers of Tennessee. Cottonwoods and willows rustled their slender leaves on the lakeshores, beckoning as if to invite us to dally and swim. Game was abundant, deer and elk, hare and prairie fowl and fish. Despite spying their scat, I had yet to glimpse any large predators – black bears, moose, timber wolves, or catamounts, not especially eager to spy any of these. I would not allow the boys from my sight, my rifle always within reach.

On the other hand, we came across no signs of human habitation; Jacob explained that the Indian folk lived far from any beaten paths, preferring their solitude. The animosity amongst whites and Indians was undying, especially since the Dakota War, as Jacob further elaborated, but it was his opinion that we had little to fear from any groups we may come across. Jacob spoke Hannah's native Winnebago, as did his children, and I was reminded of the Darvell family; should we ever cross paths with them again, would I have the courage to tell Fern I'd done my best to kill her brother? That I wished to God I *would* have killed the bastard, and made him suffer first. It was my sincere wish that we would not encounter the Darvells again in this life, despite what they'd done for Malcolm, Cora, and me.

As for Church Talk, all I could say with any sort of truth was that he would not survive much longer were I ever to catch sight of him again.

Cort and Nathaniel rode on the wagon with Tilson, or walked, by turns; they were fond of minding Malcolm's cat, Stormy, a large, purring, much-spoilt creature grown fat on field mice. Malcolm and Cora rode together on Aces, ranging ahead with Jacob and Sundog; they would ride out until they appeared as only small dots, sometimes sinking from view as they crested a rise in the earth before the slower-moving wagons caught up. Lorie took a turn riding Whistler, the first she'd attempted since our journey from St. Paul began; she stayed near Sawyer as he drove their wagon, Rose bundled into her cradle in the wagon bed, and lifted her face to the sun, letting it bathe her tired eyelids.

Tilson smoked his pipe, its scent reaching us as we bumped along; I realized it had been a damn long time since I'd craved a smoke. And, as always, Rebecca and I talked of anything and everything, eager to gain all possible knowledge of each other as insistently as our bodies craved our lovemaking. Riding along with her at my side, I could satisfy my urge to touch her by braiding our fingers and stealing kisses.

We talked of our upbringings; Rebecca's mother had been raised in Tennessee and had spoken often of her birthplace when Rebecca and her brother, Clint, were children.

"I feel as though I've been there, Mama told so many stories," she said. "Mama was never able to return, not once she and Papa settled in Iowa, but a part of her heart was always there, nonetheless."

"You an' your mama was close?"

"Oh, very much so. I am ever so grateful she was able to know the boys before she passed. I miss her dearly."

I told her of my youth in the holler, of my brothers and cousins, aunts and uncles, Daddy and Mama, all the trouble I'd raised and the strappings I'd received, of playing all day in the crik on Sundays, when we were allowed a day of rest. I spoke of riding to War and leaving behind all that I held dear for the notions of glory and honor, and the promise of a quick Southern victory.

"That night in Iowa when you spoke of Elijah leaving to fight," I remembered, tracing the back of her hand with my thumb. "I watched your face in the firelight an' I wanted to take you in my arms. I felt goddamn guilty, seeing you suffer an' wanting nothing more than to step right around that fire and gather you up. It ain't easy for menfolk to think on what they leave behind, to think on what their family's feeling in their absence. It's selfish as hell, when you think about it."

"I was ashamed at my outburst that night. And yet, listening to you and Uncle Edward speak of what you'd seen was more than Elijah ever confessed to me. He believed it was not proper for me to hear of certain things."

"I can't say I entirely disagree. I don't like thinking of those images in your mind, not one bit. But I promise I won't keep things from you, Becky darlin', proper or no."

I found such release in speaking freely to her; I'd never understood what boundless relief existed in the sharing between man and wife. She opened to me in every sense of the word, body and soul, as I did to her. There were no secrets left between us. I told her of the women I'd been with as a soldier, of the women I'd paid for use of their bodies. I told her of the nightmares that stalked me, of killing and desperation and bitter hopelessness. Of the ache of the loss for the family that had raised me, the forfeiture of kin and homeland. Of how the promise of our own family, mine and Rebecca's, eased that ache and fulfilled my heart, in turn planting a small seed of hope that perhaps in time the animosity between the opposing factions of the War would wither and die, never to return. Her listening was a blessing I could not have imagined.

"I believe Jacob shall not be able to refrain from riding ahead." Rebecca nodded towards the scrap of color on the horizon that we knew to be my uncle, to the left of Malcolm and Cora.

"Believe me, was I so close to the promise of you, I'd be hell an' gone ahead, just to get to your arms. Uncle Jacob's been a right miracle. That night we came across him as we rode into St. Paul I thought I was maybe seein' things, that it couldn't possibly be my mama's brother just ahead there. Then I saw Cort an' Natty…and I about tore apart the wagons searching for you."

"Mary had only just told me that you were alive. And knowing it, I felt as though I had been given wings."

I lifted our joined fingers and kissed her knuckles, one after the other in a path along her hand. Nightly, before the boys retired to the wagon to bed, I inspected her stomach, slowly allowed reprieve from my fear as the wounds healed with no gathering infection and where only puckered scars now remained. Her ribs had healed as best as Tilson could figure; she kept careful in her movements and I would not allow her to tote water or lift heavy things, and she'd mended well, thanks be to Jesus. Lingering there in the dimness of our wagon I would kiss her soft belly, following a path down to the center of her, where her skin was salty sweet against my tongue; with renewed vigor, I imagined the bedroom I would construct for the two of us, in which we would not be forced to rush through a blessed moment of anything.

"I'm right here, darlin'," I promised, resting our joined hands against my thigh. "I ain't going anywhere again."

That night we gathered at the fire and the mood was rife with gaiety. Accompanied by Jacob on his harmonica, I played for a solid hour, the stars rowdy with no moon to overpower them. A rose-washed sun sank into a sky of dusty blue hours since and the heat of the day had thinned, leaving behind an evening the likes of which I wished I could tuck away for safekeeping, so fair and fine it was. Brown bats darted above our heads, feasting on the mosquitoes that feasted on us; fireflies glinted and winked in the tall grass beyond the fire while Jacob and I played with great and unrestrained joy; how I loved the feeling of Rebecca's smiling eyes upon me as she clapped along.

Lorie leaned against Sawyer with Rose on her lap, the baby wide-eyed at the noisy excitement, as Malcolm, who would have once coaxed and begged until Lorie danced with him now spun Cora in an untutored waltz. Lorie, no doubt thinking the same thing, caught my eye across the fire and between us passed a depth of awareness, a warm acknowledgment of all that had led us to this moment. Neither of us would be here without the other. Cort and Natty danced together, tripping over each other's toes, laughing all the while.

Tilson smoked his pipe, grinning to observe the commotion, while Stormy prowled about our ankles.

"By this time tomorrow, we'll be home!" Malcolm enthused, twirling Cora as 'round and 'round they went. "Can you-all believe it?"

I winked at my wife and the kindling in my heart glowed all the brighter. The lesson was one it had taken me a damn long time to learn, but I finally understood. Surrounded by those I loved, recognizing the grace of this fortune, I said, "We's home right now, at this here fire."

THE END

❀

THE STORY BEGUN in Heart of a Dove was born long before I ever wrote it, and so to have typed the final sentence in a trilogy based on an idea that sprang to life in my mind as a young girl not yet twenty is something of a wonder. Twenty years later, as a woman who just edged past forty, I am overcome with a sincere, humble sense of accomplishment. I love these characters as dearly as cherished friends whose lives I've shared now for years. Imagine an old-fashioned film reel projecting flickering images across a faded screen. You hear the clickety-clacking of advancing film; observe the sepia-toned, spot-flecked and disjointed pictures. Then, all at once, the reel jams – bam! the film is lodged on a smudged and slightly grainy scene of a wagon on a prairie.

You step closer, curious to see more, and suddenly sunlight from another century altogether touches your face with its dusty warmth. You smell sweetgrass and horses. You hear distant laughter, carried to your ears on a friendly trail of wind. And the prairie becomes a sweeping, sprawling panorama of life, no longer a two-dimensional image on a screen. Sensations pelt you, along with nostalgia; in fact, you know you belong here. You aren't certain how you know, but that's all right. It's not important in this moment. You glance down and spy in your hands a tattered journal with a pencil tucked between its pages, misshaping the binding and begging you to take up where you left off with the story last night. And so, with a grin, you do.

So many people are involved in the production of a book. I must thank my publisher, Michelle Halket at Central Avenue, for continuing to accompany me on this book-making journey. Without her words of encouragement, suggestions, and overall moral support, I would not be the writer I am today. Further, I must thank the amazing people at Independent Publishers Group, whose dedicated work ensures that the words I write reach bookstores in lands near and far. I would love to thank those incredible bloggers whose kind and inspiring reviews also keep me busy curled over my keyboard – most especially Mary, Shannon, and Bri!

My family, as always, deserves a huge debt of gratitude for sharing me with the characters who roam and stampede through mind on a daily basis, not to mention steal me away for hours at a time. (Thank you, frozen pizza, for being readily available for dinner). I want to send a special note of love to my oldest daughter, Ashley, whose global travels (she currently resides in Lima, Peru) and insights about life and wonder and the world in general inspire me each and every day. I want to thank my dear and wonderful writer friend, Molly Ringle, with whom I exchange frequent emails and who remains the number one person I want to meet in Real Life, rather than via online communication. Thank you for all your support! Two other kind souls whose wisdom I count upon are Roger and Kristin – you have helped me more than you will ever know, and I thank you both.

And finally, to Boyd Carter, whose story I feel privileged to tell in Grace of a Hawk. I hope you enjoy his voice as much as I do.

Printed in the United States
by Baker & Taylor Publisher Services